CW00735851

# Melusi

## Book Two of
## The Heirs of Anarchy

### By G. Lawrence

Copyright © Gemma Lawrence 2020
All Rights Reserved.
No part of this manuscript may be reproduced without
Gemma Lawrence's express consent

To an old friend,
For the story you told
On a dark night of isolation,

And for reminding me of dragons

"I tell you: one must have chaos in one, to give birth to a dancing star.
I tell you: you still have chaos in you."
**Friedrich Nietzsche, Thus Spoke Zarathustra**

"Our greatest blessings come to us by way of madness."
**Socrates**

"Among all the kindes of serpents, there is none comparable to the dragon."
**Edward Topsell, 1658**

# Prologue

**Petit Quevilly**
**Rouen**
**Normandy**

**September 1167**

"Let me be, I will be well. Many more striplings than you have I outlived, and will again."

They smile as I say such things, as I try to fend off their flapping as they tend to me. Many I have outlived, it is true, but I shall not outlast these children serving me who think they are adults. It is as well. I have lived longer than many I loved and loved not, and too many children have I watched die.

My servants remove themselves, growing fearful of the glimmer of rage building in my eyes. Peace granted at last, I sit near the window, gazing out over the royal park. The Seine is in the far distance, sparkling grey and gold and green in the light, seeping rain. There is a haze of water and warmth in the air, flowing about the river. I think of the fishponds and the novices I saw only days ago. I miss the Abbey of Bec, but I will not return again. Not in life. I will not have that chance. I have said farewell. It is more than most can say they managed when it came time to depart places sacred to them.

My fever is returning, this new companion I have acquired these past few months. That is why my women and men assault me. The first days of September have seemed long, soon they will be short. I sigh as I gaze onto the water. I am tired. The ado of people makes me only more so. Sometimes the only company one needs is oneself. People are such vexation and noise, so fearful of listening to the voices inside themselves that they prattle and boast, trying to avoid the silence in which truth might speak, whispering what they never want to know. The world has too much noise. That is why the places of silence are sacred, beautiful.

A twinge of guilt flutters in me. I, like most women, hurt a little when I insist on taking my pleasures first. Ridiculous as I know it is, and much as I have trained myself not to, still it is there, guilt when I do not put others before myself. But I am old and as I ignore aching bones and creaking blood, I have learned to ignore foolish guilt put upon me as a cowl by others when I was young and knew no better. There is no reason I should not want what I want. Peace is a worthy impulse, and I have spent many years' serving others. I also, where possible, did the same for myself. That is something I got better at over the years.

Most of the time I indulge the people who attend me, allow them to fuss, to flutter hen-like and hectic about me. Flapping as fish feeling the finger of Death pressing at their gills makes my servants feel better. That is why they do it. They are trying to solve a problem, cure me of that which cannot be cured. They bleat at me to stop, stay in bed, sit down. One would think I was a hound at times. Rest, rest, rest, young say to old, thinking they know anything. They do not understand; the reason I have lasted is due to activity, not repose.

They want to fix me. They always do, people. They see sadness and want it gone, witness illness and try to cure it. Some conditions, however, are not to be cured, they should not be, cannot be. Some conditions of life, and death we simply learn to live with, then die by, symptoms managed, never cured. People like to think there is one single and simple answer to each problem, and once it is found all will be well. The truth is things are never all well, and rarely is anything stable for all time. The sooner we understand that, the less disappointment we suffer and the more we learn to cherish good days.

They want to make me well, and cannot, for what I suffer is age and no one recovers from age. There is nothing wrong with me, I am simply dying. It is not abnormal. In fact, it is one of the commonest things in life. I do not fear darkness closing. Sometimes I am tired of life. Part of me lusts to see what lies beyond, what comes when I close my eyes and my heart falters, what follows after the pain and fear as my chest weakly tries to rise, and fails. I will fear the pain and the shame that comes as we pass, but not the end. What is there to fear when one is dead? There are more friends waiting for me in Heaven than I still have here on earth. I fear not to see friends once more. I fear not to stand in the light of my brother's soul.

My servants fear these things; illness, age, disruption. They shiver to see a reflection of what they may suffer, to hear an echo of what will come one day for them. They fear change, and death is the great change, and the one we know so little about. My people think normality is stability. It is not. They think what is calm and tranquil benefits humans most. They are wrong.

We are not beings of calm, but chaos. The same is true of the world. Chaos is within us, an ever-changing state of light and darkness, possibility and madness. It is not to be feared. It is power, and power may be of good or evil, as we choose. Chaos brings forth purpose. Works of the ancients speak of rivers flowing with darkness from which life and light were born, the long night before God spoke the Word and brought forth light. People fear their own personal chaos, they try not to look into it, but it is there and it is strong, and it is the root of all that is possible. Chaos is where creation comes to life. Darkness is where light is born.

Chaos brings forth wondrous invention, ushering in what is meant to be. The start of new and loss of old is not always to be grieved for. Harnessed, chaos is an astounding element, creator of creations, bringer of life and death, the endless circle.

And it is everywhere. I look at the world now, through the eyes of an old woman, and I see a broken world of broken people. And clearly, this is as it was meant to be, otherwise it would not be. We are not beings created for a stable, safe life where the track runs always smooth and path perpetually clear. We are not beings made for idle repose and nothingness. Even monks in closed orders have tasks to be done each day. The way to death is the path of inactivity. We need occupation, goals, trials and tests. Life is work. It is not people that keep us alive, but purpose. We are broken as the soil is; the rivets where the plough cuts through earth, the place where life springs from darkness. We are the falling dusk, waiting, holding its breath for night. We are that space where dreams intrude upon day, the moment as the wave curls upon itself, waiting to crash. We are that moment of possibility made flesh, granted bone and blood.

And we are monsters.

They have it wrong, men with busy, inventive quills who draw maps. *Here be monsters*, they write where land and sea become unknown and unknowable. Perhaps there are creatures that defy explanation hidden in rolling sea or sun-swept shore, in black, dripping cavern and cave, I know not, but I know where else they are. Inside us all are creatures, many. Some are good and some are bad. Some are presently undecided. That is the nature of the chaos within us; it may act on either impulse, it may become anything.

In legends and stories we separate monster from man, make monsters flesh, make them hideous so they might easily be recognised. We send out valiant knights, better knights than ever there are in life, to fight these dragons and water wyrms, these great snakes, all kin and cousin to one another. Always they are fought, always defeated. Good triumphs, evil falls.

That is not the way of things. Some monsters do not die, and I have come to think in my long life that not all monsters are evil. They are what we make of them. The world, men who craft laws, the Church… they have tried to make it seem all monsters, dragons, wyrms, are wicked. Perhaps they thought to distance themselves from our ancestors who carried such beasts proudly on banners of war, who built ships with dragons as their heads, leading men to distant and undiscovered shores. The Romans flew flags in the shape of dragon heads to signify five hundred men marched beneath. My Viking ancestors displayed dragons on longships, the terrible roar of their purpose seeming to float from the carved wooden head, across the sea, to infest those they would fight with terror.

But the word *dragon* is Greek, I am told. It means to look terrible, or to gleam. These things, I wonder at. All that gleams dazzles, and that which appears terrible may not be, in fact.

Legends speak of maidens offered to monsters as sacrifices, or those who are guarded by dragons. Those monsters then fall in love with their prisoners, guard their virtue, protect their bodies. But I wonder if the ways we read such myths are as they were intended. Sometimes I think maidens are of two souls, all women are, all people are. With men it is easier to see the monsters within; those dark souls brought to bear in battle, unleashed in violence, sometimes in marriage. With women, demons are more subtle. Many women hide away the dragons within so none will see, none will suspect what lies beneath; what power and fearsome darkness there is hidden behind the blushing cheeks, the downcast eyes, the veil over our hair and faces. The monstrous within them women must hide, for it is the part that the Church, that men, that the world fears in us. Yet it is not always a thing of evil, just power, and the power of women is feared. All that upsets what is normal is feared. At times I think we should fear what is normal, or what is perceived as normal. It too is a story and often a dangerous one.

Monsters are another part of our souls, something denied that hides within, something that guards what is valuable, what is dear to us; the gold of our souls. We know not how to face certain parts of our souls, so we make them into things external, demons to fight. Sometimes we do more harm by refusing to see our true natures than we do by accepting them. To deny a dragon is not a thing wise.

The monsters we carry are born of chaos. Sometimes they are rebels we need. Often they threaten not life, or virtue but normality. They would bring change. When what is normal benefits someone they want to retain it. Anything which dares to trespass outside of that created normality becomes monstrous. Some heroes of folk tale and legend were thought demonic, many women of old were. If we make what we fear into a monster, we are allowed to kill it. If we pretend monsters live outside, not inside us, we can pretend we know not their darkness.

There was much in me that wished to trespass. Much men thought monstrous. I was different. I was chaos unbound. And yet I, like so many others, followed the tracks of a story already told.

The line of the House of Anjou was brought to life by the union of a lord with a spirit of water, a demon, a woman of dragon-tail, water magic and serpent soul. They say the Count of Anjou was wandering in the forest, that realm joining kingdoms of here and there, at twilight when he came across a woman of such beauty he cared nothing for her name, family or origins, but proposed marriage that moment, wanting to possess her. He did not know she was the fairy Melusine, daughter of the King of Albany and the sprite Pressyne. Pressyne had stolen her three daughters, half mortal, half fae, away from their father for he broke his oath never to watch their mother bathe. In Avalon, kingdom of mist and magic, the three sisters were raised, their spirits infused with power, souls with boldness. When she was older Melusine was told of her father's betrayal, and she and her sisters captured him, held him in a cave in a mountain, along with his riches. For this, her mother cursed her. On certain days, Melusine would reveal her monstrous side, become a serpent, a dragon of water.

But since she took care to hide away on such days, the smitten Count had no need to know about her transformations. Melusine and her Count married, and she bore him four sons, but the Count found it strange that never would his wife hear Mass. Melusine would enter church, but leave before Mass was sung. One day he had four of his men grab Melusine and hold her, to force her to listen as the priest sang, but the woman of magic escaped. Taking her two youngest sons by the hands, Melusine transformed into a dragon and flew from the church. She and her sons were never seen again, but the eldest heir who remained with his father, became Count after his father's death. So the blood of Melusine flowed through Anjou's ruling house. Sons of the dragon ruled the people of Anjou.

Into this house I married. Into this story I walked. Life is pleased by spirals, wending about as water, as the weaving threads of *wyrd* formed by the Fates to become one cowl of destiny. A Count of Anjou married a demon of water once, perhaps his descendant did again. Child of water was I, as was Melusine. Both bound to duty but not to whim of man, we were. And both of us were woman, as we were something else; something older, something mighty; dragon of the darkness, the power of flame and wave within. Something man tried and failed to tame.

I had a monster within me. All people do. We cannot reveal our darkness to just anyone, and often deny it ourselves. If left without companionship it can become something of evil, but often the monster, if dealt with fairly, does not evil do. Often they are misunderstood.

*Here be monsters*, they wrote. But I feel the monster within, spirit of water, spirit of freedom, something of chaos born which gave purpose to my life. Old though I am, there are still nights I hear my monster lift her head to roar. And on certain nights, I hear her answered by other dragons; heads rising in the darkness, maws open, teeth as metal shining in starlight as a river of noise which no untrained ear may hear floats in the night, bonding us, one and all.

*Here be monsters,* they wrote. Perhaps they were right. Monsters are everywhere.

# Chapter One

## Le Mans
## The Norman-Angevin border
## Normandy

### Summer 1128

I stared.

Blue-grey swirls drifted slowly about his face. Bubbles of air floated, teasing green curling weed dancing about his wrists, his arms, in the flow of the water. He was staring at me, face pale, yet eyes unchanged from when we were children and I would catch him smiling at me as we sat under our tree in Westminster, the green-gold glow of sun and leaves flashing back at me from eyes so like mine. A twist of weed fluttered near those eyes, gently licking his face. My fingertips itched to reach out, place my palm to his cheek, feel his skin, his warmth against mine one last time.

How was it I could see him? My brother, long years dead, body and perhaps soul lost in the sea?

Usually I saw him in my dreams, on a beach, his body laid out, wrapped in linen. I would send him out on a boat to sail to peaceful shores. I watched from the beach in those dreams. This was not like those dreams.

I was in water like him, yet I did not seem to move. I could feel water about me, yet not as in life where one is weightless, floating. I seemed bound, held by water, a prisoner. My brother was free. Had he called me here to the place his soul rested, the place death had claimed him? Was I dead? Were we, two children in whom one destiny had combined, never to be free of each other in life or death? Not that I wanted to be free of him. Not that ever I would. Some chains do not bind, but embrace. Some tethers do not restrict, but keep a person steady in a world of turbulence and change.

I watched his face, trying to see if there was accusation there, if something in my brother resented me for taking his place, becoming heir to England's crown. Did he sense me walking towards the throne he should have occupied? Did Will hear the whisper of the crown that should have been his moving towards the hair on my head? Did he hear our father, a thunderous voice not slowed or stopped by storm or wind or sea, as he named me his successor?

Yet although there was much for Will to resent, there was nothing in his eyes that suggested hostility, only love.

"Will," I whispered, voice lost, becoming a stream of bubbles pouring from my lips, floating to the writhing surface of the sea. "Brother, where is your soul?"

Of all things, this, I had wanted to know when he died. Was Will in Heaven, or, denied last rites, deaths in battle lying heavy, dirty upon his conscience, was he lost to God, banished to the seabed for eternity?

He shook his head. Perhaps he did not know. In my worst times I had thought his body lost, soul bound to earth rather than freed unto Heaven. My brother's body was still upon the gritty floor of the ocean that had swallowed him. Fish would have eaten flesh by now. Will's skull would be grinning in the grimace of death, white bone on sand and rock, weed and water, for all time. But where his soul was, no man could say. Did I speak now to body or to soul? To ghost or to man?

Yet I had hoped him safe because of the dreams of shore and boat and winding cloth, because of a fantasy captured from dreams dreamed upon his death which repeated many times and nights after. Because over and over that slumberous form of me placed my little brother in a longboat, draped his body in linen and in gold, placed herbs in his hands, about his head. Every time I came to that shore I sent him to sail upon the top of the sea past long, wide cliff-tops of bright grass moving in the wind, the blades gold. Past crumbling stone above and under shrieking gulls cresting in a sky of innocent white and water blue, his death-ship sailed, sails moved by a wind that swept under my hair and across my brow as I stood on the beach watching water steal my brother away. *Men under heaven's shifting skies, wise though they be, cannot say surely who salvaged that cargo…*

I had set him in that ship like one of our ancestors of old, like a hero of a tale still sung, echoing through a warm hall, dancing above a glowing fire when ale and wine flowed deep into the darkness of night. I had set him there, soul if not body. I had watched that boat sail out, had known that place. Those dream-shores I had walked a thousand times, sand on my feet, sometimes snow in my hair, in countless dreams where I had watched that boat over and over as it sailed away from me. Therefore how could my brother be lost? If that shore was of my dreams, he was at least within me. I could not see how he could be lost when I knew where to find him. When I watched him go into that ocean, boat riding the waves, I felt loss and I felt peace. I believed he was heading for the Kingdom of God. But, seeing him here, under the water, I wondered if part of him was still prisoner to the sea. Was the reason I had dreamed his death-boat sailing over and over because he had not made it to Heaven? Was my brother in limbo? Still a wanderer upon the waves? Was Will bound to life because his destiny had become mine? Because we were now tied by a shared fate to one another?

"What would you tell me?" I asked.

At his feet, weeds were thick. As branches of a tree they curled upon each other. I could almost see the Confessor's tree-tale in them, a trunk split, carried far away to graft to another. Was my brother that tree, or was it me? For something told me I was once more far from the land of my birth.

*Normandy*, said a voice. *You are to be married today*. I looked at my brother, but it was not he who had spoken.

Will opened his mouth, eyes bright in the gloom. He was about to speak. About to answer me. I would know all I had wanted to know. I would hear him as my heart had ached to since the day I was told he was gone.

And then nothing, then darkness.

I opened my eyes, for a moment thinking I was still in water. I choked, pushing covers of linen back, afraid of the weight, of suffocation, of water pressing upon me. I could feel it in my mouth, clouded with the taste of my brother's body, rotting skin, the panic of the drowned. I could taste my brother's fear on my tongue. Grasping my throat I screamed, thinking there would be no sound. There was.

I realised they were covers, not water. The woman in the bed beside me stirred, blinking against the dim light in confusion at me. "A dream," I said. "Just a dream."

For a moment I felt better, sinking back upon the bed, gasping in air, until I realised I was not being suffocated by water, but the world, wyrd; fate pressing upon me to do something, something I never wanted.

That day I rose, dressed, went to church and was married, for the sake of politics and present, to a boy.

*

Dust plumed into hot air, a curl and waft of gritty smoke. People coughed, some laughed, many cheered. Horse and rider thundered past, emerging suddenly from a cloud of white and yellow dust, hooves churning ground, the flash of metal glinting in the sunlight blinding my eyes. Looking to my side, I wished I could be blinded for longer. Wished all of my senses, those under skin most of all, might cease to operate for a time, at least until I made it through the night. My fingers strayed to the adder-stone, the last present from my brother when we were children, which hung in a pouch about my throat, hidden under my clothes. I asked it to bring me strength. It was said that to look through it into the setting sun would allow the bearer to see the future. I had not held it up to that light. I feared the near future.

I sipped my wine. Perhaps that would help. If I could maintain an appearance of sobriety and decorum on the outside, perhaps I could drink enough to dull my senses inside. So I would not care, would not feel his hands on me when to my bed he was brought by his men that night. I set the cup down. There was grit in the goblet of silver, thrown there by the riders. The wine tasted of resentment.

Another horse flashed past. Knights of Normandy and Anjou were competing in glorious events, mostly feats of mock war, although there had already been a few injuries, and more than a few serious. Deaths had been rumoured, but if they had occurred my father and Fulk, my new father-in-law, were busy keeping them quiet so death and pain and disapproval of the Church, who liked not these kind of entertainments, would not intrude upon the image of perfect harmony they were seeking to create. It was all a farce, there was no harmony here. Men of Normandy wandered past those of Anjou, the word *Guiribecs* whispered on their tongue, an insult. It could be seen in all the tournaments; melees where men lined up as in battle, although fewer in number, rushing at each other, hacking with sword and spear. Every sword fight had a cloud of hostility upon it, every eye held the determination to best men of the other side, kill if necessary. These were not brothers-in-arms. They were enemies pretending to play nicely. A blow here, harder than it had to be to win, a strike there more dangerous than it needed to be for simple show… There were many dangers here, for all men. When night fell and there was drinking, the perils only increased. Men knew it.

They were not venturing about the camps, these forests of cloth and gold and blinding colour, alone. They roamed in packs. This was war wearing a mask of festival. This was pain pretending to be pleasure. That was as true for what was to come for me as it was for these knights. Something of the horror in my mind had been torn from me, to become not flesh but a miasma of polluted air, seeping into men, making them enemies, as my husband and I always would be.

*Husband,* I thought, a trickle of disgust running from nape to groin as I considered the boy. *Never will I think so of him.*

Married before I had been. This boy was a marsh light to the glaring sun that was Heinrich, Holy Emperor, King of the Romans, King of the Germans, chosen of God. What was Geoffrey of Anjou, not even yet a count, to the man I had loved and lost to death? He was nothing.

My marriage would be as fraught as the battles and melees being fought before us, and not only because men of England resented my new child-husband, not only because men of Anjou and Normandy had no trust in one another, but because we two, wed to one another to secure my father's kingdoms, despised one another.

But that would not prevent this boy coming to my bed. For all I knew, hatred might well encourage him, hasten his steps, for whilst I was his superior in title and blood, I had sworn an oath to be compliant to his will in the bedchamber, an oath only women had to swear.

*Long you wore the mask of Empress, now you must wear it in marriage*, said my heart. *Maintain control. Do not let him see fear. If he only sees disgust, he will not win.*

That was what this was about, in part at least. A child I had married and children want to win games. Geoffrey had small sense of self, and what there was, was fragile. He pretended confidence, but it was as false as the Pope's teeth.

Geoffrey found me a threat. It was easy to see, his hackles spiked each time he saw me. I held grand titles, was older, had ruled great lands. His experience was small. He found other men with higher titles unnerving. That a woman, his wife of all women, outmatched him, was a great threat to that crumbling sense of confidence.

There were other troubles for his soul. I had been married a long time, to a man who was twice a King and once an Emperor. Heinrich had been a proved knight, a respected warrior and a man of seemingly boundless power when to my bed he came. Geoffrey had only just been made a knight, had little experience in war or in love. Oh, he had tumbled with women of lower status, servants, daughters of peasants, but at least a part of him must have been aware they had a limited ability to say no to the Count of Anjou's son and more than one reason to pretend affection and desire. I did not doubt there was fear in him when he thought of my bed. He was about to complete with a ghost.

But Geoffrey also feared me.

Perhaps not me, exactly, but his desire for me. He wanted me. He did not want me to know, but I did. Men are poor at hiding when they desire women, whether they like those women or not. Desire is a different creature to friendship. There does not have to be respect in it. My boy-husband wanted me, and did not want me to know. Such knowledge might grant me power over him. More than anything did the boy fear anyone having power over him.

I saw him lean forwards, bright blue eyes blazing like the blinding skies of winter as he watched the other knights. On his gold and purple coat was a yellow sprig of broom, something he wore often. Like the lions he insisted were embroidered on his clothes and leopards that were embossed on his shields, the broom was becoming part of his costume of nobility, this boy I had married, dressing up so men would think him a man.

My just-turned fifteen-year-old husband was not to compete that day, so the people might see us, the *happy* couple, side by side on the joyous day we had been joined. Geoffrey resented not competing. He was due to tomorrow, after he had proved himself a man in my bed. I had no doubt Fulk had already talked to lords Geoffrey would face, telling them to ensure he won. There had been competitions before our marriage, and for his youth Geoffrey had done well, but there had been moments I had thought I had seen the knights back down. If it were another man they would have pressed on.

Fulk would not grant his son a too-easy win. He would instruct his men to press the boy hard, test him, but in the end Geoffrey would win. It was important the people had faith in Geoffrey, and that he had faith in himself. Fulk was to leave Anjou in a matter of months to claim his new wife and prepare for his promised throne in the Holy Lands and when he did, Anjou became Geoffrey's. Fulk wanted Anjou safe in the hands of his son, and feared it would not be. So Fulk wanted Geoffrey confident, but not a slave to the impression life would toss gifts in his lap. The new Count of Anjou needed to know the strain and fear of battle before he faced it in truth, alone and without his father. Besides, it was traditional for lords to win tournaments. Sometimes they did so from honest skill, more often from true terror. When you hold power of life and death over people in real life, strangely you often find they let you win when playing games.

There was a cheer. I glanced up, thoughts broken by noise. The riding of the knights, a race I had witnessed little of due to the dust and my own preoccupation, was at an end. They rode off into another cloud of their own making, bearing fluttering banners aloft. Others assembled to begin the melee, a dangerous contest. Two sides would rush at one another and fight with sword, spear, or another chosen weapon. Two-handled axes were common if one side were pretending to be marauding Danes or Saxons. It was popular with men, and although I could see the attraction if one were fighting, as a spectator I often found it hard to see what was happening. Men so often think of their own pleasures first, ignoring those of others.

The melee was not as a bear when baited with dogs, where one could see the fight in its entirety. This was a clash of creatures and noise, a glare of sword light and a rumble of men shouting, metal grinding, shields bashing. Even those in the midst often had no idea who had won. I preferred to see one man pitted against another, for at least then the skill of the individual could be witnessed. When the melee came I often found my mind wandering. The men fighting thought we all watched, enraptured, but men often are deluded when it comes to what goes on in the minds of women. It would be cruel to tell them we are, so often, not thinking of them.

Not wanting to think of my present, I was considering the future.

Heir to the throne of England I was, barons of Normandy and England sworn to uphold me as Queen when my father King Henry I died. My father wanted it, desired his blood on his throne, wanted a dynasty created with him as the founder. I was the instrument of this. My marriage would grant me children, blood of King Henry who would rule England and Normandy for the rest of time.

All men want history to remember them. They want to be a story told by memory, want men sitting about a bright fire on the eve of battle to speak their name and recount their glories. They want bards and minstrels to lift their voices and sing haunting tunes of their deeds and lives and wounds and joys. It is a way to cheat death; if always we are remembered never can we die. If our names are perpetually upon the lips of man, we remain real, not ghosts. I was the vessel by which my father's blood would be poured upon the crown, a stain of red never to be removed by touch of man.

Perhaps it was fitting, then, that the stud chosen to seed this dynasty with me had hair that was red and gold. No King was Geoffrey and if my father and his men had anything to do with it, never would he be. Yet on his head was the red of blood and the gold of royalty.

My head, like my father's, was smoke and shadow. My eyes were grey-blue, like water. People called me beautiful, which pleased me, but I had always thought beauty a passing fancy, an outside show. Heinrich had not been handsome; honesty would have named him plain, yet his head and heart had been unique, special in a world of glaring, tedious ordinariness. My new child-husband expected people to love him for his sweet face, but I knew how well masks may work; spiders hide behind pretty petals.

I hoped men of England and Normandy might come to see my inner soul and not concentrate on the outside. My *outside* was particularly troublesome for them. Breast and shapely hip were all very well for breeding, but not for leading. My father's barons had sworn to uphold me as Queen but they did not welcome the notion of a woman on the throne. It was not the normal order of the world. A woman wielding power was an aberration. Only sometimes, when ruling for absent husband or young son, should women hold power.

The barons had agreed because in my father's plan of the future I was only a guardian of the throne. A son of my womb would emerge, and become of age to be King, hopefully before my father died. Father was a hale man, hardly ever had he been sick a day in his life, and even if he passed sooner than he wanted, if he could cling to life for a while I might only have to rule a few years. Then another man could take over. I was but a bridge, a hasty construction linking two solid banks. When the procession passed, they would knock my timbers into the water. I would be forgotten.

That was what men of England and Normandy thought, but often men are wrong. I intended a different future, for the throne and for myself.

But ruling as I wanted to, as a king, would not be easy and it would be impossible if I had no support. I intended to show them I could rule, and continue to rule until I died, as a king would. When I was dead a child of my body could claim the throne. My father's ghost might wail, for that was not his plan, but he would be gone. The dead may not command us, their time is done.

I had won the respect of some barons already, and felt I could count on them, call on them. As for others, if they could look past the body, see my mind, hear my thoughts, know the courage that was in me, perhaps they would accept me as Queen, as they had my father as King. He, too, had not been intended for the throne at first. He had been a younger son who claimed the throne by luck, held it by wit and will.

I had as much spirit as he. I had looked Death in the eye and had not flinched. I had lost all that was dear to me, all I thought I could not do without and I had survived. I had done my duty, married where I hated for the sake of England and Normandy. I might not have fought in battles, but I had wielded power, had managed countries, men, politics, and I had never faltered. Never, in all the trials I had faced had I surrendered. I had full as much courage as a man, perhaps more, for women must face all men do without sword in hand or armour on their bodies. All I had to defend myself with was my mind, my wit, integrity and my courage. I had faced men who meant to enslave me, men who would lock me away until I did their will and oftentimes those men were those who were supposed to love me, want the best for me. I had seen all I dreamed fall to ashes, and a new fire I had built, many times.

Yes, I had courage. In time, men would come to see that.

I blinked. The melee was in full swing, roars erupting from all sides, clash and clang of metal on wood and hide filling the air. But the noise was not what had woken me from my thoughts. There was a flash of blue, as though the sky threw itself into my eyes.

I had caught him staring again. Geoffrey did not like it when I caught him. He tried to stop himself but he could not help it. Over me those rebellious eyes wandered, over skin, flesh, lingering where his mouth, lips and hands wished to linger too. I could hear his blood throbbing painfully, brutally, inside his hot veins. I could smell his lust. It made me feel sick.

I sighed and he looked away. In the distance I heard a lark singing. Into the skies she winged, delighted by the heat and light of the day. Larks are not known for letting a chance to sing pass them by. She sounded joyous, so happy that my sorrowful heart thought it might break from envy.

Night would soon fall. Owl would replace lark, calling into empty darkness, longing for an answer. There would be feasting, dancing, people would cheer in the warm, glowing great hall. Smoke would rise from the fire in its centre, pluming up to the wooden roof. Cups of ale would pass hand to hand. Wine, warm with spices and honey would be shared. And I would be taken to bed, washed and perfumed, set between the sheets to wait for him. Geoffrey would drink with his men until his young blood was awash with the courage he needed. It was courage he could not rouse in himself, so would find at the bottom of a horn of ale. Heinrich had been sober when he came to me. He had been attentive, careful. Geoffrey would be none of those things.

I breathed in, setting my teeth. No matter what I faced this night, I would face it undaunted. This stripling could not frighten me. Thus far he had taken only girls to his bed, or wherever he pressed them to accept his over-eager shaft. This night he would find a woman, one who knew what a true man would be capable of, and who wanted him for one thing, seed. When that was done, so was my duty. I was not about to bow and scrape, show fear to this child.

I lifted my chin, and began to clap as the winning team of the melee came to bow. Men stood proud, blood and dust on their sweating faces. I was the one who handed out their prizes. I was the one they bowed to first. It was traditional for the Countess of Anjou to praise and pamper knights, but I liked that I was the one all eyes were on, rather than Geoffrey.

*That,* I thought, *will be how it is for all the time we are together, this fragile boy and me. And never will he be allowed to forget it!*

I would be on the winning side in this fight, not only in marriage to this fool of a boy, but in my quest for the throne, to become Queen in my own right.

# Chapter Two

## Angers
## Anjou

### Summer 1128

A breathless pall of heat hung on me as we rode along the winding track. Oppressive as marriage was the sun, harsh as fate. I gazed upon the back of the man I had been shackled to, wishing he would tumble from his horse, break his neck. A swift crack of spine, and I would be free.

Child of summer and sun was Geoffrey. That month, as we travelled into the heart of Anjou where he was loved, I had watched the sun's radiance alight on his red-gold head and thought of his birth in the dawn of summer. I, daughter of winter, child of water was an offering of bitter February, something torn from a belly of ice and skin of stark water. He, child of light and warmth, spoiled by father and fate was a creature of summer and sun. A beast of ease, not burden.

When one has been handed all one ever would want, one comes to think that is the way life is. That is how it is for children of summer, especially noble ones like Geoffrey. All should be easy as the summer breeze, rich as the harvest his hands never had to gather.

I do not deny some born in summer do not think so, but in him shone a golden self-importance, a warm bluff boast. In his soul was the hum and buzz of bugs hovering over a field. He was the sun-haze, blocking out what was real to be seen or heard with the force of the lazy, liquid season of heat. There was little under the surface, the earth of his heart baked dry, plants that might have grown in his soul withering. Child of summer, yes, the exhausting, suffocating, sweaty season before the glorious harvest, sunny stranger to the wondrous chill of misty, rich-scented autumn where frost lies on fields at dawn, then the grass is ablaze with sunlight by midday. Geoffrey was the stifling summer, a season many looked forward to and then remembered why they liked it not when it arrived and they bathed in sweat each day, and were unable to slumber by night. Golden son of the sun was the boy I had wed; a being that glittered bright and burned my skin.

His people saw his fair looks and thought that meant he was good inside. People always believe fictions about their rulers. The thought they are evil is too hard to bear, and to be handsome is a fine disguise. Many a hard heart has been hidden by fair face.

We were night and day, moon and sun, and those elements are not supposed to exist at the same time. Where we crossed, dusk and dawn, was where it was said borders between world and otherworld were to be found. There was danger. We should not have been matched. There was a darkness in me born of sorrow and experience, it showed most keenly when light shone on me. When the sun climbed or fell, casting shadow, my shade could be seen only darker and stronger for the light at my back. And yet there was light in me, I knew that. But next to this golden boy of the sun it would not be seen.

"Le *Bel*!" They called as he rode through their towns. Hands waved and heads bowed. Priests walking, robed in dark colours, stopped to pay respects, their hands making the sign of the cross in the sweltering air. Young women looked on with admiration, for Geoffrey was handsome and rich, recently made a knight. What dreams cannot be made from such mysterious substances as sunlight and fantasy? Women dreaming of another life, one of less hardship, perhaps even of love, are spinners and weavers, just as the Fates are. From small threads maids may make blankets most glorious to drape over their lives, to cover themselves in wishes. I saw them turn their eyes up towards him, some coy and some silently begging that he might notice them, fall in love, that heady substance that when it falls upon men may change the world. A peasant woman had attracted my great-grandfather, Robert the Devil of Normandy, leading to her being taken into his castle, and to the birth of my grandfather the Conqueror. Why should something so wondrous happen once, and not again? There was hope in their eyes as they watched him. Geoffrey affected to see nothing. He saw them, though, of course, and liked it. He felt admiration pouring upon him as we all felt the sun streaming upon our heads. As the sun feeds flowers, so adoration fed Geoffrey. Perhaps that was why he found me vexing. All I had to offer was darkness. There was no sustenance for him there.

Our horses' hooves clopped slowly through the gates of cities surrounded by high timber walls, and through villages and towns so all could see and admire and adore their soon-to-be lord. My falcon, *Faith-Breaker*, called out, fractious and hot in her cage in the wagon, even as the man who tended to her fed her water and flesh. Past rows of merchant's houses, their roofs glinting with stone tiles, we went, past shops with soft silks and linens fluttering outside to tempt customers in. In central squares our horses stood a moment over dull patches of brown and black; blood from a cockfight dried into the dust. Children stared with wide, beautiful eyes at Geoffrey, nervously fingering their clothes. Narrow, tall houses of the rich with small windows covered in waxed parchment seemed to stare down enraptured, just as the people were. Sparrows chirped from under shadowed eaves, as though they too welcomed their fair lord. I could not deny Geoffrey was pleasing to look upon. His soul was less so.

It was like the country we rode through, like all kingdoms. Much beauty there was, and ugliness.

On the gates of cities were the blackened heads of criminals executed for treason, or more petty crimes, on spikes. Heads hairless and par-boiled pink, goggle-black eyes staring endlessly out beyond life to death, they were displayed as warnings to others. *This is the path you walk, and its end,* whispered wide-grinning skulls as magpies and crows picked clean mottled flesh from white bone, scraps fluttering in the light wind, the sun crisping what was left upon them, maggots dropping curled and soft and white to scramble away into the dust out of reach of foot and hoof. Inside towns the streets smelt of piss and shit and cooking and sweat. Bakehouses made pies and bread, women brewed ale. Incense burned from noble houses to drown out the stench, but always it was there. The air was polluted with the din of pigs grunting and geese honking, indignant chickens scratching, flapping, horses snorting. And always there was shouting in towns, sounds of music from inns and good houses. Always there was silence filled. Outside, along roads through the countryside there was the sound of the birds, the hum of insects, a crackle of grain stalks ripening. These were the sounds of beauty, solitude, of a moment apart from the world of man, his noise, and his unquiet, violent presence.

Yet there was beauty man had made, or at least had aided. We rode past glittering green-gold fields of grain, oats, barley, rye and wheat, stalks and heads fluttering in the wind, silver and golden light flickering, teasing the eyes.

Here and there a field was fallow, sheep, pigs or cattle wandering on scrabble grass and dried, cracked mud imprinted with hooves. They were grazing on the tired shoots still left, pausing now and then to look up at us, jaws never ceasing to move, eyes fixated yet uninterested. Long valleys of grapes we rode past were lush with life, cool air blowing across them, keeping the fruit at just the right temperature. Anjou was famed for its wine, particularly from Bordeaux.

Past villages where thatched roofs and spires of small churches were the first things we saw, we went. Smoke rose, vanishing, into cloud. The scent of pottages of wild herbs like daisy, colewort or sorrel, and spare bones put in for marrow was on the air. People tending beds of beans and turnips looked up, hands covered with dirt and dust, dried mud in every crease, shading their eyes as on our bright banners and huge numbers they gazed. Barrels placed to collect rainwater stood guarding houses, as hens, released from their own little houses, pecked and scratched in yards.

Carts trundled the roads, stopping to allow our procession of men and knights, horses and wagons to pass, for they saw Geoffrey's banners. As we rode past, dust heaving into the air, horses dropping leavings of manure, the people bowed low, respectful. When they rose they stared first at their lord, hope in their eyes that he might be a kind man, a just ruler, and then they all tried to see me, their new Countess.

Pale interest and bright alike alighted on me. Some thought nothing would change with the coming of a new Countess, but some who dared to dream hoped much would. Fulk had not been a bad ruler. He was a good man, but he had pursued war and glory to enhance his name, and for his people that meant taxes, the loss of their sons to military service, and danger of invasion. With the coming of a new Count would come a new time, for better or worse. Geoffrey was young and handsome, it was easy to place hope in him. With pretty vessels it is tempting to imagine what is stored within is sweet. And he came with a new wife, and since wives often interceded between husband and mercy, there might be thought to be more hope. If I could influence him to forgiveness, peace and justice, their lives might be easier. If I could not, little would change.

Some bowed and waved, some cheered, a fragment of hope in their voices. Some looked shocked, for it was a long journey and I had refused to ride as women were supposed to in Normandy and Anjou. Like a man, but with a riding skirt to preserve modesty, I rode. Geoffrey had not liked the notion, but my father had laughed. "My daughter has much spirit of man in her," was what he said.

Always, if something was good it was masculine, bad if feminine, and usually if either sex transgressed those borders it was also bad. At times, however, women were lauded by being granted traits supposedly male, as long as we did not trespass too far. It was nonsense, but there was no sense in arguing with any who said such, as these things were truths universal. That did not make it any less irritating, or erroneous.

When we reached outskirts of towns and villages, there still were people. Past fields where young men practised archery, preparing for times of war when their lord would call them to battle and death for Anjou, we went, the zing and thump of arrows hitting targets of hay and straw echoing along with the song of the birds. Buzzing bees swooped close to ears then away again, swift as a love forgotten. People gathering waybread and other wild herbs from ditches and the edges of forests looked up. We rode past one manor and saw beehives draped in strands of black cloth. There had been a death in the family and as was traditional the family had informed the bees. It was an old tale, that bees were connected to the living and the dead; messengers between the two realms. It was not a wise idea to leave them uninformed. If they were not paid the respect they were due, bees would fly away never to return. They were also told of marriages, or births of children. Rather than bring black cloth or sing sad songs, people of the house would bring bride cake or flowers, and set them about the hives until the bees came, to listen and to feed.

At the boundaries of the manor we found people gathering wood, twigs and branches, a favour granted by their lord. They must have been tenants, for manorial lords would grant the right to no others. Further on were men burning coppiced wood for charcoal, others building fences for livestock. Burbling streams and faster flowing rivers had to be crossed either by bridge, or by wading the horses through. Once we came across men seeking a villein who had run away from his lord. Villeins had two ways to gain their freedom, be set free by their lord, or run away and hide. If they were not caught for a year and a day they became free. We had not seen the man, and they rode away up the hillside, searching. A voice in me prayed they would not find him, that he would escape. I knew what it was to wish to be free.

From time to time I glanced at my new husband, as different to the first as it was possible to be. Frequently I let out a sigh through my nose that others could not hear, just to release tension in my soul. At others I touched the hidden adder-stone, asking my brother's spirit for courage.

Our wedding night had been an interesting affair, one I was not sure Geoffrey remembered. Drunk as a Viking he had come to my chamber, borne on the shoulders of his friends, all fools like him. Most brides were waiting in the bed, but, deciding this would set me at a disadvantage I had stood in the centre of the chamber wearing my nightgown, my cape and an icy expression. Young lords of Anjou had burst through the door, red-faced and chortling, and been confronted by a wall of snow and shiver. Ice and disdain were my glittering armour, sharp was my sword of disgust. Distaste, thick and yellow as morning piss stored stinking in the bladder poured from me, contempt billowed from my every pore.

"You can leave," I said to Geoffrey's friends.

They left, suddenly mirthless, as though each man had met his grandmother and been scolded by a scalding tongue. I stared down my nose at the boy. "Come," I said, my voice stark. "Let us to our union go."

He had no idea where the words had come from, why would he? They meant nothing to him, but using the words of Matilda of Canossa, warrior Countess, soldier of the Pope, brought heart and courage to me. She had not wanted her husbands, either.

"Take your gown off," he had said, smirking as he stumbled into the inner chamber where the bed was. Despite his drunkenness, there was a cat-like calculation in his eyes, for cats are creatures of their own comforts. He was thinking how to best pleasure himself, using me.

"As you wish." Removing it, I stood before him naked. Clothed in ice as I was, he could not touch my soul even if he would my body. He stared at me, stunned. I think he had expected I would refuse, that we would fight. I think he had liked the notion, mistaking assault for passion. "Let this be done," I said. "I would go to my rest."

Turning from him I had walked to the bed. I could feel his hesitation in the air, a moment of being lost, not knowing what he should do. "You will need to at least pull your nightgown up," I told him, pulling back the covers. I heard a curse invoking God's fingernails, which almost made me laugh.

I had lain down in the bed, heard him pulling the last of his clothes from his body. As he came to the bed I blew the candle out and steeled myself. As blessed darkness fell, I tried to imagine the fumbling, drunk and overexcited youth was Heinrich. It was not possible, and had I been a maiden the experience would no doubt have been horrific, but I was somehow distant of it all. I set my mind apart, told myself to endure and soon it would be done. I was right.

Geoffrey enjoyed himself, I knew that from the strangled cry he made as his frantic, short-lived thrusts came to an abrupt, shuddering end. Upon my body he collapsed, trembling, gasping. He almost kissed me, a hand reached up as though he would stroke my face, and then he remembered who he was upon and in. To one side he rolled. I could feel he was angry, not so much with me but himself.

In darkness I smiled. I almost laughed again, truth be told. Partly it was relief the encounter was over, the first one at least, but Geoffrey amused me. The cry he had let out he had not meant to emit. Although clearly I was not the first woman he had bedded, as despite fumbling hands and rough ways he knew his way into a woman's body, I had greatly excited him. He had not wanted me to know I had such an effect, and my regal disdain had made him want even more to make it appear as though this were all business for him as it was for me.

*Almost* he had succeeded, but not quite. The frantic rush of lust was too hectic, hands too wild and excited, and that last cry had held all the desire of months of waiting, all the times he had imagined this moment. He knew that I understood that he found me as desirable as he found me disagreeable.

He rose from the bed in darkness and threw on his fur-trimmed robe. "I shall come again tomorrow night," he said, words slurring from his lips.

"Come every night," I said, striking a flint and fire steel to light my taper then candle, not looking at him. "And you should stay this night."

"You want me to stay?" A note of hope escaped his wine-stained lips before he could restrain it.

I gazed at him coldly. "The sooner there is a child in my belly, the swifter this unfortunate duty may cease," I said. "Then I can enjoy nights of peace, and you can to your whores go and listen to them scream false rapture."

The scowl on his face as he left was marred by the glint of excitement in his eyes.

I rose after he left, washed and sat by the fire, watching firelight flicker on the walls, the lapping tongue of a dragon. Outside I could hear our guests still celebrating. The noise went on into the early hours in the great hall. Men cheered, no doubt wishing their young lord well as he bedded his wife. They thought he would mount me over and over, as most men did on their wedding night. They did not know he had gone to his bed already, duty done.

Duty done, indeed. And now the union was legal and binding. Consummation was required to make marriage legal, and in that brief coupling it had been done. Because of spare moments of Geoffrey upon me, I was now tied by fate to this man until one of us died.

Somewhere below my chambers a door opened and a burst of song and laughter escaped. It closed, music and mirth contained again, prisoners.

Down winding corridors came echoes of guards moving, peals of laughter from the halls and from outside buildings where men had persuaded women to head for adventures more pleasurable than mine had been, or so I hoped. I hoped I was the only woman of the world so unhappy.

I had washed again, smearing soap of lye and ash on skin, rubbing hard. I could smell him on me, a scent that made me feel sick, as though perfume of sweat and lust and wine had marked me as his. I was his property now. I did not need to smell him upon me, scent sticking to my skin.

Each night after the first he had come, determination on his face. As bells tolled for dusk and white owls prepared to make their steady, gliding graceful flight through the skies, there he was at my door, the light of ceramic oil lamps on the walls dancing on his face. He was always ready, as though the thought of night had been in his head all day, infesting his manhood to excitement. Sometimes he lasted a long time, taking pleasure in rutting upon me. More often it was rushed. As time went on I thought his lust would fail but he grew only more eager. The more I withdrew in spirit the more he wanted me, as though to push himself inside my body would allow him to somehow reach the part of me I kept separate from him, from these trysts. The part he could not touch was what he wanted. The colder I became, the hotter his blood burned. Some nights he was feverish, consumed by a flame I lit in him.

Sometimes, in daylight I would catch him watching me. Although he despised my pride, he was proud of me. My titles reflected well upon him, and my behaviour in public was impeccable. I referred to him as *my lord*, praised his skill in tourneys that occurred each day as our kingdoms celebrated our union. I was gracious to his men, polite to his friends. In all ways I was the perfect model of a countess, of a Queen.

But it angered him too, for in our bedroom I would not allow him the upper hand. I treated him as though he was a vessel to deliver seed, which he was. In public there was nothing for him to find fault with. In private I made no secret that I despised him, that our coupling brought me no pleasure.

He found it insulting. I wondered how hard and high maidens he had lain with had faked pleasure. Women grow talented at deception, not that it does anything to improve the performance of the men. Perhaps some had enjoyed it, found him desirable, but I faked nothing. I endured and I made that plain. He wanted me to want him as he wanted me, and he knew I did not. That stripped away some of the pleasure he took, and much satisfaction. Had I been frightened, shown fear, he might have taken pleasure in that, for there was a cruel twist to his soul, but I showed none of the fright I felt. And there was some. I had no wish to be with him, still less to have him inside me. But I would not allow him to think that by bedding me he was mastering me. My body I had sworn to offer up for duty. My soul was my own.

"As a soldier in war, as a maiden sacrifice to the dragon," I had muttered to myself one day as I stood gazing from the window in the castle of Le Mans. Perhaps that was what those stories meant, that the maiden of the tale, offered as a sacrifice, was meant to be the bodies of women, by law not our own but property of husbands, fathers, brothers. And the dragon was not the beast that would consume us, but the spirit we kept inside, the part that was ours and no others.

I remember as I watched from that window, a kingfisher, blue and silver, flashed down into the water. They say the kingfisher lays its eggs in the ocean, calming the sea. Some used it to predict the winds. If hung by its head, its beak would turn to the direction of the wind. I had watched a while, hoping beauty would return, but the bird was gone. Ugliness followed as night fell.

Each night Geoffrey arrived, hoping to see something in my cold face. Taunting eyes searched mine. "Always you are ready, waiting," he said on one occasion.

"I have sworn to do my duty. My oaths I keep," I said. "No more, no less."

"No more, no less," he said, eyes glinting with a spark of anger, as though he expected that at some stage I would fall to his feet, fainting for want of him, admitting slavish love.

He had other women for that, so why he wanted it from me I knew not, but for to win the game between us. There were mistresses already. I saw them on his arm. I ignored them and him when he was with them.

I sighed, looking at the road ahead, trying not to think on my present. All roads lead onwards, to somewhere. I had to think of the future, of England and Normandy and my claim to their thrones. The present was not something I could control, but perhaps the future was. This would pass, things would change, and one day I would be free, free of this mauling kitten in my bed, free of much man had imposed upon me.

# Chapter Three

## Angers
## Anjou

## Late Summer 1128

"I wish you would stay," I said to my bastard brother and my friend.

Robert and Brian Fitzcount were heading to England, called home by my father who was already there. Tarried long enough to know I had been wedded and bedded had my sire, then back to business in England it was for him. Until there was a child for him to use as he had used me for politics and power, there was little for him here. Robert and Brian had remained behind, a stay allowed by my father on the understanding that Geoffrey's temper was unknown. The presence of men who cared for me might hold the child back from striking me in a tantrum, so it was thought. But even that protection was about to be removed.

"Fulk will not allow Geoffrey to hurt you, Domina," Brian said, his fingers clasping shut a ring-brooch of silver on his shoulder, holding his cloak in place. It had come undone.

"Until he too rides away," I said. "But you are right, and my father-in-law is not leaving for a time." Fulk was due to depart Anjou in the year coming. For a while I had someone I could rely on.

"You know we would rather stay, sister," said Robert, taking my hand. "There is no welcome task waiting for us in England."

I smiled. Our father had sent for my two kinsmen and friends because he wanted them to undertake an audit of the treasury. It was to take at least a year, for they were to look at many things, the ancient *danegeld* included, a tax put in place in ancient days to raise tribute when Vikings attacked England's shores, and maintained long after they left because England's kings found the money useful. Robert and Brian would have clerks, of course, but for men of action spending a year overseeing a dusty, dull task was not a jaunt of pleasure.

As I said goodbye to friends, I was called on to do the same for an enemy, and kinsman. "He is dead?" I asked. It seemed impossible.

"The wound was thought nothing, Domina," said the messenger sent from Flanders, bowing as he spoke. "A cut to the hand, by all reports not a serious one. The Count withdrew from battle, fever set in. The flesh turned black. Five days later, Clito was dead."

William Clito, my cousin, son and only heir of my uncle Robert Curthose, was dead. The formidable enemy who had waged war against my father, who had become Count of Flanders after being a penniless wanderer, the proved knight who many thought should be Duke of Normandy, even King of England, the man who many thought should be named heir instead of me... was dead.

A cut to the hand. A fever. An accident and my greatest rival was no more.

And this twist, this cruel little curl of fate just six weeks after I had been married. Had my father paused just a moment, my hated marriage would not have been required. Anjou had been needed to stand with us against Clito, Clito was no more. I could have married elsewhere, wed a man rather than a boy, a prince rather than a count's heir. I could have been free of the curse of Geoffrey, liberated of a country that men of my homeland despised. I would not have had to endure all this... all for the sake of forty days.

Had I not felt like weeping, I might have laughed.

Clito had been busy after my father had forced the retreat of his ally, Louis of Francia, from our Norman borders. My father's harsh trade sanctions, imposed upon Flanders, had caused damage to Clito and his people, but my cousin had taken to laying siege to castles near his lands that stood allied with England and my father. Thierry of Alsace was Clito's great rival, for under the bitter weight of damaged trade with England, men of Flanders were turning to Thierry, who had a claim to the kingdom, hoping he would become their lord. My father supported Thierry, and towns of Flanders started to declare for him. Clito made war on him.

There was no spirit in Clito that would permit surrender; something inherited from our shared grandfather, the Conqueror. Tirelessly, with relentless spirit and feral skill in battle, Clito pushed his forces onwards. He did not have the numbers he needed, yet from reports it had seemed to matter not. His men believed in him so completely he was as God to them.

There had been reports of him, silver in armour and red, awash with the blood of his foes, fighting as Mars come to walk amongst mortals once more.

Clito had been attacking the castle of Thierry of Alsace when he was wounded, when fever fell. Then he was gone, in the beat of a bird's heart. Clito, the man who had wandered and conquered, who had made much of the slight hand Fate dealt him, who had been praised as a soldier, a knight, even as our grandfather reborn, who had shown more promise than a thousand men who became kings, was no more. He was but twenty-six when Death stole him away, a man who might have made the world tremble to hear his name.

Before he departed life, Clito sent my father a letter, begging forgiveness for all he had done. My father was happy to oblige, relieved that his great foe was no more. My reaction was more complicated. The danger to me was gone, yet my repulsive marriage was superfluous.

"I wonder at times if there is a curse upon male kin of the Conqueror, indeed," I said to Elisabeth, one of my women, "if the curse of the New Forest haunted men of my line not only in that forest, but elsewhere. My uncles Rufus and Richard died by accident, Curthose was ill-fated, my brother drowned, and now Clito, dead of a wound to the hand."

"Yet, Domina, your father lives, and prospers," Elisabeth said.

*Some would not think so*, I thought. His greatly loved heir dead, only a daughter to replace the son he had reared so carefully for the throne. My father had been denied children with Adeliza, my stepmother who was more like a sister, particularly in age, to me. Accident may not have stripped my father of life, but accidents had marred it.

It would of course be hard to find a person not scarred by life, but it could not be denied my father had suffered much.

I heard many tales of my cousin after his death. Often this is the way. When people die they become perfect, faultless. They can make no more mistakes, so perhaps that is why. I heard of Clito's passion, the intense and .loyal friendship he inspired in men, his high spirits which never could be dampened. I found myself thinking a dispensation should have been sought and I should have been married to him. At least I would have had a warrior for a husband, rather than a boy playing knight.

Clito had no sons; neither of his marriages had begot children. Without their leader to inspire them his men fractured. Some headed to make peace with my father, the rest sought their fortunes in the Holy Land, some as mercenaries and some joining orders like the Knights Hospitaller, defending holy sites wearing the black surcoat and white cross of their order. Overnight, the entire political situation altered. Because of the fever of a wound, my life was changed. Much of the time I felt I was by water influenced, but this time fire changed my fate.

Thierry of Alsace became Flanders' Count, and was approved by all. Later in life he was to wed Clito's widow, Sybil of Anjou, sister to Geoffrey. As Flanders and England renewed treaties of trade, my father surprised a few of us. He commanded Stephen of Blois to pay homage to Thierry as overlord of Boulogne. There had been talk before I was named heir and even after that I might be replaced by one of the sons of Adela of Blois, Theobald or Stephen, but this made it clear that whilst in England Stephen owned much land, in Europe he was the lord of a small kingdom, and owed homage to both the King of Francia and Count of Flanders. My cousin Stephen was guardian of the northern borders of Normandy, a worthy ally, but he was not destined for kingship. I wondered if this was revenge inflicted by my father for Stephen making peace rather than war with Clito whilst he had lived.

A week later from England came a letter from Robert, informing me of the death of Clito, and of something else. On the day Clito died, Curthose, his father, had dreamed a dream of portent. In slumber he believed his arm had been struck by a lance, and the flesh upon it died. When he woke, Curthose told his guards his son was dead. At the time most men thought it a lunatic thing to say. Although Clito indeed died that day, his men kept it secret a long time, so no one knew for a while that Curthose was right, and his only son died on the day he woke from that dream.

Curthose was not alone in his dreams.

I had a dream after Clito died too. I was standing on the familiar shore where often I came in dreams, watching the boat carrying my brother sail away, past green-topped cliffs, heading into the boundless sea. It was as it always was. I was alone, sand running past my bare feet and over them, my gown and cape snapping and floating in the light wind, arms crossed across my body, holding myself in a lonely embrace. I watched my brother's boat borne away by wind and wave, by curling white froth, by the gentle yet insistent pull of the hungry sea. Always I stood there, alone, watching Will and his ship. Many nights I was alone with grief, with the sound of water sliding on wet sand, the twist of the wind's voice curling in my ear. Always I watched.

This time I saw something. At first it was a play of light on water; a dragon scale of light flashing, twinkling, and then I looked up and saw it was not a play or trick of light. A swooping creature, like a bird, was in the skies, red against the blue fire of the heavens. I thought for a moment it was plunging to attack the ship bearing the body of my brother, but as it fell from the skies and its serpentine tail arched in the wind, I saw it was not. It was protecting it, accompanying him.

I knew it was a dragon; there was something that suggested such in its shape. But it was not a threat to my brother. The creature had joined him, would guard him, perhaps guide him.

I think that night, in some realm of dreams where the living might visit the dead, I saw two heirs of the Conqueror meet, find each other. It was not because they had been friends; had my brother lived Clito would have been his greatest enemy. They met and met there, in my dreams, in the realm of possibility, because they had held much in them that never had been used.

How many children of men and kings and gods are lost to us, purpose unfulfilled? How much that could have been do we lose, the chaos and possibility they held inside them falling as ash to the ground? What of fire is lost to smoke?

I felt I saw something that night. Something of where dreams go when they die, where those who could have altered the world go when they fall.

Would they watch as we lesser mortals struggled to do all that they might have done with ease? Would my brother, my cousin witness my deeds, and know pride in me, or only sorrow? What of potential, of possibility was lost with men like those I and the world had lost? What might the world have become, had fate allowed them to succeed?

That is the sorrow of ghosts, not death, but us. Unthinkingly we live, not seeing it is a gift, and one of limited time. The dead mourn our lack of concern, our fecklessness, our waste. They grieve the time we flit away, squander, for they know what it is to stand outside that bright, warm, glowing hall of life, looking in. Grendel did. That is why the monster turned savage, why he slaughtered so many. The dead know what it is to be a border-walker, a never-belonger, never kin, never welcome. What it is to be alone.

And those like my brother, like Clito, knew what they might have done, had they been granted a chance. It is not surprising we fear ghosts. The realm of spirits must be full of fury, of eyes watching how we waste life and love and potential, how we fools use the small time we have.

# Chapter Four

## Angers
## Anjou

### Summer's End 1128

"I need no woman to answer for me!"

I closed my eyes at the shrill scream. It grated on spine and soul. The adder-stone, warm in its safe pouch, heated my skin, offering comfort. "I merely put forth my opinion. I would think you would appreciate a voice of experience, no matter if it came from man or woman."

"*Experience*," he spat.

"I was Empress of the Holy Empire for more than half my life, regent of Italy at the age you are now. I watched over the kingdoms of the Emperor when my husband was at war," I said using a deliberately mild tone. "Experience is something I possess."

Matters might have been aided had I not added, "unlike you," under my breath.

Geoffrey turned a face of fire upon me, rage rode his breath. "You will know your place as my wife, as a Countess and as a woman." I could see a vein throbbing in his forehead. He was not as handsome when he was angry.

"My place ever before this time was to be partner to my husband and ruler," I said. "I may have been demoted in title by becoming *your* unfortunate wife, but depleted in intelligence I have not been. A wise man would use all the resources he has."

"A wise woman would know when to hold her tongue." His fists were clenching at his sides. A spark of fear flew in my chest.

I faced him full on. "Strike me, boy, and I will slap you right back."

As he was fire and fury, I stared at him with winter in my eyes. At the moment we were a fair match. Muscular though Geoffrey was, for Fulk was training him as intensively in sword craft as in politics, I was as tall as him and my temper was more than a match for his. He might do me more damage in the end, but the mere idea that he might bear a mark of my hand upon his face, for he knew I *would* strike where it would be seen, was enough to make him hesitate. The idea men would see that his wife had struck him brought intense shame to Geoffrey. Hitting me would not trouble him, he was itching to try, and law of man and men of God would support him in chastising his wife, but he had no wish to bring dishonour upon himself.

He had been about to attempt it. Those hands bunched at his sides, twitching to hit me, longed to be unleashed. I could see the desire in his eyes as keen as his lust for me at night. Beating one you cannot best with words or spirit is the last preserve of the weak in soul. He thought knocking me to the ground might make up for the fact I was more intelligent, more titled, nobler than he was. If he could stand over me, I was no more above him; a childish leap of logic and one all too common.

I had no doubt he would eventually do it, as I had no doubt I would indeed strike back. It might make my beating worse, but I was not about to allow the boy to think he could best me, in this or any other way.

At times I pitied him. I could see Geoffrey was intimidated and not only by me. Geoffrey might boast and brag he was ready to rule, that he would wage war upon enemies, bestow the kiss of peace upon friends, spend nights drinking ale and days swathed in a cloak woven of the sinew and blood of his foes, but the truth was he was scared. His father was preparing to leave, and this boy of only fifteen would then be in sole command of a kingdom, which, like any land, had enemies, many of them, and borders that would need defending. Men would think to test the new Count of Anjou, and might test hard, thinking his age and lack of experience would make the kingdom weak, easy pickings for ambitious ravens. Geoffrey had been trained well, he was not unintelligent and he had potential. From the age of three, although he would have had no idea of their significance, he had been witnessing charters with his father. Fulk had involved him in the administration of the kingdom as well as tutoring him in war, and this had only increased in intensity since our marriage. But Geoffrey also had many poor characteristics and without some calm influence upon him was likely to indulge what was rotten. Something in him knew he had the potential to fail, and fail with breathtaking speed and depth. He feared that, as he feared men seeing into his heart.

Geoffrey would tell the world he was ready, and yet he was not, for what man can truly say he is ready at so young an age to command a kingdom, lead a whole race of people? What man can tell you he is ready to be tested by enemies of greater experience and age, perhaps rebels in his own kingdom too? Tests were coming, and they would be of blood.

Failure, of course, scared most men for failure as a lord and master often meant death at the hands of another knight, ruler, or rebels. But Geoffrey was scared of failure itself, for being seen as a child, incompetent and foolish. He feared to be laughed at, looked down on. He feared that all would see how unprepared, unready, and ill-suited he was. He feared men would look upon him and see him as he sometimes saw himself.

And this was why he did not look with favour upon me, aside from when I was naked. When he glanced into my eyes

Geoffrey saw himself reflected in a way he feared more than anything else. In my eyes he saw not lord or knight, not warrior or count, but a pathetic boy.

Think not I was utterly devoid of sympathy. One reason I had intervened on this particular day, offered an opinion about what Louis of Francia might do now Clito was dead, was because I had seen Geoffrey had no answer for his men when they came before him. I made no attempt to shame the boy in public, he did that well enough on his own, but I was as accustomed to offering my opinion as I was utterly unaccustomed to dealing with a man like Geoffrey. Truth be told, I was not doing well. Dealing with men with flirtation and subtlety, as Adeliza did, was not one of my talents. I had always been frank and in the Empire had been encouraged to nurture that characteristic, in private at least. I found deception often a simple waste of time, and if men were permitted to speak honestly to one another, why could I not do the same? Sometimes I forgot I was a woman, and the rules were different for me.

Yet even women could be heard, if they were high enough. As Empress I had been called upon to know all and everything about my kingdoms, to offer reasonable and informed opinion when required. Geoffrey wanted me to sit, dumb as a statue, at his side. He did not want me to appear more intelligent or learned than him. Since that was hardly a Herculean task, he wanted me silent.

I pitied this fragile confidence he struggled to hold on to, whipping and tossing like a rag on a fence in a storm, but I was not about to alter who I was to appease this boy.

It should have been unnatural that he responded to me in this way. His mother, Eremburga, had acted as regent for her husband, and oversaw much in the country at other times. She had not been a silent statue at Fulk's side. Geoffrey did not mind when I undertook tasks obviously female; the welcoming of guests to the hall, offering of gifts, all works of charity; these acts of hospitality, expected of all noble men and usually worked by their wives, Geoffrey was not troubled by, but because I could do those acts and those he could do too, he was threatened.

I tried to remind myself of the patience Heinrich had demonstrated with me, of lessons Bruno had taught. I had been telling myself to deal with Geoffrey in the same way, to be calm, clever, to lead him as Bruno and Heinrich had me, but a guiding hand from his wife he did not want, and I grew fractious with ease. I was not a teacher born, as Bruno had been, and Geoffrey was not an ideal pupil. His staggering lack of respect for me and wealth of contempt granted me no reason to actually *want* to help him or show patience. I resented him and my marriage, and resentment is not a fertile field to grow grace and patience in. Failing those who had taught me so well in the past, I did not make the effort I should have. Geoffrey did his part, but I made an insecure child feel more insecure, and my refusal to back down when he, the hound of raised hackles and bared teeth, growled his way towards me, only made him more determined to silence me, and one day reduce me. Backing down would not have been a wise notion, for bullies scent blood and tear wounds only wider, but there were things I could have done, as the elder in the situation, which I did not. We all must accept responsibility for the pain we cause. The truth was, Geoffrey and I made each other more childish, and more dangerous than we needed to be. We were a bad match made, and we made it worse.

"You would not dare strike me," he said, eyes narrowing.

"Do you wish to test that theory?" I asked.

Out of the chamber he stormed, not fool enough to try his hand against me. I took a shaking breath and leant against a wall. My eyes rested on a candlestick, the bottom in the shape of a stag. I thought of my uncle Rufus, fallen to forest floor and to death because someone mistook his shadow for that of a stag, if the tale was true. A shadow against the sun, man indivisible from beast, and the world had changed. Stag walked away, as a King fell.

I would not let Geoffrey see it, but I was scared. He would strike me eventually. He was a growing boy, soon to be a young man in truth. At some stage he would be more than a match for me. On the day he realised that, I would know pain.

"But I will not surrender," I whispered. "I will not."

I gazed from the window, trying to fix my eyes on something to steady my mind. I saw a tree beyond the gates, gilded in dusk sunlight. Shadow faded to green, green to gold as up the tree my eyes went. The purest light was upon the top branches, where gold became white, part of the skies.

"Surrender I will not," I said again. I touched a brooch at my chest, an eagle depicted in gold, his feathers rubies. It had been Heinrich's, but was a piece older than him, than the Empire. Something in it sung of days lost, of Rome.

I had faced Heinrich when I feared him, and had not surrendered then. This boy certainly could strike, but even if he knocked me down I would not admit he was my master. I would rather have died.

That night I dreamed. A knight on a white horse killed a dragon of water. As the beast fell, I dropped to my knees at its side and wept, hot tears mingling with its red blood.

"Do you know what you have done?" I whispered to the knight. "Would you destroy all more powerful than you?"

He did not answer, but just walked away and I knew he was leaving to find another, another being of power he feared, that he might slay.

*

It did not help Geoffrey's fragile sense of self that men of letters had been dedicating books to me. It was customary to seek patrons for tomes and the patron was not necessarily a person of wisdom, but a dedication made them appear so. Authors benefited from a wealthy person supporting them, patrons from the appearance of wisdom.

Books had been dedicated to me when I was in the Empire, mainly because of my title, as many had been dedicated to me when I was a child with no reputation for learning. But when I came home to England I had been contacted by the monks of Malmesbury. One of their own, named William, had written a tome, *Gesta Regum Anglorum, a History of the Kings of England*, which had been intended to be supported by my mother, but upon her death required a new patron. The monks had sent an appeal to my uncle, King David of Scots, asking him to approach me with the book and speak well of their messenger. The monks said they pinned much hope on me as the legitimate heir of my father, and as a woman with a bountiful reputation for mercy and goodness. They hoped I would support the book, especially as it was about my great ancestors. Seeing the book might teach me what lessons to follow and which to avoid from those my ancestors had to teach, I had agreed to the dedication.

Another, which more recently had come to my hands, was a book by Philippe de Thaon, a man who had lost many lands in England. I believe he was hoping flattery could win them back, and this was the prime reason he meant to dedicate a book on the prophecies of the Sibyls to me. Adeliza had already written to me from her royal seat in England to say that he had approached her with other requests for patronage, so I knew it was not for my own personal qualities I was selected.

Geoffrey however had fumed, albeit quietly, about this. It was perfectly normal that the Countess of Anjou be approached for patronage, and it was a compliment to him that I be so. It was the place of noble women to encourage arts of literature and painting, music and dance, and the more that happened the more cultured the Count would look. But, much like my father, Geoffrey was simultaneously proud of such honours offered to me and angered by them. What angered him more was that I did not restrict myself to the sphere of *gentle* arts, but knew much of warlike ones, which he thought he alone should understand. It was true I had never swung a sword, but I had read much of military history and theory, and I could talk with clarity and wisdom on the subject, which annoyed him as much as it surprised, and in some cases delighted, other men.

"My daughter has *such* an eye for strategy," Fulk would tell his barons as he called me over to discuss battles of ancient Rome or Greece. "Most women concern themselves little with such matters, as is fitting, but the Empress of course had to understand such when in the Empire. You will find her thoughts illuminating."

My high title was a reasonable excuse for a woman knowing anything of war. But Fulk, excuses though he made, never sounded shamed by me knowing such things. Geoffrey tried to ignore the fact I knew anything. Men dedicating books to me called attention to the notion that wisdom *was* one of my virtues, so whilst in public he said nothing, so the honour to his house remained great, in private he seethed, miserable and bitter that I should be respected. What the boy wanted was to lower me so he could stand taller. Others were not supporting that plan, me least of all.

I tried to turn from politics for a time, thinking that if I concentrated on my household, on domestic matters, and left Geoffrey to rule for a while then he might feel less threatened. Fulk was still in Anjou, so there was little trouble Geoffrey could get himself and the country into after all. If the lad could gain confidence perhaps he would not continually try to steal it from me.

I had no chancellor, but in the Empire I had shared Heinrich's men if they were needed as witnesses to charters, so that was not unusual. I had four chaplains, my own body of household knights and my ladies. I had, too, my own cooks in the kitchens who were to make food just for me. This was, Fulk said, because he knew that Heinrich had done the same for me when I was Empress. "I wanted you to have some familiar comforts," he said.

"You are kind, lord father," I said. And I meant it.

I had many to serve me, of course. Almost everyone was a servant to another, and the higher you were the higher was the person you served. The women in my chambers were daughters and sisters of great lords, knights and barons, the mothers of future counts and earls, dukes, perhaps even kings. The knights of my household guard were not as elite as those in Geoffrey's, being the third or fourth sons of noble houses of Anjou where his were the eldest, but their blood was noble and I thought they had more potential. They had always been passed over, which made them more eager to prove themselves. Something I could well understand.

"The fire to be noticed will mark you out," I said to them on the day I met them. My accent sounded odder in Anjou than in Normandy, inflections of the Empire and lingering notes of England floating upon it. "Into your hearts it will burn, spurring you on. Remember, sons of Anjou, some of the greatest men of history, the most feared kings and conquerors, came of humble origins. My grandsire was the Conqueror, William of England, but he began as the bastard son of a duke and a common woman. He fought for all he took of life. You, serving me, can do the same. Fight for me, as my men, and on the day I come to the throne of England and Normandy, you will know greatness and glory."

My men had roared. I was told later they were drinking my health, and their future wealth, in the great hall.

Whilst I had sworn to step back and allow Geoffrey to rule, I could not help but gather knowledge. I did it quietly, trying to tiptoe about my husband, but I read of Anjou and her people.

It did not surprise me that the country was not so different to Normandy or England, or the Empire for that matter. The structure of society often was the same. At the top were kings and princes, counts and dukes, then barons, lords and knights. Then came tradesmen, then peasants, and, at the bottom, villeins.

Villeins, men and women who were not free but were not slaves, occupied land owned by us, their masters. Villeinage was a common Norman practice that my grandfather had carried to England. Although pockets of slavery still existed, and no doubt an underground trade still went on, in two generations the practice was, at least legally, wiped from England as it was in Normandy. Villeins might be said to be in no better position than slaves, since their masters owned the land they used and the bodies they wore, and they worked the land as slaves had before them. They supported themselves from land loaned to them, and their masters could sell them to other lords, decide who they married, take their children. Their rent for the land they occupied was their labour, and most of their produce. I could understand.

Although I wore silk and linen, although I slept in a castle and had enough to eat, I had no choice over who I married or what happened to my life. My father chose who entered my body, not me. My husband chose how many children I would have, and all of them belonged to him, as did my property. By marriage I was owned, by sex I was constrained. I lived an easier life in many ways, but in others I was no freer than men who scraped a living at the bottom of the scale of society. If I was permitted a voice, I had one, but that was not freedom. It was a leash loosened for a moment; a condescending nod allowing a child to speak.

But one day, that might not be the case. A crown might set me high enough to set me free.

# Chapter Five

## Angers
## Anjou

### Autumn - Winter 1128

"Your father names *you* in yet another charter and refuses to acknowledge me!"

The door banged hard against the wall, a powder-light shower of dust floated down from a beam above. On the head of the child it fell, like snow, or like the mist hovering over Angers that morning. Had it not been for the rage in his eyes, Geoffrey might have looked angelic.

*Faith-Breaker* hopped on her silver perch, roused from half-slumber by the infant wailing. I glanced up from the letter I had been reading from my uncle David. For months he and I had been in regular communication as he kept me apprised of matters in Scotland and England. Before leaving for Normandy and this ill-fated marriage I had asked him to send word of both countries. I knew I might not get the full tale from my father, and if I was to rule I needed to know all. I had decided to use the time I had been granted, much as when I was a child and Heinrich sent me into Bruno's schoolroom to learn all I could before I could take my place at his side. This time, to my father, was about me gaining an heir in my belly to make me an acceptable guardian for the English and Norman thrones. He would stay alive, he had said, so I could achieve this. To me, the production of an heir was but one goal. The other was to glean all information I could so when the time came I could claim the throne *and* rule until the end of my life, as kings did. Then, I would pass country and crown to my son and heir, if I had one.

Despite Geoffrey's nightly visits to my chamber, however, no matter how enthused, there was no sign of a child.

Since there was no peace in the castle because of my husband, and none in my mind for worry that common wisdom had been correct all along and I was indeed a barren wasteland, I found refuge in work and in planning a future; news from England, Normandy, Scotland, politics and passions of court. I welcomed letters from David, Robert, Brian, Adeliza and my father. I found even news of hard times and measures soothing. My father's clerks merely reported all doings of the state, but David often asked for my opinion. As I was finding it taxing to get Geoffrey to see me as a person and not just a hole to insert himself into at night, being treated by another man as a person with a mind by was welcome.

I set the letter in my lap. Winter shadows danced blue on the walls. "What my father chooses to do or not do is up to him."

"He insults me!"

I said nothing, for in truth Geoffrey had a point. But what he failed to acknowledge was that my father was trying to make one too. Before we had been wed my father had dropped hints aplenty that he might name Geoffrey King if I became Queen, or at least that the boy might become Duke of Normandy, taking control of one side of the kingdom as I ruled in England on behalf of a son. Since our wedding those scraps of hope had been reeled back in, snatched away. I was frequently and routinely associated with my father in charters, letters and royal documents, Geoffrey was not. No attempt was made to increase Geoffrey's power or standing with nobles of England or Normandy, no further offers of elevation, lands, or mentions of titles were made. Not even all my dowry had been handed over; castles in Normandy that were promised to Geoffrey remained in the hands of my father. Exmes, Domfront and Argentan, strategically placed castles along the borders of Normandy and Anjou, should have been Geoffrey's now, and were not.

To all intents and purposes, Geoffrey had vanished from the glittering realms of power and shady halls of politics of England and Normandy on the day we had wed. It was a shameful reversal of roles for him. Usually it was the woman who all but vanished, lands and titles merging with her husband's, her legal identity as a free woman gone. Under the cloak of the man went the woman usually, yet in our case it had happened to the man, and what Geoffrey did not welcome, aside from the potential loss of all dreams of glory, was that others would note this too, and laugh at him.

I knew the truth he had not been told. Having met and appraised my husband, my father wrote that Geoffrey was, at the most, to be a commander for my interests. There was likely to be trouble in Normandy and Anjou in the future, there had been much over the past few years, so as I ruled in England as Queen, Geoffrey was to be my soldier in Anjou and, to a lesser extent, Normandy. Robert and Brian, too, would act for me in Normandy as they were more popular than my husband. Geoffrey was to be relegated to a lower position. Unless he showed real promise, there he would remain. Anjou would be his main concern, and my father's only true concern with Anjou was ensuring it remained allied to Normandy and did its part to protect the borders.

Now that Clito was gone the danger Anjou presented was not as great as before. Had Clito lived, Geoffrey might have languished longer in the fantasy that he would one day be King or Duke. But now, since he was not as important to the present of England, my father did not see the point of putting energy into deception. And the child, dullard though he was, was not blind. Had my father been crafting the clay of Geoffrey's spirit for governance, for kingship, he would be making it obvious *now*, whilst he lived. That he was not made it clear that there was one heir to England and Normandy: me.

Of course, Geoffrey was not to be told this outright. My father was fond of dangling possible rewards over the heads of those he sought to control. He had smothered Geoffrey with honour to begin with, granting me to him, making him a knight, and now began to retract and conserve the treats, slowly, training the young hawk to peck at his hand for scraps. I could see it so clearly. It was how Heinrich had trained me, with praise, with love, with responsibility, with power, all offered generously and then infrequently, so all titbits became more valuable for their rarity. I wondered if men were taught this on purpose by their fathers, or perhaps just by experience, by the same being done to them and their mothers so they learnt how to wield this power, exert this cruel and effective control almost by accident, turning to it naturally when needed.

But whichever way it had been taught to my father, he was expert at it. He knew just how much flesh to offer the falcon, how to keep it hungry. He knew the sweetest scraps, what each man and woman longed for the most. My father was a master manipulator, and it stood him in good stead as King. He knew how to keep my husband pecking, and he knew how to keep me on his glove. That I saw what he was doing did not make it any less effective. My father had power over my future. At his whim I could lose my title of heir, and he might hand it to Robert or my cousin Theobald, Countess Adela's eldest sane son.

"You should intervene, *insist* that I am named in charters with you!" shouted Geoffrey.

"I thought you did not want women interfering in your affairs?" I asked mildly, although my voice bore a sharp edge. "You told me I was to remain quiet, and now you would have me send commands to my father, telling him how he may use his God-given power? You would have your place in royal documents won by your wife?" I looked to the window. A raven was on the wing; touch of night on skies of day.

"And where are the castles I was promised in payment for taking you as my wife?" he demanded, ignoring what I had said.

"Again, this is nothing to do with me," I replied. "You are a man, so deal as a man with my father over matters agreed between you."

"You are useless," he said. "I wanted a wife and countess, and I got a barren hag without dowry or wit."

I clenched my jaw. Respond, and I would allow him to know he had hurt me. I would not, but inside, the barb lashed and caught on flesh of my heart, pulling it. The lack of a child was now as a constant thirst in me. I yearned for a babe, and not, anymore, so people would cease to slander me for lack of one. I wanted a child.

"I think you have uses for me," I said. "I think there are times you are *most* glad I am your wife."

I meant the bedchamber. As fleas were trapped in bowls of honey, so Geoffrey was to my bed. As the weeks and months of our marriage went on his fire for me had not died. Often he stayed through the night, sometimes he tried to get me to respond with passion. Much as he might say he had no use for me, he would not have wanted to put me away. I infuriated him, it was true, but that only seemed to increase his passion for me, and the cries he let out when riding me, hard and wild as a stallion, could not lie. In bed, I fascinated him. He was addicted.

"There are a few times I am glad," he said. He looked sullen, but I had to admit there were times he was capable of truth, and admitted surprising things.

"You are not alone in your regrets, husband."

Geoffrey left. I could hear him complaining to his friends as he strode down the hallways, no doubt on his way to his new mistress. I pitied the girl; fair face and hair, plump of breast and wide of hips, she was in all ways my opposite, which was why I suspected he had chosen her, to make a point to me about his preferences. Her differences to me, sadly, were why he was not as interested in her as he was in me. When with her, at dances and feasts in the great hall or in his chambers, he was distracted, talking to his men. When he was with me, for good or ill, rage or desire, Geoffrey was fixated. There might have been no one else in the world when I walked into a room. I knew it, as did he.

The fair maid of light he had made his mistress was enamoured of Geoffrey, many women who were not me were, but I pitied her. She had to endure his complaints about me. Listening to a man you adore talk endlessly about another woman is never pleasant, and it comes to mind eventually that the complaints are sign and symptom of an obsession. Geoffrey wanted me, and he wanted to alter me. If I had changed for him he would have lost interest in a moment. As I remained myself, he was stuck to me; flea to honey.

I also imagine the poor girl had endured a great deal of angry coupling. Sometimes his lust was rough with me, although he did not dare be too rough. I had no doubt that with her he was less careful.

What I did not want to show him was that there had been times when he had managed to excite me. I had to hide my pleasure. Other women faked joy, I concealed it. Detachment was one of my only defences against the boy. I was not about to lower it.

Hearing that Geoffrey was far away, footsteps on stone and rush vanishing into the dark innards of the castle, I turned back to my letter. My uncle had been busy with the Church and with fighting, two things that might seem opposites. Perhaps they were, yet with my uncle always they were linked.

David was not alone. Men who went to war, to the Holy Lands, who killed many, spent much time in church before and after, attempting to mitigate their sins with penance, with prayer. To be a man of war was, of necessity, to also be one of God. War protected man's earthly rights, prayer and penance sheltered his soul, the soul he risked by inflicting death on others.

David was working on the consecration of new churches, the first being a community of Tironensians he had moved from Selkirk to Kelso. This order was his most favoured. Another affair of Church he was working on was to consecrate a man named Geoffrey, prior of Christchurch Canterbury, as the first abbot of Dunfermline, an appointment which aligned David with the foremost royal monastery of the north. It was clever to keep close links to the Church, and to separate men of the Church from those of state. As I had seen in the Empire, when a prince mixed the two it led to disaster. Men should have power in one sphere or the other, not both. Worldly power and divine combined make men believe they are invulnerable, which makes them ambitious. I had seen that with the Pope in Heinrich's struggles with Rome.

In terms of fighting, David was attempting to keep the north of his kingdom under control, an ongoing struggle. The west was also a problem at times. *"Keeping all barons and lords and men loyal is one matter,"* he wrote. *"Keeping an eye on all men, another."*

I smiled. I enjoyed my uncle's lessons, for he had a wry spirit which pleased me. David's kingdom was diverse in many ways. The land of my Scottish kin's birth was a kingdom of vast, sacred highlands, rolling mountains, wide, clear rivers, long marshes and stunning coastlands. David described Scotland in a way that made my blood itch to see it. It was not, of course, without problems as well as beauty. Men of the north, from across the seas, claimed mastery of isles about it, and men of England and Ireland owned other parts. Often they raided David's lands. Often he raided theirs. It was the way of things.

David had problems of loyalty too. Some lords on his borders thought deals with close neighbours more valuable than oaths made to their King. And David, who had spent much of his youth in England and owned much English land, was seen as a foreigner by some.

That was of course just an excuse. Men will find a reason to rebel if they want one. Usually it conceals other reasons. The poor rebel out of desperation, for they rise against men who are better armed, who ride horses, who own castles, and that is not a thing of sense to do. But rich men rebel because they want to be richer, in general. Sometimes it is because of the tyranny of the lord they are sworn to, but more often because they want more, more power, more coin, more land. Branding David a foreigner was a way of making him different. If someone is different enough, if they can be made a monster, then men feel they are justified in not following them, keeping loyal, keeping promises. I knew this well, for I was different. I was a woman claiming the position of a man. To many, I was a monster.

*

Winter was waning. Trees on the hillsides were purple in their starkness against the dark blue skies of dawn and dusk. Sometimes the mornings were fire; bright crimson and yellow behind the skeletal black fingers of the trees. Sometimes they were sombre, clouds and air pondering something serious. Catkins were staring to show, first leaves daring to poke soft, downy green heads from the tips of twigs. Ravens winged black and cawing into low skies, and still there was a threat of snow on the air. A strange time is the close of winter. There is threat there still, and yet promise too.

Taking my eyes from the bleak splendour of the day, I saw there were letters waiting, voices that had travelled from other lands to comfort me with their friendship. David's quill had been busy again, but writing of kin this time. Stephen of Blois and his wife, another Matilda and a woman I much admired, had had a second son, named Eustace. The country was rejoicing, but their first son Baldwin, David wrote, was not hale. In other problems related to the same house, David told me that Theobald, Stephen's brother and eldest son of Blois, was unhappy about my marriage. "He is not alone," I murmured to the parchment.

*"The Count of Blois believes your new husband will supplant him in the order of precedence in the eyes of the King, your father,"* David wrote. *"For more than twenty years the Count has been at the side of the King, fighting for him in war, supporting him in peace, and, Domina, now he feels betrayed. He has said nothing, of course, to your father, but I mention this to you, Domina, in case resentment should birth mischief."*

I breathed in, gazing from the window. Mist was creeping closer. Anjou was a kingdom where mist lived long and merry, thick rolls tumbling down green hillsides and falling into valleys, where it would linger. Smoke from cooking fires joined it in the skies, filling them, mist and cloud and smoke dancing. Sometimes sun shone through the mist, separating it, illuminating it, sending fingers of light to separate the cloud of fog, like a mother's fingers through a maid's hair. Some did not welcome the mist of Anjou, but to me it was not a thing of gloom, unless I was in a truly poor state of mind. It made me contemplative. There was something about mist, the way it obscured all beyond, that made me feel I was separate from the world. On good days I would welcome this distance, thinking it gave me the space to see events and people clearly, and time to ponder matters that would come. On bad days, it made me feel I was the sole person in the world; I had wandered into a realm of ghosts. The living were on the other side of the grey-silver mist, and I could not reach them.

Autumn is the time of ghosts; barriers break, the mist frees wanderers to walk, borders are traversed, what was lost comes back to be found. The dead seem to walk in the moonlight, the fluttering light of stars over them, the scent of falling and fallen leaves rising as though those phantom feet could still crush them, as though the dead could still make an impact on the world. Perhaps that is why the dead walk at times, why ghosts cannot rest; that fragile, mortal voice in all of us screams to be remembered, to be significant, to never be forgotten. We wish for immortality, in memory if not in reality. We wish to become immortal in the minds of men, to become a story told so we do not become lost in that darkness, not alone in the black and seamless coldness where all is nothing save us, where our souls are naked, bared.

I let out the breath I had been holding and frowned at the letter. I liked not this warning about Theobald, although I was grateful to have it. This was one of the things I had feared about this marriage my father had forced upon me for reasons now superfluous. If Theobald was indeed threatened and angered by the idea Geoffrey would supplant him, whether it was true or not, he might not become my ally when I needed him. I wondered why my cousin of Blois had the notion in his mind, but it did not take long to conclude that my father was dangling scraps over Theobald's head as he was to others. Perhaps he was using Geoffrey as a lure to make Theobald do something in particular, or just a warning, to make the Count of Blois behave as he wanted him to.

Or perhaps the threat of Geoffrey was real, and I was the one being deceived, drawn into thinking I would be Queen when my father intended to put a crown on Geoffrey's head. It was hard to know for sure, when it came to my father. He was as slippery as the lamprey he loved to eat.

But either way, Theobald feeling threatened and hostile towards me was not in my interests. I needed men loyal to me. I could not claim this throne alone, even a man could not do such a thing. Whilst my father was alive, barons and noble lords would be kept in check by the force of his almighty character, but what of after? Few men would fear me, still less would fear Geoffrey. When my father was no more, would the husband he had saddled me with prove to be the wedge that would drive itself between baron and crown?

I knew not, but I feared.

Perhaps it was a surprise, therefore, that when I went to my bed that night I was not thinking only of how to appease Theobald and draw him to my side without him knowing I knew of his complaints. I thought of Stephen and Matilda in Boulogne, of their children. I tried to be happy for them, but in truth what I felt was sorrow.

I did not feel incomplete, as some women say they do when childless. But I felt lonely; as though I had a friend somewhere I could not reach. As though there had been a presence in my life that had been precious, important, significant, and now was no longer there. Perhaps mingled with my sadness at not having a child there was, too, the sadness of missing Heinrich, or Bruno, Will or my mother. I know not. I only know that is what I felt; that once I had a friend and that that friend was out there somewhere in the world and I could not find them.

# Chapter Six

## Angers
## Anjou

### Winter 1129

I jumped. A warm-tinged wind, early herald of spring's coming was at my neck, tickling skin. Rustling spare leaves, rattling the bare bones of trees made naked by winter's touch, the wind came. My heart thumped, painfully loud, in my ears. It had sounded for a moment as though there was a step to my side, in the bushes. I froze, staring with wide eyes into green darkness. For a moment I thought I saw eyes, a person. But it was my mind, trying to see faces where none were, trying to protect me against a threat that had been mounting as all the best ones do, bit by bit, moment by moment until I was surrounded. I was under siege, not in a castle, but in my own mind. I was under constant attack. It was causing strain on my mind and nerves.

Some think a surprise attack the best weapon to disarm an enemy. They may have a point, a storm can cause much to fall fast, but another way is to come gradually, advance whilst seeming to be only a small threat, to invade little by little until the essence of threat is everywhere, in all things. Then something thought distant, unimportant, becomes all you can see. You are surrounded, the walls close, the breath of the enemy is on your neck. In such a way had danger crept upon me. My own bold promises of courage and fortitude seemed further from me that winter than they had in summer. Slowly, little by little, I had become afraid, and each little fear had not left. As a jagged fence collecting wool from passing sheep, fears had snagged on me, in my soul, suffocating it. That winter I had become afraid, and slowly it was wearing me down.

I shivered, and hurried towards the castle. Past emerging flowers my feet scuttled, past little blooms just starting to show courage. I had little left.

When I think back on those months in Anjou, I think often of pain. That is the impression that stays with me. From the jumbled chorus of the birds in the first dawn light, thrushes warbling and jackdaws cawing, to the end of night and the whistles on the wind as the same birds settled, all that time there was pain. It was fear become a sword in my side, slowly digging, digging in.

It was not because my husband beat me, he did not dare for one reason and another, something for which I have always thanked God, but there are other ways to inflict pain. Fist, strap, even sword may not always be the best weapon. There are ones more insidious, more lasting. Creep into the mind of a person and you can wreak untold damage. There are no scars to show, no bruises to display, yet there is assault. There is no blood to wipe away, no swelling to treat, yet there are wounds. By God there are. The manners in which people are able to hurt other people are so varied, so disparate, so creative. We are creatures of great, unbounded imagination, especially when it comes to inflicting cruelty.

So it was then, for me, with my new husband.

It had started in little ways; cruel comments begun in private started to creep into the public sphere, shaming me. He stood close then closer to me when we fought, screaming into my face, clenching his fists. I faced him, pulling courage into my heart as a shield, but week by week the boy was becoming stronger. The fear of him striking me was worse, I think, than if he had just done it. At times I felt myself provoking him, trying to force him into action, because at least then it would be done. The anticipation of being beaten was a strain upon my soul.

At other times I took to my knees to pray. In my private chapel, surrounded by the fug of incense pouring from cages built of silver and brass, I prayed, I thanked God that Geoffrey had not hit me. I stared at wooden carvings on the walls, the fall of man, Adam, his hand on an apple held out by Eve. Below them all the animals of the world looked on, eyes steady as they watched the destruction of innocence. On windows the raising of Lazarus was depicted, gold on painted glass. Surrounded by suffering and redemption, I prayed.

I thanked God and the Virgin I had not been attacked by Geoffrey's fists, or by other parts of him. But no matter, he was gaining ground in my mind. I felt him there now, all the time, occupying a corner he had claimed as his own. I felt violated, for he and fear, boon companions, had invaded my borders. Places that should have been safe, been mine, my mind and my heart and soul, they were not mine alone anymore.

I tried to ignore his snide comments, all the little insults that came each day. I tried to not show I was intimidated by his growing muscles and lengthening frame. I put from my mind the fact I was in a foreign country, alone and friendless but for Fulk. One day I found *Faith-Breaker* was gone. The leather strap for her leg had been cut, the window left open. She had flown. I blamed her not for wanting freedom, but wondered who had known how deep her loss would cut me. I became nervous about my wolfhounds, worried someone would set them loose, or kill them.

When Geoffrey started rumours I was barren, something he knew cut to the core of me, I tried to pretend I had not heard them. I tried to remain aloof when he was in my bed, in me, but each day it was harder. Each morning I woke more and more tired, as though I had not slept. At times I did not, found myself staring at the hangings about my bed, listening for his step, wondering if he would come back again, bed me again and I would have to put on the exhausting mask of courage and pretend I was distant, untouchable. Other nights I slept so deep I did not dream, and I fell asleep in the day. My mind was becoming fogged for lack of sleep, then too much.

I drank vervain and betony, trying to calm my nerves, my blood was let to clear memory and mind, but I was becoming more and more anxious. Summer had been bad, but winter, stuck in a castle with this man who hated me and desired me, and of whom I was growing increasingly afraid, was a slow, subtle torture. I went out for walks, for rides, but there were hours upon hours where I was within walls, the stones of the castle seeming to press upon me. I was drowning, and there was no one to talk to, to express my fears. My new ladies I liked, but they were daughters of Anjou. They would tell kin what I had said, those men would tell Geoffrey. I could hand him no excuse to abuse me. In public I was the model Countess, if a touch pale and less communicative than before. In my private mind I was a tapestry, one end cut through, loose strands floating free, coming apart.

I had thought being strong meant I was impervious to fear, that courage meant I could not be worn down. But I was as a grindstone used so much and so rough that in two it might snap, falling, rocky shards bouncing across the ground.

Fulk was my only friend. But even with my father-in-law I could not share all. I know he spoke to Geoffrey, told him to be kinder. I think that made the boy worse.

Just outside the castle, in the light wind I stopped and shivered. I knew there had been nothing in the bushes, but I felt as though there were. I felt watched, hunted. Calling my hounds to my heel, I hurried inside. I tried to attend to business each day to distract myself, so I would not end up merely staring at the walls, nothing but thoughts silver-sharp with fear or darker ones of despair in mind. There was another missive from David on my writing desk.

David sent letters, hearing misery in the ones I sent to him. He tried to distract me with tales. *"Men of Orkney say they have* seen selkies," he told me. *"Coming from the sea as seals, they shed their skins on the beach and transformed into women, dancing all night about a bright fire, laughing. Men would often, in days of old, capture their skins to hold them prisoner, make them their wives, but I am told that all the men who watched the selkies dance that night were wed already, and thought their wives might thrash them for bringing home a bride of the otherworld."*

I put down his letter thinking that all these tales of myth and monster had much in common: the capture of a woman, of this world or another, by a man; unions forced; the power of the woman limited. Thinking of my present situation, it made perfect sense to me. Someone had my skin, holding me captive under the power of a man of whom I was becoming increasingly afraid.

\*

As the months went on and we shared space and bed, I became agitated. Even when I slept I barely rested. I was on edge, always, for the threat of violence was always upon me. My mind tried to make what was bad worse, trying to prepare me to face the most awful outcome so I might *be* prepared, so I could survive it. When someone learns to tap into that area of your mind an unlimited source of horror drips down, feeding nightmare, fantasy, setting nerve endings on edge and the soul into torment.

That was how I felt. To his face I was the embodiment of courage. I knew if I allowed Geoffrey see that he was starting to scare me it would only encourage him, push him to greater cruelty. He was a child still. People like to think children are sweet and innocent, but that is just the way they act when before adults. Many children are embodiments of the worst of us because the best they have yet to learn. They control other children through coercion; through bullying, through cruelty. Long months this child had fought to become my master. If he knew he was scaring me then he would have won.

But inside I was a hare frozen on the hillside, the crimson light of the dawn igniting upright ears so they became spears of blood. Eyes wide with fear when I heard him outside the door, I was the hare who feels the hounds close, the fox near. I was twitchy, restless.

It was not fear of Geoffrey alone. Although he seemed to grow day by day more muscular and well-formed, for he was training with sword and lance and on horse as a knight each day he could, I thought I still had enough in me, enough influence and enough pluck to stare my husband down when by himself. But he was not alone in this court. He had companions, all young, all reckless like him.

"My friends say you should be beaten!" he shrieked once at me.

"You have no friends," I said, hands on my silver girdle, thinking I might strangle him with it.

"I have many."

"I have lost more friends to death than ever you have known in life," I said. "You are so alone, Geoffrey, so alone that you fear to face that truth, but it is a truth we all must face. Those minions at your heel, they are not friends. There is no union of soul, no challenge to intellect, mind. They are fawning, bleating creatures of feeble will and power. You gather them as wool about you to block out the whisper of the world as it tries to induct you into adulthood, to tell you truths. They aid you not, for they keep you a boy and not a man. They are false. The way you choose to live is false."

"They are true to me," he said. "They are loyal."

He had a point, for there are different kinds of loyalty, and although true to Geoffrey they were not, not in all things and situations as those truly loyal are, Geoffrey's fawns were loyal to his *position*. He was fire, they kindling. They would keep him burning whilst it suited them. And they were dangerous to me.

There might come a night, I knew, when, drunk and fractious, he would complain and they might suggest something to shame me, humiliate me. He might agree. I doubted he would allow them to rape me; he took too much pleasure in me and was jealous of any other man looking at me for that to be agreed to. But what of a beating they witnessed? What of them holding me down as *he* did things to me? Of that I could not be sure. Of him I could not be.

He dropped hints, hints of violence, physical and sexual. Seeds sown, plants of darkness grew wild and twisted in my mind. The threat of him polluted my thoughts, making me feel stupid. I know not that any of the abject horrors that occurred to me during that time truly entered his plans for me. Perhaps he never thought of such things and would be insulted I had thought it of him, but men of power have the luxury of thinking well of others. Women, peasants, people under the legal control of another do not. If we do not think the worst, we find ourselves blamed for complacency, for not taking measures to defend ourselves when the worst comes. And the worst comes to be more often than people like to believe.

There were other things Geoffrey might do, if influenced. If he thought himself robbed of the chance to be King or Duke by my father, if I still had provided no child, would he think to kill me in some subtle manner? He would not seek an annulment, since my father and his would not allow it. But death is a foolproof way to rid a man of a wife he wants not.

Poison is easy to come by; it grows in fields and along hedgerows if you know the shape of leaves, the scent of flowers. Slipped into wine to hide telling bitter taste and strange colour, poison may enter body and blood, speed to the heart. I started to shy from food and some drinks, found myself wary of pungent tastes, found my nose sniffing things. All food and drink was supposed to be checked in the kitchens, cooks taking a little of each dish themselves. If they did not fall down dead it was sent to us. But what of poison that took its time? Socrates imbibed water hemlock and chatted pleasantly to companions until a moment before death. Would I feel a creeping numbness come, or worse, die a dried husk of myself, voiding all contents of stomach and body through mouth and rear?

I became suspicious of spices. They might be used to conceal darker substances. I started to lose weight, unable to eat from fear and then from lack of interest in food. It seemed the enemy. I sent out enquiries for men to find me a segment of unicorn horn, said to sweat when poison was near. I had to issue my instructions with care, so Geoffrey did not find out. "Often it is found on beaches," I told the man sent to find it. "Unicorns are thought forest creatures, but perhaps when they die they go to the sea, for that is where fragments of horns are found."

I had an emerald ring, which I passed over dishes I did eat, for it was said to rid foods of poison. I bought a stone on which a scorpion was engraved, for the sign of Scorpio was a sign of coldness, and might protect against poisons that brought fire to guts and mind. And I kept my brother's stone close. It had no magical power, but I felt protected by it.

At night I prayed to Saint James, kneeling before the golden glove which held the relic of his hand, holding the scallop shell badge of pewter I had been given by my lady Maurelle as a gift in the Empire, so long ago. I asked my personal saint to protect me.

I became cautious of my cosmetics, lest something be added that I would smear on my face and hurt myself with. I used little in any case. Some women, skin ridden with dips from pox, filled in ravaged faces with wax or human fat stolen from the corpses of criminals, and covered that with a white paste. I was fortunate my skin was milk and unmarked. But I had kohl for my eyebrows, a grease and plant mixture for my lips. I stopped using them. I washed only in water, without scents that might cover something other than perfume.

I found myself listless. I ceased to take an interest in trying to aid Anjou. I did not read dispatches, did not attempt to speak when sitting at the side of my husband. I did not insist I witnessed charters of Anjou as I had before. Dully I read missives from England and Normandy, or Scotland. They had ceased to mean a great deal to me. Those lands, that future, seemed far away as though the distance had grown greater in winter, snow stretching land until it was so vast there was no way to cover it. There were times I felt the castle thick about me, times I was wrapped in despair. My menses became irregular. Under my clothes I looked like a skeleton.

The only thing to cheer me was my father-in-law, and Fulk was concerned about me. "You are losing weight, daughter," he said one morning when he came to take some wine by my fire. Soon it would be stripped out, glowing logs replaced by blooms and branches. But I was cold. He was right that I was thinner. "Your cheeks are pinched and their bloom is pale," he went on, pulling a cushion to his back. It ached when it was cold, an old injury from a broken bone in his shoulder. "Are you not well?"

"I am not sick, but have no appetite these days, my lord," I said. My eyes were caught by a spider in the wooden roof, her web silver and beautiful, crafted with patience and perseverance. She was a lesson sent to me, I think.

"I can send my man to bleed you, Domina," he said with a worried brow. "It is good for the digestion, bleeding."

"If you wish it, I will undergo the process," I said, my fingers straying to a brooch of emerald and gold at my shoulder, holding thick furs in place.

"You need to come from these chambers, this castle," he said. "Your women tell me you have not hunted in a while."

"I feel no urge, my lord. I am happy enough in here, with my books, my embroidery."

This concerned him more, I could sense it. Men so often fail to see what is in the hearts of women, but Fulk knew something was very wrong with me. The fire in me was fading. Always I had loved to be outside, but of late I had retreated into my rooms. I felt the cold with little fat on my frame, and I felt safer where I was. The walls were close, but somehow whilst I feared them, whilst they suffocated, I also felt unsafe outside them. I had become a bird in a cage that knows not how to fly, the sky is too big, the world too large. The small world is suffocating, but safe. I was becoming small of self. I had done what I had said I would not. I was retreating, close to surrender.

"I am going to the Abbey of Fontevrault soon," he said. "I want you to accompany me."

"If you so wish, my lord."

"I do so wish." Fulk smiled, his handsome face lighting up. "I am to see my daughter, Mahaut." He stopped and did not go on to say more. He knew it would pain me. Mahaut, also known as Matilda of Anjou, had been my brother's infant wife. They had never shared a bed, for she was a child when he died, but they had been married. She had been one of the last people to see him alive. Because of her youth, my father had taken her on his ship, considering the *White Ship* too raucous and wild for such a young woman. That caution had saved her life.

"It is not often I am permitted to see her, and I take her brothers, Geoffrey and Helias too. Before I leave for my new kingdom and wife in the Holy Lands I am to go. I wish to say goodbye to my daughter, my family at my side. It is likely I shall not see her, or indeed my sons again."

A trip out with Geoffrey was not welcome, but if others were there it might be preferable. Helias, Geoffrey's younger brother, was much the same as Geoffrey, but he was more a child than my child-husband, less a threat. "Or me, my lord," I said, attempting a smile.

"Or you, Domina and daughter." Fulk leaned forwards and touched my hands. His were fire against the coldness of my skin and I saw another flicker of consternation flit across his eyes. "I would that you would come and see the Abbey. It is a wonder of beauty. I think it will revive your spirits that have been set upon by the winter."

I smiled, knowing it was not winter, but a child of summer who had assaulted my spirits. "If it is a place you love, my lord, I would love to see it."

He sent salted boar for my table that night, including a message that the rich flesh would improve my health. There too were leeks in pepper and wine, spiced pork balls and blood sausage. Fulk was trying to boost my spirits and my health.

That night I slept better. In dreams I saw women on a beach, dancing free and without shame, naked, about a fire. Light bounced from smooth grey rocks, shimmering with water, which stood about them. Light moved graceful and gliding over their bodies as they twirled, over their hair as it fanned out in the air. They were beautiful, free.

Many nights after that in my dreams I heard bare feet on shifting sand, felt grit between my toes, felt the salt wind brush skin, face, normally hidden by a cloak, a disguise. I heard selkies as they danced, as they sang. Sometimes with them I danced, naked and unafraid, free and freed of bonds of blood or duty or disdain. I was shameless and at liberty, dancing under the light of moon and fire, under the glimmering silence of the stars.

# Chapter Seven

## Fontevrault Abbey
## Anjou

### Winter 1129

*This woman was once my sister,* I thought as we rode towards Fontevrault.

*She still is,* said a voice within, *just bound by another bond.*

Never had I met her before or when she was married to Will, this Mahaut, Matilda I was now related to because I had married her brother. Her union with my brother had not troubled my father in terms of consanguinity between Geoffrey and me. Will's marriage had not been consummated, so Matilda of Anjou had been sister in name alone to me. And yet she had been my sister once, and was now again. Although it had no legal tie or moral bond, I felt closer to her for her attachment to Will than that created by my marriage to Geoffrey. I wondered if she had loved my brother, if she had mourned him.

I was soon to find out.

We left early one morn, to make best use of the day. Along the roadsides was evidence of moles, *moldwerps,* as my mother's ancestors called them. Earth ruffled, tunnels dug, under the ground they toiled, making long and greedy traps for worms they hunted. Along the road our procession went, banners of leopards flowing in the wind, as underground the moldwerps hunted. We stayed at an abbey on the first night and continued the next day. Geoffrey said little to me. In front of his father he always behaved himself.

Wild birds of prey were wheeling in the skies, watching for emerging vermin, or for the first lambs, creatures too weak to hold them off if left behind by the flock, or if they fell helpless into a ditch.

As we rode towards the Abbey, I knew Fulk was right. I had been shying from life inside the castle, drawing into myself in fear, in weariness. I had been becoming like a wizened apple or pickled walnut, shrinking small. Being outside was like drinking an elixir. And as we approached the Abbey a sense of peace and wonder came upon me, slow at first and then rushing as wind in my ears, water over my hands. The sight of its lands, long fields of crops being sown, animals grazing and vines glowing green, brought upon me that same feeling I had felt as Heinrich and I had ridden closer and closer to the Alps; a sense of awe. This Abbey was no mountain, but something in it called with the same voice I had heard on crisp, cold nights beneath those mountains as a youth; an echo of the almighty voice of God, trying to tell us something always never quite heard.

Stone walls which encased the Abbey hummed with heat and seemed to murmur prayers to God as we rode past on the way to the main entrance. A sense of peace surged from it, strong and sound as the wind that blew along the wet road. A Benedictine order, Fontevrault housed both nuns and monks, and was dedicated to the Virgin.

The eyes of the Virgin held a draw for me. Perhaps she called to all women, representing the sacred part of us that, if sold in marriage, we had had to surrender to men. She had not surrendered, but had been chosen.

The Virgin had not had to sacrifice her maidenhead to have a child, had needed none but God to carry her from position of sacred maiden to sacred mother. That was why she was special. It might seem to some that she was an impossible model for women. How were we mortals to live up to a woman who could be mother and maid at the same time? Yet to me her purity was not in her virginity; that was but a symbol. Her purity was in her independent sacredness, in God singling her out, keeping her free of men and their sins. In her was maiden, mother and death-crone, for she had given Christ to the world and she had held his body in death. All women she was at all times.

She had not been tainted by touch or ownership of man. If men had thought on her for a moment, they might have noted that her purity was the absence of *their* touch; that *they* were the ones who soiled women, and not in terms of sexual union, in terms of ownership. Husband she might have had, but God alone was master of Mary, as He was of us all. She was freer than any of us.

The position of the Virgin, untouched by hand of man, appealed to me greatly, as I am sure might be appreciated. The sister-in-law I had not met before, did also. I thought after that perhaps this was why Fulk had asked me to come. The glories of the Abbey were welcome, but perhaps he thought his daughter had much to offer me too.

"You are doing as you should with Geoffrey, Domina," Mahaut said as we walked in the physic garden that afternoon. Clouds as black smoke were pouring over a light blue sky. Dusk was on its way, but still there was warmth, light.

Rain had fallen whilst we were inside the Abbey, meeting each other. Globes of water, tiny and perfect, lay on the grass and made stones of the pathways glow. There was a smell of freshness to the world; God's element of water washing it clean of sweat and toil. Herbs good for kitchen and for healing were all about us; fennel, marjoram, thyme, rosemary, sorrel and sage. There, too, were beds being readied for tiny lettuces for stews.

I looked up, surprised, as my sister-in-law spoke. I had said nothing of my troubles. Perhaps Mahaut could read them on my face. She nodded as she saw my eyes widen and then narrow. Mahaut was younger than me by some years, but grief had given her maturity, and her time in the convent had brought wisdom. Books were much honoured by Benedictine orders, and reading was encouraged. It was, indeed, one of the duties of the order to keep and improve a monastic library. Nunneries everywhere encouraged education, and they taught as many girls as boys. Closed orders were more restricted, but there was a respect for education here, something I could almost touch in the air.

"I always knew if he was matched to a woman of spirit it would either make or undo him," she went on, fingers trailing in a rosemary bush, the oily, rich scent seeping into moist air. "When we were children he held great promise, but always he was selfish, inward looking. He picked on me and Helias, as is often the way. Geoffrey boasts, as I am sure you have seen, Domina, but there is a frightened boy hidden under all that bluster. He needs someone like you otherwise he will become not a great lord as our father wishes, but a bad one. That will not be good for the country, or our future." She patted her leg. Her pet dog, a small creature who clearly doubled as a ratter for the abbey, wagged his tail and came to her, licking her hand before bounding away to investigate a hedge.

I swallowed. "I am afraid any influence I may wish to have is unwelcome."

"Are you afraid?"

I lifted my chin and shook my head.

"There is no sense in falsehoods," she said. "Women, under the power of a man, as we always are, do fear. Courage is when we fear and stand to face danger despite that. You have great courage, I see it in you. I understand why you do not wish to admit fright, especially to him, and I think you are right. A bold front may work better than a fragile one, for he is a dog who sees weakness in another of the pack and nips its heels to steal its meat, but you do not need to pretend to me."

"You are his sister."

"I am a servant of God, first, and always. What God wishes for Anjou is different to what my brother believes. The health of a country depends on its head. The head of Anjou is the Count. My brother needs to become a man, fast, and leave boyish things behind."

I pulled at the brooch holding my long, loose tunic in place. Gold, covered in flowers of gold, it reminded me of the crown I had been honoured with as Empress. "I do not think I am the one to make a man of him."

"No, that is his task." We walked on. "There is not a person on earth or in Heaven who can alter another person," she said. "God granted free will and men use it. The only ones who can make changes to their souls and hearts are people themselves. Wishing and wanting, asking or pleading for alteration does nothing. Geoffrey must change, and he must do this on his own."

She stopped on the path and put her hand to my sleeve. "You do not love him," she said. "But do not, because of this, or because of his poor treatment, wish ill upon him or his country."

She meant more than simple wishing ill. Although it was rare, noble women had sometimes rebelled against their husbands, or encouraged rebels. My grandmother, Matilda of Flanders, had sent money and arms to her son, Robert Curthose, when he was in revolt against her husband. Mahaut was asking me, in a covert way, not to become a danger to Geoffrey, but more importantly to Anjou.

"I do not. I have no wishes that are ill for this country." I looked about the garden. "There is much here I have come to love."

"That is good," she said. "And I would offer you some advice."

"Which is?"

"To leave him."

I stopped and stared. "Leave, and do what? Flee here, to a nunnery? My task is to have children."

"No children will you bear whilst you lose weight in this manner," she said, waving a hand over my thin frame. "You have lost your menses, I think?"

I flushed. I had. They had been spare, weak and then they had gone. I had told no one. I had smeared blood stolen from the kitchens upon cloths so that those who took my garments to be laundered would not know. There were spies everywhere and nothing I did was secret. I had thought that if it was known I had lost my courses I might be more in danger. If I was thought of no use, I was more at risk of being poisoned. I tried to avoid her eyes, her brutal and direct words, that frank observation, but Mahaut shook her head, her eyes kind.

"It is nothing to be ashamed of," she said. "It is the loss of weight. It is not uncommon. A woman must be of reasonable health to bear a babe, and your body lets you know that this is impossible whilst you refuse to eat by withholding blood. I have studied much in the way of medicine. There are texts some ignore, written by women, on the subject." She inclined her head. "Your fragile frame is one reason you do not conceive, but the other is that you find no pleasure in it. It is said in some wise tomes that there is a seed released from both male and female in the marriage bed. Men find seed easy to release, but women must know pleasure. You find none with my brother, so no child will come."

She breathed in. "That is why you must go, Domina. Leave; go somewhere for a few months, a place of quiet and calm where you can recover. As my father departs Anjou, leave Geoffrey alone. It will allow him to gain confidence as a ruler. Allow him to become the man he needs to be. You are both young. When this is done you can return and set to the task of getting a child and heir for Anjou and for England."

"It would be a scandal."

"A short scandal now is better than you wasting away or Geoffrey becoming a monster," she said. "And it does not have to be a scandal. Make an excuse, visit with your father, tour estates in Normandy, anything, but get yourself from this situation. With time, with distance, you two may be able to pull yourselves from this brink on which you stand."

"You see so much," I said.

She looked around at the covered stone hallways of the cloister, at the plants in the garden, the sunlight. "Removal from the world has its hardships, at times," she said. "When first I came here, even though it was my choice, my soul rebelled against the quiet and the silence. I would lie awake at night feeling like the only person left alive. The rush of the English court, my marriage to your brother... I was so young when all that happened. I had such dreams of life, of being Queen, finally marrying the man my infant heart loved, of having children."

It occurred to me, as I listened to her, that her life had mirrored mine, in youth. I too had been sent away at a young age to wed, to another court, to another kingdom. I thought of how I had loved Heinrich, such innocent and painful passion, and I wondered what I would have felt had I lost him as a child, as she had lost Will. Was it worse to lose fast and quick before dreams had a chance to root, so that love was always innocent and perfect in the mind? Or was it crueller to leave a maid with dreams that always would be perfect, so nothing else could compare? I knew not.

"And then those dreams, that life, were gone," she said. "I did not want another husband, did not want to start again, to risk heart and soul and life all over again. I had not the courage or the spirit. I needed retreat, and I retreated here." She smiled. "You took another path when your husband died, you chose another road, and I think it was the right one for you."

"Our lives have similarities," I said.

"Many do," she replied. "We are all more similar than we ever believe, and yet we can alter our parallel paths so easily, walk away from one another. I chose to come here, and in quiet reflection I find I can think on the world better than I could when I was within it. There are some here who say this is not as it should be, that my mind should be dedicated to thoughts of God alone, but God is in everything, everyone. In time I have no doubt I shall linger more on the mysteries of God, but I am young, only recently a bride of Christ; my mind is tied still to the world. But perhaps that is a good thing, for now. If it allows me to help you, or my brother, it is perhaps in God's plan."

"Did you love my brother?" I asked.

She smiled sadly. "I did, sister," she said. "He was a son of sunlight and wonder to me. I worshipped rather than loved. Perhaps that was why I came here, needing a true God rather than the one I had created. But Will was good to me. He would have been a great King, but God must have a plan. Perhaps He wishes you to be Queen."

"I hope to prove worthy."

"Prove worthy to yourself, not to others, and God will be pleased with you," she said. "And remember this is a long race, and you must take care of yourself. You are not, now."

"So you think I should leave your brother?"

"Take time away, recover. Leave Geoffrey to become who he needs to become. Then return, make an heir."

"There are some who say I should do that now."

"Some who know not what they talk of," she said. "There is time, Domina. Time for you two to come to a place where an heir may be produced, but that time is not here and not now. There are moments in life we must stand away from the rush and hustle of life and of expectations and make our own plans, form our own strategy. We all must learn to survive in life, and many a time we must find our own way to do that. The way you and Geoffrey are making is not working; another path must be sought."

She touched my hand. "Come now," she said, the briefest suspicion of mischief in her eyes. "At first men are simply glad women are away talking to one another, but after a time they become worried. Let us return before they grow scared."

We did, and it was a quiet evening. We dined on barley bread with leeks and sops in wine. In the morning I rose when darkness still held dominion over the skies, and I went to the guest chapel. There I prayed to the Virgin for strength.

On the walls of the chapel the Queen of Heaven was, painted at the moment the angel Gabriel first appeared to her. Mary was drawing back, afraid of the apparition, of the power and trust being placed in her. I wondered if she was shrinking, modest, as men thought her, of if she had seen the wealth destiny held for her, and wondered if she could be enough, enough to carry such joy and sorrow; if she could love a child so deeply, and surrender him to death, for the good of the world. Hers was a sacrifice deep and painful, yet never had she turned her back on the world of man when man killed her child. In Mary was the awesome power of which love was capable.

At her feet were other women, nuns of the order, staring up at her, hands clasped. They were there not to worship, but support her, so I thought. The best that women are capable of, that mankind is, is when we hold others up.

We departed the Abbey, but it was in my thoughts, always, as was my brother's widow.

*

I was so taken with Fontevrault that when my father offered a charter granting a generous donation, I confirmed it, and meant to do more in the future. The charter was brought to me in Anjou by my father's men, Richard and Ralph de la Haye, sons of my father's steward, and was one of many my father was sending across the sea, keeping me tied to England and reminding her men that I was heir. Geoffrey was not pleased to see it, pleased less still that he was not to sign.

The payment my father offered was to cover the food of the nuns, from the produce of Winchester and London. When I signed my name to the charter, I thought of the circle that gratitude might make. I was signing something that would sustain Mahaut, this woman whose sage advice I was pondering. Yet she had begun that circle, seeing into the centre of my soul, offering counsel and friendship to sustain my spirit.

When we returned to Angers, it was late January. Days were short and cold, yet although I was once more inside the castle for days, I did not feel so encased. I was thinking of what Mahaut had said, wondering if it were possible, or responsible.

Fulk departed one day in February, riding out into the crisp air, ice cracking under the hooves of his horse. The sound of him leaving Anjou was as the trumpet blast of the four riders of the end of time to my ears.

As soon as his father was out of sight, Geoffrey became unbearable. The hope I had felt in the Abbey left me. Fear and concern returned. I felt weak and tired, hunted and hounded.

One night something woke me, it often did. A state of fear is no place to find sleep. Exhausted, I would fall quick to slumber then wake at two or three of the morning, and lie there until dawn. But this time something woke me, some dream unremembered, gone and forgotten in the moment I woke to find myself staring into an abyss, a darkness complete that did not in nature exist.

Man builds his own darkness; walls, windows, shutters. There is no darkness like this elsewhere, out in the forest, in the mountains. In the night there is light, sharp and brilliant, sometimes hazy and floating. Even in caves there is a mouth to the outside, green-glowing plants within. Man makes darkness. It is an illusion, a box in which we place ourselves, a space in which to hide, and it is easily conquered by man himself. Light a fire, light a candle, and we see the darkness we have made is not complete, not all-powerful.

I rose and took a glowing ember from the fire, the end of a piece of wood. I sat by the hearth, it in my hands, and I could see smoke rising into the air, smell the acrid scent, feel the warmth of it. In darkness it glowed, a light I kept alive, blowing on it from time to time to see it flare. And shadows danced on the walls, on my hands, shadows cast by darkness, but yet also by light.

Perhaps what it was I should fear was not darkness, for in darkness there are things, people, much that is good. What I should fear was the void opening inside me, the emptiness which threatened to swallow me. It was a lack of myself I feared, truly, not a darkness in my soul. There were uses for darkness; it was just another teacher, as light was. But in the void opening inside me, created by fear, nurtured by the loss of self and courage and strength, there was nothing. If into that I fell, I would not climb out. In that nothingness I would be lost, indeed.

# Chapter Eight

## Angers
## Anjou

## Spring 1129

"You will never be King!" I screamed. "Never Duke, never *anything!*"

I froze. The silver pomander shaped like an apple which hung from my waist banged against my leg, releasing scent. It was the only sound for a moment. I cursed my impetuous tongue, my unbidden, reckless rage.

I had been told to hide that truth, keep it hidden so the puppy would keep dancing, so the falcon would keep feeding at the outstretched hand of my father. Now it was said and could not be unsaid. I could feel disbelief floating on the air of the chamber, coming from Geoffrey's open mouth.

I looked to the window, breathing hard, heart pounding. Blackthorn was in blossom, a vast expanse of white bloom heralding another snap of cold before summer came. Herons were hunting fish, and frog spawn, light and bobbing in water which was still, in places, covered by a sheen of thin ice. Here and there fluttered butterflies, young and first-emerging, the braver of their kind. There too were bees, ruffled black coats and fluffy bellies bobbing in the air, making their way about plants whilst there was time between falls of rain. Outside the window birds chased each other, tiny balls of feather and fury whipping across roads and in front of un-shuttered windows. Air and light poured into the castle, long dark and stuffy from winter. Lettuces were emerging, delicate, waxy leaves just starting to poke their heads from the ground. They had been nurtured with care, covered at night with pots to protect them from frost. The walls of the castle kept the inside gardens warm. Lambs were in the frosty fields, calling in tones of soft desperation for their mothers, their voices rising clouds in the frozen air. Spring was come, yet I felt as jaded and tired as I had through the endless winter.

I was at the end of my patience, the end of my strength. My soul was ragged, spirit ripped. Since Fulk had left, Geoffrey had become the monster his sister feared he would. About court he had begun to parade mistresses, forcing me to speak to them in public in an attempt to humiliate me. His friends called me names that were hardly even whispered. All of court knew them. They said I was barren, I was unnatural, I was not a woman.

I felt eyes on my back wherever I went, eyes that judged me for my lack of a child. Even those who had welcomed me, supported me as Countess when first I came, had grown less friendly if not overtly hostile. My father failing to hand over the castles in Normandy, my promised dowry, was one contention, and my childlessness another. I was taking hardly any part in the affairs of Anjou. I spent most days in my chambers. It was said I was not a worthy successor to Geoffrey's mother, that I did nothing for Anjou and did not love her countrymen. Geoffrey encouraged the rumours, the slander, and his long walk towards physical violence I felt was nearing an end. I was at the edge of what I could stand.

I had grown more afraid of poison. Sleep was a stranger.

We screamed at each other often, it was a release for me in some ways, and I welcomed it. Sitting and trying to work on embroidery or reading books had become torture. Because of lack of sleep and an overdose of worry, I could hardly read more than a line before my mind turned off, could not sew without making mistakes. I had to unpick my work often, making me feel more like a failure at everything. Often I just stared, at my hands, at parchment. Inactivity made my fears worse. Sometimes a screaming match was a relief.

This particular argument had come about because of my father, again. Just how long he thought he could continue to exclude Geoffrey before the boy noticed it and said something I knew not, but Geoffrey was noticing.

My father included me in all his charters, in his charity too. I confirmed his commands, demonstrating that I was his heir. All that came to his hands was sent to mine. A stream of letters flowed from my father to me, all business, tips and hints and inclusion in ruling so I was prepared when the time came. But to Geoffrey came only silence. The message could not have been clearer.

Until the moment I said it aloud, that was.

Up until that slip my father and I could always have argued that Geoffrey was going to be included, eventually. That my father held back now, sending matters to me because Geoffrey was occupied with his new lands in Anjou and I as his wife should shoulder the burden. But not now. Not now I had made this mistake, told him outright. I cursed my tired tongue and shattered spirit.

"What do you mean?" he asked.

There was no sense in denying it. A surge rose in me, anger and satisfaction, a dark monster of spite. "You will never be named King of England, or Duke of Normandy," I said. "That was never in the head of my father for a moment. All he wanted you for was a secure border and seed. You are a breeder and border holder, husband, not a king, not a duke."

"You lie," he hissed.

"What need is there for lies between us? Those who love one another lie to save the other pain, but with us there can be honesty, for all we have for each other is hatred. Hatred may be as honest as it likes. It cares not for who will be hurt. It enjoys it."

"You are a monster."

"Then to you I am well matched."

He reached out, hand flying before he could stop it. He struck me across the face. My head snapped to one side, and my hand lashed out before I knew what I was doing. I struck him across his cheek. I had a good, thick ring of gold and garnet on. It cut into his skin, slicing a slender gash just under his cheekbone.

He stood staring at me, a thin line of blood running down his face, cheeks flushed with anger and shame.

"I told you I would strike back," I said. I tried to keep my voice steady. I was scared he would attack me. If I faced the bully down, he might back down. "And now you know the truth," I said. "The lands to which you aspire will never be yours. You, my lord, are the wife in this marriage and I the husband. You were bought for your lands and for your body, not for power."

"I will rule those lands."

"The barons never will support you," I said. "And my father will name you not. I am his heir, and my son after me."

"You will have no sons from me," he said.

"I have none now. You have done your task poorly, my lord."

"Into a barren desert, no seed may sprout," he spat. "You are the one at fault, not me."

"If that is so, seek an annulment, release us of our combined misery. Marry that poor pale whore you keep parading about court."

"England and Normandy are mine."

"They are mine," I said.

I left the chamber. I glanced down as I marched the halls. My hands were trembling. I was not sure what was growing stronger in me, the hatred I had for this boy teetering on the edge of manhood, or my fear of him.

There was a tale of old I remembered, of a dragon that lay under the world, chewing at the root of the great World Tree which linked the realms of man, heaven and underworld. The dragon chewed roots, and he chewed souls.

There were times of late that I could feel his gnashing teeth under my feet, and inside my soul. Sometimes it felt as though the ground was not beneath me, that I had lost what tied me to the earth, that I was not part of this anymore, that I had lost myself.

*

My feet crunched stones upon the path. I stopped, flashed about, eyes wide as my hounds, *Hope* and *Courage*, growled, a threatening rumble, at something behind us on the path. I could see nothing but shadow.

"Come," I said. They would not move. My wolfhounds of Ireland stood, guarding me, hackles up, hair rustling in the light wind.

"Come," I said again, authority and annoyance in my tone. They turned, reluctantly, and came. *Hope* and *Courage* knew who fed them, whose bed they were to guard by night and body by day. Ignore a second command and they would go against nature and duty, but their hair remained on edge. Every now and then another rumble came from their long throats.

I wondered if my anxiety had climbed, a creature of flesh and blood, a snake, from my throat, from my chest, slithering out of my very blood so it might stalk me in the outside world.

Fear was a companion at that time, not a feeling. It had ceased to be inside me, and had come to stand at my side, walk the same paths. I could feel its breath, at times cold as snow and at others hot as flame, on my neck, down my spine, a whisper in my ear of words I could not quite hear. I ran hot and cold as though I stood beside a fire in the night, scorched by flames on my front and frozen by winter coldness and dark at my back. Dragons can breathe either water or fire if they choose. Fear has the same power.

Distantly I caught the scent of meadowsweet, blooms emerging nearby. It was a heady scent, sweet and heavy, even from the first hesitant flowers. It was said if a person inhaled too deeply of the scent they would fall into a slumber from which they would not awaken. In the Empire the flower had been thought unlucky, associated with death, for the blooms were often dried and placed in coffins to mask the smell. Here in Anjou it was a strewing herb for floors.

Sometimes when I smelt it in the castles I shivered, the beautiful scent bringing ghosts to my mind. And now, with death on my mind, with fear a cloak upon me, it seemed a herald of something dark, something dangerous concealed in a mask of sweetness. *Like your husband*, my mind whispered.

I walked on fast to leave fear behind, pulling my cloak lined with fur about my thin shoulders. Never had I felt the cold before, but with nothing on my bones that winter and spring had been cold in Anjou. "This cannot go on," I muttered to myself.

If it did, I would soon not have a mind.

# Chapter Nine

## Angers
## Anjou

## Summer 1129

Not long after milkmaids decorated their wooden pails with marsh flowers to mark the start of May, I walked into the chamber of my husband and told him I was leaving.

"I will to Normandy go," I said, "to the lands of my father. I am unwell and need time to recover. I will say business of my father and his kingdom calls me away, so there is no gossip in court about me going."

"You will go nowhere," he growled. "You think to shame me!"

"I think to save us both," I said quietly. Truly I meant it. Together we were wending a path towards the destruction of us both. I cared not for him, but Geoffrey was the lord of Anjou, and I had no wish to contribute to the destruction of a country. Together we were no good, not for ourselves and not for others. The darkness in me brought out that in him. The light he was capable of was being smothered. And I was vanishing before my very eyes.

"Save us?" He laughed. "What do I need saving from? You think me a maiden with a dragon at my back?"

"I think you a dragon," I said. "And you will become so in truth if I stay. I do not bring out anything of good in you. You return the favour when it comes to me. For the sake of Anjou, for the sake of my sanity and what chance you have to be a decent man, let me go. I will recover, we will spend time apart.

Perhaps later, as strangers we may meet again. Perhaps we may as strangers come to know each other better."

"You will go nowhere," he said again, although something in his eyes caught, as though my words had stroked something in him. He behaved like a fool often, but Geoffrey had brains. He knew what I said was true.

I will spare you the length and tedium of the argument that followed. There was nothing of interest in it, for both of us said the same thing over and over at each other. This truly was our great fault, both he and I, we could not allow the other to have their opinion and we could not leave the last word alone. He told me I would not go, I said I would. Eventually I used my final threat, and felt weak for doing so for I called on the power of men, of fathers, like a child who threatens to tell on a sibling for a crime of the schoolroom.

I stiffened my thin shoulders. "I leave freely, or I will send word to my father and to Fulk that I am being held captive."

He knew I would, and he knew I would make trouble for him. It was trouble he needed not, for there was a small but persistent rebel group in Anjou. Soon he would have to deal with them. He needed no other men interfering in his business, and the notion of either my father or his sending rebukes for his behaviour embarrassed him.

Geoffrey said I would take no one with me. In the end a poor escort of only a few who were most loyal to me gathered. Geoffrey would allow no good, secure escort for his wife, his Countess, not if I was leaving. He thought it would hold me there, but I had faced hard roads and long journeys before. More did I fear staying, wasting to nothingness.

His was a fool's game, in truth, for denying me a good escort of knights and guards and ladies would make people talk. I had taken care to protect his reputation, something he never reciprocated for me, by saying that I was going to Normandy to attend to business of my father. Not providing me with an escort made it obvious that I was leaving without permission. People would gossip now, but that was not my fault. I had done all I could.

On the day I was to depart, I went to take my leave of him. I barely got a word out before he came at me, so fast that a scream rising in my throat died in my mouth. He shoved me roughly against the wall. For a moment, as he pulled at my gown, I thought he would rape me, but his purpose was theft.

His hand reached into my gown and underclothes, and ripped the pouch from about my throat that held the adder-stone. Desperately I grappled with him, hands flailing, eyes wild, but he danced backwards, eyes alight with glee.

"Give it back to me," I said. My heart was thumping. My brother's stone! My last, precious gift from Will and now it was in the hands of Geoffrey! Would he throw it into moat or river where it would float away, this precious piece of memory, of love, so I never would hold it again? Would he keep it so I would never again feel the rough-smoothness of the stone in my hand, feel the warmth of it, something I could imagine still lingered from Will's hand?

"I shall not give it back," he said. "All you own is mine, including this stone…" he paused, eyes glittering. I could see the dragon. "… including England."

I blinked back tears. He could see them. He knew this theft hurt me and even though he did not know, could not know, what the stone truly meant to me he knew it meant something. It was important, it was hidden, never did I speak of it. It was not a gem, so had no worldly value. It was sentimental, personal. No doubt he thought it a gift from Heinrich and that was why I treasured it. He would not give it back. If I told him what it was, he would only derive more pleasure in keeping it from me. It, like so much else, was lost to me.

"Nothing of mine, nothing of me is yours," I said.

I left the chamber, all but running to the courtyard. My poor escort, all who were loyal to me alone, were assembled, barely enough men to mount a guard for me and my ladies. Although they were not far from each other, the road from Anjou to Normandy was long enough. We would face dangers with so few, but I had little of my own money to hire more, for my money was controlled by Geoffrey. I could pawn my jewels, but that would take time and merchants and moneylenders might refuse, on his orders.

Hired men might prove a danger to us in the wilderness in any case. They might decide I would be worth more as a hostage, kill my loyal men, and abduct me and my women, sending word to my father for gold in exchange for me.

We had to go as we were, that was all we could do. Stay here and I would die, perhaps not in body but in soul. I would be vanquished by this boy in the end. He would destroy me.

"Leave Anjou now, and never will you return," Geoffrey shouted. I turned. He was standing in the doorway of the castle, the stone in his curled fist. There was shadow on him. I could not see the expression in his eyes or on his face. There was something in his tone that suggested sorrow as well as rage, but it was only a thought. I had no proof.

"Then never will I return," I said to the shadow.

A warm wind blew in my face, scented with bloom and broom. It was gentle but rushed; a young lover eager to please and hasty to begin. Yet there was, in that warmth, in that perfume, a hint of force coming, a promise of violence; the curled fist of a storm stirring, racing towards us.

I stepped away from the shadow of Geoffrey in the doorway. If I left, there was a chance that he would become more than just a shadow, more than the monster I was helping him turn into. If I left there was a chance for both of us. There was none if I stayed.

I went to my horse and mounted. Geoffrey was still in the doorway. I turned my horse, and away from Anjou I rode. As we clattered into the road a shadow flew over my head, a hawk. In the shadow of the sun it looked vast, wings long and broad as those of a dragon. There was a call on the wind. It sounded as though the creature of the skies was calling to me, urging me on, encouraging me.

Melusine had taken flight, winged into the skies to escape her Count. I did the same, with mine.

All stories are circles, an ouroboros, a snake eating its tail.

# Chapter Ten

## Rouen
## Normandy

### Autumn - Winter 1129

In the garden I stopped, a sprig of rosemary in my hands. Golden light of autumn was warm upon my back, a gentle hand pressing between my shoulders, relaxing muscles, soothing mind.

Not far away, hillsides were bright. A fire of heather seeped up them, bracken and bloom red and gold as flames. Women were gathering leeks from raised beds in the gardens for the kitchen, and to combine with cow bile to make a balm that prevented fever and swelling in wounds. The castle was busy, people flowing through and about it like water. Watching them, you would think they all spoke of their paths, for so fluid and graceful did they flow. Do people ever understand how they become as one with others with such ease?

Lifting the rosemary to my nose brought back memories, not all good. The scent was a smell of funerals. Rosemary, an evergreen, symbol of everlasting life after death, was often carried by mourners. If there was a funeral in town or village, palace or castle, there would be the scent of rosemary and other pungent herbs on the wind, blocking out the scent of death and the salt tang of tears. It brought the past alive in my mind. Nothing has more power over memory than scent; it is its King.

A flash of memory, sharp and sweet and bitter, leapt into my mind; Heinrich's hands touching my face. I could almost hear him whisper "*amata*", his breath hot, perfumed with fennel on my cheek. If I closed my eyes I would feel his lips brushing my skin, would smell his throat, warm skin touched with oil of rosemary.

For a moment, I had him again. He was there with me, as real and tangible and touchable as I was. I could feel his breath, that condition of life, upon me. A moment more and I would feel his lips, feel the love he tried to show me as he pressed them to my skin. And I felt the weight of all we had been to one another. It fell upon me, heavy and solid. A weight yes, but at the same time light like some kind of breeze lifting my hair, my spirits. That history, every memory, jests shared only between us, moments of intimacy not only in bed but everywhere, his fingers touching mine as he passed a missive to me. These were the things of our life, moments that made our life, things that now were gone.

How strange it is that all this of him and me could have and had existed, but I was now the only person who knew of it. That I was the sole witness to a life shared, dreams dreamed, plans made. That now there was no one I could turn to, share a moment remembered, smile about something merry in the past. He alone could have understood without explanation. Now only I could. How strange it was that those memories meant nothing to anyone in the world, but me.

For a sweet moment I had him again. For a moment he was there, real as anyone I saw from the window, passed in the hallways. And then he was not. Heat from those phantom hands was gone, the scent of his skin vanished, the whisper of his endearment drifted away. I lost him all over again.

The smell of the plant in my hands did not alter, yet it seemed to, moving from one memory to another; his sheets on the day I had washed his poor, wasted body, his cold skin, wrapped him in linen, rosemary laced between winding cloth layers covering the stench of his illness and then his death. That scent, so powerful was it that it could transcend such borders, link such things as life and all its fire and fullness, and death, and all the empty darkness of the void that state ushers in.

What weapon could be more powerful than one that could bring the dead back to life for a moment, then snatch them away again the next? That could bestow such comfort, and then such cruel coldness?

I dropped the rosemary and all but ran inside. Through the thick wooden door, along cramped, close corridors of stone lit only by small windows through which cold air gusted, I marched swift. My steps sounded like my heart; rushed and disordered, on the edge of panic, as they struck the rushes and stone beneath. I reached my chamber just as I thought I might lose control over myself. Brushing aside the greetings of my ladies I went to the window, gulping in crisp autumn air, trying not to smell the lingering scent of rosemary on my hands.

*Wicked plant!* my thoughts cursed. I had been content until the moment I smelt it. I had hardly been thinking of anything, then rosemary saw fit to remind me of love and loss, tainting my day.

*And yet not wicked*, I thought as my breathing was restored. Sweet and sad and lonely was the memory rosemary brought to me. Perfect and beautiful for a brief moment was my mind as Heinrich was there, with me. I could still feel the warmth of his breath. Was memory curse or blessing? Something to drive one to madness, or was it only sane, if not comfortable, to remember and honour times of happiness no matter how they were tainted by grief? Rosemary, keeper of memory, did it offer me comfort or curse? I knew not. It was said our ancestors, Norse men, worshipped a god called Odin, and on his shoulders sat two ravens. Their names were *Thought* and *Memory*. Wise Odin said he feared to lose either, but *Memory* most. Was memory more important than thought? That the past was treasure to be protected, to place guardian monsters about in a cave so it could not escape? Was thought, the present, not as important? Even if not, it was as powerful, for with memory gone and present restored, what I had now was grief.

It is in moments such as this that grief reveals its cruel nature; moments where for a brief second the person lost returns, as alive and vibrant as the sun rising. And then they are gone; shadows fall, coldness seeps. The world is dimmer without their light and the rushing weight of all that we had that now is lost falls on us again. The first moment of loss returns, fresh wounds sliced atop the first. The cut runs deeper, new blood seeps then pours from the wound sorrow made in our soul. If we are not careful, infestation comes, blood is poisoned, the soul dies.

I shook my head, stepping back from the window. The scent of hot piss was on the air, women washing clothing and sheets bearing stubborn stains with it, for it was the best tool to remove marks. At least it blocked out the rosemary. As I looked to the autumn skies, not an hour ago gold and amber, I saw not only garments of the castle's people were stained.

Gold and amber were fled. Black ink was smeared in the skies upon clouds of grey, impenetrable blackness beyond. The river beyond the castle was ominous green, black waves, tiny, turbulent, rocking its surface under the hand of the autumn wind and the rolling grey-black skies. A storm would break by nightfall. But the storm I had felt in Anjou I had escaped. Ahead of it I had ridden, breathless with fear that any day we would hear horses coming after us, that Geoffrey would dispatch soldiers and knights, we would be overtaken, my meagre guard murdered. I thought I might find myself a prisoner of my young husband, locked away as many wives are, or that I might, instead, die on the road, my head bearing no crown as one destiny wished for me, but instead a diadem of earth and bracken, as I was thrown in a shallow grave that none would ever find.

Each step of our horses on the road had caused my ears to prick and skin to burst to life, sweat pearling under the heavy cloak and gown I wore, snaking down my back. The boy was in my head. Each night spent in some inn or tavern, abbeys when we were fortunate, saw me lying awake or wrestling with the covers, feeling hands on my throat, about my ankles, trying to drag me backwards or squeeze life from me. Even when we had reached the border I had not felt safe. When I had entered a castle owned by my father I had jumped at shadows, at the sound of people walking stone corridors, slippers echoing on stone flags and along the winding walls. It had taken long days for that heightened anxiety to lapse, for me to cease to feel like a hare exposed on a hilltop, ears lit up, blood-flame in dawn sunlight.

Here in Normandy I was safe. I was recovering. My appetite remained poor, but I was riding each day and that was welcoming hunger back, an honoured guest, to my belly. It came bit by bit, little by little, as a she-wolf feeds cubs, as a weak monk, feeble with fever, sips broth. But it came, and with it came courage. It is a wonder how sleep and food and rest can restore spirit as well as body.

But as my body grew stronger, my lonely mind was falling to distant visions of the past. Heinrich came often, memories of little things like his hands, the scent of his breath, the way he had held me at night, the smooth touch of his skin. There was no reason this should be. He had never been to Normandy; there was no association with him in this kingdom. Yet here he was, stronger than he had been for years. I was unhappy, lonely, sad, so my mind tripped out memories of happier times. Perhaps my mind was trying to comfort me, perhaps it was a trap I would fall into, become lost in the past, in a time I had been respected, nurtured, loved. In fantasy I might drown.

I wanted to escape misery, and I thought at that time that all my sorrow was bound up in Geoffrey. It was not actually so; he was not the cause of all problems in my life, of many, yes, but not all, yet he became the root of the plant to me. If I could dig him from my garden, throw the weed over a wall, perhaps I could be happy. We like to extract what we see as evil and trap it in a body, that we might recognise it, fight it. He had become to me all that was ill in my life.

"In Wales," Adelaise, one of the women serving me, had told me, "I have heard it is commonly accepted that in the first seven years a married couple may separate if not suited to one another. For men the reasons are varied, but I heard it said a woman of Wales might leave her husband if he was thrice caught with other women, if he were a leper, or if he had bad breath."

I had laughed, and then fallen to sick envy of the women of Wales. I doubted it was so anymore. Wales was a kingdom ruled by many princes, but most of those princes abided by the rules of the Church. Tentatively asking men of God if Geoffrey and I might find a way to separate, have our marriage annulled, I had found no good reason we could. He had only struck me once and that was not enough. I could prove no cruelty of mind, had no proof he was thinking of ridding himself of me by murder. My dislike of him held no weight in terms of law. I cursed my brother's marriage to Geoffrey's sister, for had she been older and the match consummated, Geoffrey and I would have been related in God's eyes. Never would we have married. I became obsessed with the notion of freeing myself, and depressed to know I could not. Hunted I had felt by Geoffrey in Anjou, and now in Rouen I was haunted.

It is a thing strange that we look at our lives and think changing one external thing will make us happy. We are creatures who always seek simple explanations, but the truth of all things is that they are more complicated than we would like. Happiness and sorrow are two elements of life that seem simple and are not.

If I have learnt anything, it is that the happiness brought to us by things and people external is fleeting. Happiness itself is. We humans are better suited to conflict and change than peace and stability. Our brains lust for problems to solve. If things become too easy and there are no hills to climb, we become bored and start making trouble for ourselves, and others. That is why we fell from grace, after all, our insatiable curiosity. We are restless animals. Therefore we are rarely happy. Perhaps we were not meant to be, for happiness is better valued for being rare. I do not mean that we are doomed to be unhappy or should pursue that sad goal, but that we should not always lust for happiness thinking it may cure all ills. It is no kingdom we may travel to, no bed we may make and tuck ourselves into. We would be happier creatures if we accepted there always will be toil and trouble, challenges and mountains, and set ourselves into the task of doing those things, and by doing so become at ease with life, happier with the way things are.

The trouble is, we often think of happy as a particular state; a realm of few problems and much pleasure. Since life is like this only for few, and those few will find themselves unsatisfied with that state in the end, to chase such a dream will only lead to nightmares.

But we humans, we are dreamers and dancers. We think we can alter the world because we want to. So we wish for what we think we want. If we are fortunate, we never get it.

The happiness I sought was not in another. It was something only I could grant myself, and, stuck and dissatisfied in life I could not find a path to contentment. I had thought leaving Anjou and coming to Normandy would make me happy. It was better, certainly healthier, and I was feeling a vast deal more sanity upon my shoulders, but I was still unhappy. I was unfulfilled. No person could make me full, besides me. But I thought picking the tick that was Geoffrey from me would make me merry. If I was to achieve this, I needed help. I had no charge of excessive cruelty to lay at his feet, no proof he bedded animals and we were not related to any degree that might separate us. I needed men with influence to aid me.

I spent my time not only riding and walking, but writing. Endless letters of complaint headed from my swan-feather quill to my father and my uncle of Scotland, all asking that I be released, that a reason be found to annul the marriage, that I be made free. My father wrote back from his seat at Worcester, sympathetic yet vague in his promises. The only time I sensed panic or any sense of true emotion was when I told him Geoffrey had threatened to leave Anjou and go on pilgrimage. Then, my father was worried. Firstly, it would make it clear to all that we had separated perhaps permanently, which might make the barons reject me as heir and ruin my father's plans for the future. Secondly, if Geoffrey went to the Holy Lands or somewhere else sacred, there was even less chance we would make an heir, and lastly Anjou might not be as much of a threat now, but if its lord left it could easily become one. Father wrote to Geoffrey, telling him to stay where he was.

It mattered not. I had no intention of leaving Normandy. Geoffrey might as well have gone to the Holy Lands, or wandered, feet sore and boots broken, to pray at a shrine in a dripping forest, hidden deep on a mountainside. People with no intention of reuniting are as far as it is possible to be from one another. Distance becomes meaningless. My husband was only over a border, but we might as well have been on opposite sides of the world.

My father had more success than me in commanding the boy. I know not what he said or threatened, perhaps promised, but Geoffrey's clerk sent a stiff note to me not long after. It said the Count would not leave Anjou. Geoffrey had intended to go to the shrine of Saint James in Compostela, said the note.

I wondered why. James was my saint, not Geoffrey's. It seemed a strange choice, especially since his father was in the Holy Lands. There were multiple places he might have visited there. Perhaps Geoffrey did not want to see Fulk, but selecting my personal saint's shrine struck a curious chord. That which is not explainable often does.

I glanced up as a flash of light whirled in the skies. Lightning: the mouth of a sky-wyrm had opened releasing light and energy. The heavens were cackling like a madman, thunder rolling, light flashing. Maids and boys hurried to put up the shutters, locking out the rushing wind. They blocked out the sight of the storm, but still I could hear it, rolling and crashing through the night, in my dreams.

*

Autumn became long-toothed. The season of Allhallowtide was upon England and was celebrated too in Normandy. Lasting from October the 31st to November the 2nd, it was a time to honour the dead. Lone walkers and riders would carry rowan branches or dried berries in pouches for protection, for whilst the dead were honoured, in some parts of the world it was said they walked, too, the same paths as the living used at this time of the year.

It was fitting I thought so much of Heinrich at that time. It seemed then that the dead were with us always; mist creeping through fields in the morning and evening, as though a legion of wraiths were stealing upon us. Bonfires were lit many nights, blazing fire against the darkness. People danced about them, surrendering to a call older than the religion they followed in daylight. The fires honoured the dead, but kept them away too, enticing ghosts and revenants towards the light in the darkness, rather than their phantom feet heading to walk through the towns. The dead would bless crops and fields for winter, if we honoured our ancestors well. In Wales they would be watching for hounds of the underworld, said to cross the borders between their realm and ours at this time, to hunt in the world of man.

"Anyone who hears their howl is doomed to die," I told my women, gathered at the fireside like children, hugging their knees and staring wide-eyed at me as I told tales my mother had told me. Flames leapt, yellow and orange in the fire and when a log cracked, they jumped. "Arwan, King of the Underworld leads them, sometimes Gwyn ap Nudd, King of Fae. At Glastonbury, Kings of the underworld hold court, and their hounds guard them as they talk."

As December came, and men headed out into the orchards to offer ale to trees in return for a good harvest in the coming year, I had more letters from my father. Geoffrey was complaining that the castles promised for my dowry had still not been handed over. In truth, although I had no affection for the boy, I was starting to find the situation embarrassing. The string of castles along the southern edge of Normandy should have been released to Geoffrey's men. Instead, my father's followers held them. Geoffrey was demanding them not only simply because they had been promised, but because he needed them. With Fulk gone, rebel factions in Anjou had risen. Anjou and its new Count were being tested. Many lords saw the weaknesses in Geoffrey. His enemies thought to expose and exploit them. There was also trouble in Maine. If Geoffrey held those castles in Normandy, he would have more power, more options and more authority. That my father refused to hand them over was infuriating for Geoffrey and potentially dangerous for Anjou.

In one of the letters, Father told me to return to Anjou, smooth things over with my husband, get a babe in the belly. I shook my head at the letter. Quite aside from the dangers erupting with rebellion and rebel lords, return was not in my mind.

My father thought it such an easy thing, to return, but he had never been afraid of the person, or in his case, people, he shared a bed with. There was no point, in any case. I was plumper, feeling better, but my courses had not come back. Until they returned there would be no child, and a child was the only reason I would return. If he wanted me to, my father could force me. Until then I would remain in Normandy. I would be married, yet alone. As I understand it, this is a state many married people find themselves in, whether they are in the same house as their spouse or far away.

I did not mind being alone. There was a pleasure in solitude. No company is better than poor company. I found a routine, and each day fell into it, my hands and mind walking routes well-worn and smooth. I rose, I washed, dressed, walked in the frosty gardens. I ate lightly, went riding. In the afternoons I read, I walked some more, I stared from the window, attended to business, wrote letters. My duties were lighter than before, although my father sent me plenty on laws and current events to read. I went to bed early. I slept well and deeply, often without dreams. I was happier without dreams.

My loneliness became not something I feared, but a companion. It had arms and legs, a heartbeat and breath. If I reached out in the dark of night I could touch it, fingertips trembling on its cool skin, feeling the soft hairs on its long arms. It was my only true friend, besides the darkness.

I had come to think the darkness was not an enemy as people said, but a friend. It was not the same creature as the void of emptiness inside me that had been threatening to eat me. Darkness was something good which seemed fearful and was not. It was where I learned much I could not in light.

I stood often outside at night, no matter the cold or if it rained. I stood on battlements, under the stars. I felt I belonged there. I was a border-walker, a transgressor, a wanderer. Between worlds I had walked, through possible fates I had climbed. I had roamed what was normal and natural and always stood apart, never within. I was Grendel more than I was a man of the bright hall. I was monster more than I was mortal.

With the darkness I was with a friend. The blackness of the night mirrored that darkness within me, but in the night there too was light, as I hoped I still held. Nothing and no one is but one or the other, always we are both. As I watched dark skies and hazy clouds gathering about the hoary moon, the brilliant darts of light that were stars, I was at home. I was content. Here in the shifting dark, the roaming light, I found more peace, more acceptance, than ever I did in light.

In light I felt watched, judged, condemned. In darkness I was myself, whoever that was, bare, naked-souled to the air, unafraid to be seen. I was a dragon in her careful cave, a selkie dancing on the shore, skin bare to the biting wind and salt breath of the sea.

In darkness there was not judgement but acceptance. There was not constant examination of my imperfections; how I had no child, how I disobeyed my father, had left my husband. How I tried to rule, think and behave as a man would when woman I was born. The night did not condemn me as daylight did. Darkness was acceptance as the light was rejection.

In darkness, I was safe, and I was me. And as the darkness and the light of night wrapped arms about me and held me safe, so too did my loneliness, this creature now more real to me than many people, and one I knew better. In their arms, those friendly arms of darkness and loneliness, I was held, rocked as a mother does her child, my head against chests through which I could hear heartbeats, thumping echoes that rang out through time, through eons, from the first moment of creation and into and through me.

Somehow, although that sound held loneliness so great, solitude so complete in it that I felt it might shatter my heart, there was comfort in it too. Because, somewhere, inside wind and world, darkness and night, something understood me. I was connected to that source of life. In eternal loneliness I was not alone.

At times it seemed there was a message in that call, in that touch, that whispered that even if I did not understand it now, I might one day. As though in all this chaos there was purpose waiting that I would one day see, understand, and touch. As though this, this now and here, was not all there was. As though I was unfinished, and held potential within me, possibility in my heart, and in my soul. In darkness and loneliness I found something I had thought lost.

Hope.

# Chapter Eleven

## Rouen
## Normandy

### Winter - Spring 1130

It was the 2nd of February when I found myself considering that I was creeping fast upon the heel of thirty years of age. Time I might have needed to recover, but time was no friend to my body, or my desire for a child.

It struck me as I was carrying a candle to the altar, the cold air washing along my arms, covered only with a thin layer of cloth. In a line we processed, women of my court, taking candles to the altar to honour the Virgin. Candlemas was her day, one of several that honoured her. It was the day the baby Jesus was presented to the temple, the day the Virgin was purified from birth, although many asked why she would need to be purified since she was without touch of man or sin. "My eyes have seen your salvation," the priest said in Latin, "which you have prepared in the sight of all people, a light for revelation to the Gentiles and for glory to your people of Israel."

We knelt before the altar as the priest blessed the candles we carried symbolising the light Mary had brought to the world by being the chosen of God. It was one of the days of the Church where women took a sacred role, and therefore it was special to us. So often we were spoken of as though we were monsters, but on days of the Virgin we all seemed to reflect a little of her light. It was often said that the Virgin's day marked the beginning of spring.

Perhaps spring was tarrying late that year, or the Virgin was not ready, for wild winds broke on the night of her celebrations, tearing trees from roots, creating caverns in the earth. Shelters for cattle and hens shattered, the animals set loose in the dark confusion of night, some captured by predators or thieves by morning. There were more winds to follow, many storms. I sat inside the castle at the side of the bright fire embroidering with thread of gold or crimson as I listen to the wind scream outside. It sounded hungry, eager to reach us. At other times it sounded as though it had claimed the world, yet abandoned us. Such a wild thing had no reason to want to enter a castle, a chamber. It would be out of place. Outside in the chaos and lunacy of the storm it was free and complete. It screamed as it wished to, its voice loud, claiming the very air itself. We were in the centre of its storm, yet left alone, unwanted, for it had no use for us.

Births and deaths marked the start of that year. Although these comings and goings of life affected me and my destiny, it felt as if nothing could touch me in Normandy, as though in coming back to the home of my ancestors I was becoming infused with the spirit of the dead, of victors, those who had passed blood and bone to me. My spirit was returning, my will and courage too. I looked back at the frightened mouse I had been towards the end in Anjou and she seemed like a stranger. It is remarkable what fear can do to wear a person down. I had never thought I would fall so hard and fast from all I was, that a child could taunt me until I wore away, chaff in the wind.

I went to abbeys and churches that my grandfather the Conqueror and his wife, Matilda, had ordered to be built. I slept in castles they had shared, walked hallways they had wandered. Some ghosts brought only pain, but not my grandmother of Flanders and grandfather of Normandy. I felt they were with me, walking beside me, telling me to stand strong. But as I walked in the past with ghosts, my husband was busy creating the future.

A bastard was born to Geoffrey and his mistress. I kept my face straight and impassive when I was told, yet something hard and sharp and thick hit me in the gut. Geoffrey had a child, a son. I had nothing.

Little as I wanted his child, I wanted a child. And grief was not alone, for he brought shame to me too. I knew I would see this bastard child in the eyes of people when they looked at me from this day onwards; a reproach. Geoffrey had good seed. He could make children. Other women were capable of bearing his sons, but not his wife. Still I was defective, broken, unnatural.

Unless you have been the same as me, you know not what it is to be looked at as though you are a scorched patch of earth where green shoots have perished, blackened and withered. You do not know what it is to feel the washing, bitter gaze of pity float over you, and feel that pity turn to loathing, for you not being the creature you should be. You know not what it is to start to accuse yourself, until you have another enemy, one living inside your own mind, telling you that you are broken, useless, abhorrent.

At times, it was as though I had been turned from the realms of man and Heaven, as though I were Cain. Thus did men gaze upon me, thus did I regard myself. I was something cursed.

I found myself reading myths, sympathising with dragons, wyrms and serpents. They knew what it was to be stared at as though they had no right to walk upon the clean earth of God. I understood why they hid in caverns and caves, underwater and on the top of mountains. I too would have fled to such places had I the wings to carry me away. I too might have surrounded myself with gold, purest of metals, so unadulterated light might wash away the dark, accusing eyes of man.

So as Geoffrey celebrated, I mourned. I made no public show. I took from the example of my mother, and never would I blame an innocent child for the pain inflicted upon me. But I mourned. I wept tears in private for all the children I had never borne.

The need to have a child had become a raw ache. There were times I looked on women feeding children, that natural, beautiful moment of connection, and I hated them. Envy rose, a dark, bitter miasma in my mouth, threatening to choke me. I thought I might perish for the effort it took to hold that darkness in, to not let people see it. Had I unleashed it, the gulf in me might have swallowed the world. It was a vicious, wretched, broken feeling. Day by day, look by look it grew inside me, as much a canker as the growth that had snatched life from Heinrich.

Death did not come for me, and at times I felt life had not either, as though because of my state of marriage and not marriage, childlessness and yearning, that I was in limbo, not alive and not dead; waiting for something, and I knew not what.

The hand of Death stole others away. In the spring we had word from Rome that the Pope had died in February. Gregory Papareschi, named Pope Innocent II, was elected and, I was informed, had been consecrated on the 14th of February, but a large group of cardinals declared the swift election was invalid and contested it. Only eight cardinals had elected Innocent. Many thought that not enough, and the election too swift to be legal.

"Another Pope has been elected, Domina, by the rebel cardinals," the messenger informed me, bowing low. "Pope Anacletus II, Pietro Pierleoni, as he was before."

"A son of a rival Roman family," I said. Although the knowledge was distant and rusty in my mind, I recognised the surnames of the two new Popes, and I knew their families were foes.

"Innocent has fled the Holy City," said the messenger. "Anacletus has control of the Basilica."

"Is there word as to where Innocent has gone?" I asked.

"To the Empire, it would seem, Domina. There is word Lothair III will recognise him."

"In return for being crowned Emperor," I said, dry cynicism in my tone. Heinrich had held the Pope captive to gain his crown. Lothair would exchange support for a crown Imperial. The sanctity of the Empire and Emperor, Pope and Rome… where had it gone, if ever it existed? I had thought when Heinrich forced the Pope to crown him he was justified and the Pope was wrong. Now I saw all these games for what they were. God and the saints, orders of the Church I would honour and uphold, but the papacy was a palace of princes like any other, as corrupt as any other.

It was as I foresaw. Lothair traded support for support. It was traditional. My father wrote and said he would support Innocent, and I was to too, but in a vaguer way. If political winds turned we could switch Popes. The world had two Popes for years after that, with Innocent in Pisa and Anacletus in Rome. Most of the Frankish clergy, led by the influential monk Bernard of Clairvaux, supported Innocent as did my father and the Empire, but Anacletus held Rome.

Now that a bastard, young Hamelin as he was called, had proved him a man, and me barren, Geoffrey set himself from life to death. Determined that other men would see him as the knight he had been dubbed already, he set about quashing the rebellious factions in Anjou and Maine. A series of skirmishes and sieges went on. Geoffrey led his household knights and called men to his banner. From what I heard, the boy had become a man, and a warrior. He led his men well, learned fast, and was using that intelligence, so long only employed in cruelty towards me, against his enemies.

All was reported to me, including an injury Geoffrey took which led to wound fever. Although he was better swiftly and the injury was not reported widely in case his enemies took it as weakness, I knew that was one of the first times the boy might have felt truly vulnerable, not in control of something because of his position and ancient name. Sickness is a great teacher of what it means to be in the hands of fate, how wildly out of control our lives are, how there is nothing we can do and no control we can exact if Fortuna decides to frown on us.

But soon, if faced death he had, Geoffrey was up and racing away. I imagined his men had treated his wound with moss, a fine material for soaking up pus and other noxious liquids that seep from wounds. They would have packed it tight with old bread, whose mottled green-blue moulds were known to clean wounds, some said because Christ was the bread of life. Geoffrey's *Miles*, knights, might have strapped clean spider web over it, the strands drying with time to seal the wound and keep it from evil airs. Spider web made wounds cease to bleed, kept open wounds from festering. However they treated him, his recovery was quick and soon there was news of more victories.

"The young Count shows promise, Domina."

I looked up at my clerk and nodded. He had been reading another letter about Geoffrey's exploits to me. Strangely, I was pleased. There was a time I would have rejoiced at any humiliation or pain for Geoffrey, but I did not feel that way now. I wanted no revenge. I was glad he was growing in spirit and in fame, glad the promise my father had seen had had the chance to blossom, the man to grow. Anjou needed him.

I listened as I was told of Geoffrey's command of his armoured horsemen, knights who made up his heavy cavalry, how they used their spears and swords in combat at close quarters. I heard how he used archers well, and with wit, keeping them far away to keep them safe, but close enough to inflict damage. Few were the fights out in the open. Pitched battles were a risk, since if you lost, an entire army as well as its lord, as at Hastings, was lost, but when there were such battles Geoffrey pitched weight against weight, armour against armour, and the boy employed some unexpected tactics, such as holding troops back to use them in surprise. His knowledge startled me.

There were reports of strange weapons used by Geoffrey's men during sieges, and when I heard I almost smiled. Incendiary weapons, the like of which had not been seen since the days of Roman and Greek domination over the world, were being wielded by his troops. People spoke of his innovation, of the dreadful fire he unleashed on castles under siege, and marvelled at the knowledge of the young Count. But I knew where he had the idea from. My library, brought with me from the Empire, that was where. Several books in that collection had been copies of texts penned by ancient masters of Rome. They talked of such weapons. There were variations, and his use of them was imperfect from reports, but Geoffrey had sought out knowledge and used it.

Dragon fire, for the son of the line of dragons. The secret of such weapons taken from books I had left behind.

Which made me think... Geoffrey had been in my chambers, then. Had he been there to clear out my effects, throw away more that was valuable to me than just my lost adder-stone? Had he stripped my chambers of books, cloth and ornaments to send as gifts to his mistress? Or had a lonely boy gone there by himself to leaf through belongings I had left behind?

At night there were times I thought I could almost see him, sitting in a chair, one of my books in his lap, and the stolen adder-stone rolling back and forth in his fingertips. I wondered if the boy I had married regretted much, now that he was becoming a man. I wondered whether he had gone to those rooms not so he could strip them, desecrate them, but because he missed me.

When spring arrived in earnest, as braised greens graced our tables by night along with civet of hare and fig and raisin cream, I started to eat more and better. Maids and gallants were found in the gardens, dancing and courting to the music of flutes and harps. Men took gaming tables out into the sunlight to wager against each other's skill. I was not with them, my court. I was in the woodlands more often than the palace. I left the castle, where often scents of cooking from the kitchens and hot piss from women dying clothes with berries and bark, lichen and leaves would waft on the air of spring, mingling with flowers and sticky buds opening. I left smells and tasks of the everyday behind as I rode for the forest, to bathe in the light and shadow of trees.

In the castle courtyard, darkness soft and cold about me, I put on my gloves to ride. The soft leather, treated with copious amounts of dung and human shit before being perfumed with thyme and sage and anything that would block out the ill scents of its past, was smooth upon my hands. Large rings held the gloves on, slid on top of the fabric. As I rode hard and the sun shone down on me, scents of orange blossom and rosemary floated up as inside the gloves my hands began to sweat, but always in the background of such heady, sweet smells there was an echo of dung. The past never leaves. There always is a trace.

From the castle we rode; me and a spare guard. Along streets in the town in the early morning light we clattered, past dung piles waiting to be cleared, shining, diamond-laced with dew. The morning kept out the worst of the smells, those that would rise from shared latrines and piles of offal thrown by butchers and fishmongers during the day to sweat on the streets, and be stolen by cats and rats who would run hissing or squeaking to safety in the close-packed alleyways to protect their smelly, scant prizes from other vermin. People tried to stay away from areas affected by the worst smells, those where tanners worked, for there it was said the miasma of scent brought illness upon a person. Some thought the opposite, stating that men of smelly professions rarely knew illness, and those people gathered in the midst of such men to breathe the same air, gain a cure by prevention.

But in dawn light, a fresh wind blowing, those smells were far from me. In some ways it felt everything was. I felt apart from the world even though it was all about me. Separate even though I was surrounded.

I was alone, truly, but although I felt lonesome at times I was in company with myself, and I was gentle with myself, perhaps more so than ever I had been every other time, every other day. For this was not the everyday. That time in Normandy was a time without time, life without living. It was a time to recover and find peace, sit still a moment and think. It was a time to be quiet, and listen to the world. This was a space, a breath taken, a pause and for that moment there was no world but the mind, no reality but the air held in my lungs. This was a moment of pause in a busy-lived life, a moment of reflection when so often all was rush and noise. And it was a gift, one few ever have. For fear I had fled here, but for sanity I stayed.

There were few sounds, although people were already abroad. The grunting of pigs being herded to woodlands outside the town gate rose in the distance. The honking of geese being thrown the first scraps or grain of the day floated on the air. Soon would come the time of the bells, rousing those who did not leave their beds of hay and straw with or before the dawn. From outside the town there was the sound of singing; maids on their way to market with fresh milk in their heavy pails, flowers on the handles which they had picked along the way.

The warm, inviting air was an elixir after so long indoors with mistress smoke and master candle my only companions. I rode into woods of hazel and hornbeam, elm and elder, past coppices of ash and willow, but often I did not hunt. I walked beside hidden streams burbling with fresh blue water, watched lone butterflies only recently awoken flit through ground ivy and emerging flowers. When I passed the edges of fields my eyes would light on fire for on the grass were a thousand suns: celandine. If they could whisper they would tell us spring was here, winter gone. Celandine are heralds of hope.

When looking into one river, I saw a coin glittering in the mud at the bottom. I almost stooped to pick it up, but then I saw another and another. Eyes now awake to this sight, it seemed all I could see; the bottom of the river bed shimmering with coins, some rich, some poor, but all thrown to appease some spirit in this flowing water. Beneath those coins, deep in rich red-brown mud, I wondered if there were other offerings. I knew of places where swords had been found, blades rotted, broken. I knew that in the days before we offered prayer to God at the altar and money to His Church, we sacrificed to spirits in springs, our eyes on waterways, recognising the power of a path wending through soil, the path of a spirit not of earth.

My mother had told tales of knuckers and water wyrms. The Golden Dragon of Thebes, son of Ares, had guarded the Castalian Spring. Beowulf's dragon, his last and fatal foe, had guarded treasure, but only had attacked man when man stole from him. King Arthur's father, Uther, was said to be of dragon born. I remembered my mother telling me of the white dragon upon the banner of Harold, last of the Saxon Kings, which had fallen along with its master at Hastings. But if the white dragon fell that day, others still lived.

Sometimes creatures who could take human form, like Melusine, haunted waterways, some benevolent and some decidedly not. Like their kin in caves, dragons of water liked treasure, offerings. Here, seemingly in the middle of nowhere, people still were appeasing a water spirit, a god of old.

I remembered too, tales of dragons who guarded temples, like that of Delphi. A dragon-serpent named Pytho, son of the earth goddess Gaia, guarded that palace of priestesses until he was slain by Apollo. Pytho and Gaia were gods before gods, killed by younger gods who came after, jealous of their power.

Once, creatures such as Pytho guarded not the riches of men but our sacred places. Perhaps the gold that had gathered in places like here, like the caves they were said to haunt, was not gathered by the beasts themselves for greed, but had been brought to those places by those who came to offer to sacred spaces. Did dragons stand guard over gold because it always had been their task, or because it reminded them of their holy masters, now gone?

Perhaps dragons and their kin were not guarding gold, but gods. Perhaps man had simply forgotten this, and thought them creatures of greed when they were, in fact, sacred guardians of places and beings once divine, now forgotten.

Did we remember so much so badly? What of tales of women of magic, of women in general? If wrong we were about dragons, could it be that tales of Eve and the wickedness of women, long used to keep women subordinate and low, were false too?

Were we all, monster and maiden, misused by memory of man? Were we once sacred rather than sinful?

As I thought this, my hands trailing in the water, I seemed to hear a laugh. I rose and turned, but I was not afraid. The guard who had come with me was still at his horse, wiping his horse's shivering flanks with wool. He had not laughed, something else had, but it did not feel malicious. It was the laugh of a friend.

There was a whisper in the trees. But I felt not as I had in Anjou. I felt safe, protected, as though these woods held me, as though the spirit of water that lived here watched over me. I never saw the person who laughed, if ever they were there at all. I stood a while, heard nothing more.

Mayhap it was Melusine, and this forest was where she had flown, as I had, to escape a husband who respected her not, who feared her power. Perhaps she too was tired of being seen as a monster and found freedom in darkness, in solitude, in a space where once creatures like her had been guardians of sacred places, and sacred creatures in their own right.

# Chapter Twelve

## Rouen Castle and
## The Abbey of Bec
## Normandy

## Summer 1130

"News of Fulk," I said to Juliana, one of my women. She looked up from the window where she was sitting with her embroidery, slim silver needle dipping in and out of the fabric, lacing golden thread into one of my azure gowns as though it were the waves and she goddess of the tides. "He is named heir of Jerusalem."

The news was of some time ago. Fulk had made it to the Holy City by Whitsun of 1129 and had been wed. This was his official naming as heir, as the next King.

"A fine thing for the Holy City, and the people of God, my lady."

A standard phrase, and praise, for a woman of her station to make in honour of a man of Fulk's, yet my noble companion was more right than she knew. The wild youth flush with adventure and battle had become a wiser older man, and he was kind when he had the chance, something not often seen. *It did not pass to his son, for instance,* I thought, an old bitter echo in my mind.

*You have not seen the boy for some time,* a voice in my head, which sounded surprisingly like my mother, rebuked. *He may be another creature by now. Many people change a great deal in the time you have missed.*

I was never one to argue with my mother. I breathed in the air coming from the un-shuttered window. Rich with fragrant flowers and pollen rising from the herber, my small enclosed garden, it was. Later in the day, I decided, I would walk into that garden, sit on the soft mead of flowers I had commanded to be planted that spring. Surrounded by rue and sage, basil and violets I would read more letters, or a book. Vines planted over the mead brought shade so the sun could not burn me. Life had become gentle for me in Normandy; I had crafted it that way.

The summer air was thick that morning. It felt like a blanket, like it had texture. If I reached out I would touch thread of heat and pollen, sewn with sunlight. Peaches had come to grace our tables, along with trout and hare. Butter and milk were fresh and rich, sweet with grass, and plentiful. The castle smelt of fruit being baked into pies with honey and cinnamon, which floated on the thick, summer air.

I read on, eyes following the black letters on creamy parchment. Baldwin, the present King of the Holy Lands was yet living, but he was not hale. Fulk might soon be King, his new wife Melisende at his side.

There was news that morning, too, of David, in England. In the spring my uncle had gone to the court of my father, initially to act as a judge in an important case, but he had remained, visiting his estates and manors, overseeing matters in his manorial courts, attending consecrations of churches. Then, there was news of Scotland. His wife, Matilda, had died. He wrote to inform me he was riding back to take care of her last journey.

I had not met his wife in life. I would only now in death, yet she, another Matilda of my family, had been good for David. She had shared his religious devotion, and her gifts to the Church had been generous. She had transmitted northern lands and manors in England to David, and through him to the line of the Scots throne. Because of her the King of Scotland would always now be linked to England. I could only think that a good thing.

*"She will be laid to rest in Scone priory,"* David wrote. *"For there, once she told me she felt the true presence of Christ, a feeling of humble wonder. I think her soul will be at peace there."*

David was heartbroken, something I could well understand having lost my husband. Unlike my father, unlike most men, my uncle had been faithful to his wife. There were no legions of bastards fathered on other women. David also confided that although his men were already talking of Matilda's replacement, he had no intention of marrying again. *"She was my wife, there can be no other. I loved her as I never will dare to love another. In truth, niece, my heart could not take risking such love again. I fear it is not strong enough."*

Rolling up his letter in my hands, I pressed it to my chest hoping David might feel the sympathetic tug in my heart. If only I had been free, I would have chosen not to marry again. But whilst I had had no choice in that matter, I had a choice over my heart. Like David I did not want to dare to love again. Once I had loved and loved with all I had. It had taken much. I had surrendered much of what I was and might have become for it. I had not the strength nor will to attempt such a feat again. But in some ways, perhaps my own marriage was good in this respect. My heart was in no danger from Geoffrey.

Before David could return to his northern kingdom, we heard rebellion had broken out in Scotland. A nephew who had risen against him before had gained support. With David in England, and with the death of his wife, his main supporter in Scotland, David's disloyal nephew rose up. The King of Moray joined with the rebels, a dangerous affair since he had his own claim to the kingdom. David raced north as his constables went out to meet the rebels head on. My father wrote to inform me that David had requested and was to have support from men of England. *"Your uncle reminded me that he was first of all laymen to swear loyalty to you, daughter, when I asked it of him. This I can hardly deny, and I would not have held back from offering support in any case, but he shows his wisdom in reminding allies of their duties to one another in times of peace and war."*

I lifted one eyebrow at the letter. My father and uncle were bent on teaching me, no matter the situation, it seemed.

"My lady?" A knock and scratch at the door made me turn.

"Yes?"

"There are reports of a sickness in the city, Domina," said the messenger, making a hasty bow. "Some think it a plague."

I nodded. It was not uncommon in summer. There usually was a surge in late spring and as summer rushed in close and hot, there would be more. Some plagues brought on sneezing and fever, others vomiting or boils. It rarely mattered which. The same measures had to be taken.

"The court and I leave for the country within the hour," I said. "Only the few who attend me will come, a skeleton guard. Vinegar is to be used to exchange coin in the towns and markets. Close the baths and brothels. Tell the sick to stay inside and the hale to avoid them. Food will be dropped in doorways to the unfortunate. Those with a mind to leave the town will do so today, otherwise they stay. Send word to the abbeys and churches to pray for the people and ask God to forgive the sin that has caused this. Tell them I will send offerings. Have the watch keep a curfew, all to be in their houses by dusk, and no one abroad in day without good reason."

"Yes, my lady," said the man.

To the country we went. It was the safest way. I stayed away from all but those who I knew had not been into the town.

Fortunately it was not a plague of high deaths. We lost people, but many times I knew it had been worse. The quicker we could contain it, stop people wandering city to city and town to town, the sooner such spirits of sickness departed, heading to another kingdom to test another race.

We seem like creatures of such power and might, yet often, I think, God decides to humble us, sending something small to demonstrate how fragile we are. It does not do for those who rule to grow complacent. Death is as true for a king as it is for the race of man. Every now and then something so small it is unseen and unheard comes, and we are rendered helpless before it; every now and then we are reminded how small, how fragile, how delicate we are.

*

"I know peace here, that I know not anywhere else," I said to the abbot.

"We are honoured, always, Domina, when you wish to visit."

"Thank you."

I doubt not he was honoured in part because of the rich gifts of money, relics, fish and game that I brought with me often. I liked to sometimes turn up with little, a trifle, and sometimes with much. It kept the monks on their toes, their abbot not expecting too much, becoming greedy.

But I would not inflict hardship in any way on the Abbey of Bec. I had come to love it, perhaps as much as I loved Fontevrault. When I came, I stayed in the guest quarters, ate barley bread and cabbage pottage with the Abbot. I prayed in the guest chapel. I found peace, for a while.

Founded by the once-knight, Herluin, Bec was a place of peace, beauty and learning. Where possible, all learning should be surrounded by beauty and when not, learning grants beauty to its surroundings. Herluin, fighting man that he had been, had welcomed a scholar-monk named Lanfranc. Lanfranc had established Bec as a centre of learning. He was also a good friend to my grandsire, the Conqueror, and was the man who convinced the Pope to sanction my grandfather's conquest of England.

It was my father's once-Archbishop of Canterbury, Anselm, who had made a continued success of Bec. Anselm had been a sometime tutor to me and my brother when we were very young, and I remembered the old man with affection. He was good, too, at leading orders. Under him the abbey and its daughter houses had grown and flourished. Upon his death Bec was known as a house of God *and* great wisdom, not always two things that went together. Young men, many the younger sons of noble houses, flocked to Bec, for it was said that its walls were the first to witness leaders of the future of the Church. A man looking for a high position in the service of God should spend his youth at Bec.

Its older members, too, knew lives different to those of other monks, for they were sent out to other priories and abbeys to govern them. Bec taught men letters, prayer, and management. Anselm and my father had not always agreed, indeed the Archbishop had come close to ordering my father's excommunication, a dire sentence only prevented by the machinations of Adela of Blois, my aunt, famed peace maker and shrewd politician, but none could doubt that Anselm had been a man of wit, intelligence and foresight. Bec was a wonder.

It was also one of my father's favoured houses of religion. That year he gave the monks four houses in the city for their use and was working on plans to build himself a residence next to the monastery, for when he was in Normandy he spent so much time at Bec that it was only sensible. The daughter-houses at Envermeu and St Neot's were also under his eye, and there was another being built just outside Rouen, which his beloved mother had planned in her lifetime but not had time to begin.

A good relationship with the Church was vital to any king, as my father and indeed my late husband could have told anyone, yet it was not just politics that tied my father to Bec. There comes at times some essence that takes hold and pulls us by the soul towards things, places, moments, people. We cannot explain it, for such tugs of spirit influence our lives in ways that remain unexplained. There are no words for these moments and times, places and people, and perhaps there should not be. Some things defy explanation, flout the human urge to put all we feel into words and lay them out so others may understand us. In my long life I have come to think that moments we cannot explain are not supposed to be explained, that God grants them to us for reasons deeply personal. We may never understand them, yet they aid us. I had felt it in the night breeze, with the call of ocean and earth when I stood on a beach aged eight winters, and in sunshine that fell upon me on the day Heinrich died. I felt it when I stood under the mountains, and at Bec, I felt it too. I believe my father did too, and that was why he spent so much time at Bec.

At times I felt I was starting to understand the soul of my father, perhaps he felt the same, some connection between us not forged of blood and bone shared, but in soul and spirit.

One night, as I went to my bed in the Castle of Rouen, I was brought a message. The rider had come late through the gates. I was surprised; usually information arriving in the evening would be saved until the following morn. Thinking it something of grave importance, a death or outbreak of rebellion, I broke the seal swiftly, and found myself holding a curious letter.

"The King wanted it placed in your hands without delay, Domina," the messenger said, bowing as he wiped a weary brow. He did not look as though he had stopped for rest from England to Normandy. Looking at him swaying on his feet, you might have thought he had swum the sea as well as ridden the roads. "He would not say aloud what it contained, so I hope you understand the entire contents?"

"I do," I said. "Repair to the kitchens, they will serve you food, ale. I will ensure there is a good bed for you. My man will show you." I waved a hand to one of the young boys at the door.

"My thanks, Domina," the messenger said, bowing again.

As he left I looked back at the letter. Not a missive of death, but dreams.

My father had been having nightmares. They had shaken him so badly that he had to share them. In one, he wrote, he had been alone, and threatened by a band of peasants demanding their rights. Over him they stood, screaming at him. Another followed the next night, where he was surrounded by knights threatening to tear him to pieces, thundering the same charges at him. On the third night men of the Church had been about him, gnashing teeth and snarling, accusing him of plundering lands of the Church. *"Those who pray, those who fight, those who serve,"* he wrote. *"All, all men of all society before me, lashing me with furious anger and resentment. Each time I dreamed, I woke in darkness and leapt from the bed with my sword in hand, and found no one there. Thinking after the second that some flux of spirit was upon me, I asked my physician to watch over me, to see if he could see demons or spirits. He watched and saw nothing, but has advised I should grant alms, do penance, for some sin haunting me."*

My father must have been troubled by his conscience before this, for he had been increasing his efforts with the Church for some time. A new cathedral had gone ahead at Rochester that year, and there had been gifts to Bec and other abbeys. All were generous. I wondered if these dreams alone were what he had experienced. He was getting older, everyone was, but he was older than many dreamed of being. It was possible it was simply the slow, steady march of years starting to weigh upon him, but he was a hale, active and energetic man, never sick. There was another reason he had sent this letter. A reason he had insisted it be placed in my hands the moment it reached me. A reason he wanted to forge a connection with his daughter.

Sometimes setting out fears onto parchment or paper makes them smaller. Because they have been laid out in black ink, shrunken to fit the words we use to describe them, our fears are not permitted to grow in our minds. When left unspoken they become larger than we can cope with. There is sense in the phrase that to share a problem is to reduce it, for even if the one we share it with has no solution we reduce the power of fear by speaking it aloud. There is magic in this. Gods of old feared men learning their true names, for knowing the true name of someone grants you power over them. This is true for fear, too. Father wanted to share his fear, reduce it, by showing it to me. He trusted me.

Touched as I was, I was also disturbed. My father feared what these dreams meant, and was right to. Dreams of portent had come before Rufus died, when the Conqueror went to sea, when the last Viking King failed to invade. Some portents are good and some bad, but there seemed little that was good in this one. My father saw it as a warning, set into his head by God. Perhaps it was, but one had to ask, was my father to beg forgiveness for what he had done to his people, or what he had done to his brother? What sin truly was he to give alms for that they might cleanse his soul? Why did he suppose God was frowning upon him? My father was haunted, and I wondered if ever I would know what haunted him, or whom. Would he trust me enough to tell me one day, or die with the secret shared only between him and God?

# Chapter Thirteen

## Rouen
## Normandy

## Autumn 1130 - Spring 1131

That autumn, as common people and rich alike ceased eating berries of brambles for the Devil had spat, or done other unsavoury things on them, and as our harvest was gathered in, two men came to Normandy. One was my father. The other was one of the two Popes the world presently possessed.

Before leaving England there was a rush of appointments made by my father in the Church. Perhaps he wanted it secure, or perhaps it was a part of this new rush of offerings to God, in order that his soul might be cleansed. I think he feared rebellion, thought that was what the dreams foretold, and with the Church on his side he had an ally.

My father did not hasten to me, although I had no doubt I would see him in time. He stayed at Bec. He had a man to elevate to the archbishopric of Rouen. Hugh was the present Abbot of Reading, another religious house my father favoured as he had founded it, and this promotion would secure Hugh as a man of influence, working for my father within the Church. My father went on to Vernon-sur-Seine, where he held court with my Blois cousin, Theobald, for some time. I had no doubt he was attempting to appease Theobald on the matter of Geoffrey, although by that time most of the world knew we were living apart so perhaps my cousin of Blois knew Geoffrey was no threat to his power anymore. Many were wondering if there would come word Geoffrey and I were seeking an annulment from Rome. I was thinking the same.

Men started to smoke fish and flesh in smoking houses, beans and peas were gathered in to dry and store. The first chestnuts were dropping from the trees and mushrooms erupted in the earth. And then Father came to me.

"Your wisdom I have appreciated when I received it by letter, daughter, in the time we have been apart," he said after we had greeted each other formally before others. We had come swiftly to a private chamber. I narrowed my eyes. He was speaking carefully, a little too much so, and flattery only fell from my father's lips when he wanted something. He was preparing me, lacing the bed with wool so when he asked what it was he wanted to ask, or commanded, it would feel softer.

"I shall not to that boy return," I said bluntly.

"What did I say that had anything to do with Geoffrey?" he asked.

Oh, that a face could look so innocent yet be so crafty! I laughed, half amused and half annoyed, and shook my head. "You speak with the tongue of flapping flattery, lord father. It rings false as wisdom from Geoffrey of Anjou's mouth."

He laughed too, his head tipping back and hair catching the light from the window. He could easily be called silver now, rather than grey. The thought made me sad. My father, almighty force that he was, was aging fast. Were it not for the power of his personality he would look like an aged man. Winter was upon him.

I did not let him see that I was sad for the thought of losing him. My father would use anything, especially anything vulnerable, for his own benefit. That included love and affection, sadness and joy. Heinrich had called him a fox more than once, but sometimes I thought my father a magpie, pecking at shiny things, collecting what was valuable for his nest.

"You have to go back to Geoffrey eventually," he said. "You need a son. My time runs shorter each day."

I looked from the window. The woods far away were a smear of russet smoke and ash on the horizon. Out in the bailey there was an autumnal celebration going on; a white bull garlanded with flowers was being led about. Barren women would stroke its flanks for a fertility blessing. It would be walked from castle to abbey, and it was said when it reached the house of God the prayers of those women would be answered. *I should be there, stroking his legs too,* I thought.

I turned my head to my father. "He struck me."

"From what I hear, that strike was returned."

"Does that make *his* strike justified?"

"Justice was exacted on the spot," said my father. "An eye for an eye. You were struck, you struck back. What matters is not who started it, but who finished it. That, I understand, was you, daughter."

I met his eyes. There was pride in his. He would never admit such in public, unfitting as it was for a woman to defend herself against a husband, but he was proud I had refused to be bested.

"The boy should not develop bad habits, such as beating women," I said.

"As you should not develop equally bad ones, such as running from your duty."

I looked away, playing with a ring of emerald on my finger. "The threat of Clito is long gone, Father. Anjou is not needed so as a friend now and we two are as incompatible as oil and water. We never will rest easy with one another, and the more time we spend together the more I am certain we will destroy each other if forced to remain married." I paused and looked at him. "I have been asking for advice on whether an annulment could be brought about."

"So I heard," he said.

"You heard?" I was shocked, even though I knew my father had men in all corners of the world. I had thought I had been subtle. Clearly not subtle enough if the old fox could still outfox me.

"Why do you think I am here? You will not find a man who would support it," he said. "Matilda, sorry as I am that the boy proved too much and you had to come here, he is your husband. Your marriage was witnessed, and it was consummated. The time it would take to gain an annulment, then negotiate a new match is more time wasted for you in trying for a son. You are not getting younger, daughter."

"But you are to meet the Pope," I pointed out. "I imagine you will make many a deal with him. Could not one of the bargains struck be for me?" *Can you not this once be on my side in this fight of life?* my heart called.

He breathed in. "Even if I managed it, there would be some who would doubt it, some who would contest an annulment because of the present nature of two Popes walking the world. That means that if I did arrange this, and you separated and married again, any son, any child you had would have their legitimacy questioned, therefore their right to the throne." He shook his head. "Give men no reason to question your children," he said. "Troubles enough they will have without that."

"So you want me to go back to the boy, to be struck again, worse this time perhaps, to be ignored as a person with a mind, to be humiliated as he parades mistresses at court before me? You know not how hard I came to fear I might be poisoned, how he shamed me, his men calling me barren, unnatural."

"I want you to gather your courage and return, get a son in that belly and use that son to forge a future, for you and for England," he said. "Many times in life we must do the unpleasant to attain our goals. Geoffrey will never make you happy, you two may hate each other, but he *is* capable of giving you a child."

"What if I am not capable of bearing one?" I asked quietly. My hands strayed to a rope of pearls about my throat. Soft, glimmering light graced my sorrowful face. "He came often to my bed, and nothing. And nothing with Heinrich. What if I am what men call me; a barren wasteland?"

"You are not," he said.

"How do you know?"

"In my dreams, I have seen your sons."

My head shot up. "You dream of my children?" The awful rawness of wanting burst open in me.

He inclined his head. "In dreams that brought comfort, after the ones I had that inflicted misery."

"What did you dream?"

"I dreamt of you," he said. "Sitting upon a mound of earth covered in camomile and thyme, in a garden. There were roses there, birds in the skies, flowers all about you. You looked up at me and smiled. You were beautiful, young, as you are now. There was a child at your breast and another playing at your feet, hiding behind your skirts and then uncovering his face and laughing. I saw you look down with such love upon that boy that I thought I would weep."

I swallowed a hard lump of longing and sorrow and hope in my throat. Worst was hope. When one has given up there is nothing to lose. When there is hope one can still be hurt. "My sons?" I asked, my voice rasping in my throat.

"And they had red-gold hair," he said, "which no son of yours would get from you."

*

I knew not if my father lied when he told me that story. He was talented at falsehoods and at reading people. It was entirely possible he knew how desperate I was for a child, so created that dream to make me do my duty and fulfil his plan. Yet I cannot deny that tale, that possible lie, brought me hope, made me dream again. My dreams hurt, and brought me comfort at the same time. I wept at night, and treasured the tears.

Hope can be a terrible thing, a struggling, flailing wretched thing. But at the same time, it too is a creature of survival, of toil. Perhaps it is both at the same time, for that which struggles on survives. My hope was indeed ragged and wretched, a bedraggled creature clinging to life, wandering lost in a storm along a road unknown. Friendless, it was, and yet with my father's story it seemed to see a light, and made for it.

I feared to hope. The darkness that had held me safe a long time was threatening to lift. If I let light in, and lost again I was not sure I had the strength to carry on. Well did I understand from my time in Normandy why people retired to abbeys and to convents when they lost wives or husbands. When Heinrich died the thought had come to me, but I had promised him I would not, and there had been another path open to me which had offered hope for the future. Now, a wife separate from her husband, Countess without country, the only light in my future was the throne.

Yet perhaps the Fates were drawing threads of my life together. I wanted a child, and I knew my chances of the throne were slim unless I had an heir. I had a husband, my father had dreamed I would be a mother. But I would have to return to a man who hated me, who now was a proved warrior and warlord. The danger would be greater to my life, but without a future what good was my life? All I wanted was bound up in all I did not. All that might set me free was tied to that which might kill me.

We feasted on the night of that conversation in the great hall, ate cheering dishes laced with saffron shipped from Essex and Cornwall, and rich pies fat with fruit only recently gathered from bulging orchards. There were oysters and mussels and whelks, brought by barrel from the coast. Garlic mustard and sage ran through thick sausages of pork and hog blood. Minstrels played, music on the warm night air floating along with scents of food and wine. Jugglers and acrobats came to perform between dishes being brought out, and after all stood about the edges of the hall, bellies full, horns and goblets of ale and wine in hand.

"I will consider what you have said," I told my father when we parted for the night.

"That is all I ask," he said.

He was kinder then than at any other time I remembered. It could have been that he, with that keen sight for people's emotions, saw I had truly been scared in Anjou, or that I was tortured for want of a child. It could have been the situation he found himself in. This was the first time in a great many years that he had come to Normandy without it being an emergency of some kind. Touring, spending time at Bec, planning to meet the Pope and bargain with him, these things were not work as war and battle were for my father. He ate well, drank deep and hunted. He did not go to bed late, and we spent many evenings talking. He prepared me for England, for the throne. We were closer then than at any other time in my life. Part of the reason, I cannot deny, was the hope he had offered me. Wretched though it felt, it was a light kindled in my soul.

Robert and Adeliza were in Normandy too. When not with my father I was often with Adeliza during the day. We spent time sitting in our chambers, pretending to embroider as we caught up on the last few years. There had been letters, of course, but stories flow best when they trip from the tongue of a friend. We spoke of all we had been doing, great and small. There are some people who you can spend a day away from and feel awkward when you meet again, as strangers, and then there are people you can not see for years who you fall into conversation with as easily as if you had been apart an hour. Adeliza was one of those, the best kind of friends, for me.

Robert was another.

"You seem happy, brother," I said to him.

"Happy to escape the treasury," was his reply.

"Still you and Brian are doing that task?"

He chuckled. "No, it was done a while ago, yet like a ghost still it haunts me. I am happier doing things not of that nature. Brian too." He smiled. "He told me I was to send his regards and best wishes, and sorrows for the state you find yourself in."

So word had spread to England. "Everyone knows?" I asked.

"Officially our father has said you are in Normandy on his business, but yes, Domina, everyone knows. The barons are nervous."

"They will not support me without a son."

Robert said nothing, but from his eyes I knew it was the truth.

\*

It was early January before my father went to Chartres, capital of Blois, to meet the Pope, the wind blowing wild and snow fluttering across the roads like the tiny souls of children lost before God could claim them. "I will be some months, perhaps," he said. "When I return, I want you to come to England with me. It is time the barons re-swore their oath to you, and time that you see your people once more."

"I would be honoured," I said. I wondered if he wanted the barons to swear again because they were anxious, as Robert had said, about my lack of a child. I could not imagine my father would want to repeat the ceremony unless there was a reason. It was not unusual that barons and lords, knights and the clergy might swear more than once to uphold the King's chosen successor, but I felt an urgency hidden beneath the surface. My father was worried.

"And when you return from England," he said. "You must return to your husband."

My face hardened. Although I had been thinking of it, I had no wish to be told what to do with my own safety and life. "You said you would not force me."

"And I will not, but you have to go back. Something in you knows that. Whilst we are in England I will dispatch messengers to Geoffrey. I will tell him that you must be treated as you deserve, not as he sees fit. I will threaten, and with the barons of England re-sworn to you, you will be in a powerful position. We will see you returned, *and* see you safe, daughter. You will get your sons, and the boy will not think to harm you again."

He left on that road, heading through the snow. My father knelt and recognised Innocent as the true, if exiled, leader of the Church. I have no doubt promises were made in private on both sides to bring about mutual benefit.

As I waited for his return, mutual benefit was on my mind. Could these children my father had dreamed of truly exist? If I suffered in the present, could I bring about the happiest of times for my heart in the future? Could I have all I wanted, all I yearned for so badly I could taste it in my mouth, on my tongue? I feared Geoffrey, but hope I feared more.

Allow hope a mouth and I might be eaten by my dreams.

# Chapter Fourteen

## Rouen Castle
## Normandy

## Spring - Summer 1131

As orchards of Normandy burst blazing into flowers of glaring white and maiden-flushed pink, the Pope came riding to Rouen. It was an honour, even if it was one *many* were receiving. He was making his way to every area of Normandy and Francia so it seemed, so he could gather support. Some said the Pope was constantly on the move so moneylenders could not catch him; his exiled-Holiness was so poor he could offer only prayer in payment for bread. His only means of making his way in the world was to visit barons, lords and princes, and trade on his contested title. Those lords hoped they would be rewarded in the future for extending hospitality.

"Men like to trade in hope," said my father as we walked the halls, watching preparations for the visit of the Pope. "It is a flexible currency."

"It is how you deal with me," I said.

My father rolled his eyes as we walked the dim stone corridor between towers in the castle. I repressed a snort. My father could roll his eyes to the very base of his skull but it was the truth. I would have a summer, a little time in Normandy and some in England, and then I would be back with Geoffrey, if my husband would allow me past his borders and into his country again. I had a feeling it would happen. My father would be persuasive. He often was. He had forced me to stagger into this hellish limbo of a life. Geoffrey might have sworn I never would return to Anjou, but my father would make him take me back. Not long after, however, it seemed any efforts enacted by my father might not be needed.

"Geoffrey has *asked* for you to return," Robert told me later. Father had sent him to me that we might go over lists of meat and vegetables, wine, ale and grain needed for feasts that were to go on in honour of the Pope. Stewards had counted what they thought would be required, and we were to check their numbers and add to them. This was to be a glorious occasion. No expense was to be spared.

"Did Father tell you that?" I asked, not looking up from a list of animals to be butchered. "Or just tell you to *say* that?"

"The Count wrote to me," he said.

I glanced up. "To you?" I handed my brother a list of requirements for cheese, butter, honey and milk, unwilling to let Geoffrey and my hateful return to Anjou distract me from the business at hand. Something in me did not want anyone to know how the mere mention of Geoffrey could threaten to unseat my nerves. If I acted like a creature made of courage, perhaps I would become her.

Robert took the list and nodded. "He asked me to persuade you to return to Anjou. He has sent letters, too, to Father and Queen Adeliza."

"Adeliza said nothing."

"She thinks it should be your choice, but to many of your friends Geoffrey has written, swearing if you return he will treat you with the respect you deserve. I doubt not some of his motive is for shame that his wife is living apart from him, and some for want of an heir, but something in his letters rings true."

I raised an eyebrow. "You are not going to claim he misses me?"

"I think he has strong feelings for you, and they remain with him."

I looked away. Robert busied himself with the lists. He was a sensitive man, my bastard brother, but not one to intervene in people's lives. Robert was one who only offered advice if asked for, a rare thing in a world where many throw opinions into any conversation, whether they possess any knowledge or not. He was feeling uncomfortable for having spoken without me asking for his thoughts. I went on to the requirements for fuel, charcoal and wood. I too was uncomfortable.

The thought of going back to Anjou was not only fearful because of Geoffrey. I had become another person there, a feeble, frightened one. I had lost strength and courage, felt helpless and lost. It had taken a long time to lock that person away, yet I felt it might not take much for the key to her prison to be found. All want to be free, even the frightened. I did not want to become her again.

Yet at times, I could not help but be curious about the boy I had left behind. Years had passed and when one is young there are more changes to character and soul, as well as body, than when we are older. Had he changed?

*Does it matter if he has?* my mind asked. *Do you want to care about any changes to a person who treated you so ill?*

I busied myself with the papers, for in truth I had no answer for my own mind.

*

Readying for the Pope's visit took time, and we were also to host many distinguished men of the clergy. Suitable chambers for archbishops, bishops and abbots were being prepared in castle as well as city. A sea of tents had to be erected for all the servants of those men that we could not fit inside the city walls or castle. Kitchens of almost every noble house were in a roar, preparing food. Once the commands were out, I only had to oversee problems as they arose, and my father left much to me and to Adeliza. Robert he stole away to aid him with tournaments. It allowed Adeliza and me to spend more time together and have a common goal to work at, and I know few women who do not relish the task of organisation, though many may not admit it.

In between plans, we had time to wait, and my father filled it with stories. I have found that as men age they seem to live more in past than present. It is only to be expected. They have more past than future. When we are young there is no past, only future; an endless summer devoid of clouds or rain, or so we seem to remember. The mind of the youth is not to be relied on any more than the brain of age.

I am not guiltless. I sit now, at a window in a castle, remembering, not caring to think how much I have forgotten. I wonder what slipped out of my father's mind; how true all I was told during those few days was.

Father told me of battles fought before I was born, and of squabbles. Although I had heard it before, Father told me of the incident in L'Aigle that started his brother Robert's rebellion; Rufus had pissed from a balcony onto the head of Curthose, leading to him threatening to kill both Rufus and my father.

"Father stepped in, hand on sword," he said. "The only reason he did not kill Robert for threatening us was because our mother was there. He never liked Robert, perhaps because our mother liked him so."

"And Curthose left, and rebelled?" I asked.

"That very night," he said, eyes lost in the past. "He stole from the castle, rode off with his friends, and rose against Father." He smiled. "And his rebellion would have failed sooner, had our mother, your grandmother, not supported Robert with funds." He shook his head with admiration. "She was the only one, besides Robert, to ever cross our father and live," he said. "And because of her he and Robert reconciled. When she died they drifted again. Indeed, Robert made more trouble in league with Father's enemies, but when she was alive our mother held us all together."

From childhood he went on, telling me how he had supported Curthose and Rufus in their struggles when one was Duke and the other King. "I was too young to take possession of the estates and manors my mother left me when she died," he said. "And after our father's death, they were claimed by my brothers, so I had no choice but to work for them. Warrior and politician I was, whatever they wanted me to be, for years."

"People never speak well of Rufus," I mentioned. "He must have been hard to follow as a lord and master."

"He could be hard to like," said my father. "But I liked him. Rufus was daring, brilliant in battle, rash and impulsive at times, but his mind was quick and courage boundless. People said he had scant respect for the Church and they had a point, but he was not as loose in morals as some liked to believe. To friends, he was loyal without question. There was much good in him."

I saw sadness in his eyes. "Not so in Robert?" I asked.

"Robert," said my father with a sigh. "There was much good in him, a great deal of promise, but his life was tainted by our father. Always Robert could do not enough. Always he was trying to live up to an impossible standard, which always changed, getting loftier, when Robert reached it. It was a race he was never to win, for the end post changed all the time. He scrabbled for our father's love, but our father resented him."

"For what?"

"Our mother, Matilda, loved Robert greatly. I think our father was always envious of the love she had for him, for any of us. He feared she loved her children more than him, and it was proved, in a way, when she supported Robert's rebellion. She chose her children, not her husband. There was something dark and jealous in our father that could not accept that. He could not take revenge on our mother, she had command of his heart, so he slaked his rage and envy on Robert." My father sighed, stretching his back. "And Robert knew it. Our father's lack of love stained my brother's life, affected all he did. He was always trying to be more than he was, always trying to best not man but expectation of man. The monster in my father's heart birthed a son in Robert's. Because of our father's dissatisfaction, Robert could never be satisfied with himself. He was trying to live up to someone else, someone who hated him, and that was only ever going to end in sorrow. Had he proved his worth to himself, Robert might have been content, might not have been so feral and feckless, but he kept trying to make our father proud by outmatching him. It was a mountain without a top that my brother tried to climb. And he fell often, exhausted."

But Curthose had moments of brilliance, I was told. He had faced his father in battle, man to man, had bested him and had spared his life. And once under siege in Rouen, the very city we were in, the troops of Rufus about him and peril on all sides, Robert had sent for aid and many responded. "I was one of them," said my father. "I came to the call of Robert, even though Rufus was the brother I liked more. But Robert had granted me lands in Normandy and Rufus had only stolen and kept those in England I was promised."

With reinforcements Father had come, joining Robert in Rouen Castle. In a lunatic advance to break the siege, they had charged from the castle. "As I fought, running with my men into the fray, Robert made for the water with his. People said he ran from the battle, but it was a part of our strategy. Robert was the one they wanted. Capture him and all was over. Get him out and the war carried on."

"Rufus's men fled?" I asked.

"They did. We were strong and new and eager to the battle. Only a slight time had we been inside, so we were lusting for freedom. Many within the walls had become reliant upon them. Sieges can be like that, some people accept and welcome the walls and others rebel. We were the rebels, not wanting to be contained. Rouen was a slaughterhouse that day. It was not a good day. It was a good battle, but often that means not a good day. There was a song of mourning, wailing mothers and wives and knights, for a long time after. But we won."

"But people did not like that Robert did not fight," I said.

"No, they understood the strategy when they heard of it, but the actions Robert took were not what the people thought the Duke of Normandy should do. The Conqueror was in their minds, an image of a man who fights without surrender or tricks. The idea people have of heroes is so false, no true hero of old ever fought that way, they all used tricks and traps and escapes. But that glittering knight who will never surrender, who fights to the end even if it costs him life and title is in the heads of people, so no matter if it was the correct choice to run, Robert's choice was not respected."

"But you gained their respect." That day was often spoken of in Rouen. Although the people had borne a huge toll of life and blood for victory over Rufus's men, my father and his courage were remembered. From that day he was in the hearts of the people of Normandy, their son and lord.

"I was. Yet mine was the foolish path to take in battle." He laughed. "Often we respect what is foolhardy, as long it risks death. Strange creatures we are. We do not respect those who do all they can to preserve life, but those who rush to meet death we think wonderful." He shook his head. "We are an idiot race," he muttered.

"Curthose became better respected in the Crusade," I said.

"He did. It was deserved for Robert did much worthy of respect, but you will find, daughter, mistakes are what men remember. Talk of the Siege of Nicea or that of Antioch, and men will nod a little, but talk of the Siege of Rouen and men will recount all details of battle, all that shamed my brother."

"And Tinchebrai," I said.

"My great day," he said. There was pride in his voice, but also bitterness. It had been my father's first great battle and victory, and he had won grandly, but many he had known had died, and that day had marked the start of Robert's captivity, something I felt weighed on my father's soul, in honest times.

"I learnt of that engagement from Archbishop Bruno," I said, "as an example of how a pitched battle should be fought."

"A rare compliment, since they should never be fought," he said, nodding and rubbing his nose, red at the tip from the sun. "Pitched battle is too risky. Lose that day, in that place and the whole campaign is done, over. It is a foolish way to make war."

"But you won."

"I did. It was hard fought. Helias of Maine and his knights won the day for us. He broke the back of Robert's cavalry. So fearsome was his charge that not only did more than two hundred men die, but Robert's reinforcements turned tail and ran. I had planned my troops well; had many unmounted, solid lines of knights to withstand the charge of Robert's cavalry. Knights are the best troops for a cavalry charge, taken from their horses, braced, ready, they can withstand the impact of the enemy's cavalry. Knights know where to strike horse and man, so if any can withstand such an onslaught it is them. I had made three divisions of my troops, which was one more than Robert, but in the end a lot of my planning was almost superfluous and it was the knights, and one charge, that made the battle mine."

"I hear men often claim it is knights alone that win or lose a battle."

"Cavalry charges can be devastatingly effective, but they are hard to repeat and if the men you charge at know what they are doing they can repel you. Helias gave the enemy no chance. It was the strike of a dragon, fire breath. They stood no chance because his charge was so vicious. But in other battles, often infantry, archers, many more segments of troops come into play. If you can deflect the first cavalry charge, the battle opens up, possibility is born. Helias and his men exacted an almost perfect assault. The battle was down to them, down to pure aggression."

"And then captivity for Curthose," I said.

"I could not bring myself to put him to death," said my father.

I wondered if that was true. It might be. If my father *had* arranged the death of Rufus he might baulk at murder of another brother, especially one done in public, for it might add to his reputation as a kin-killer. Or perhaps Rufus died by accident, and my father would never have thought of murder in return for a crown. Perhaps my father imprisoned Curthose because he had once loved him and could not be the author of his end. It was hard to know. Liars often are hard to know, and my father was one of the best.

When at last we got to the present, or the near past at least, Father was scathing about Stephen. My cousin of Blois had disappointed him by making a pact of peace with Clito rather than war. "Once I thought that boy as promising as his brother," my father said. "I knighted him, you understand?"

"Stephen is not a boy, Father, and is indeed a capable man."

There was a barking laugh, sour and irritated as a festering wound from my father. "His wife is the better ruler. A good King she would make."

"And his people note nothing of his flaws as her abilities cover his shortcomings, therefore they are a superb team," I said. Stephen and Matilda ruled jointly in Boulogne. That was clear enough from their charters, as both always signed. It was also clear if you knew them, where Matilda's hand was; often guiding her husband who could be short on attention to detail. "Stephen is a good man, Father, a man of honour."

"Good men make poor rulers," my father said. "He has not dirt enough in his soul to make a good ruler."

I wondered not for the first time if my father had considered Stephen as a successor. If he had it seemed he did not anymore. "You think I have enough?" I asked.

My father looked at me and nodded. "There is darkness in you," he said. He did not sound ominous, just reflective. "Men think darkness the enemy, but it is not. There are lessons to be found there, some more valuable than those learned in light. But it takes courage to go into the darkness, to face it. In darkness we find ourselves, raw and naked. It is not something everyone can do, for we find the best and worst of ourselves when no light is upon us. But for a ruler, it is imperative. Stephen will never go into that darkness, so will never know himself."

"But you think I will?"

"You already have."

# Chapter Fifteen

## Rouen Castle
## Normandy

## Summer 1131

It was a glittering time, the time of the Pope in Rouen. Days of prayer and Masses were followed by afternoons of entertainments and blood. Nights of feasting came fast on their heels, roaring men who had been victorious in melees talking loudly with priests who had thundered out rousing sermons. Roasted boar and heron, peacock and rabbit came in their hundreds to our long tables in the great hall over those nights. There were fat capon, their skins gold, glistening and brown decorated with blackened lemon slices still hissing from the ovens. There were bream in green sauce, roasted rabbit and pigeon slathered in honey and pungent mustard, slices of venison rolled and stuffed with oats and herbs, custards and tarts of pork, apple and egg. Pottages wafting steam laden with parsley and rosemary, mace and saffron floated before each course of meat, and after there were wobbling puddings of sweet custard, rose petals and honey, almond and nutmeg, cinnamon and lavender.

I found the Pope himself about as impressive as I thought I would. Rather than fawn at his feet as so many did, I was respectful and dutiful, but I did not throw my soul at him. I had learnt how easily Popes come and go, and if the Church is sacred the men who seek to rule it often are not. There was no sense in putting great energy into one Holy Father, they changed too often, and my father had said I was to be a little aloof, in case we needed to switch allegiance in the future.

I watched him, this Pope without a throne. He held himself as though he were the chosen of God, when not all mortals had chosen him in truth. Men find it so easy to suppose themselves divine. They see themselves in God, for God is the image of them and they of Him. Where is woman to find herself in the eyes of God, in His soul, when all there is, is man? Women, formed of scrap of man, find God not so easily.

*The divine is not outside you,* something seemed to whisper. *That which is sacred is not always easy to see.*

*

I was glad when the celebrations were done. Exciting as it is to have nights and days of entertainment they grow long and old and tired, as most things do in time. After the Pope rode on by mule to his next haunt, to test the purse strings of yet another nobleman, days were spent packing away linen and clothes and bedcovers into chests, taking furniture apart and checking horses, so we could make for the coast, and then for England.

We came to that hated place, to Barfleur.

My father seemed suddenly all business and nothing else, trying to fill his mind so he did not think of the past, of Will, of his other children who had died there, alone, cold and terrified. It is a response of insanity, working like a fury to avoid thinking. All it does is to put off evils haunting the mind, saving them for later by which time they will be larger, stronger, harder to best. But in times of trial people throw themselves into task and toil, and tell you they feel better for it. What they mean is that they have not allowed themselves to feel anything, any of the emotions riding them as a knight on a whipped horse. They have taken their fear, or pain or sorrow and thrown it aside a while. But creep back it will, wearing all manner of strange disguises, hoping to trick you, trip you. Emotions demand to be felt, and they will eventually, no matter how long it takes or how you try to numb them.

Wallowing in pain and misery does not help one either in times that come to try the soul. The best solution is to face the darkness head on, as my father said; understand the agony that hurts you. There are things inside us that must be embraced if sane we wish to stay. And as my father noted, not everyone can do such a thing. Many times it is easier to bury oneself in work, to look the other way, live in fantasy, than to gaze into the eyes of the dragon within your own soul.

And here at this port there was much that we did not want to see. Here were many ghosts. Much that was lost. My father had much dirt in his soul, but this place was too hard for him to bear. I did not think badly of him for turning his eyes from the monster, from this coast, this sea. Here was where all failures of his life, all he might feel guilt for, converged as the lapping waves upon the sands did. Wash after wash of evil came for him here. My father buried himself in work so the dead would not find him. We all find ways to survive in hard times.

But I heard them. I walked in the darkness waiting for me. Dreams dead and buried beneath the sea were here. Whispers in the darkness of what might have been could be heard. I could feel the thread of the Fates passing through their hands, as their eyes examined the lives of me and Will, as they chose to cut short his destiny and keep the thread of mine flowing through their hands. I could feel *wyrd* about me as water, that essence that cares and is careless, that moves and shapes us. Here my brother's story had ended, and it might be said mine had begun. If my brother had lived I would not be heir to England. He had died and I had been offered the destiny that should have been his.

At night I dreamt of a white ship upon the water, rails as white bones against the grey-green crashing sea. The snapping sails were formed of skin and hair woven together, pickings of the dead. I dreamt of voices calling, pleading for help, of hands reaching out for me, hands I could not touch. I woke often in the night, awash with sweat, thinking there were hands on me, touching me, clawing me.

In daylight I walked the shore. My ladies did not want to, they heard stories it was haunted. I went with my guards. Even they crossed themselves when we saw movement in the water. Ghosts walked there for everyone, I think. Most families had lost someone, kin or friend, when the sea swallowed my brother.

"Will," I said to the water one day. "You died in a fruitless quest, brother. You died trying to outmatch our father, to impress him. With all I know now, I know it never would have been. We, neither of us, can achieve the impossible."

The sea did not answer, neither did Will, but I knew I was right. My father might look down on his father for the way he had treated Robert Curthose, but the same pressure had been upon Will, and was now on me. Will had died trying to impress Father. I would have to live, and outlive him, in order to do what my brother could not. In order that I might impress myself first, and thereby break the curse.

I stared at the surface, the water silver and iron. It was blinding, yet I did not look away. A cold, moist wind blew, ticking tears from my eyes. I stared for a long time at the place they told me the ship had sunk. My mind almost thoughtless, I watched short waves curl and crash, saw glimpses of the rock that had lain, a monster under the water, to rip the belly of the ship, to drown my brother. As I turned to leave I thought I heard voices, phantoms calling for help, screaming in terror.

I was glad when my father's ship, the *Esnecca, the Serpent* was ready and we could leave.

And then, we almost died.

# Chapter Sixteen

## The *Esnecca*
## The English Channel

### Summer 1131

The *Esnecca* tossed again, pitching side to side, side to side. I could hear boards moaning, rigging wailing; outside, wind shrieked, hungry and alone, desperate for friend and for food. Soon the sea might not be so lonesome, not hungry with all of us in its bottomless belly.

"Lord Jesus, Lord James, Holy Mary, Mother of God..." My lips were barely forming prayers, just names. That was all my mind could call forth, names, cries in the darkness and the tempest pleading for someone, anyone, to help us.

The ship rocked violently. Adeliza retched again, her lady trying to keep her upright, hold her beautiful face out of the vomit that splashed into the bowl and out of the stream that raced, frothy and pungent along the floor, seeping into the water already there, sloshing in from above us.

Another heave of ship and of Queen and we rocked, hesitating just a moment too long on one side of the ship. I had my hands together, trying to pray, yet there was nothing in my head. Not one name could I recall, not one word could I mouth, I was so terrified. Fear was a bright, white light in my mind. I could see nothing else.

I was about to die. About to join my brother. The ship fell back, slapping on the waves and rocking the other way. My head knocked against a post. Adeliza heaved again, nothing coming out now but froth and tears flowing from her eyes. She grasped for my hand, hers slippery with sick and water. The ship charged recklessly into a series of smaller battles against roaring waves. Men above us shouted, screamed.

*The same crossing, the same crossing,* was all I could think. Will was below me somewhere. His ghost grown lonely and hungry. His hands would reach for me through the sea, taking hold of my ankles to pull me to the bottom. Any moment now I would feel cold fingers wrapping about my ankles, my flesh plunging into water, closing over my head, and then down, endlessly down, into darkness, into the depths. And there we dead would dance with the weeds, with those long dead of the court of Normandy and England, under the sea.

This was the end of the story, our story; the story of the heirs of Henry I. I had thought it two tales diverged and it was not. All this time it had been one and I had not known. Old men telling it would say, was it not strange how the sea took them *all*? How the prince went first, then his sister, named heir after him? Was it not fated that they took the same path? The waves were hungry, water thirsted. Failed it did to take them all the first time, so it waited, and was rewarded. Fate was a sea serpent. She opened her mouth. We were, neither of us, fated to rule England. We had known it not but both of us were cursed, doomed to end our lives in the same stretch of sea, but for what sin? A sin of the father, it must be, the old men would say, for both children of his line to die in the same way, in the same waves.

This was the end of the tale, the twist in the plot that none saw coming. The sea would have her dues, always. Old men would whisper as they came to the end, telling children that on cold nights of autumn brother and sister both, those lost children of England could be heard, ghosts seeking each other in the sea.

*This is the end,* I thought. There had been times I had wished for death. A safer, quieter end it is than life. I had wanted to see Will again, Heinrich too. Yet then, at that moment I feared to see my brother's eyes. I feared to die.

Should I have feared so? Perhaps death was better than what I had in Normandy where I was alone, cast off, a life lived unloved. Perhaps it would be preferable to die rather than go back to Anjou.

Many times I had wanted death, that easy end. And then, I found I did not.

When I faced death on that day I knew I did not want it. Not that death. Not that fear, not that terror, not that itching under the skin of inescapable horror. I wanted to flee storm and tide, the waves and the pale, drawn faces of people I loved. I could not. Where could I go? Into waves? Perhaps swift death would have been a better fate than waiting for the ship to tear apart in the thrashing wind and the busy hands of the thrusting, teasing, mocking water. Perhaps to die fast and join my brother in the depths would be preferable to that torture. To watch people I loved bound in fear and fright, watch them clasp hands over one another's silently, tears in their eyes for fears they did not dare express lest they came true. To watch people I loved unable to tear their eyes from the water, from the creaking, groaning boards about us, was torture. I saw them waiting, always waiting for the moment the ship shattered and water flooded in and we were torn apart, hands waving over the white crests of waves until all were gone, until we were alone in the icy sea, all we knew gone and dead.

Perhaps death would have been better than waiting for death, but I had no wish for it. I had been numb. All this time I had been numb, thinking that death might be better than living because life had so little to offer, but in that moment of clarity I knew what a false, wretched thought that was. What a vanity! Life had given me everything. What had death offered but pain? Death was a black hole into which my brother and mother and Heinrich and Bruno had fallen. I wanted none of it. I wanted to live.

There are times fear is not a bad thing. It is there to make us move, get away from danger, to alert us to things suspicious that our rational, cultured minds miss. There are times fear may wake us, shake us from a sleep of soul and mind. That was what I experienced that day. Fear took hold of me and ragged me like a hare in the maw of a hound. Fear woke me from a slumber of the soul. I had been dead for years. There, facing death, I was alive.

All the years I had been in Normandy, perhaps more, perhaps all time I had lived since Heinrich died, I had been unconscious. I had retreated into a cocoon not knowing what to do with the grief inside me, how to manage it and carry on, how to be the person I thought I was or was supposed to be. Grief had made me step from myself, protecting me so all I had felt I had not felt, so I was sheltered from the weight of my emotions. I had thought I mourned? I had only allowed myself to grieve in part. A part of me always was withheld, so I could survive.

In that moment, in all those awful moments as our ship was thrown about the sea, I knew the silver-sharp dart that my mind truly was. Compared to what it had been as I lingered as Geoffrey's wife, as I had all but retired in Normandy, my mind now was an arrow shining bright and glorious against a flat, black hole. The purpose, the single-minded purpose of survival was so sharp I thought it would cut me open from the inside. Every drop of my blood, every shard of my bone was screaming at me to live.

I had never thought I wanted life so much, not until I stood in the very shadow of Death himself. Not until my brother was so close I could smell the salt scent of his breath upon my cheek. The bright dart of life and light kindled in me. Darkness had held me, but as a mouth opened before me and I saw the dark throat and belly beyond, I knew I wanted safety and numbness no more.

"Lord God in Heaven," I screamed, my voice louder even than the storm. "Protect your children! Do not call us from this world!" *I am not ready, Mary, Queen of Heaven,* my mind shouted. *I have only just opened my eyes to see.*

From about me there were cries; the same prayers shouted by other people. Voices lifted from all about me, even from Adeliza, on her side, weeping and praying on the floor. From above I heard a noise. Those still on deck, those not swept away, were praying too. My father staggered down the steps into the covered deck, lurching and teetering. He stumbled to his wife and pulled her into his arms, cradling her against his chest as though she were his daughter. He looked into my eyes. I saw more than fear. I saw guilt.

Was history about to repeat itself? Was the snake to eat its tail? Perhaps ancient gods of the sea, spirits of water, had not been after my brother at all on the day he perished. Perhaps they had wanted my father. He had been supposed to be the one on board that ship if destiny and a good story had had their way. Had demons of water taken the wrong prince? Did they think to end this tale as it should have ended all those years ago, by taking Father now, and to ensure the death of our line, me too?

There were ghosts in my father's eyes. He thought something was after him. Something angry, dead but not forgotten.

I heard him calling out prayers, bargains made with God. He would not collect *danegeld* for a year, my father called to the wind. He would build churches, give alms. Endless men and women would be dedicated to the Church. He would make a pilgrimage to the shrine of Saint Edmund. God would be well paid if He spared us.

The ship tried to turn, and I wondered if these King's promises were enough, if what haunted my father would surrender. *If it is Your will, to Anjou I shall return,* I said in my thoughts. *If You show me death to make me do Your will, spare us and I will know it is Your will.*

All that night the hungry wind moaned. I lay on a bed, too weak from fear to kneel and pray. I was ready for it to end, to give in, give up. Ready to take Will's hands and float to the floor of the ocean so we might swim amongst the weeds together, tell stories to the fish. I surrendered to water. I felt as though I were floating, already with Will. When I felt that, fear was gone. All was gone.

I will never know if I dreamed or if I was visited, but I thought I felt ice about me, melting. Free, I floated in darkness. I felt the smooth tail of a creature close, wrapping silken and wet about my waist. I rose in the water, floating up, always up, to the top. My head broke the surface but I was not out of breath. I had breathed in the water, and water had sustained me. I looked to my side and there was the ship, sitting peacefully on the calm surface of the water, a dawn of blue and puddles of indigo, silver and streaming pink spreading out slowly at her back.

I went to swim to it, and saw something in the water. It was the tail of some serpent of the sea. It rose in the water then dropped, vanishing beneath the white-topped, gentle waves. For a moment, as sunlight streaked up the smooth skin, the tail seemed to wave. It looked like a salute.

I opened my eyes to the sound of weeping. I tumbled quickly from my bunk, thinking the end was closing… only to find myself racing across the floor. I looked down in amazement. The ship was still, unmoving. Boards were creaking gently, but their voices were called from them by sunlight, warm and golden, not by crashing, surging waves. We were not dead. The ship and sea were still.

Bewildered, I looked to the source of the noise. It was Adeliza. She was on her knees, weeping for joy.

# Chapter Seventeen

## Westminster Palace
## England

## Summer 1131

When I think back to that journey by ship where I, my father, Adeliza, and Robert almost died, at times I recall all of it, every second. At others all I have are flashes. In dreams I hear groaning timbers and smell the salt rush of grasping waves. I hear prayers wailing upon wind. At others, I see such small things; eyes, wide and white, pupils distended, staring not at me but beyond, looking for the Creator who made us, asking that He would not steal us from life.

I see fingers, knuckles white as bone clinging to wood. Often I see hands on one another. I remember this most; at the moment of ultimate and suffocating fear what each of us did was to reach out to touch, feel skin against skin, know the comfort of the warmth of flesh. Adeliza in my father's arms, I recall a great deal.

And I remember I reached for no one.

Think not it was not for yearning. More than anything I wanted to touch, to feel, to know I was not alone, yet I did not reach out. So alone had I been for so long that the thought of skin to skin was as fire to flesh. Closeness had become alien. I had feared to love again after Heinrich and that fear had become manifest, something built inside me, shielding me from others. I could offer friendship to a degree, but always something was held back to protect myself. I saw then, facing death, it was sheltering me no more. It was harming me. I was alone at the moment of death because there was something in me pushing all others away. I could not risk to love, therefore in many ways I was already with my brother. The Bible says he that loves not abides in death. The past was upon me, a cloak, a warning, keeping me from love, and life. In the moment of death I knew I wanted to live. As clouds cleared and skies stretched wide and blue and white above us the next morning, I stood on deck thanking God for our survival, and wondering what that meant for me. Was survival not what I had been doing all this time, rather than living?

I had not known I was frozen, until water thawed me.

Could honour and duty, a throne and power ever truly be sufficient for the human heart? Could I live with those things alone? My days could be busy, my life stuffed with purpose, yet I would bear a heart that would grow colder and more isolated each minute, every year. What hope was there of love and light for me? My father was a distant figure even when at my side. Adeliza was warm, but often we were apart. My friends I did love, as far as I was able, yet I knew I could carry on almost unchanged without them. I had before. There was a husband I was joined to, but he despised me. I had become self-reliant to a point where I had made myself alone. This is not what reliance upon self should mean. I should have been one of many friends and companions I had, not the sole one, not the lone one.

I stood on deck that morning thanking God for my delivery, but wondering what purpose He thought I might serve. Life, service, toil I could offer, but at what cost? Would my soul ever know the comfort of bonding to another again? Would I abide in death, because I could not love?

He had spared us, and I had promised I would return to Geoffrey if He did. Whatever would come of my future, it would be found in Anjou. That was all I knew that morning.

"God is merciful," Adeliza said, joining me. Her face was pale, and I doubted she had eaten anything, but her eyes were bright. Greener than the sea or grass, those eyes shone with life.

"We were fortunate," I replied. *I hope God and Geoffrey both will be merciful if this path I must walk,* I thought.

For a moment there was silence. Adeliza's eyes were lost on another path, one inside her mind. Wending down that endless labyrinth we all wander within. It is a thing wondrous that humans manage not to fall over all the time, considering how absent we are, lost in our thoughts.

"There is another purpose for you," she said. "That is why we were saved, why this was different to the past."

It seemed I had not been the only one thinking of my brother, or of the future.

I smiled and touched her hand, but in my heart I wondered. I remembered stories of old told at Christmas, tales of men of the North. Their gods were not merciful and benevolent. Those gods had played with the lives of men, for sport. There were times I wondered about our God.

*

They stared at me, that mixture of condemnation and pity in their eyes.

I was so accustomed to seeing it now that the pain it caused was familiar, almost a friend, one who hurts you over and over yet you cannot help returning to them for the comfort of the familiar, even if you must endure the wound you bear tearing open again, just a little more, just a little deeper, each time.

I was on my throne in the great hall of Westminster. The long, echoing chamber was full of men, all with pity and judgement in their eyes.

Barons of England had gathered, standing before me and my father under the vast domed roof of wood, so they could swear to uphold me as his heir, again. It was a tactical move on my father's part. When these men had sworn the first time I had not been married. Many had protested about my father's choice of husband. Having them swear now I was married meant Father was destroying a loophole they might think to sneak through. If the barons swore loyalty to me *after* my marriage, there was no backing out by saying their oaths were invalid because they objected to my husband. My father had commanded they come, and they had, falling to the power of his almighty will, but that did not mean they were merry about it.

I could feel bitterness. It was on the air. Like sweat and the scent of sodden wool rising from their cloaks I could smell it, a sour tang riding the draughts running along the stone walls. My father's will held men of England in check, but they had been promised much by him and he had gone back on his word by wedding me to Geoffrey. I have no doubt many of them had wanted to marry me themselves and he had dropped hints they would, little games to keep the children looking one way as he made plans the other. They would not have wanted me for *me*, no matter if they found me pleasing. Barons who might have thought to marry me wanted me because I was a path to power and money, influence and advancement. I was a kingmaker they need not obey after a king was made, a stepping stone that could be kicked aside once they had crossed the churning river.

But one thing my father did not insist upon, which appeased the English barons and more than anything would reveal the truth to Geoffrey when he heard; oaths were sworn that day to me and children who would follow me. Nothing was promised to my husband.

If my father intended any role for Geoffrey beyond the borders of Anjou this was the time to declare it. On the subject he was silent as snow. The exclusion of Geoffrey defused some of the anger of the barons, dissipated it as though it were smoke in a storm. These men of England were swearing themselves to me and my children, and who knew? If children never came and I became Queen, mayhap there was a chance to make a man a king when my father was dead, if an annulment could be achieved. There was still a chance I could transform from woman to stepping stone when the force of my father was gone from this world, when I was alone, defenceless.

They would uphold my children, they swore, those mythical beings I did not possess. My children were tales told by men and by me by night, to comfort ourselves. But no matter, it was done. They had all sworn, voices ringing down the long stone hall of Westminster, bouncing from the great throne Rufus had built for himself before bleeding to death in the wilds, skies and trees his only company as Death came for him.

They had sworn, and then they demanded. I was to return to Geoffrey. I was to get a child, if I could.

And then they all turned their eyes on me. I stood awash in their pity and judgement, a woman not a woman, a person part monster for being outside the borders of what was natural, and normal. *Grendel they named this cruel demon,* my mind whispered, *creeping from the moors, haunting the marches, came this God-cursed beast…*

Almost thirty years of life had I, and no child to show for it. What was woman without child? What was I as heir without a *male* heir to pass my claim to? But it was more than the affront of being thought worthless for my defective womb that hurt. It was more than being passed over as a claimant in my own right because I had a cleft between the legs rather than a shaft, that grated. It was because more than anything, sometimes more than food and air, more than water did I want a child. When I was gazed on with that condemnation and pity it was as though I was being told this curse was my fault. I could not have what I wanted most in life, and that was my fault. I did not deserve to be blessed, to be happy.

What sin was mine that the double pain of wanting and being thought unworthy of that wish was upon me? What had I done? Perhaps it was for not obeying Geoffrey that I was being punished, yet I had obeyed Heinrich and a child had been denied then, too. Was I so unworthy in the eyes of God that I should not be granted a child? I had seen mothers who ignored and abandoned children, who passed them to other women to raise. My grandmother had let her servant beat my mother and her siblings mercilessly, yet she had been granted children. My father had broken vows of marriage and love, as well as promises to his people, and he had been granted children. Geoffrey had been cruel to me, and yet he had a son. Why I was less worthy than all these others? Than all the sinners in the world able to have their pleasures and reap rewards too?

At times I wondered if I was too bitter a soil to grow a seed in, that I would wither that which tried to grow. At other times I thought the fault was my heart, too weak and frail to love again. God would not send me a child lest that child die of lack of love. Yet people who treated love with scorn could breed. Others with base, cruel natures could sire.

"If there is to be hope of a male heir, the Empress must return to her husband," said Roger of Salisbury. The Bishop was one of my father's most trusted men, who often had acted as governor of the realm since my mother and brother had died. "God will not look kindly on England or on any of us if a wife stays away from her husband."

I tried not to scowl. Father liked the Bishop, I did not. Roger had supported Clito for the throne over me, even though he never had admitted it. I suspected he was more uncomfortable than most about the notion of a woman as his sovereign. He did not like that I had been wed to Geoffrey, either, but since I had, obviously he thought I should get on with the duty of children. He was one of the three most landed men of England, the other two being my bastard brother Robert and my cousin Stephen of Blois, therefore I had to hear him, even if I did not trust or like him.

"I agree," said another of my cousins, Henry of Blois, now a man of the Church who was both Bishop of Winchester and head of Glastonbury, one of the wealthiest monastic foundations of England. Henry was the youngest son of my aunt Adela of Blois, and the most unpredictable. He was rumoured to own fire as temper, and ambition as blood. His men followed him loyally, and he made men rich so many did follow, but I was not sure where his loyalties to me stood. His kinswoman I was, which might aid him in goals of further advancement, but he was a slippery one, Henry. "If we wish the Almighty Father to gaze upon us with clemency, the vows of marriage must be upheld," he said.

*My sin becomes their sin?* I thought. I wondered if God looked kindly on me at all. Many had been the time I had thought myself Cain, or Grendel, cast out of realm of man. Woman was part demon to many, especially to men of the Church like Henry and Roger. Did God think me a monster? Had the Almighty stared into that darkness inside me, into the dirt my father saw, and thought it too dark? Would I birth monsters, made of monster soul torn from me?

Pain piled on pain as around the hall men nodded, agreeing I had to return to Geoffrey. Pain was what I had from those eyes, those pitying eyes I hated so. What shame may be inflicted upon one by people feeling sorry for you! But always that sympathy came with accusation, always with condemnation. I was no woman, but a non-person. I was no fertile field, but a barren wasteland, fire burned so hard and deep into the earth that nothing grew or ever would again. When they looked at me people saw a destiny unfulfilled, and the only destiny that would make me a person, a woman, something of worth.

And the worst of it was, part of me agreed. There is in each of us a part of us that hates the rest, and how could I argue with their logic? To give life to the world, what greater thing was there that I might do? If I lived one lifetime I might achieve much, but breed and I would sire a line of kings, a line of England, of Normandy. I would send children out into this world, eyes would open, the story of the world might be altered. Little as I liked being judged for my womb, I longed for children.

At night I would dream of them, my phantom children. When I woke, I could feel mouths at my breasts, the heat of their bodies next to mine. I could smell the scent of their heads. Each dawn I would swallow tears that came, asking to be wept. I would hide shaking hands that longed to hold a child. I would lift my chin and stare pitying glances in the eyes. I would not flinch, I would not weep, would not surrender. If any of those men in that hall had understood the strength it took to show nothing of the pain I felt, they would have known I had the strength to claim a crown and hold a throne. Unleashed, the power within me could have ruled the world. The courage of my heart could have won a thousand wars.

But they did not know. What did these barons and lords know of me in truth? People are so fond of judging by the outside shell. What the barons saw was woman, soft of body and feral of nature. No matter what alternate proof they had in their own lives, the courageous wives they loved, strong, intelligent mistresses they discussed politics with, wise mothers who had raised them with duel strengths of love and mercy, those men saw women as they had been told to; weak, foolish, feeble of heart and mind and body, creatures to be contained and curtailed, not obeyed. It was the tragedy of men, the thing that would haunt and hunt them, keeping them from wisdom and for many, from love.

But I needed a loyal baronage and clergy. I needed men to support me. They could see me as guardian of the throne first, and then as the crown itself in time. If I could unsex myself in their eyes, there was a chance. First I had to prove myself. I never would stop proving myself, something that was true of any ruler, but especially for me. A loyal baronage and clergy would keep me on the throne and peace upon England. I would have to do as they said now, so they would do as I commanded later.

But there were problems besides form, and prejudice about that form. Female royalty was always an accompaniment to male, not a replacement. Grafted to power we were, not the main trunk. There were problems of sword and law, too. I was no warrior, had not been raised as Matilda of Canossa to wield sword and axe, to lead men into battle. Call them to arms I could, but I could not fight beside them as a king would be expected to. That brought my authority into question. It was also the duty of the King to be the lawmaker and keeper of that law. Women could appear as witnesses, sometimes litigants, but there was no place for a woman in the making of English or Norman law. I had acted as judge in cases of manorial courts as Empress, but people could claim I wielded that power on behalf of the Emperor. The true position of a Queen was to influence her King to mercy. Showing mercy always, as people might well suppose I would, being a woman, would unpick the seams of justice and law, turn my father's empire into a realm of chaos.

Yet if I had a son, they could see past these problems. If I had a son they would see past the problem of me.

"To Anjou I shall return," I said to them. "Though it grants me no pleasure, I understand my duty."

Heads nodded. They liked that. Of course they did, who does not like it when another obeys them? These lords were accustomed to obedience, especially from women. The question remained however, whether, when the time came, they would obey me.

It was something my father understood. When I left that hall and those men, we went to Woodstock, his hunting lodge in the country. I think he saw that I needed peace to prepare myself to return to Anjou. We walked in the gardens, through small pleasure parks where groves of trees sheltered game. Blackbirds hopped along the ground and linnets sang. Often I was silent, contemplating the beauty about me. My father was not. He talked, and taught.

"You must be to men of England and Normandy not woman, perhaps not even person," my father said, his fingers trailing above, through low-hanging twigs on a willow tree. "You must be an emblem, their banner held aloft in war. You think they obey me for fear, and certainly a little of that is true, and for favours, but the real reason is not any of these things."

He looked away from me, to the countryside. England was buzzing with the sound of bees and insects on their merry way, gathering food, fighting to survive. We had been walking long that day. It was still hot but the light of the skies was dimming. Dusk was tramping along the skies, blue light pouring in to join with yellow and amber in the heavens, making indigo and red streak as hares across the distant, wide horizon. Trees were moving gently, whispering secrets as they brushed leaves. There was a sense of stillness yet motion, waiting and expectation on the wind. Often I have felt this surge at the times day changes to night and as dawn rises. Anything may happen. It is the same at certain times of year, the turn to autumn as summer twists her head away from us, and that to spring, when one morning winter is suddenly swept away and warmth is prancing in the still-cool air. These are times of magic. The changes of the world infect our blood. Borders break. Possibility ignites. There are, for all of us, a thousand moments in life, in each day, when something may happen, when accident or adventure or both may come to life. There are a million roads to take, thousands of fires to kindle and countless stars to see if only we lift our heads for a moment from the muddy path we walk, and gaze up, seeing open skies above.

"The crown, the throne, the king… these things are not real, you understand?" my father went on. "They are constructions, titles, baubles of gold, a chair dressed up to look grander than another that men might call it a throne. These are things we have made, constructs of human imagination." He looked at me. "They are stories," he said. "Men need stories. We breathe them, we eat them, they sustain us. If you can become to men of England what they need, you will succeed. If you can be a tale they rely on, food they put in their mouths, they will uphold you."

"You tell me to become a fiction," I said.

"All people are fictions," he said. "To each other, to themselves. We all tell stories of ourselves, what we are, what we want to become. If we are good storytellers the tales become true. If not, we fail, as do our lives. Become what they need, create a tale you become. Give them the emblem they require, the banner they hold up in battle, the light they follow. Men need food and drink, company and slumber, but they need, too, a reason for life. The crown, the throne, the King..." he smiled, "the Queen; these things are a light in the darkness. They are the sword that will protect, the hand reaching out, telling frightened souls they are not alone. They are order made from chaos; the stable and unchanging point in a world where all is turbulent."

"The calm sea," I said, almost as a whisper.

He looked at me, tears in his eyes as he took my hand and squeezed it. "The calm sea," he repeated, "when so many are lost, shipwrecked."

# Chapter Eighteen

## Westminster Abbey
## London

## Summer 1131

I stared at the light. A small chamber to one side of the main church, a place I had not known was here was where I stood. I had come to pay respects. They told me that pilgrims came here often, sometimes to see this tomb rather than others, like Holy Edward the Saxon King who lay in peace not far away.

It was a chamber in which my mother's tomb stood. On her stone tomb burned candles... more than I could count. Smooth, glossy white wax dripped; silken tears. It was here and there on the floor. Much had been scraped up, to be used to make more candles, perhaps the ones burning even now. There was a cloth protecting the tomb, this tomb of blazing light in the darkness of the Abbey.

We had ridden to London from Woodstock the day before. My father and his court often were on the move and he had business to attend to in London for a few days, perhaps a week. We would return to the country after, he had said.

I was glad, for although London was interesting, Woodstock had taken us in as if it were an old dame, arms open to new life entering her ancient hall. Woodstock gave me a space I needed to collect myself, nurture peace in my soul so I could plant it there, take it with me to Anjou. I had toured my father's menagerie, marvelling at beasts and birds sent as gifts by kings of other lands. There were lions, sandy and thin, with terrible roars, and a porcupine with long, wavering spines. I marvelled at camels, who ate only iron it was said, and at a northern white bear, still quite young, but with eyes of dreadful doom.

My father's birds were stunning, with bright plumage and long tails. As they sang, songs that I thought might break my heart, I wished I could do as men of old had and taste the blood of a dragon's heart, so I could understand words spoken by the birds.

I had walked outside, past trees where rooks created kingdoms in the tree tops, those untidy, chaotic masses of sticks and grass and moss, of wool stolen from hedgerows where thorns had torn it from sheep. Nature is full of thieves. Added to each year, those nests could become rambling and huge, castles built by birds. Their caws of defiance clattered from the trees as the sun died in the skies.

We had seen men shearing the last of the sheep, women outside spinning wool, other men preparing to cut hay, sharpening long-handled scythes on stones. As I walked along one day past fields planted with barely and rye, and others with vetch for fodder, a flash of light on the ground had caught my eyes, and I had found a stone, polished and sharp, in the shape of an arrow. Tumbled from a plough rivet, it was covered in clumped earth yet immediately I could see it was something unusual. One of my ladies had seen it in my hand as I cleaned it and gasped. It was, she said, elf-shot. "One of their arrows discarded," she said. "Shot at a person to make them sick, Domina. It must have missed."

"Is it dangerous?" I had asked, turning it in my hand, admiring it whilst trying not to allow the sharp sides to cut me, in case it was. I had heard of people being elf-shot, of course. It was a common illness, and many sicknesses, wide and varied, could come from that injury. I had not known mortals could find their arrow heads.

"Fortunate," she said. "There is no danger in it now. Many a cure can be made from elf-shot, Domina. You should keep it, my lady, set it aside for a time you need it."

As I tucked it into a pouch at my side, my heart ached as though shot through by the sharp flint. I thought of my brother's stone. No doubt it had been tossed into a puddle in Anjou. All I could hope was a little boy had found it and had given it to his sister, as Will had for me.

We had come back to the palace, although Woodstock was more hunting lodge than castle or fort. We had passed a priest on the way to the gate, his golden-eyed sparrow hawk upon his leather glove, her scaly yellow legs hopping impatiently. He had paused to bow as best he could, his eyes nervously watching our guards.

I had shown my father the elf-shot and he laughed. "The fae are here, indeed," he said. "People of the villages say they see them, out stealing children and milk by night."

"Do you believe in nothing of the strange?" I asked.

"Many things," he said. "But not all."

I put the elf-shot in a pouch and wore it about my neck, as once I had with Will's adder-stone. Sometimes, when first I woke, I could almost believe it was my brother's last gift, still upon my throat, unlost.

Then to London we had come, along the roads from Woodstock. And then to Westminster, to pay respects to my mother. I had not found myself ready to come the first time I had returned to England. I had prayed for her soul in the Abbey, but not sought out her grave. I had wondered how I would feel, how I would manage the old grief. My mother had been the first person I had lost, the first wound. She was my oldest grief, the first, the fall as I lost innocence and knew what it was to lose those I loved to death. I thought it would be hard to stand at her graveside, for all griefs I had known would come thronging. I felt in some ways it would do her a disservice; I should come and grieve for her alone, and until I was ready to leave all others I had lost at the door, it did not feel right. My mother was a Queen. She deserved to be honoured as one by me.

I had thought I would find darkness at her tomb. The oldest wound is the one that often never heals. I thought here I would find the start of the darkness in me, the shell of the monster who had hatched within.

It was dark, indeed. But something else lived here: light.

Soft light, yellow, amber, ochre, white, flickered before me. Behind it the eyes of the saints and Christ and the Virgin upon the walls seemed to blink, watching me. Fragments of glass set into those eyes made some look as though they wept. I might have wept too, when I had asked why the candles burned.

"Your father ordered candles to burn for your mother from the day of her death," one of the monks had said. "There are large payments for the candles each year, Domina."

I had nodded to him and smiled, and away he went, feet scuffing the stone floor, brushing glazed tiles. As the noise vanished into the air above me, I turned back to gaze upon those lights burning so bright against the gloom. Never had he said, never had my father protested when I had all but accused him of not loving my mother that he had done this for her soul, in her memory. And why had he not?

Because he had no reason to prove anything to me. He had no need to prove his love for her. Because he, perhaps he alone, knew it was real, how deep it had bored into his soul, how his heart bled now that she was gone.

And this was private. Perhaps even she had not known how he loved her, the depths, the heights. I wonder if she could feel the pain I could feel in this chamber, the silent, aching sorrow of a heart once given, never reclaimed.

I watched dripping wax running smooth and slow down long pillars of more wax, collecting in silken pools at the base. If I touched it, it would feel like moist, supple skin. I could almost feel the heat, residual, lingering, in the fallen wax. Shadows danced and tallow and wick, wax and fire mingled, taking hands to prance.

The light and dark, the play of red flame and yellow, the shadows dancing gently on the walls, all this was his love. All this was his pain, in life and in death, for he had said he never knew if she loved him, but he loved her. I wondered how often my father came here, how often he knelt not in the presence of God in truth, but before the soul of the woman he had loved. Did he weep here? Did quiet tears shown to no other soul but hers creep from his eyes in this place of dancing shadow and light? Or did he stare into the red-gold light before him, hoping that somehow she would see him, stare back? Did he ask her ghost to come to him, touch his hand one more time as so many of us wish so we might treasure that last moment of life. Were we to know moments were the last we would have, we would make them of significance. So much of our lives pass by. We forget so much.

Often enough I had spoken to the night, hoping Heinrich would hear me. I did not suppose I was alone. Millions upon the earth have lost someone they had thought they never could do without. I was not alone in holding on to memories, even to dreams. I, like thousands of others, was held in warm arms in dreams of people I loved.

Not alone was I in lingering over these moments, trying to remain asleep as the fug of dreams ended, as I lay in bed with my eyes closed trying to return to a moment more comforting in dreams than life ever could be. Thousands weep each day, each moment, and thousands more are sad. If all of those who mourn upon this earth could be heard at the same time, the skies would break for the pain.

The saddest moment, often, in life, is the moment of waking from a dream of one loved and lost. The moment you pass from the realm of dreams and know you are awake, that slumber-comfort is gone. You know they are not there, and you will, once more, wake alone. There had often been times, mornings and moments, when I had wanted to die for feeling the loss of Heinrich, sometimes of Bruno, my mother, my brother, all over again. The cruellest dreams were ones where all of them were, smiles warming my soul, until the moment sleep released me and back into body and mind I fell, alone, having lost them all over again, grief fresh as rain and acid as vinegar upon me.

But it is with places like this, with silent and quiet and private places hidden away in darkness, where none can judge and none can stare, that we survive. These caverns we make, in churches, in our homes, in our hearts, this is how we live on when those we love die. We make sacred spaces; into them we place ghosts. We guard them with love, and we keep them secret.

We come to worship in darkness and peace, where none will see us, where we can not only be with grief, but become it, allow sorrow for a while to suffuse us, to become us, overwhelm us. That is the secret of the darkness, it is a place where we can be as we wish, where no eyes stare or eyebrows lift or mouths smile with cruel amusement. Darkness is where we may hide until ready to come out. The warm hush of shadow, lightest play of light, this is what we need, at times. Here is where we place our dead, these quiet tombs we make in the world and in our souls. And here is where we hide ourselves, a sanctuary to bring solace, to bear up our courage, to defend us against the glaring light of day.

This place was the cavern my father made, the sacred place my mother would be worshipped eternally. This was where he came to make the truest prayers to God, for he would ask her, not the saints, not the Virgin, not even Christ to intervene for him. He would ask her. I knew then, sure as I knew anything, that she was the intermediary he prayed to. That in death as in life he saw her as his partner on the throne. She had died after a mortal life, and had gone on to become a saint. That was how he saw her, because to him, her face illuminated by his love, she could be no lesser being. To him she was sacred.

I thought fire fitting to symbolise this love he had had for her. A flame lit, never to be allowed to go out, passing candle to candle, wick to wick, by the hands of men of God to whom she had entrusted her soul in life and in death. And my father had ordered those flames to stay burning for her. I wondered if something similar burned and always had burned in his soul for her. Wondered at the force love may exert upon a life, that even if we come to hate the people we have offered our hearts to, something pure and purifying always remains within us. If there is something eternal not only in the soul, but in love, and that, like the flames of the candle never allowed to extinguish, cannot die.

If anything should be eternal, it is love. It was for love that Christ died upon the cross, for love that Mary gave up her son to death. It was for love that I gave all I was, changed who I was, for Heinrich, for the country he brought me to as a child. It was for love the world has been changed and no doubt will again, many times.

For what heart, when touched once, cannot always be by that person who managed to penetrate the core, dust fingertips lightly upon the flesh and blood of that immortal organ of life? What heart is it that when it has loved, and loved truly, honestly, painfully and vulnerably, can deny that a part of it always will love no matter if that love is possible or not? What soul is there in this world that when it has been offered to another will not always be, at least in part, in that person's hands?

There would always be a light, a shadow, an echo. There would always be love. It was a footprint on wet sand upon which waves never would break and wind never tear away. It was an echo of a call in a wood, reverberating down passageways of mountain, tree and stone. Love was as a light lit on the day of death, tended by the tender hearts of men who, having loved, were love's willing prisoners, always.

We can deny all we want in the light of day to a person who has hurt us, to a world that would judge us, but the truth is that once there is love, and as long as it has not turned, Janus-like, its face to hatred, love lives always in a heart that has loved. Plenty protect themselves, will protest that what I say is not so, but they will know in themselves the truth, no matter how bitter, how painful. There is a surrender in love, a part of the soul torn from the whole and placed inside the person you love, and once given this is a gift that cannot be taken back. Always you are a part of them and they of you. For better or worse, in sickness and health. It is not marriage those lines talked of, but love. For there is a part of you that roams with the one you love, in their lives, forever more, as you carry part of them in you. I felt Heinrich at times, bleeding out of me, in the water of my eyes and the words on my tongue. I felt as though he was beside me and I wanted to show him all I could do, things he would have been proud of. As water that had filled me, becoming a part of the river within, so he flowed in me and through me. He might be drops in a vast river, but he was there, part of me that was not me but him, part of my soul.

To myself, I could not deny this, though I told no one else. In some ways, although it brought great pain, I welcomed him inside my soul. The pain of loss was bitter, but would I have given up knowing him, loving him, no matter how imperfect it was, and accepted the hole that would have been, without his presence in my life? I think not. If love is about anything, it is risk. The risk that we may give ourselves to another and they may hurt us, for in one way or another people always do, and yet know that to risk nothing would hurt more. The more we love, the more we tear our soul to offer to people, but the more they offer scraps of their love, their hearts, too, to us. As we rip ourselves apart through life, so we are made patchwork by the souls of others coming to us, enriching us, feeding us. That is the secret of love, that a soul may be torn and yet mended in the same moment. That we will love and lose and know pain, sometimes more than we think we can bear, sometimes so hard and painful that we struggle to breathe, but so we can, too, know moments of great, abiding and eternal joy. We can touch the infinite, and for a moment in this life of cruel and grasping grief know comfort, even happiness.

Hearts, once joined, do not break bonds, no matter if the bond is become rotten with hatred. Always it is there, no matter what we do. We cannot destroy the part of us we gave away, cannot call it home by the sound of our voices, or shrill of the hunter's horn. I could not call back the part of me I had lost with Heinrich, the part buried in the old stone tomb in the Empire. I could not give away the part of him travelling in my heart. As much a comfort was that thought, as torment.

But seeing evidence of my father's love, here, in this glowing place, I felt the depths of my own heart, my own ability to love. There was in me, a glowing place. There was light in the darkness within.

Any heart that could deny, detract, disengage, from love was not a heart as mine was. I had loved in life and beyond the shadow of death. I loved when there was no hope of love being returned. I loved those who had not loved me. I still did and always would, for in me the fire lit once did not die. And this was not weakness, it was strength. It was something that would survive without sustenance, something that would light the innermost parts of my soul for all time. There is no sin in love. It is God's light made emotion in us.

A heart that could abandon the love it had for one once loved would be a cold one. My heart was not cold, no matter how I appeared on the surface. Had any of my detractors thought for a moment they might have considered that this calm surface hid a wealth of emotion, deep and long, too private and painful to be shared. When I thought of that, I thought of my mother again. When I was a child I had thought her lacking emotion and heart. But now I knew, for like her I had become; a creature who hid her heart, who masked emotion. But that did not mean I did not feel, or that my heart was cold and dead. Standing there, I did not feel ashamed of loving who I had loved. I was proud of it. I did not sorrow that I had loved. I honoured that I had had the courage to risk so much.

Heinrich would always be etched into my heart. No matter that he was dead, no matter that I had come to see our marriage as not the perfection I had thought it when he lived. I had been a different person when with him, one still growing, not formed, and yet, different person though I was now my heart would always love him. There would always be a light in my chest, burning for him. When we came to meet again in the light of God, that light would burn only brighter. Always there would be something in me that was him.

"I love, Bruno," I said to the ghost of my teacher. "It was not so, that perfect tense. I was right after all. It is not *I have loved*, it is *I love*."

I stood before that altar, the smoke of the candles in my nose, my lungs. I did not want to leave. Something of my mother's soul burned there, some wisp of smoke curling up, cresting into the dark air above her tomb, up to the wooden roof above. It was my father who had ensured that, bound her spirit to this place. My father, whose love for my mother always I had questioned, whose love for anyone I had wondered at, had kept these candles burning, and never had told me, never used it as proof that he had loved her.

But I knew now he had. Deeply, painfully, he loved her. To a man who had loved many, shared many beds, broken untold hearts, there had seemed little that was special, small feeling in him that ran deep. Often I had wondered if he loved me or if I was simply a means to an end, part of his plan, and this had led me to question if he was capable of love. Yet he was, and not surface love, not trickery to obtain a place between a woman's thighs. These candles were that love, something quiet, yet bright. Something hidden yet seen.

Often it can feel, when one lights a candle in a room where the light has dimmed, that this is the only room, you the only person, the candle the only light left in the world. Sometimes it is that way, too, for love, for who can understand a heart and the yearnings of that heart for another? Who may hear its call, taste its wildness? Perhaps we find love always a shock because it is a surprise that souls should dare in a world of sin, cruelty and fear to ignite with something as shattering and vulnerable as love. Yet hearts love, and candles light. Everyday miracles are these, as the rising sun is. As life is.

I could feel it. It was here, a love that burned still, for a woman long dead. As this room was her soul, so it was too his heart.

I stood there long hours. I know not how many. For the first time in my life I felt I was with my parents. Perhaps neither of them would know. My father might never hear of this, and my mother was with God, serving at the side of the Queen of Heaven, for that surely was her place in death. But even if they never knew I was there, I felt I understood them better than ever I had. In that room I could feel the essence of their lives, bonds that had tied them, devotions that had bonded them. In that dark chamber they were more alive to me than in life, for there, in that sanctuary built to protect my mother's soul and my father's love, I found union with them.

There was a place like this inside me, a sacred space I had built and in it was love. I was not joined to my parents by duty and blood alone, for there, in that chamber, I understood them. I saw love and loyalty, sacred and abiding. I saw suffering and pain and survival. Something of the pain and love held there reached out a hand in the guttering light and touched my heart, and my heart reached back, understanding all that was left unsaid with perfect, painful clarity.

In the darkness of my father's heart, my mother was his light. Always she had been.

# Chapter Nineteen

## Woodstock Palace
## England

## Summer 1131

"I find your thoughts on war refreshing, in honesty, my lord," I said to Miles of Gloucester. We were opposite each other on wooden stools, a chessboard between us. Miles was a deft and surprising player of this game that was now so fashionable. I was keeping up, but he would beat me in the end. I did not mind. The struggle was the interesting part, along with his conversation.

"So often," I went on, toying with a pawn, "especially when one talks to young men, the advantages of battle all seem to lie in knights and cavalry, yet I hear from my father and I read of many instances where archers or infantry are thought more important; the spine of the army."

"A worthy point and excellent manner of expression," Miles said, looking up from the board with glittering eyes, nodding furiously. "What young men fail to remember about cavalry, and using them in a charge, is that whilst it can be crushingly effective, destroying a line of infantry if done well, it is hard to repeat if not fully effective on the first go."

"My father said as much," I said, moving the pawn.

"There are other problems with mounted knights," Miles said, immediately taking my pawn. "Horses run in the heat and noise of the battle, and often *keep* running. A rush of cavalry means you must commit to an early attack too. It could be said such an endeavour risks all in the battle. The infantry, if prepared and ready with spears, can inflict great damage on mounted men if they have the courage to stand and the wit to attack the horses of knights. Archers also are most important for they can kill horses, knights, and create panic, and all at a distance; all without a general risking all his best troops in the first moment of battle."

Often Miles forgot terms of respect due to me in his excitement in our discussions. I minded not. It had nothing to do with respect or lack of it.

Miles found talk of battle and war, strategy in particular, so fascinating that his mind forgot rank and order. In many ways it was a compliment. He talked this way with my father. They both became so heated and excited that there was no time to insert "my lord" into every sentence. It was proof of the friendship they shared, for Miles loved my father and had great respect for him. He owed all he had to the crown and, unlike many, had not forgotten that.

Since we had come to Woodstock, Miles and I had found a shared interest in discussing battles of old, and in the writings of Roman and Greek generals on theories of war. Where I could not see the battle strategy spoken of in books, Miles helped me to. His descriptions of battles he had fought, and those of history, were so vivid I felt I was standing with him on a hilltop, looking down upon men clashing with sword and shield, spear and horse. With Miles I did not feel like a woman, and not in a bad way. I did not feel I was one sex or another. I was simply a person. I was not judged for having, or not having, I could never be sure which was worse, female characteristics. With Miles, I felt like a mind removed of body, so my sex mattered not. What mattered was my thoughts, my passions, my wit. It was a freeing experience, one I had come to treasure.

Miles had followed both his father and grandfather by becoming Sheriff of Gloucester, and my father had made him keeper of his castle in that same county. He possessed a sharp mind and an enquiring spirit, and loved history. We got on well. Sometimes I half imagined Miles would entirely forget I was a woman and ask me to spar and drink with him.

I would like to say I felt that way with all my father's men. Sadly, it was not so. Even those who were friends I had some troubles with. Brian FitzCount, for example, was my good friend and I had been most pleased to be reunited with him in England, but if he ever was capable of seeing me as a mind and not a body was another question. Think not he judged me harshly for being a woman. The truth could not have been more different.

The trouble was that Brian saw me most certainly as a woman, one he desired, I believe. I did not know for certain and did not ask. I invited nothing that would lead him to reveal any truths. He had a wife, I a husband, and I had no interest in offering my heart to any man. All there was to be found in that pursuit was unhappiness, since I was to Geoffrey bound. But Brian would not have offered anything, or attempted it, even had he thought I was attracted to him. He was a rare man, one who took vows seriously and that was as true of those sworn in marriage as those to his king. He did not love his wife, but he had respect for her and therefore took no mistress that I ever heard of. Perhaps there were women in a casual sense, but nothing permanent and certainly nothing obvious. Few and precious were men who took no lovers but their wives. My uncle David was another. I did not doubt that since the death of his wife he had at times welcomed company in his bed, but during her lifetime he had been faithful, and would not marry again, for love of her.

In some ways, I think it was not so much my physical attractions that drew Brian to me, although they played a part. We had a similarity of fortune, or misfortune. He and his wife had no children, a sorrow he felt as keen and deep as she. Some men are born to be fathers and are denied that responsibility and pleasure. Some men, too many, deserve no such role yet are handed it all the same. God must have a plan; perhaps children of poor parents go on to raise babes with deeper love to make up for the love they lacked, I know not. We are all granted trials to test our strength, improve our courage, for God knows what Fate has in store, so we must grow, be tested, grow again, to prepare us for the worst of times in the future. But at times I knew Brian, like me, struggled to understand the mind of God; times he too buckled under the strain of wanting what he could not have. Brian threw himself into work. He was a wealthy landowner now, with vast tracts in Wales, and the lordship of Wallingford in the Thames Valley. But it did not satisfy, not entirely. He, like me, longed for children.

Mayhap this struggle taught him that what we want and cannot have is the thing most worthy of our love, and that was why he was drawn to me. I could understand. The same had been true for me much of my life. It may be said to be common to all humans. If God wants us always striving, content with our lot we cannot be. The fruit just out of reach is always more tempting than that in the bowl. A love denied is always more attractive than one waiting with open arms. We like to punish ourselves, I think, but we also are creatures of ambition. Seeking the highest mate leads us to fall in love with people who often love us not. We are creatures of hope; we fall in love with cruelty, hoping it will be kind.

Sometimes I caught Brian staring. In his eyes I could see a dream trying to flee before I could catch sight of it. It was as when you catch a glimpse of light and movement, whip about to find it gone. It was a ghost of emotion in his eyes.

It was then I knew. No man needs to hide his eyes from a woman if he cares not that she knows his thoughts. Brian did not want me to see his thoughts. They would betray him.

For the most part, however, my friend kept his emotions in check and I enjoyed his company. Brian was literate and well read, polite, and he gave excellent advice. Other men could be said to be more troublesome.

Ranulf of Chester was one. I did not know quite what to make of him, but it seemed few did, so I was not alone. His father had been a traitor, and had had his lands confiscated by my father. Ranulf had been granted them back, and had become Earl of Chester. He was wed to my brother Robert's daughter. And yet for all that, no one trusted him. Ranulf still wanted Carlisle and Cumberland, more of his father's lands, returned to him, but my father was not quite willing to do that yet.

Roger of Salisbury, man of God but more often man of the world, was another I did not trust. Although he was my father's man, and had been his Chancellor, I did not think well of him. Roger lusted for power and had found it through the Church. It was not unusual, many sons of England and Normandy did the same, but Roger was hard to fathom. He was vague often and on purpose, and I had the distinct impression he did not like me, so might work against me.

I was a frank soul, and preferred men who were the same. Those I could not read well, snakes who kept their tails hidden, I did not know if I could trust, and therefore I did not.

*

As summer rolled on and men took the last of the milk from their sheep before Lammas Day, as I got on with learning the names and characters of my father's men, Adeliza was busy with charity. She was beginning to draw up plans for the building of a hospital for lepers. Dedicated to Saint Giles, it was to stand at Fugglestone St Peter, near Wilton.

I came to her chambers often, and we talked as we looked over her charts and lists. One morning I arrived as she was talking to a messenger sent by my father. It was customary for him to send a servant to wish her a good morning and ask after her health. She was busy so I waited. Spread out on the table I could see her hospital taking shape; rooms for healing and recovery, chambers for permanent patients, and places where chambers were removed to places of greater peace, for those about to die. Those chambers had gardens below them.

In the last moments of life those men would smell flowers and herbs, hear birds. They could watch beauty unfold about them, perhaps forget for a moment their bodies were falling apart and death was coming fast. It was a touch most thoughtful, typical of Adeliza.

Adeliza smiled, nodding to William of Albini, my father's man. "Thank you, William," she said gently. "My lord is well this morning?"

"The King is in excellent health, as always, my lady," William said, bowing.

"Even after all those lampreys yesterday?" I interjected. "They always disagree with my regal father, yet he always eats them."

William allowed himself a short smile. "The King is accustomed to the aches the little eels offer, Domina," he said, bowing to me this time. "And always says no good or great thing comes to a man without some pain."

Adeliza laughed. "My husband is a wise man," she said. "Please send my best wishes and love to him."

"I will, my Queen," William said.

As he bowed and left I caught a moment of honesty in the poor man's eyes as he gazed at Adeliza. Queen she was indeed, to him; Queen of his country, wife to his lord and clearly ruler of his heart. Adeliza noted nothing. I thought it best to say nothing too. Obviously love for her was something the unfortunate young man was desperately trying to conceal. He must have known it was doomed.

"Men will bless your name for ever more, for this," I said, my attention leaving yet another man in love with my friend and stepmother and returning to her hospital.

"I think not," she said quietly. Her finger lingered against one of the charts; a brushing touch of affection. This project was dear to her.

I glanced at her and she touched my arm. "I am no fool, though many think me simple," she said. "Your mother will always be the Queen of your father's reign. She, not I, will be remembered, I know this even now. I am not fated to be so remembered, to be so blessed as she was. Ever since first my father broke with me, when your father sent word he wanted me for his wife, I knew that. There are some who etch themselves into the mind of a country. They remain in memory; stained glass blazing in a window as the sun sets behind it. I am not as she was. My deeds will not be remembered as hers are."

"You are a good Queen."

"I hope I am, my friend," she said. "But I stand in her shadow. I have always felt it, as perhaps at times you feel that of your brother bearing upon you. We do not feel such ghosts upon us because your mother would wish me ill or your brother would want anything bad for you. Their ghosts would not be so cruel. But it is the way people see me, and there is no changing that."

She smiled. "There was a light cast by your mother and when there is a great light there must come a corresponding darkness. That darkness has fallen upon me. I stand in it. It is not evil, but obscurity. Your father, his men, they have love for me, many have respect, but always there is shade upon my face, always my acts are not as great as hers. Since she died, your mother has become only greater in their minds. The only way I could compete is to die after providing a child for the throne, and I think I am not destined to be mother to a king." She nodded. "And I have no wish to die, even if it would make men think well of me."

"I do not wish you to leave life either, but you would be a good mother."

"So would you, my dear friend. I know your pain well, for it wounds me too. Something we share."

We were silent a moment, the hurt rising as so often it did, the familiar shock and pain that we would swallow. "I think indeed sometimes men look at me and see me stand in the shadow of my brother," I said at last.

Adeliza nodded. "Perhaps at times. It is natural for men to look up to a throne and want to see a reflection of themselves. That is why they worship kings and fear queens; in women men cannot see themselves, so they lose heart. It is the same with God. If men cannot see an image of themselves in a higher power they lose hope and faith, ambition. But I think it is not as true for you as for me, or is becoming less so."

"I do not feel it lessening."

"There is a place for all of us in this world. I have taken up my place as well as I can, but you are carving out one. You are one of the rare ones, Matilda; given a place you were, yet you will make it your own too. You craft fate, or perhaps weave it. It takes power and devotion to do such a thing, for it will not come without pain."

"And if it is too much, and I fail?"

She chuckled. "Fail? What is this word to those of your blood? You, if nothing else, are your father's daughter. If you fail, it will not be the end. It will be but a hump in the story, something the hero must overcome to triumph in the end. You will fall and you will put your hands back to the earth at the same moment and push yourself up. Fall you will, we all will, old friend. Fail you will not."

I laughed. "I hope I do not fall too often or hard."

"You have fallen many times already, because of fate, and it has not bested you. Life, I think, is not so much about times we walk strong and fast, or times we stumble and fall. It is about our hands, about our willingness to press them to earth and climb back up. Life is about learning to rise when we fall, learning how to go on when we thought we could not."

"My father is indeed good at that," I said.

"As you are. Much you have lost and gained, then lost again and gained anew. It happens to all of us, but some learn that is the way of things and so make a friend of the earth, so it will cradle them each time they crash upon it. Others make an enemy of the ground, they curse it, fight it when they fall. There is nothing more pointless than fighting earth, for always it will win, but to make a friend of it, that is wise for when we push down, it will push us up too. Perhaps it may even remain steady a while as we walk, might be softer when we fall. Some struggle against destiny, blame all and everything on someone else. Some get on with walking." She looked into my eyes, her green ones vibrant as the grass of spring. "That is your father, Matilda, and it is you."

# Chapter Twenty

## Reading Abbey
## England

## Late Summer 1131

"A gift worthy of a king," said my father as we walked from the Abbey. "Are you sure you wish to part with it?"

I tried to dismiss my irritation as we left behind the echo of our leather boots in the winding stone walkways of the cloister at our back. He had asked me this many times over the past days, ever since I had announced my intention to leave the hand of Saint James in its glove of gold and jewels to Reading Abbey. "I am sure," I said, for perhaps the hundredth time.

I had possessed the hand a long time. Stolen from the collection of the Emperor, it was not mine in truth, but I felt like it was. Saint James was my personal saint, there to guide and aid me. I had been crowned on his feast day, and there was a tradition of relocating artefacts like relics if one thought they might be better treated in, or suited to, another religious house. When leaving the Empire, the thought of leaving the relic of my personal saint in the hands of an ungodly man like Lothair had seemed a travesty, so I had stolen it. Now I was handing it back to men of God.

It was a favour for the English Church, indeed; a rich prize for them to have. It was not of course the first gift I had ever made to a religious order. Father and I had sent numerous gifts to abbots and bishops, fine fish for their table, servants to care for them, as well as grants for food or other necessities for monks and nuns. In the Empire I had approved grants and privileges, and had recently sent a candelabrum to the house at Cluny which now stood before the new High Altar. On a pedestal seven feet high, it was a magnificent arrangement of gold and silver and jewels, holding many candles to emphasise the image of Christ as the light of God. I had also sent gold crucifixes and embroidered vestments to men of the Church, and a set of bells which had a novel timbre created by the metals they were cast from. But the glove and hand were more sacred than any of these gifts or grants, and now the hand of James was in the keeping of the brothers of Reading. They had been almost stupefied to receive it, knowing full well its worth and what it would bring to their order.

I had granted it to Reading as it was one of my father's favoured houses. It would please him and it would curry favour for me with the Church whose support I needed if I was to rule. A less cynical reason for the gift was that I liked the place. I was fond of Benedictine orders, something about the black hoods and ways of worship spoke to my soul and I admired their stance on education, but this was not the only reason. My final reason was the most important; I wanted the glove and the hand of my personal saint safe. I was going back to Anjou soon. Geoffrey had taken one of my treasures. I would not have him steal another.

It was right that the hand be in a house of God in any case, so people could come to see it, pray to Saint James and draw comfort from it. The hand would bring pilgrims flocking to Reading, and they would grant revenue to the monks, which could be used to maintain the abbey and to aid the poor who lived near it. No matter the comfort it offered me personally, it should be where people could see it and worship it. Relics, like books, were things that should be shared.

Reading was my father's great abbey. It had been established in 1121, and he had heaped rewards on it since; lands and manors, estates and farms as well as riches and influence. It was a Cluniac order, founded by monks of Cluny. They prayed for the soul of my brother, and mother. In many ways I think Reading was part of my father's penance for not keeping Will on his own ship that fateful day, and for not keeping his promise to our mother to keep us both safe. I wondered if he had asked God to take Will into Heaven so my brother did not remain beneath the waves for eternity, and Reading was the payment offered to ensure that.

My father wanted to be entombed at Reading and he kept a tight hold on it. Reading was different to other orders. It held its lands by free alms tenure rather than knights' fees and was forbidden to create knights' fees on its lands. New abbots were selected by a free election amongst all monks, and its offices were not hereditary, which eradicated nepotism. The Benedictine custom of child oblates was not permitted. Only free and consenting adults were allowed into the order. Much of this was reformist in nature, in keeping with reform in other houses about Europe, but traditions were maintained, such as the Benedictine rule of charity. The brothers were to shelter and feed travellers, as well as pilgrims and the poor and unfortunate. Reading, positioned near a busy road and busier river, was ideally suited for this kind of charity, and my father was intimately involved in this side of the abbey's business. He wanted his personal abbey to become famed for its good works. The hand was a great boon for his abbey to possess. It would make Reading more famous than it was.

"You are sure?"

"I am," I said again, almost absentmindedly as men led our horses to us. Outside the abbey birds were swooping in the skies, fast as the Devil seeking souls. There was warmth and light upon the air, a haze over the cobbles. The sound of our horses clopping to us seemed almost too loud, too abrasive. "The hand brought comfort when I needed it most. Let it do the same for others."

*

"And what of defences here?" my father asked, one finger on a small blob on the far left of the map.

"Many castles lie there," I said. "Pembroke, Manorbier, Carew, Haverfordwest, Arberth… many were wood and now some are stone. They stand in good places, held by good men."

"How do you know they are good?"

"You chose them."

My father laughed, a touch of scorn on his breath, but I could tell he was pleased by the compliment. That morning's lesson was on Wales; dangers posed, defences, the men and the rebels, secret hiding places and fighting tactics. Many thought men of Wales wild and untamed, but they were often the best soldiers in an army *if* an English King could convince one of their princes to support him. Their bowmen, in particular, were notorious for skill, strength and precision. No men had eyes as keen, nor arms as strong, as the Welsh, it was said.

There had been many lessons of late. I had come to think this whole summer in England had been one long lesson. I had met my father's court, toured palaces so I knew them and what I could expect from manors in times of peace and castles in times of war. I had spent time with his men, hunted with his court, so I was now friends with many and had some idea who I could rely on. Before I returned to Anjou to get on with my duty of lying on my back and trying not to vomit as a man I hated rutted between my legs, my father wanted as much education as possible thrown at me, to prepare me for the throne. I also thought he was preparing his men. This season in England had been about letting them meet me, understand what skills I had, to set their minds more at rest. I believed I had done well. Those who were opposed to me would likely remain that way no matter what I did, but I thought I had made some friends.

My father perhaps was also trying to set his own mind at rest. He had become nervous of late and not without reason. There had been a plot discovered within his own household to assassinate him. An old retainer, a chamberlain of low birth who by my father's grace had risen high, had been uncovered in a plot to kill him. The man was blinded and castrated, but because of his affection for him in the past, my father did not hang him. Other attempts of the past, including one by my half-sister Juliana, who had almost shot him, echoed in Father's mind often. He changed beds sometimes halfway through the night, increased the guards about his chambers continually, and slept with a sword in his hand and shield by the bed. He would not allow Adeliza to stay with him. He went to her chamber each night, and left after he had coupled with her. If an assassin came he did not want her put in peril.

His fears were not unfounded. There were people who wanted him dead. Yet his response to this threat was growing larger, more anxious. I think in some ways his lessons for me were about both ignoring threats upon his own life, and settling his mind so he feared less for the future, when he was not here. My father was not a man to surrender control. It was alien to his nature. He wanted to have a ghostly hand upon my back when I ruled England and Normandy; his phantom directing me, so I ruled not as myself but as an extension of him. Sometimes I wondered if there was any man in the world who did not look at a woman and see an appendage rather than a person.

There would be more lessons, as there had been before, by letter when I left. But now, we could do this in person. I was reminded with a painful sweetness of Bruno, of being a child in his schoolroom. My father taught in a similar way, by asking relentless, unending questions and every answer I offered led to more. Tired though I was by the end of the day, during the hours he quizzed me I felt nothing but exhilaration. I thought it akin to the spirit felt in battle, when men are exhausted yet fight on with the strength and remorseless vigour of bears. My father roused a fighting spirit in me; he teased the dragon. When he challenged, I screamed defiance back in his face.

This was something the Welsh, too, were known to do. This perhaps was why he had such respect for them.

Wales was always likely to be a problem for an English ruler, since the Kings of England believed the land was theirs and the Welsh did not. My grandfather, the Conqueror, had made strides into the kingdom, this land shared between different princes. The Conqueror had built castles, fought battles, placed his own men in positions of power, but Wales had not been fully conquered as England had. Marcher lords, men who held border lands and castles, kept the Welsh penned in to an extent, and deals had been made with Welsh princes, warlords and chieftains. Such men did homage to the English crown, but in their own kingdoms they ruled, and they raided lands of other princes, and lands of my father.

It was a fertile land of milk and meat, with great mountains and long, beautiful shores. Its men knew how to use the landscape, the forests, hills and marshes, and a Welsh army was hard to beat for they would strike and fall back, stalking prey like wolves, vanishing as wraiths into the long, green valleys of mist. Fortunate it was that the Welsh often were more divided than allied. Bonded together, the forces of all the Welsh princes could be a great danger, but they distrusted each other almost as much as they did the English.

It was said Wales was a nation of farmers and fighters, that when the war horn screamed every man in the fields would drop plough and race with spear to the fight. All free men had the right to bear arms. Accustomed to being outdoors in poor weather, for Wales was a kingdom of rain and storm, they were hardy in a long campaign. Many travelled barefoot, their feet hard as leather. The Welsh were frugal and could do without food for a long time, and they were patient in war. All those things made them dangerous.

Often lightly armed therefore swift of foot, and with generally only rulers and their *Teulu*, or warband, on horse, men of Wales made wise use of infantry and cavalry. Long spears were favoured, perfect for bringing down charging horses and knights, and men of Wales understood the earth beneath their feet, so laid traps where knights and their horses would stumble, or have to charge uphill. There was wit in the warcraft of the Welsh. They might not have had the resources of the English crown, but by God they knew what to do with what they had.

And their bowmen were fearsome indeed. It was said they could strike any target, and the strength of their arm was as deadly as their aim. There were tales of Welsh bowmen hitting men's thighs through armour of leather and iron, of them pinning doors of oak shut as men tried to escape through them during sieges. Some said Welsh bowmen had shot through wooden saddles, and managed to kill the horse beneath, or stuck men to saddles with arrows. And all this was done with bows not of yew, considered the best wood, but elm. Welsh bowmen did not polish and adorn bows as other men did. They were tools, not trinkets; there to serve and be cast aside when the bow broke. Racing after a retreating troop of Welshmen was an exceedingly bad idea, as they were as good at firing backwards whilst they ran, as they were at firing forwards, standing still.

Each prince had his war band, his *Teulu*, made up of the sons of noble Welsh houses. The word *Teulu* meant *family*, and many who rode with the prince were kin. They were armed, mounted, and ready to defend their prince to the death. Although the most we heard of in such a band was only around one hundred men, they were dedicated, loyal and brave. When they could be persuaded to become mercenaries for the crown, they were amongst the best soldiers of the army.

"*Never* are they discouraged by defeat," my father said. "Always they return to fight. If they have to retreat, they do, then they come back all the stronger the next time." My father had faced the Welsh many times, in meticulously planned campaigns. It was claimed he had been shot once by their bowmen, but he had refused to believe it, because the arrow had missed inflicting a fatal hit. Father had found it easier to make deals and peace than to try to make war. Much of South Wales was sworn to him in fealty, although admittedly that could alter in a moment. North Wales remained a problem.

"Like you," I said quietly. He looked up. "That is why you admire them," I went on. "I hear it in your voice. They are kin to your spirit. You understand men who do not surrender, who strive, because they are like you."

"Surrender I have always feared," he said. "That is why I will not do it. In all times when hardness hit, I found the worst thing ever I could do was to sit still, allow myself to feel pity for myself. Even when I felt I should be paralysed by grief, or by terror, I would not do it, because I feared more to sit still, to become washed away by the tide of life upon me, than I did to move."

He scratched his nose. "Not always have I moved in the right *way*," he said. "But I would rather walk ten miles on a wrong course and then correct it, than stand still for ten years not daring to choose which path to take." He shrugged. "I cannot say my way is the best or the only way, that what I think is always right, but I can say it was right for me. Inaction is death, to me."

I nodded. "There is wisdom in that," I said.

"Let us look at campaign and strategy," he said. "Why is it sieges are so effective?"

"People are starved of food and water, but also freedom and company."

He nodded, eyes glimmering with that always slightly concealed pride. "Isolation is a tool most dangerous," he said. "More than food or even water it can prove a castle's undoing. After time, people grow reckless when they are thrown into captivity. They take risks, trying to prove they are free, and to feel free. That is why there are tales of such foolhardy bravery in sieges; gangs of young men steal out by night, lead attacks. Young men are often subject to lunacy, but under the right pressure it grows, overcomes them. The strain of the mind is more powerful than that of the body. People begin to feel walls, stones as weights upon their souls, their lungs. We are creatures born to resist captivity, and when we feel it close we become rash. The walls are too close, the sky too far away, air thin, weakening. And we are creatures of company who seek out others. You are right to add freedom and friendship as essentials of life. Never underestimate the strain upon the mind during a siege. It is a potent weapon."

I nodded, thinking that I clearly had *not* underestimated the potency of isolation, since I had mentioned it, but understanding my father loved, as all men and fathers do, to pass on his knowledge I said nothing. And it was true he had more experience than I when it came to this. He had been inside siege castles and had besieged them.

There was more, more on castles and defences, more on the Welsh. I left that day with a sheet of parchment on which the houses of Wales were drawn out so I could familiarize myself with the princes, their likely successors, although many might be deposed by enemies. It was not uncommon in any realm, certainly not in Wales.

I found myself thinking of the Welsh as I studied the chart. I thought of my father's eyes as he spoke of them; half irritated and half awed. I think it is often the way we feel about an enemy. If they were easy to beat, we would not name them enemy, after all. There is an equality of strength, respect even, granted as we name a man a foe.

People called them savages. Perhaps they were, but no more or less than other knights and men of war I had known. Their bows might have been simpler, but simple obviously was effective. Unfettered by armour, by polishing bows, by tarrying on what was unimportant, men of Wales were warriors to be reckoned with, and they had one more weapon that was as inexhaustible as the sun: Determination.

That was why my father admired them, why they were like him. They did not surrender. If they failed, they tried again.

*

As we came to the end of my time in England, and I pondered lessons I had been taught, an unhappy thought came to me.

Not a scrap of England was mine.

I should have been named *designatus*, as my brother had. I should have been crowned as heir. The barons had sworn to uphold me but had not been asked to pay homage to me. I had no lands in England and no castles. The castles promised to Geoffrey in Normandy had still not been handed to him, or to me. I had no hold on England or Normandy other than by word of men.

My father thought oaths of the barons enough, but I wondered. Oaths were sacred, such as those God swore to Abraham, the Covenants. These had established God's duty to His people and theirs to Him. Calling on God to bear witness to a promise and then going back on that promise was to make God a liar, an upholder of false deeds and words and men. That was why it was a thing cursed for a man to go against his word, although plenty did. The word of man was a fragile thing to base so much hope on.

And perhaps men would not have confidence in me, if my father showed it not. If my father had confidence in me why not crown me heir, offer me lands from which I could make a base if ever there was need, where I could be known and supported by people of England before I came to the throne?

Perhaps he did not want to offer me too much power, even now. There was a chance I might become a threat to him, or Geoffrey might on my behalf. There was always a chance an adult heir might try to supplant their father. Perhaps he feared me.

But I think the answer was simpler.

I think my father was waiting for a son to come from my body, so he could offer honours to my child, not me. It made me wonder if, even now, he looked at me and saw but a stepping stone, dull brown rock rather than glittering gold.

# Chapter Twenty-One

## Angers
## Anjou

### Winter 1131 - Spring 1132

Trumpets blared into air, slicing birdsong and icy wind. The sound of all the hooves of all the horses upon the road was deafening. People lined the waysides, thick as summer grass, as towards Angers we rode. Despite the cold wind and the feeling of frost in the air, people of Anjou were there, hands raised and cheering, welcoming their Countess home.

Had they all turned into pigs and danced, I could not have been more astonished.

Pomp and glory, people cheering, a procession greeting me that was so grand I could barely see road or horizon, was not what I had expected. I knew my father had struck a deal with Geoffrey that I was to be well treated, but this was more than what I had thought. I had been surprised, amazed would be more accurate, at the size of the escort sent to bring me safely from Normandy to Anjou. I had ridden away from Geoffrey's kingdom with barely enough men to defend me and my ladies if we were attacked. The retinue sent to bring me back was enormous.

What was that snake up to?

"The Count is to meet you ten miles from Angers, Domina," one of Geoffrey's men told me.

Ten miles... the same distance I had ridden out to greet Heinrich when he had returned once from Rome. The miles were a compliment. The nobler the guest, the further out on the road the host came out to meet them. This was an honour to my title as Empress and my station as Countess, but I was suspicious. To go from no respect to all?

As Geoffrey met me on the road, I heard the song of a wren. In hot, sweating summer or long, stark winter always wrens sing, often on the wing as they flash, dipping tree to tree. Dull the wren looks from afar, but close up it is beautiful, ruddy feathers and bars of black, its lower parts grey and brown. White bars on the wings catch any light, and it is a bird of fierceness and fury when roused, but one of mercy when it chooses. Wrens attended to the dead, covering the fallen with leaves if there is no one to cover them in earth.

I had hoped for mercy from Fortuna and her wheel when I came back to these lands. It appeared I might get more than mercy, for I was greeted with magnificence and munificence. Although I was suspicious, something gnawed at me, some sense of understanding. This was akin to when my father did something wrong and rather than saying sorry did something for me instead. It was the gesture of a man who has trouble expressing regret.

And on the road was one who had much to regret, although I wondered if he did. Riding towards me was a boy I had feared.

Yet as he came close, walking beneath fluttering banners of Anjou bearing leopards, I saw much. The boy I knew was no more. Geoffrey was eighteen. It was a man who dismounted from his great horse and walked towards me as I came along the road. My eyes barely recognised him. Geoffrey had ridden out with the entire court to meet me and a sea of tents had been erected to shelter us.

"God speed, my lady wife, Countess and Empress," said Geoffrey, bowing. I noted his voice was deeper than before. "All of Anjou rejoices at your return."

"God speed, lord husband," I said, dropping to a short curtsey. "I am overjoyed to return."

Before we rode for the castle, this stranger who was my husband took me to a pavilion to eat and drink. There was wine as well as an infusion of mugwort, to relieve weariness from a journey. This was a curiously thoughtful touch. I found my nose surreptitiously sniffing the hot liquid, but told myself this would be a *most* public way to poison me, and would hardly endear Geoffrey to my father.

For a while we sat, making polite conversation, and what amazed the most was that it *was* polite. I kept expecting Geoffrey to laugh, smirk in that horrible way, to insult me. He did not. He asked about England, the roads, my father. Then he sent his men away, so we could talk.

For a moment as we came to be alone, there was nothing but the sound of the wind battering the tent flaps. A peg was loose on one side; I could hear it thumping against the canvas.

"The years have made you only more beautiful," he said. His tone was gentle.

"What is all this?" I asked, suddenly angry, wondering if I was walking blindly into a trap. "Do you mean to disarm me then harm me again? I tell you, I have come here for no more games. I am tired of them. I am too old and too weary to play fool's games with a fool. I came back for one purpose and I will accept nothing from you but respect. If this… " I waved a hand at the tent. "…is some route into game or trick you may as well tell me now. I know you of old, Geoffrey, forget that not."

There was silence a moment, thick and hard.

He nodded. "I treated you badly," he said. "I understand your fear."

I snorted, pulling my cloak lined with rich, thick northern fur of squirrel about my shoulders. "I do not fear you. I found my way from that state long ago. Touch me in a way I do not like and I shall call on the barons of England, for many of them are friends and sworn to me now, and they shall make you pay. Threaten me and I shall leave again. Gossip about me and I shall send word to my father. Treat me as you did before and I shall make you regret it."

Geoffrey was silent, watching me. He sipped his wine.

"I came here because you and I are stuck," I went on. "We are unlikely to be granted an annulment and my father's men tell me that even if we were, it would likely be contested as would the legitimacy of any child I went on to have with another man. Divorce will aid neither of us, for you will be without an heir, and I too, and we will not be permitted to remarry. So we are stuck with one another. The best must be made of a bad situation. That is why I am here."

There was silence again.

"Here." I looked up to see him holding out his hand, palm up. In it was the adder-stone. A shock and a thrill hit my heart. I had trouble keeping my jaw closed. I supposed he would have thrown it away long ago, so Will's last gift would become just a stone amongst stones, a fragment on a mound of rock or at the bottom of a weed-strewn moat.

I watched his face, thinking that if I dared to reach for it he would snatch it from me. Had all this pomp been to play me so he could taunt me with my brother's last gift once more?

"Take it," he said. "It is yours."

Hesitantly I reached out. I cursed my fingers for trembling. I wanted that dull stone more than anything, more than a child, more than mercy or peace or respect. I could almost hear Will as I looked on it, almost see those eyes as he had handed the stone to me so long ago, in a past only we had shared. I could smell the scent of my brother's skin warmed by the sun on the day he had presented it to me.

The brush of my cold fingertips on Geoffrey's hot palm shot through me. I all but snatched the stone from his hand, clasping it to my heart. The beat and thump of my blood echoed in my ears, throbbing against the stone. I fought to control myself. As though my brother's heart was beating in the warm stone itself, I felt Will's soul against mine. God forgive me my weakness! I could have fallen to the floor and wept for the rest of time. But I would not, I did not. I pulled my shoulders back with an effort that tore my soul, pressed the stone to my breast and stared into Geoffrey's eyes, mine cold, my jaw set. "Thank you," I said.

"I should not have taken it," he said quietly. "I did not understand what it was, what it meant."

I did not ask how he had found out. "You understood enough to know it would hurt me," I said.

He nodded. "Yes," he said. "I was talented at seeing that." He bowed his head a moment, then looked up into my eyes. "The past cannot be changed, it is what it is and there is nothing I can do to alter it. But I can swear to you that much will be different now. You are my wife, my Countess. Empress and Queen consort you have been. I was a child when you left, but I am no more. I have had time to think on my past cruelties, and to regret them."

I stared, shocked and suspicious. "You… were not alone in blame for the failure of our marriage," I said stiffly. "I was impatient, insulted, full of pride which did not become me."

"It is good of you to say such," he said. "But the fault was mine. I did more harm than you. I cannot excuse it, but I can tell you I was not grown, not as a man, so was incapable of being the husband you needed, and deserved. The way I treated you dishonoured not only you, but me. It will not happen again."

Something haunted his eyes. I seemed to catch sight of myself, not then and there, but in the past. In his thoughts was a memory, of a moment when he had realised that all would never change between us no matter what he did, no matter what he wished; a moment where he had understood that dreams he harboured were not real. It was a moment of us, of truth, and of loss.

It was a rare moment, a time when one might look into the eyes of another and see truth. So often all we see of others are masks hiding the person who lies in the cage of flesh before us. We conceal so much from others, are honest only rarely with ourselves. There is too much darkness there to share, even with our own minds. Too much to face. A depth too long and darkly lit to stare into. Our darkness is something we must face if we are to grow, to learn, but many never do so. It is too hard and lonely, too long and deep. We fear what lies at the grimy base. We fear what lurks at the back of the cave within our souls.

Yet in that moment, I saw to the core of Geoffrey, to something he had understood. As a boy he had thought all he wanted would come to pass, and he had been taught that was the way life was and should be. What I saw then was a moment of awakening, of adulthood; a realisation that just because we wish something it will not make it come true. Tales of wishes are true only in stories of fae and dragons, where right prevails and evildoers wear horns so the good may spot them at a distance. Age is understanding others are not to be altered by our wishes, and we cannot change the way other people think. They must do that.

What I saw was a moment of fatality, the death of a dream, the end of innocence. I marvelled that I had taken his innocence, not in terms of virginity, but in another way more stark, longer lasting.

He watched me stare at him. "You do not believe me," he said. "I cannot blame you. It will take time, but I will prove I am a different man, that you left a child when you rode away, and there is a knight now in his place. There was something growing in me, something I did not like to face, something I saw in your eyes when you looked at me. I have done my best and will continue to do my best to keep that creature captive."

He was right it would take time before I would believe that, before I would cease to see a snake in his eyes. There had been a monster in him, there still was, yet it might be that in seeing it Geoffrey had found a way to recognise and contain it. Myths talk of monsters dying when they face their reflection. Perhaps this was so. Denying monsters offered them power over us, recognising them brought about their ends.

Do monsters that live outside of man become terrible because they are a part of us we have cast aside, a part of our souls with which we deny kinship? Some say dragons and man are brothers, perhaps demon is too, a part cast away, as Cain was by God, a wanderer standing outside the glowing halls of light, looking into a world of fellowship and brotherhood denied to him. And does that monster grow stronger because of our mistreatment, because of our eyes that turn from him? Would these monsters be not so monstrous if we were willing to look upon a part of ourselves we fear and admit kinship?

Geoffrey had faced the monster within. He had gazed into his darkness. That did not mean he had beaten it, but he knew its face. Perhaps that would keep me safe.

He had changed, that I could see. Those who have seen death are different to those who have not. Facing rebels and sieges, Geoffrey had stared into that dark cowl as once I had. He knew the long void of death, the terror of standing alone in that pitch black tunnel. But he had also stared out of the glowing hall and seen Grendel watching him. He knew now he was both man and monster. When men learn to see their own personal monster they have two choices; surrender, or learn to keep him in check. No one may rid themselves of the creature. It always is there, it sometimes is a strength we need, but never can it be dug out. Even men of God never have succeeded, and saints know their weaknesses better than any of us.

We are the dragon, and we are the cave the dragon is kept in. We are innocence sacrificed in pursuit of wisdom. There is no knight to save us. It is as well. The only ones to save us are ourselves. Dragon and innocent must be one, powers combined, essence accepted.

"If you say you have changed, and we may treat each other with respect, I will attempt to believe you," I said.

"That is all I ask," he replied.

On the ride to the castle, Geoffrey was courteous and polite, pointing out changes to the country that had occurred whilst I had been away. Fenland had been drained for farmland, and woodland turned over to coppicing and lye production. He asked my opinion on agriculture and politics. Frequently I was at a loss for words. It was like meeting another man, although I knew the face and other parts of this one with more intimacy than his mother. In many ways it was most confusing.

And if handsome he was before, he had become only more so. The boyish beauty he had possessed had become rougher, his charm more smooth. He was honey and grit bound together. Had I known nothing of him, had we had no history, I might well have found my heart falling for his charms. Many women did. But they left me cold. To me he would always be, at least in part, the boy who had terrorized my soul, who had made me feel reduced and humiliated. Geoffrey was an emblem of the humiliation and fear I had been forced to endure, of my lack of choices in life.

My time away from him, from marriage had taught me much about myself. My grandsire was a man for building castles and perhaps something of that spirit was upon me. Inside me were walls. I did not want to love again. I had enough chains upon my life without adding more. I wanted to be free.

Although when I thought of Heinrich there would come a surge of beauty and wonder in me, there too was confusion. Love had been my puppet master and I a glove, neatly fitted to his hand. I had been a falcon blinded and seeled, trained in darkness with sweet songs and tempting treats. By love I had been tamed and kept tame. I did not want that again. Any man I loved would become master of me, it could not be otherwise. When man holds all power, all money, all property, law and right of the Church and God and man, what is left for woman? It was enough to be tied to a man through marriage, or by blood as I was to my father. Binding one to my heart, to the one space that was mine and mine alone, was too much, too much a risk, and too much to ask.

I had loved once, and that was more than most people did. I had been fortunate, even if the love had not been perfect, not equal. That was enough. I would not risk my heart, my soul, again. I would have a space in me that was free of men, which was mine alone. I would have freedom inside me, until I could carve a space for it in the world.

# Chapter Twenty-Two

## Angers
## Anjou

### Spring - Summer 1132

"You have become a general of renown," I commented one morning as Geoffrey told me of his exploits against the rebels in Anjou whilst I was gone.

I turned from the window. I had been watching the day and its industry. The baileys were busy, people carrying water from well to kitchen and stable, men sweeping away horse dung piles, children running errands. A young woman had snuck surreptitiously from a small house where the cunning man lived, carrying a love potion, perhaps, or a charm hidden in her hands. I had been admiring apple trees in the pleasure park near to the castle, awash with pink and white flowers. The grass was thick and verdant, the fields bursting into life. Clover, purple and red, were everywhere and so were bees, bumbling balls buzzing happily, sometimes impatiently if someone came too close. People were gathering wild herbs, thyme from the hillsides, watercress from ditches, sorrel from waysides to make tangy green sauce for fish.

It was busy and the people were merry. There were old songs on the air. Peace had fallen upon Anjou after a long time of rebellion and campaign. People were content now. Out in the fields near the town people were gathering and preparing, ploughs dragged by oxen trundling up and down, the cold ground broken so new life could spring. On smaller plots men without beasts to pull the plough were dragging it themselves, brows pealing with sweat which was rapidly cooled by the cold air. That they had fields and crops, that their homes were not burning or being looted was down to their lord, Geoffrey. His achievements could not be denied, yet what surprised me was that there was only a little pride hovering about him. Only a slight swagger. He had gained confidence, therefore had no need to make a show. Men who possess confidence not will never understand how calm and quiet, how humble a thing confidence is, in truth. It never needs to boast or shout. It is the man who stands upright and still in the room, who says nothing and yet to whom all eyes are drawn.

"It is a feat remarkable that you learnt so much, so fast," I went on. "All I speak to at court talk of your wisdom in warfare, gleaned during so few campaigns. You appear to have gained a lifetime's worth of experience in the span of a few years." My hand went to a brooch he had presented me with. It was a ring-brooch, standard for holding capes and tunics, gowns or cloaks in place. It was silver and on each side were two hands, holding each other. It was a symbol of our new friendship, he had said.

"Not through experience alone did I learn," Geoffrey said. At his breast a dried segment of broom flower shone in the light from the windows. It was his heraldic device now. I had never asked why, but his loyalty to the flower made me wonder. It was a flower of magic, love and protection, said to repel witches and attract lovers. I did not ask which he wore it for; love or protection. Perhaps it was both.

When I looked at him, brow quizzical, he smiled. He walked to a chest, took out a tome and handed it to me. "It is yours," he said. "*De Re Militari*, by Vegetius."

It was one of the books I had brought with me from the Empire, one of few I had saved. It had been a favourite of Heinrich's. The copy I had was no original, but a well-thumbed book of strategy in war. "You read it?" I asked, taking it in my hands.

"Many times," he said. "As you said I should, and you were right. It taught me much. There was a time I was unwilling to learn, for I thought I knew all. When you left, when I opened this and other books, when I went to war, finally I understood how blind I was. I knew nothing, and I still do not."

"I think you underestimate yourself," I said, trying not to show my confusion. Geoffrey confounded me so often then. Much of me screamed that I should trust him, that he was another person. The rest of me told the part screaming that it was a fool.

"That is kind," he said. "But the more I learn the more I understand Socrates."

"The only true knowledge is in knowing we know nothing?"

"Indeed."

I shook my head, handing the book back. "I find you much changed, lord husband."

"I am pleased," he said.

For a moment he looked so handsome I almost caught my breath, but managed to stop myself. Still I did not trust him completely, could not, and the fear within me made the perfection of his face something to distrust. There are many things that are beautiful that are also dangerous, and just because something has a pretty face does not mean it has a good heart. Often the opposite is true, for those who possess physical beauty learn it is a blinding light. There is much they might do in the shadows that light casts.

But for all my suspicions, our marriage was a better arrangement now than before. We each found the other pleasing in body, and were not waiting for a miracle to occur and bind us in love, so our marriage became an arrangement of mutual duty and aid. At times there was fire in our bed, need, but in the light of day there was nothing but business. Geoffrey treated me with deference and respect, and distance. We were together for all formal and court functions, and he came to me each night. At times I wondered what my father had promised him in lieu of the crown… Normandy? At other times I thought I did Geoffrey a disservice. Perhaps he really had changed.

It was a thing strange to find myself once more married. Although I had not stepped outside the bonds of my vows in Normandy or England, although I had been married for several years, I had not felt that way whilst away from Anjou. I had not felt free, either, but absent from my husband I had been, and now he was here, and he was a changed man, in most respects.

So I had a husband, one who felt new and was yet familiar. Once, Heinrich had become a stranger to me, transforming into a man hostile, contemptuous of me, frightening. The opposite had happened in my second marriage. The boy I knew remained upon the face of this new man, but what was inside seemed to have altered. Life is so circular. How it loves to flow in patterns, running the same furrows, repeating stories using us as its players, time and time and time again.

I wondered if it was because there must be balance, always. Because Heinrich had turned from man to monster, Geoffrey had to be the opposite. Where there is light darkness falls, and the brighter the light the deeper the darkness, much as the stars and moon in the night's sky. There are so few people, in truth, who work feral and uncontrolled evil, yet there are a thousand acts of small kindnesses done every day by others. Perhaps it is part of God's plan, I am not wise enough to know, but patterns in my life came, repeating, as echoes in a cavern ricocheting backwards into infinity. Once I had a husband-stranger and now I did again. I little knew what to make of it, which was common for me in those days of return to Anjou. We get so accustomed to life being a certain way, people too, that we forget all beings are capable of change, if they want to change. We forget years turn, children grow. Geoffrey I found particularly confounding. I had a picture of him in my mind and that I could not part with, so deep was the etching. Yet he challenged my certainties often.

Where Geoffrey had before made obvious his resentment at my comments on any matter not domestic, he now encouraged them. I was still not a power in Anjou. This kingdom was his land and he was the authority, perhaps he was also aware he was not to inherit anything through me, but no more did he try to silence me. He listened with respect even when he did not agree. Where he had paraded mistresses before me in the past, I now saw none, and heard nothing of his bastard. I understood the boy was being raised with family in the country, but arrangements made for him were discreet, kept hidden from me. I was called Empress by his court, rather than Countess, and those feral friends of his that I had feared were largely gone. One or two remained, but he had more sober counsel now, older men to whom he listened. I noted his men looked upon him with respect. I also noted Geoffrey was alone more than he had been before. He had found a companion in his own company, no more required sheep to bleat around him to make him feel secure.

He had turned into a reader. Before, it had not been something he had often turned to, preferring women and wine, but now when I came to see him on some matter of business he always had a book in his lap. They were mostly military books, manuals of Rome, theory on weaponry or warcraft. It was remarkable that in such a small time he could have changed so much, but perhaps for him the years had been longer. He had been so young when we wed, a boy. Since I left he had become a man. Sometimes I mourned we had not met later. Much might have been different.

Sometimes, without meaning to, a person can be bad for another, can bring out the darkness in them. I had not seen much of good in Geoffrey when we were married, so not much good had come from him. I was not responsible for all, think not that, but I had not helped.

Some flowers bloom best in obscurity, all lights are brighter in darkness. Geoffrey could not become who he was meant to be with me there, at his side. Proving himself good enough, high enough to be my husband, although he would never admit he needed to do such a thing, had been a distraction from proving himself worthy to himself. I had been standing in the way of that. He was weak and feeble of spirit no more. Blood and battle had hardened him, they do most men who survive, but it was something else too. He had learnt to trust himself.

I do not mean to tell you for a moment that all had changed and he was perfect. No creature on this world is, certainly no human. It is flaws that make us people, rather than fantasies. Nothing is more personal and interesting that what is wrong with a person.

He still had a quick and bitter temper, and that dangerous pride, so easily wounded, was within him. Pride is a fragile thing, an egg shattered by the slightest pressure. He managed it better, appeased the poor fragile beast. I could see him talking to himself at times, placating the monster rising inside him, trying to control it, but still it was there. It probably always would be, and mastering it would be a lifelong task. It is that way for many of us. It was for me. Pride was one of my faults too, and knowing your flaws is one thing, mastering them quite another. Mastery, one comes to understand is not a single victory, but an ongoing war. Our vices and weaknesses are always there, bested one moment, victor the next. Struggling against them, prevailing where we can, this is what makes us good. This is what makes us human; creatures who strive, who struggle, who hope.

As silk-soft skies of summer blue crested over us, we met to talk of business in daylight, and he was in my bed each night. With the scent of the fresh grass, awash with life and sweetness which fell in the dusk as dew settled on it, Geoffrey came. He was not rough or too urgent. He did not demand more of me than I wanted to offer.

As summer went on I noted more. There was still conceit in him; still that longing to be known by other men, to be lauded. But this was now not so boyish and foolish as before. Now, rather than fame for fame's sake, it had turned to a desire to be known for something he had actually done. There is little wrong in that, we all wish to be remembered, it is part of our fear of death and how we combat it. To be remembered for great deeds or wisdom is no bad thing, just a human thing.

And he had promise, I could see that better than before. My father had said it of him at the beginning and I had dismissed it, my own pride not allowing me to see anything good in our union. It was true Geoffrey's deeds were not yet mighty enough to stand against those of the Conqueror or my father, but insignificant they were not. He had learnt a great deal in short time, a sign of that intelligence I had always suspected was there and could be better used.

He had done well against rebels in Anjou, and was praised, rightly, for his actions. He had proved himself brave in battle, rather than just in tourneys. Now that he had been in battle in truth, faced death, he knew the difference between mock and real war, he knew what may be lost. In truth, for a man of only almost nineteen, Geoffrey was much matured, much changed.

"If Father had waited," I said to myself one night in the chapel, as I prayed for a son. "I wonder if there might have been more to this marriage, Lord God, than business."

I glanced up at the painted walls. Saints stared down at me, their faces impassive. They had no answer for me.

I bowed my head again. "And you would tell me to forgive, and I shall try, but to forgive is not to forget. And whilst I may forgive, I cannot leave the fear and distrust of him behind."

Nor could I leave Heinrich, the ghost always at my side. Nor could I leave dreams of freedom which whispered that to surrender heart was to surrender all.

# Chapter Twenty-Three

## Angers
## Anjou

### Autumn - Winter 1132

"You are sure?"

I laughed. The delight on his face was really most endearing. My laugh surprised me, for there was abandon in it. Rarely did I allow the wildness within me to lift its head and bark, but I was suffused with joy. There was no part of me not tingling with it. "I have not bled for two months," I said, beaming. "My breasts hurt. I smell everything, every ingredient of pottage and pie, every herb and spice. I am sick every morning and ravenous after. I am sure."

Tears rushed to my eyes. A child in my belly. I had suspected for some time and not said a word in case speaking shattered the spell, this dream. Yet day after day I looked for blood and found none. Morning after morning I was sick and never welcomed the ugly sensation more. What I had almost surrendered hope of was mine, at last. There was life in my womb. All I had been thought, all I had accused myself of was untrue. I was not barren, not a stark, burnt field of hopeless sterility. I was not unnatural. I was not forsaken by God for a crime that I could not recall. I was to have what I had wished for. I was to have a child.

I made as though I was fanning myself to hide my tears, rather a foolish pretence. Breathless days of stifling summer were waning and cooler, refreshing air was coming in. Autumn was falling, great and golden, its light gentle and brilliant, glorious and subtle.

Geoffrey's face looked as though it might break in half, so wide was he smiling. He made as if to embrace me, but stopped as I stiffened. The smile on my face froze, my shoulders tightened. I felt panic on me for a moment. He stopped, stepping back carefully as though to move too fast would shatter me like a sheet of ice.

"I could not be happier," he said, hands dropping carefully to his sides. "And I thank you, my lady wife, for bringing fruit to my line."

He looked away, and I wondered if he was trying to hide the emotion within. Not delight at my news, there was no need to conceal that, but other things left unspoken. Although in bed we obviously had been in a closer embrace than the one he had just attempted, that was another place, one of darkness where that was allowed. He had not tried to embrace me in daylight and I had not given any sign I wanted such intimacy. In darkness we could couple with frantic need and in daylight be allies in marriage. That was the way of it. Confusing the two was not welcome to me. And I think in that moment I hurt him. He had wished only to share the joy we both experienced in this news, a joy of future. My reaction was a ghost of the past.

He looked to the window. Lights of rust and gold shone on his handsome face. I caught sight of the slightest silver scar on his cheek. It was from where I had cut him with my ring, the pink-silver line catching golden light from outside. Autumn was blazing in the trees, in the skies, a season of light and colour. His jaw tightened. I believed he was angry, but whether at me or himself I knew not.

"There should not be any announcement until the third month," I said, moving on so we could talk as the allies we were, ignore this awkwardness. "I am told that there is danger until the child quickens. I would not want to excite your people of Anjou, or those of England and Normandy, and then miscarry."

I swallowed. Fear that I would lose this child was tight about me. I was trying to ignore it, but it was there. It had been since the first moment I suspected.

"Nothing will be said in public until you approve it," he agreed. "But it would be a good idea to let your father know, in a private letter?"

I inclined my head. I had, in fact, already sent one, but if Geoffrey could be respectful, I would at least make a show of the same for him. "I will write to my father, as you say, lord husband."

There was silence a moment. When I looked up, he was smiling. "What is it?" I asked.

"Aside from the promise of a child?" Geoffrey shook his head. "It is just... I cannot believe your calmness. I thought more than anything you wanted a child."

I nodded. "There is nothing in me at the moment but happiness."

"You fear, too," he said, that sharp insight he often had once more taking me by surprise.

"I *wish* there was nothing but happiness," I said, amending my answer. "But yes, I fear. It brings guilt. Why should I, when I have wished for this so long, fear it when it comes? It makes me feel unworthy of such a blessing that I cannot surrender to it." I bit my lip and wondered if all mothers felt that way, or if it was just me. The thought of losing my life or that of the child was at the back of my thoughts, a soft-stealing madness. If I allowed it loose, I could easily lose all courage, abandon sense. So dangerous are our own minds, so many pits and traps.

"You fear to lose happiness," he said. "When you have wished so long for something and it comes to your hands, half of you wants to grasp it tight, never let go. The other half fears to crush it. The secret is to hold it gently, nurture it. Allow not one impulse to dominate the other. Balance your fear and joy."

I nodded. "I try to."

"Whatever I can do to help, ask," he said. "My knowledge of women's secrets is not vast, but I will aid you all I can."

I smiled, suddenly tearful again. His words touched me. Since the babe had rooted in my belly I seemed to feel more intensely. It was another unnerving thing, especially when I had relied so much on being able to mask my emotions.

"And you *are* worthy," he said. "You always have been. God delayed in granting a child for a purpose. If with child you are, now and here, this is a special child. Your fears are natural, as is your caution in surrendering to joy. When our child is here, in your arms, you will be able to feel all you long to feel." He smiled and breathed in. "And in the meantime, we will work together, allied as one, to make you comfortable and keep you in the best of health, so you may know that joy."

I nodded, not trusting myself to speak. After thanking me again, Geoffrey departed my rooms. He knew I was close to weeping and he knew I did not want him to see me at such a time. It was another moment where he surprised me. I was losing count.

I was nervous, it was true. I would be thirty-one years of age when childbed called, old to bear my first child. If my age and the normal risks of childbed were not enough, there were other dangers to consider. Sybil, Geoffrey's sister, who had been twice Countess of Flanders after marrying Clito and his successor Thierry, had recently died after the birth of her child, from a festering in the breasts. Most women who died in childbed succumbed to fever after, which no one ever could explain; a smaller number died for blood loss and for exhaustion when a babe would not come fast. Sybil had died when all had thought her safe. Her physician had told her to bind her breasts to stop her milk, of which there was a copious flow. Duly she had done so, only for fever of another kind to fall. The milk that should have fed her babe, granted life, brought her death.

I might die, might never live to see my child grow. It is strange how the moment we have what we want, we want something else. Humans are insatiable, impossible to satisfy. Yet I hoped that God would listen and not think my prayers, so recently changed, selfish or unworthy. More than simply wanting to be a mother, I wanted to be one who lived to watch her child grow up. I might achieve my former ambition of motherhood and die. Now that I was with child, I wanted more.

Wishes are never complete, never fulfilled. We always want another.

"You must take care in all ways," said Geoffrey later that night. "I have been reading. There are many who say too much air is not beneficial."

"I think it bad for women to be shut away, without air or exercise when with child," I said. "Over the years I have read much, and whilst I will take care, I will take a walk outside when I need to, I will breathe the air of the forests."

"As you will," he said, nodding. "But I want a guard always with you now. You carry the heir to England and Normandy and Anjou. This son will be a precious child. He will have enemies who might seek to remove him before he is even born." There was resolve on his face. Bow to me in matters of my own body he would, but when it came to defence of the kingdom Geoffrey was in charge. This was a matter of the future of the realm. His experience of his own kingdom was superior to mine.

But I shivered at his words, at the thought someone might try to kill my child before he had lived. Geoffrey looked concerned. I shook my head. "I am well," I said. "And I think you are right. Let us take reasonable precautions." I paused. "It may not be a son, of course," I said, warning in my voice.

"I think it will be," he said. "There are few things that you, my Lady of the English, do not succeed at." I smiled, trying not to flush. The title was a high compliment. My father was King of the English, so Geoffrey may have simply been referring to that, but I knew it was more. One of the first women who had ruled by herself, Aethelflaed, had been named Lady of the Mercians, a Queen in all but name.

"You are kind," I said. "But I feel I fail at many things."

"Not as many as you think," he said, smiling. "And you are the mother of my child and heir. To whom else should I be kind?"

It was as though he had struck me. Blood drained from my face. My heart faltered in my chest, the last beat bouncing against my ribs, my blood running weak all through my body. A ghost had spoken. Past had folded upon present, the tail of the serpent slipping into its mouth.

Heinrich had once said something so similar that it was as though his ghost was speaking from Geoffrey's lips. When had that been? Images flashed through my mind. It was when he had told me I would be crowned Queen of the Germans. *"To whom else should I be kind?"* he had said.

"What is it?" Geoffrey asked.

I blinked, suddenly seeing him. I had not been looking down. I must have frozen, staring at him. His face was concerned. His hand was reaching out to mine, but was not touching me. "Nothing," I said. "It is nothing."

*

Late that night, staring at the hangings about my bed, watching them shift and swish in draughts that came creeping through the shutters, under tapestry, I thought of that time, that conversation with Heinrich. The time before I was crowned Queen of the Germans.

Perhaps there were similarities between then and now. It had been a time of possibility and change then too. I a child crowned Queen had been honoured above all other women when I was not even a woman yet. Honoured by Heinrich, as now I was honoured by Geoffrey.

Was that the secret of this change in Geoffrey? Had Heinrich's ghost come to protect me, thrown itself inside Geoffrey's body? Was that phrase, so lightly spoken yet carrying such weight, a sign of this? Was my past coming to invade my present, and was the one I had loved and lost to death returning now, to protect me and my child?

I felt strange that night, as though something was with me. Oftentimes I had felt Heinrich, and I did then. I could not explain the maelstrom of emotion in me, sorrow of the past, confusion of the present, the joy of a child and the fear of losing that child. Fear of death for myself. It was too much, and in that moment I accepted it was too much. Too much to ponder and to try to control. I was within water. All I could do was ride the water, flow with it, try to trust in God and goodness, accept change and chaos.

# Chapter Twenty-Four

## Angers
## Anjou

### Winter 1132

I went to the church as dusk fell, needing to pray. I had my own space within my chambers, a private chapel where I could kneel for hours if I so wished, talk to God. But sometimes I wanted to feel awe, an echo of the mountains when Heinrich and I had ridden under them. I could not feel that in a private closet.

It was cold, growing colder each morning and eve of day. A wolf of winter had swallowed the sun. Days were lit with blue light and grey ash. The wind had become ice, bearing sharp invisible darts that struck through clothes, through skin, into bone. Even through furs of sable and fox I could feel the ice air. Milk was now three times the price it was in summer, for few kept their cattle in calf or sheep in lamb in winter. Yet to me treats like this were brought still, along with rose sugar, of ludicrous expense, honey cakes made from the stores for winter, and the best cuts of meat, carrying the most blood. Geoffrey wanted me fit, and any whim attended to. I found what I wanted most was pepper, spices that set my tongue aflame. That was *when* I could eat. Many was the morn I spent nibbling oat and honey cakes, for they were all I could keep inside me. Expensive ginger had been brought to me that helped with the sickness more than anything. My women kept telling me the sickness would pass, but it did not. I was suffering through pregnancy, but I kept the vision of my child in my mind, a vision of hope. In a time of suffering there must be a future, something of light on the horizon to keep eyes upon.

Soon we would leave and head to Le Mans. Geoffrey wanted me there for the confinement. I would be shut away with my ladies for weeks before the birth, so I could be still and quiet, so I could be safe. The castle of Le Mans was the one Geoffrey had picked as it was defensible, and it had comforts. The two were in his mind, joined as one, often in those days of waiting. It was important for another reason, being on the Anjou-Normandy border. This child would be heir to both until there was another son. It was right he be born where borders met.

My guard took position at the door as I walked in. I genuflected as I reached the central aisle, and walked slowly towards the altar, past tombs on which skeletons carved in stone stood, cold and still, and on others where knights lay, effigies of men in armour bearing swords upon their graves, deeds long forgotten. My breath was mist coming from my lips. Statues of saints stared at me, their eyes painted so they shimmered blue and green, brown and violet in the flickering light of the candles and torches along the walls. My steps were muffled on the fresh reeds upon the floor, yet sounded still like the loudest noise on earth.

Pillars of stone glimmered. Light from shards of crystal inside their flesh sparkled as reflected radiance from candlelight bouncing from the windows caught them. They could hold up the skies, those pillars, those trees that man must make inside churches for he can create nothing so perfect and chaotic as a tree. The perfection we make is too smooth, too careful. With pillars of stone we think to reach up, touch the heavens, the hand of God, and yet trees, wood that will fall one day to earth and rot, touch the Almighty with effortless ease. Branches stroking sky and roots hugging the dead. We aim for perfection and fail, for our perfection is too cold, too impersonal, too much of us trying to ignore the mingled natures of our hearts. God had it right with trees, with confusion mingled with order, with perfect impermanence.

I knelt at the altar and I prayed. I prayed for the child I carried, for good health and life long for them. I prayed to deliver safely, to be a good mother. But more than asking for favours, I gave thanks.

"I waited so long. I thought You were not listening. Forgive me, for all the time You were."

Tears came from my eyes. They tasted of the past. Slipping they came, falling to the marble of the floor and rushes atop it, turning dusty green to shimmering brightness, as though still those rushes were at the water side, and I the rain, bringing life, feeding the future with all the pain of the past.

*

Christmas came, the halls were decorated with evergreen, and holly, those bright red berries that surely would deter any witch no matter how powerful, would cascade down banisters and stairs, but not before the Eve of Christmas. It was bad fortune to bring it into a house before that day. It was said the green would bring fair folk calling, whose intentions not always were fair. Christmas went, and as the greenery departed our halls the wonderful fresh scent lingered for weeks.

I was eating little and often, it seemed best for the child and me. White meats like capon and blackbird, kid and partridge were thought most beneficial, and Geoffrey had sent for pears and apples aplenty, as well as imported pomegranates. I was not to eat much salt or the child might be born without fingernails or hair, and tonics were fed to me of ginger and honey, pepper and raspberry leaf to aid me when my time came. I was told not to bathe too frequently, and ignored the man who said that. I was not to stand outside too much. I ignored that too.

One night I stood outside. It was my wont, and no matter people telling me it was bad for me still I did it. There were times my soul needed air and space, even if it had to be reached from a battlement, from the confines of a castle.

Geoffrey did not like it. "You might stumble and fall, hurt the child or yourself," he had said.

"When have you ever seen my feet unsure?" was my reply, to which he had shrugged, because he could offer no example.

"Do as you will," he said.

As if I would do anything else. Men had told me where and when to marry, what to wear and how I should speak, feel, act. I would be damned if they would tell me where and when I might walk, too. But I said that not to him. If I refused one of his requests he accepted it. He might insist on various types of protection for me but when I wanted something I had it in those days. He was right that there were dangers, but I needed air and walking and space and time alone. I needed night, my companion, my solace, my friend. I would stand in blue-grey dimness and watch lights igniting in the town, hear men walking home from inns, catch the subtle sounds of rodents scurrying, horses snorting. Women tending children with coughs would be brewing stews of breast milk and powdered woodlouse, snails perhaps. Others would be scurrying from cottage to cowshed, where they would loosen the tight chest of their precious child in the warm breath of the animals. In the distance would be a hound barking, then another, and the clopping of hooves as one last weary traveller was let into the city gates before they closed to all for the night.

Yet all those noises, though part of life and my life, were far from me. There was a stillness in the night and it fell too upon me, an arm. I listened to the stars and the moon, to the whisper of light and the dazzle of black brilliance. I would lift my ears to the north wind as it sung, crisp and cold, swinging over the tops of houses, the trees, forests and rivers. Spring was coming and yet the wind was of winter still, a lingering presence of power. In its cold song was something I had yearned to hear for a long time.

The voice of the wind upon me, on skin, flesh, seeping to bone, I stood within and apart from its power, wondering, waiting, allowing it to flow into me. The wildness of its call as through trees, about stone walls, it flung itself and the feral nature of that call seeped into me.

There was something of the wanderer in the wind, something restless, some energy sprung from the first moment when chaos became purpose in this world. Something of the wind was always seeking, always would seek. There was something lost in it that did not want to be found, something that wandered for the joy of wandering, and not for any purpose but that. It was an ancient curiosity, older than that which caused the fall of man. Perhaps it had been a part of that, of the tentative hand reaching for food which contained wisdom, in the mind that could not resist knowledge, no matter how much pain and suffering knowledge brought.

I understood that call of curiosity. It was dark in nature, perhaps. Light would have been remaining innocent. I thought the story of the fall of man was not, as men of God would have us believe, a tale of sin, but one of understanding. We were happier before our minds were opened, before we knew sorrow, pain and death. But we were not alive before as we had come to be after, for there cannot be just innocence and joy, there must be pain and darkness, there must be sorrow and suffering. I thought the fall not God's punishment, for what of wisdom is wicked? God did not punish us, but allowed us to live fully, for joy and for pain. It is not evil to know, but knowing brings evils into our life that the innocent do not feel. We are creatures who learn by comparison. We cannot know joy complete unless we have suffered in truth. We cannot appreciate charity without knowing what evil is in the greed of man. And darkness and sorrow are not evil things, though often it may feel that way. They, like light and joy, are teachers and we are beings who have much to learn.

We could not remain innocent. We had to know, and to know is to suffer at times, as it is to rejoice. This is life, this chaos and possibility, this trial and joy, ease and suffering; this creeping madness and this sharp reason. There is not one thing without its opposite. No shade without sunlight, no angels without demons; no humans without monsters.

But that restless urge to *know* was in all humans and if it was there God must have played a part in its creation. If all was down to Him, He had placed it in us. He made a creation aware of its own existence as others were not, something that could marvel at the world He had made, appreciate it. We could not do that with eyes closed and minds innocent; could not understand all if only light we could see. We had to be woken. We had to come to see all. We had to know the darkness and the light, the shadows in between.

Blasphemous though it was, and a thought I would share with no one, it was a thought in me. We were creatures not fallen, but awoken. Knowing the suffering most men had seen, perhaps they thought this a curse, some punishment of God laid upon us for a sin. I thought not. And to me, the sin Christ had come to save us from was again that of ignorance. He had imparted lessons, had he not? If the natural and proper state of man was innocence and ignorance, why would the Redeemer teach us so much, guide us in ways of wisdom? God had opened our eyes to life, to sorrow, suffering, joy and knowledge. His son came to show us to the path that led on from there. God granted us curiosity and chaos, granted a restless seeking and wandering spirit to us.

And that same restless power was in the wind, in that call I heard, as it was in the child I carried.

One hand on the lump of my child growing on my front, and I knew. Something of the wind was in this child as something of water was in me. As I was calm surface and turbulence underneath, so this child was restless. Restless as the wind, feral and free, lifting its voice to call to those it passed as the night rushed in, as it flowed and flounced its way about the world, touching all, remaining still never.

"You will seek," I whispered to my child. "I can only hope you will find."

But even as I said it, I knew. Some are not born to find, only to seek. Some are not born to be still, but always are in motion. Some of us are of earth, steady and creative, and some are of wind, the seekers always seeking, wanderers who do not find home, and do not need to.

# Chapter Twenty-Five

## Castle of Le Mans
## Normandy

## Spring 1133

I screamed; a long, guttural, animal noise, rich with pain, liquid with fear. Never had I experienced agony of this magnitude. I was about to fly apart. Everything in me was screaming, blood, hands, skin, senses, hair and eyes. I was so tired, yet on it went. Relentless was the pain and the effort. I had not known this strength, this endurance was in me. All I wanted was surrender, yet I did not and could not. Agony was the only thing keeping me awake, alive.

"Hold, my lady!" shouted Ermengarde, one of my women. "Do not push!"

I screamed again. They had encouraged it, my midwives, told me to scream if there was pain or fear or frustration. It helped to release those emotions, helped to dull the pain. I had obeyed. Screaming was cathartic, it unbound the terror in my breast, allowed my pain a voice.

Listened to them in all other things I had, yet the command not to push sounded like lunacy. Every urge in me was screaming at me to push, but they had held me safe thus far, these women, and I trusted them. Indeed, never had I set so much trust in people so quickly. They held my life, that of my child and my sanity in their hands. I was a creature who found it hard to allow anyone close, yet willingly had I placed all those precious things in their palms when the pain had become more than a gnawing ache, and had overtaken everything in my mind and body. Nothing that was mine was under my control, not my body, not my child, not my life. I was out of control and therefore grasping in the dark for a rope that would drag me back to the light. Never had I been so willing to obey.

"Hold, Domina. Pant like a hound. Do not push or you will rip yourself apart." The voice was near my legs. It sounded like it was a thousand miles away.

I nodded, unable to talk. Scream I could, with ease, but to form words was a task much harder. A woman wiped my forehead with a blissful cloth of cold water and lavender. She peeled my hair, stuck to my skin with sweat and terror, from my face. Another woman was holding my hands, giving me something to strain against. She squeezed my fingers, letting me know I was not alone, others stood with me in this battle. Some of them I knew and some had been sent for to attend to me. Geoffrey had listened to my wishes. I had asked for and had been given experienced midwives, women who had delivered many babes, saved many mothers from the dangers of birth.

It was the 5th of March. One morn, as freezing morning mist was dispelled by bright sunlight I had entered the first stage of labour. That had been more than a day ago, or I thought it had. Time had become meaningless as pain had grown. All there was, was pain. Even hope, hope it would end, I could rest, my child would be well, was surrendering. I was becoming lost, and yet never had I felt so aware of my body; this spluttering, struggling wreak; this striving, fighting animal. Hard and long and darkly I had fought, entering the fray with energy and optimism, but through hours of light then of night I had struggled on, a mortally wounded soldier on his knees, thrashing with his spear. And then the bells of the churches all seemed to meld and ring as one, and all hours of dark and light were the same, shadows fell and stretched as bright sunlight poured in. There was no sense or time or space or normality. In a realm of madness and ghosts, shade and loss I was. And all the time, pain was my companion.

"The child comes," said the voice between my legs. One of the oldest women, Sybillia, was there next to Ermengarde, her head moving so I could see the silver of her hair. I was naked, my stained and soiled linen nightgown stripped away hours ago. Never had so many people seen so much of me and I did not care. Naked to the women who aided me I was, not just in body but in soul. They could see the root of all my fear and therefore of my courage too. These women could hear my mind and my emotions, knew my spirit and all I had in me. Bonded in this private world and war of women, we were as selkies on the beach, naked to the raw wind, freed of inhibition through agony and terror.

I panted like a hound after the chase. Distantly I could feel fingers on my source of life. I tried to think of anything that would stop me pushing as I panted. Never had resistance been so hard. I had been fighting pain, now I was fighting my own body.

I had thought the pain nothing at first, a dull ache, a twinge. I had almost laughed, thinking that women who complained about childbed must be weak and silly indeed, for this was nothing! I had not quite dared to laugh, however. Something whispered, some demon perched on my shoulder, telling me this was but the entrance to a long, dark path. My women had told me it would aid the child if I stayed upright for as long as I could, so I had walked about my chambers, blue smoke of ambergris and musk, oregano and mint billowing about me, herbs and scents said to be beneficial for a mother about to give birth. Those scents would also keep demons and spirits of wickedness from the chamber, known to prey on women when they were weakest, when they were become the border between before life and life itself. This was a time of danger, not only for life but for my soul and that of my child. Before my child was baptised, whilst I teetered on the border of possibility, we both were vulnerable. Transgressors, shadow-walkers, those not securely in one world or another always are vulnerable, but they have power, too.

There were crosses on the windows to keep devils at bay. The herbs burned, piles of white ash falling to the floor. Holy water, blessed by a priest that morning, therefore potent and strong, was scattered on the cloths, on me, on the chamber. The midwives muttered prayers and, their voices lower, protective spells of older days. Saint Margaret, who was swallowed by a dragon and climbed whole from his mouth to become patron saint of childbirth, was called on to protect me.

As women muttered prayers and smoke plumed into the air, the pain had grown. My back ached mercilessly and they had set me into a blissful tub of hot water and herbs. When I emerged and was dried, my belly had been massaged with rose oil, and my back too. And all the time the pain had grown, and kept growing. Each time it reached one height I thought it the worst. How could it get worse? And then it did. What a fool I was, how very little I knew.

They had brought me to a special chair, a groaning chair. I had used it for a time, but eventually had taken to squatting on the floor. Women held me up, helped me push as I bore down, pushing with each wave of pain, until they told me to stop, pant as the head emerged slowly.

"I have the head!" cried the voice between my legs. "And the shoulders."

There was a slipping sensation in my body. My child was coming. "Push, Domina!" cried a joyful and triumphant voice. And then all voices of all women of the world seemed to join with her. "Push, Domina!"

I did not need to be told again. Grasping the hands in my hands I pushed, hard and long, screaming all the way. From me, entering the world to hear its mother screaming, my child came.

"A son!" Ermengarde crowed, her voice ecstatic. "A son for you, and for Anjou, my lady!"

"He is well?" I croaked, falling backwards into the arms of the woman behind me. She held me, my sweat-drenched back against her warm breasts as though I were a child myself. I gasped for breath, my heart fit to burst not only for the news I had a boy, that I had a baby of *any* sex, but for anxiety because he was in the world and I was not holding him. All I wanted was my child in my arms.

A shrill cry rose up from the table as they washed him. "Good lungs," said Sybillia with a chuckle. "Our little lord is in excellent health, Domina. His arms and legs are kicking and punching and his lungs…" the baby let out another cry. It almost broke my heart "… are clearly hale!"

"Please, give him to me." I panted, hands shaking against the arms of the woman who gently held me. I could feel tiny hairs on her arms, delicate and silky against my wet palms.

"A moment more, Domina, and he is yours."

I knew what they were doing and they did not want me to see in case it scared me. It was normal for midwives to bless and baptise babes, sick and dying ones in particular, but all just in case, so that if they died suddenly as some children did, their souls would enter Heaven, not limbo. These women who had protected me in this battle would not risk the heir to Anjou and England falling into a void below Heaven, and they would not risk telling me, in case it struck fear into me. Both tasks they undertook in that moment were works of supreme kindness. It is better sometimes not to be told the truth, to be kept in a safe world of fantasy.

I was washed, helped to the bed. After what felt like an age, they came to me, Ermengarde carrying a bundle in her arms. "Your son, my lady," she said.

Into my eager arms he was placed, a fragile, delicate bundle so light I thought I might break him if I held him too tight. I gazed down into a red-white face, wrinkled like an old man and cross as a woman whose husband has drunk away their harvest profits. My son scowled, the most delightful, beautiful expression ever I saw on any face. He balled up tiny fists on the end of little, fat arms which poked from the covers, and he howled. Shrill and thin and high it was, his first cry of defiance to the world. It would not be the last. He was *my* son, after all.

I laughed. "Cry now, my son," I cooed softly, bouncing him in my arms. "Release any sadness you possess. I will ensure you will never have cause to be sad again. I am your mother, little one. I will watch over you."

"He cries only to leave your warm body, Domina, and enter the world. It is a good sign, for the more he cries the more he casts the Devil from him."

"I marvel that something so beautiful, so alive could come from my body and into my arms," I whispered.

"Life is the work of women, my lady. Death that of man," said Sybillia. "We are here to set right what they do wrong, replenish where they squander."

"My son will not squander," I said, defensive already for the soul of my child.

She smiled, sadly. Perhaps she was right to. My son would be a Count and a King, a Duke and inevitably a warlord. She was right, he would bring death to the world, but without death what is life? Without an end, what is there to begin?

"The Count is waiting, Domina, shall we let him in?" Ermengarde asked.

"Do," I said.

Geoffrey came swift into the room. He looked as though he wanted to run but had managed to restrain himself. What was clear was he had been pacing, and I was touched to see that not only were his cheeks flushed from this, but his hair was awry. He had been worried.

I held up our baby. "Your son, my lord," I said.

And with that, I burst into tears.

*

"I am glad he has your hair," I said.

In the distance I could hear church bells, still pealing. They had when the announcement had first been made and now did each hour. Some were ringing in between, the men dangling from their long ropes clearly unwilling to let a moment pass without honouring my son, and me. When I had fled Anjou I had been deeply unpopular with its people, barren and, it was rumoured, uninterested in the kingdom, cruel to their handsome lord. In one act I had redeemed myself. I was now beloved. I had done as I was supposed to and granted my husband a child. If only all redemptive acts were so straightforward.

People had flocked to Mass to give thanks for me, for Henry, for Geoffrey *Le Bel*. Gifts of grain and beer and gold were being sent to the castle and to abbeys all over Anjou, so the monks would pray for us. We were loved, for we had offered Anjou a future lord, and therefore a future. Minstrels were playing harp and drum and trumpet each night in the great hall where there was also great feasting. Tumblers and acrobats were thick in the streets. They had come rushing to the cities as soon as the news was heard, and they were paid well with good coin by people in festival mood. Carol singers were out with haunting praise of me and the Virgin on their lips, combined as one. Men in taverns were raising leather mugs lined with pitch and filled with ale to me and my son. Anjou was merry and determined to enjoy this time.

I had finally done as I was supposed to. In all eyes, I was now complete, a woman with a child. I was accepted and acceptable. Much as I adored my son, I liked not that I could only be considered whole when connected to a man. Yet forget all that I could, when he was in my arms.

I smiled at Geoffrey. I had managed to recover. I think my bursting into tears had disturbed my husband and he was happier now I was in control of myself again. The rush of emotion, as if by showing the child I had borne to the man whose seed had made him had somehow made my child *real*, had overcome me. Tender were Geoffrey's eyes as he had taken our child in his arms, allowing me to gulp and choke into a cloth until I had spent my tears. His praise for his fine boy had almost set me off anew, but I was managing to control myself, just.

Geoffrey looked surprised. "I thought you would prefer our son dark of head, like you and your father."

"Gold is the colour of a King," I replied. "I would have our son crowned in light, not shadow. I have known enough of that."

"There are none who walk this earth who do not," he said, jiggling the babe, who indeed wore strands of red-gold on his head, up and down. "What matters is not if we can see darkness, but if we are capable of witnessing light."

"Sometimes it is easier to see bad than good," I said.

"Our eyes are drawn naturally to shadows, to the creeping gloom. We think that is where danger lies, so learn to pay attention to it," said the man I had married. "But rare is the moment that, when there is darkness, there is not also light. Even on the darkest nights, where clouds obscure the stars and moon, their light still is there, radiating from the clouds themselves. On a gloomy day where the skies are low and horizon dark, the space around us is still lit, still we can see." He smiled as a gurgle came from his son. "People do not note light because it is always there, as common and as powerful as darkness. We pay not the attention due to light, and more than darkness deserves does it receive. We see shadow and fail to appreciate that without light such a thing could never be cast."

"When did you grow so wise?" I asked.

"Wisdom is not something I possess, but I had time to think in the years we spent apart, where I learned what it was to be a man," he said, coming to me, placing our son in my arms. About the milky throat of my baby was a small chain of daisies. Geoffrey had brought them to the chamber. Made by the hands of children from the castle, it was a gift, an old charm. It was said the blooms would keep spirits of mischief at bay.

Geoffrey sat next to me on the bed, now stripped and cleansed from the birth. Both of us looked down on our child. There was no creature more precious in the world; no jewel, no crown, nothing, could compare to my son. I had thought I was destined never to risk my heart again. It was not so. I fell for a man in the moment of meeting. From the moment my child first breathed I was his.

"I am sorry I was not there to witness it." I tucked my baby's cover a little tighter about him, worried about the draught from the window. It was not usual to have open windows in a birthing chamber, but I had wanted the air cleared of scents of blood, sweat and burning herbs.

"I think, had you been, it might not have happened at all." Geoffrey grinned sideways, and I found myself smiling at him. There was something between us. It was not love, but it was not bitter darkness, as before. Respect, friendship, alliance… we had those things, sometimes things better than love. There is less risk, more to gain.

"Henry," I said to our baby. "You have a good father, remember that."

Geoffrey had said nothing about my choice of name. It was not Angevin but English, which was an unusual choice for a lord of Anjou. But this child, of course, had a destiny outside of the borders of this kingdom. Most would think I had named my son to honour my father and because this tiny boy was now the hope of England, as once my brother had been. *But*, I thought, seeing a catch of light in his eyes, *Geoffrey knows the truth*. I had not named our son for my father.

*"Speak my name when I am gone,"* Heinrich once said to me. I had done so, had kept him alive in my heart and in the world. When people cease to speak the names of the dead, the dead truly die. My son was named for Heinrich. Heinrich now could never die.

"It is a good name, truthful to his destiny," was all Geoffrey said.

But a shadow of sorrow had passed in his eyes. A truth left unspoken fluttered in his mind. He knew I was not naming our child for the future, for destiny alone, but also for my past.

*

I wept at my son's christening. I could not help it. Never had I been seen showing emotion in public in such a way before, but out of me water flowed, marking my son's entrance to world and to Church as much as the water poured over his head did.

He had been baptised a few days after his birth, and I had not seen it. Mothers often did not. I was still waiting to be churched, purified from birth and blood, from standing on the border between life and death. It took forty days, another cycle of menses come and gone, to restore a woman. Between that time I rested, recovered, I read letters which seemed written in joy rather than ink from Adeliza. My good friend, childless though she remained, wept with happiness for me. There was not a hint of jealousy in her letters, though I am sure she felt it. *"Not one thing of this world could make me happier than to know you have a child,"* she wrote.

"Bless you, Queen of the English," I murmured. Adeliza wanted and was still denied the blessing I had, yet all she had for me was the generosity of love. There are few so good of heart in this world.

When the days had passed and I was well, it was time. To the church I went, a blazing candle in my hands, and I was met at the boundaries where the priest blessed me, and welcomed me back into the family of God.

Some said blood marked a mother so creatures of evil and the underworld could see her. Some thought churching a way to protect women; tell a man a woman is cursed and lie with her he will not, giving wives a while without a husband in their bed to aid recovery from birth. But to me, this ceremony was about boundaries. On the cusp of life women could stand, could bring new life into the world, or could die in the process. No man knows what to do with a person who belongs nowhere, so women had to wait, and be welcomed back, citizens of one kingdom again and not the other.

Missed baptism I had, but at young Henry's christening I wept as I saw him blessed with water, as he was named, shown to God and to Anjou. This tiny child one day would become an Emperor, like the man I had named him for.

Until we had other sons, young Henry was all powerful in the realms of Anjou and the kingdom of my father. It was likely if we had other sons Geoffrey might want one to become Count of Anjou, so Anjou would not become another part of the empire my father was building. We had not discussed it as yet. For now, young Henry was heir to all; the most powerful baby ever I had met.

Lent came, time of fish not flesh. My father sent barrels of herring from Yarmouth, the best place to find the finest of them, to celebrate our son. They came to our table each night in pies, flavoured with ginger and pepper. The world was fasting yet I feasted, not on food, but love. I was become transformed. My heart, not willing to open for lover or husband, had been stolen by a man, by my son. God had graced my life with love, love that was safe, for it was for my own child.

I could have spent hours at his cradle, watching him, indeed if I had not business of the realm I would have. I would have fed him at my breast, but it was not considered normal. I had to endure the silent torture of watching another woman, albeit one I had chosen for her clean skin and fair hair, feed my child. When she was done it was all I could do not to snatch him from her, jealous of the time and intimacy shared.

Each night, Geoffrey and I went to our son. We stood over his cradle and looked from his eyes into each other's. I was reminded of my father, talking of himself and my mother; of how two people may find a bond like no other when they share a child, and therefore a destiny.

# Chapter Twenty-Six

## Rouen
## Normandy

### Summer - Autumn 1133

"He will be a fine man, a worthy knight, and a great King."

"All this you can foresee by the wrinkles on his forehead and spare hair on his head?" I smiled at my father. He was by the window, young Henry in his arms. Never had I seen my father look so sentimental, so vulnerable. It was interesting, as Henry was certainly not his only grandchild and hardly the first, yet his only of legitimate blood he was, and apparently already his favourite.

"You do not think your son destined for greatness?" My father turned, the sun at his back so he looked like a man of shadow, light hallowed about him, shining as past on future.

"Of course I do, I am his mother."

"And I his grandfather, so I too am allowed."

I straightened my back. After the strain of birth it had been sore and weak a long while, and the journey by carriage to Normandy so my father could meet the heir he had waited for so long had not aided matters. Sadly, my father had left Adeliza in England, a rare occurrence, and perhaps one that spoke of his confidence in the future. Always before he had kept Adeliza with him so they had a chance to make a child. Now, there was young Henry, so Adeliza was left behind.

"One of the advantages of being a woman," I said, "is that I may say anything and not prove it. Men are supposed beings of rationality and sense, and must prove things."

"He shall be his own proof," said my father.

A man of gold was my father as he stood before that window, sunlight at his back. I could barely see the babe in his arms, cloaked in shadow, but my father was light, golden and shining. No more did he seem old. His silver hair was lit up like fire, the brilliance behind him erasing lines upon his face drawn by sorrow and by happiness. It must have been how he had looked in youth, a time of his life that never had I known. Perhaps how he looked when he asked my mother to be his queen.

Sometimes it seemed that elements of the outer heavens moved with my father as the sun stood with him now. When he had left England to sail to Normandy and meet his grandson, darkness had fallen upon daylight. There had been an hour when the sun was obscured. Men had prayed and the world had fallen silent, as though if we all did not speak too loud it would call the sun from her hiding place. Perhaps it worked, for back the light came and with it came my father. We all are tied to elements of creation that help to shape our path. I was of water made, my father perhaps of light.

He was delighted with the child, my son of the north wind. Young Henry was hale and brash, his voice bold upon the air of the world, so already he was his father's son and grandfather's heir, but I caught a contemplative look in his eyes at times, a mind that would mature into cleverness and wit, and I thought there at least I was. I was, too, in his eyes.

I had thought young Henry had his father's eyes as he had Geoffrey's hair. Bright blue they were at birth, and that way I thought they would remain. No one had ever told me that the eyes of all babes are blue for the first weeks of life; that water is in all of us, the touch of God. Henry's eyes now were blue when at blue he looked, greenish when he looked at green. Grey and gold flecks lurked in the centre of his eyes, about the dark pupils. I knew because I spent a long time staring at him. My son had my eyes. What destiny had in store for me was also in him. It pleased me more than I could say that something of me was in my son; that there was a place for me in his future as well as his past. Although my son would be the one to take my throne and crown from me in the end, he and I shared, rather than competed for, our destiny. We were bonded by more than blood. As Will and I had shared a destiny, so did Henry and me.

"The barons are pleased?" I asked my father. "I have done my duty. There is a male heir. Do they now believe I am a woman, or do they think me a monster or aberration still?"

My father chuckled. "Many think you an aberration," he said. "And they are quite correct. No more outspoken a woman is there in this world than you."

"I have more to speak about, and more chance to talk than most women."

"And more daring," he said, but he said it with amused pride rather than censure. "Yes, they are pleased. The notion that the throne will pass to you as guardian is more comfortable to them. On the night word came of you and the child, I could feel hundreds of contented men sinking into chairs so their mistresses might feed them wine and take care of other hungers. A collective sigh went up all about England and Normandy. You have done well, daughter."

"But Geoffrey remains an issue."

"He has behaved badly?" Pink spots ignited in the flesh of my father's cheeks, as much, I suspected, for the notion that Geoffrey had gone back on his word to my father as for worry about me.

I shook my head. "He is another man, respectful, courteous. I barely know him. I mean he is an issue because men will expect him to play a part in England or Normandy, in their future, now that he is father to the heir."

"He is happy with the deal we struck when you went to Anjou."

"Which was?"

My father hesitated and I scowled.

"The dowry to be handed over, his rights in Anjou maintained, his son to inherit Anjou, and future talks about possession of Normandy to be held," my father reeled off.

"That does not seem like much," I said.

"It is not as much, certainly, as I expected." He hesitated again.

"You pause more today than ever I have seen," I said waspishly. "Should I suppose your mind is slowing in age?"

"I pause for I know not if what I am about to say is truth or not," he said. "This is theory, a thought alone, you understand?"

I inclined my head.

"I think he missed you. I think he wanted you back. The deals we made were superficial, little more than he had already, but I think he believed that without some conditions I would suspect much, and not send you back." He sniffed. "I think your husband wanted one thing more than anything."

"Which was?"

"You."

I looked away. Outside, great drops of rain had started to fall. Rain storms in summer always started with the largest drops. The sunlight darkened quick as a breath. And in the distance there rumbled thunder, the call of a monster left outside and alone too long.

*

"You fought often at the side of your brothers," I said to my father. "Did you never think to make lasting alliance, since you so often were brothers in arms?"

"Lasting alliance, loyalty…" my father's voice came from behind me, from the fire where he stood "… such things as these most men can only dream of."

"That is not encouraging, considering where we just came from."

We had just come from the great hall. As he had called on men of England to swear loyalty to me in the past, that day my father had brought barons of Normandy to do the same. Now I had a son, it was time. Now they knew they were swearing to me and to young Henry, not Geoffrey of hated Anjou, they would swear.

I was gazing across the town, into fields beyond. Summer was upon us in truth. Storms that had broken in the skies whilst young summer was unsteady had cleared and the air was high with the scent of horse dung and flowers, a pleasing combination. Honeysuckle was hanging, bobbing light and carefree in the breeze from doorways of cottages and cowsheds. It was often planted around borders between homes and outside, for on houses it was said to prevent fever and the entrance of those with ill-intent. On cowsheds it benefited cattle, keeping witches away and the sweet scent making cattle clement of nature and clean of milk.

Blossom was already beginning to desiccate on some trees and bushes. The skies were lit by moths bright as stars at night. Golden hordes of butterflies were in the forests, floating as spirits of dryads. Some days, there would be sight of a wash of yellow floating in the wind; flowers and trees releasing pollen, clouds of colour. The grass was alive with spiders, legs twitching and scuttling from the feet of people tending crops and hay. Weavers, were spiders, just as the three Fates who wove the cloth of destiny, just as women were supposed to weave peace.

Even from this high window I could see green on some roofs; house leeks, planted to deter lightning strikes and thunder. They also kept away pestilence, fire and war it was said. Charlemagne had sent out a decree some three hundred years ago, ordering all people in his Empire to plant them on roofs and about houses, because of the beneficial magic within them. The practice had spread to other kingdoms. Some planted them in patterns to increase their magical potency. Often the juice was used to treat burns and scalds, as well as bites of vermin, stings of wasps and bees.

It was wounds of other kinds my father had been telling me of. Time together, apparently, meant time for him to tell tales of old. Coming back to Normandy made this happen, the halls and roads he had walked as a young man whispering to him, speaking of battles fought, sieges endured. They all were here, waiting for him to return so they could flood into his memory. Telling stories to me was a way to unleash the river in his mind, stop memories drowning him. He had just been telling me more stories of him and his brothers, how they made pacts and broke them, how he had worked for Robert and Rufus by turns, climbing up to better, higher places in their trust.

"Live long enough, and enemies fall away." He nodded to me as I turned to him, the flickering amber of the fire reflected on his face. "That is the real test of life, how long you can stand it, how long you have the energy to keep walking your path, keep fighting. The things that are lasting are not what we think when we are young. Loyalty fades, sometimes quickly when men see the light of much gold. Love seems eternal, and yet it can die in a heart. But if you can endure, there is much in you that makes life worthwhile. There is satisfaction to be found in your own company."

"I do not fear solitude," I said. "In many ways, I prefer it. It is simpler to deal with one person than with many."

"The mark of a King," he chuckled. "Granted to our people we are, brought out to make war and wear crowns, give speeches and inspire men, and yet the longer one rules the more we ache for solitude, the solace of silence."

We were silent a moment. "It is time for me to go to my bed," he said. "I find, the older I get the earlier I must go to bed, and the earlier I rise."

"It happens to us all," I said.

"You are young, daughter, old though you may feel at times. You understand nothing of what is waiting; all the aching joints and bones that know when snow will fall. All the injuries that you thought had healed which come back to remind you of past pain."

"The aged think they possess all wisdom," I said. "But you are not the sole gatekeepers. Many of us know pain. Which of us have not been burned by life's fire?"

"Goodnight, daughter."

"Goodnight, Father."

*

Each day there were more lessons. At times my father seemed relaxed about the situation, as though he trusted me to know what I was doing now, and in the future. At others there was an impatient urgency to him. I think he felt the years keen, at times. There was also a precedent for disputed succession in England which I think he was keen to avoid. The Conqueror had claimed the throne King Harold had sat upon when the Confessor died. Rufus and Robert both claimed the throne when the Conqueror died, and Robert and my father did when Rufus died. The duchy of Normandy had, too, been contested in the same way in the time of my grandfather, who spent much of his early life fighting for his title, and in the time of his sons. And I was a woman due to inherit, at least for a short time, the thrones of his kingdom. Men might challenge me and disrupt my father's future plans, and he would not be present to smooth things out. There was much for his mind to worry about, but it seemed I was pleasing and impressing him. My memory was excellent, far better than his, and I learnt much from him. There were times he seemed most satisfied, but he was an impatient teacher, if a great one.

And yet, for all that he was pleased with, still the castles promised to Geoffrey were not handed over. This worried me. I would like to think my father wanted to protect me, and knew this was a hold over my husband which would control his behaviour towards me. It might have been that my father thought to wait until there certainly was a child born from our marriage, so the future was secured, our destinies aligned. But sadly, I think it was not any of those reasons. He was thinking of himself.

My father thought he might need those castles in the present. No matter that they were important to my future claim to the throne, indeed to my ability to hold Normandy upon his death, and therefore would be better possessed by me and by Geoffrey now. No, no matter. His hands were tight on them.

My father was not good at relinquishing control. He held on with the grip of bone and blood to anything that maintained his power. Other men he trusted, but not my husband. One man with that many castles in Normandy might think to make a move for the duchy. This was what my father suspected was in Geoffrey's mind.

I do not doubt the thought had occurred to my husband. In days long passed Geoffrey might have acted upon it. When we were first married he would have, without doubt. But I thought not now. I had seen Geoffrey's blue eyes, and they were as mine, on the future. Both staring through the adder-stone, we saw not our possession of Normandy or England, in truth. We saw our son.

Think not we had not goals all our own. The crown was in my mind for me, as it was for little Henry, but unlike my father who was coming to the end of a path in the wood, we were at the middle. My father was tarrying with the last few steps as we stood considering the route, the terrain, the direction. There was more in the future for us, more future for us, than there was for him. That scared him, perhaps more than anything. When we are scared we cling to things, as my father held on to his castles, a grip that only death would shift, it seemed.

*

At the end of summer, as autumn began to show off her new cape, as green woodpeckers sang in the forest, warning of rain, there were changes upon me. I went to Geoffrey's chamber. He was visiting Rouen to see Henry and me. "I am with child again," I said.

He smiled so wide I thought his face might crack in twain. "Your father, he is pleased?" he asked.

"I have not told him yet," I said.

There was a look, almost shy, upon my husband's face. It came from his eyes, spreading to his mouth, his cheeks. It was as light come from the first day of true spring when the air is warm and the sun bright, casting out the long, weary lowness of winter. Geoffrey knew by then that I had informed my father first when I was with child with Henry. This time, much had changed.

"I am delighted, my lady wife," he said.

We went out hunting often during those long months in Normandy, into forests where dappled light glinted, flickering across our eyes in shades of green and brown and gold. My father was a noted huntsman, some men even called him *Stag Foot*, for my father claimed he could tell how many branches rose from the antlers of a stag just by looking at its hoof print on the ground. What was annoying was that more often than not he got this right.

"It is because he sends his hunters out to find and view the stag the day before," Geoffrey laughed when I told him I had lost a wager against my father on a stag. "It is not magic."

"Fool am I to be so fooled," I said.

"You are his child, no matter if you are grown," Geoffrey said. "All children believe what their parents tell them, or want to."

Dawn was when we set out, having risen in the blue-darkness before night departed and day came. Past woodland settlements we went, past houses of wattle and daub with their small patches of land and garden from which they eked a living. Sometimes we would see people out working, gathering eggs or carrying pails of the last milk of the season. Once we saw men mending a wall; thieves had dug into the house in the night to steal a hog.

The huntsmen would be ahead, dogs on leashes as the quarry's trail was found. As we broke our fast on meat and cheese, oat biscuits and ale in a clearing, the fresh breeze of the morning rose delicious and sweet with scents of grass and leaf. Then on the trail of droppings we embarked, horses walking then charging through the forest paths, and on to the end, and death.

But hunting deer or boar was a summer event. As autumn rushed upon us, we went hawking.

My father had his gerfalcons, beasts permitted only to kings. In wetlands and marshes we flew our birds, their wings beating fast towards their prey; black arcs in the sky, dark shadows reflected upon the golden glitter of water below.

One day as we rode into a forest, I stopped my horse. Ground mist broke under his hooves, slipping away along the forest floor. The others flashed ahead, hooves racing, but I wanted a moment to be still. My father and his men would notice soon, perhaps return. One guard stopped with me, his task always to be at my side, prevent capture, kidnap, attack and rape.

The forest was not still, no forest is. Leaves rustled, twigs twitched. A light, warm wind swung through the trees, wafts buffing my skin, once, twice. The wind sang as ghosts in the trees, a choir whose song was just out of reach, and all the more beautiful for that distance, that strange mystery, like the laughter of children out of sight. They may be laughing at something cruel, children often do, but far away there is no hint of malice and so what may be cruel to the close-by ear, sounds like joy to the distant.

A blackbird hopped, beak full of leaves and mud for its nest, as wide-eyed and alert it paused at the edge of a glittering pond, watching for danger. The water was gold and silver, twinkling brighter than any gemstone under the faded light. Trees covered with ivy stood near, watching me as I watched them. Ivy does not kill, as some think. It clings to life upon the tree, looking for space, for a place to belong.

I stared at a tree, its branches lit with light trickling through the canopy above, the upper part of the branches gold and white, the lower dark green, black, as though it were two trees, one of light and one of dark. I wondered if, in the place the light and dark met there was chaos and confusion as there was where those elements met in me. Or if the one rested aside the other, content, finding the friend, the complementary opposite they long had sought, and now had found.

# Chapter Twenty-Seven

## Rouen
## Normandy

### Winter 1133 - Spring 1134

Snow was laced on the ground, such a light covering. What lay beneath could still be seen, each blade of grass and diamond-lit fleck of mud sparkling under pale skies. Men of the town had been talking that morning in markets and streets. They seen a white stag, they claimed, in the woods before dawn. The story had seeped person to person, inch by inch to the castle. People had crossed themselves. Some thought it an ill omen, a sign the otherworld was near. Death rode a pale horse and creatures white of coat had significance. Sight of a white stag meant borders were being transgressed between the world of man and of not man.

I picked at a plate of bread, and honey from the barrels in the stores, not without appetite, but with distraction. In tales I had been told as a child, a white stag was a sign of change, a time when the wind altered course, when life switches path. When my life had altered course often it had been momentous. I wondered for whom the stag had come, who it meant to warn or forewarn of coming change. I wondered how many would ignore it, only for change to fall, as so often it does, without warning.

My eyes strayed to a painting on the wall. Two knights jousted, one dark and one light, one night and one day. It was also supposed to represent the ongoing battle of female and male. You would think it a simple painting but the dark knight's shield held a sun and light's a moon. Each contained their opposite.

In the stability of normality we forget how easily things may alter, how quick everything we know might change. When war falls on a country people discover this. Pestilence, too, changes the world as we know it overnight. Where once there was peace and freedom then there is perpetual worry and death waiting at each corner, scythe raised. Where there were gentle things of the everyday, laundry, cooking, gathering or planting food, there comes hiding and running, staring into a dark abyss and wondering how it all changed so fast, how we did not see it coming. We forget how fragile the lives we live and the realities in which we exist are. We forget that they are fictions all, that what is normal is not normal; it was created by us, a story in which we may live happily, ignore the constant peril of the world. The lives we live are myths we build, day by day, bit by bit, to mask the fragility and feralness that life truly is made of. And when something comes, war or pestilence, and sweeps away those fictions, we find we are as vulnerable as any lone and injured hare, as any beast without burrow to flee to. It is too much to see all the time, so we tell stories. Our castles will keep us safe, our medicines will cure us, our friends always will be there; death cannot touch those we love because we love them.

Stories make living easier.

But when we look honestly at this feral, fragile existence, there are teachers everywhere. Every part of the world has a lesson to impart, every season has wisdom to share.

The lesson of winter is how to survive, but it is something else, too. Winter shows that there may be beauty in destruction, fortitude found in times of spare hope. It shows there *is* hope, even when we think there is not. Trees, earth, they seem stripped of all life, bare and naked white bone and black twig, yet when the sun shines we see there is life, waiting. Life burns, hidden, just beneath the surface of snow and ice. The same is true of us, many times in life. There is potential there, there is change, possibility waiting for a chance to be freed so it may become what it will become. Through times of loss and being lost we come, life burning in us, waiting for the end of winter and the first sweet breath of spring.

Because there *is* beauty in winter, in death, in darkness, and there is in life, in this filthy world of such disenchantment still there is grace, goodness. We make darkness all our own just as we create light. We are creatures of hope, hope to succeed, hope to prevail. In wild, stark winters we sit waiting at glowing fires, telling tales of heroes. In ripe, lush autumns we gather food, store it, and prepare for the future. We do this because we hope, because we want to survive. And we hope for other things; to face our trials and grow stronger, face demons and learn from their darkness. We hope to live full, whole, unafraid. We hope there is love, peace to be found and joy, those unexpected moments, waiting.

That is what I thought of on the day I heard of the stag. Some feared change, feared their normal being disrupted and perhaps they were right to. But each time change had come to me, painful though many of those changes had been, they had set my life on the course it was now, and now I had a son. However much pain there was for me in change, in life, there had been a reward so great that it counterbalanced all I had suffered. I would suffer again, more, for my Henry. I understood the price of joy now. And I would pay it, willingly.

*

As we tumbled through the winter of 1134 and into its spring, the world seemed beset by tribulation. Change had come and perhaps those who crossed themselves to ward it off had been right, for all seemed bad. The winter brought such snow it seemed the rest of the world had vanished and all there was, was Rouen. A few paces from the castle and there was nothing but white, blinding and drifting, at once still and in motion. It made me dizzy to gaze into the storm too long.

My father groaned over letters on livestock from England. A plague upon pigs, cattle and sheep had swept through the kingdom two years before, making meat expensive, for few beasts survived. Heaps of burning animals were lit all over England that year and two years on the stocks had not replenished. Adeliza wrote that some feared the plague was not gone, for signs as spring came were that it might strike again. Sometimes I saw my father look at a missive from England and a nerve twitched in his eye. He might not reach for it for a long time.

As spring arrived there were floods and fires. It seemed odd that we could have the two together yet they came, hand in hand. A great fire broke out at Le Mans, started by an accident and not taken seriously at first for the roofs were thought too wet. They were not. When the fire reached a high temperature, it bounded thatch to thatch like a sprightly demon and only grappling houses to the ground made any impact. There were more fires that year in Chartres, Alençon, Verneuil and Nogent. A spate came, as though someone had annoyed a wyrm of fire, who breathed doom on cities of man.

My father had decided to remain in Normandy when he learned I was with child. "There is no sense rushing back to England only to have to return in a few months," he had said. "Your brother Robert, and Roger, Bishop of Salisbury can keep the strings of government in hand."

"You do not have to be here for the birth," I said, my fingers touching the jewelled girdle at my thickening waist.

"I wish to see my granddaughter," he told me.

"And you know I carry a girl this time?"

"It would be a good thing to have one of each," he said, "as your mother and I did. You have gone the other way around, but I think you and I follow the same ways, the same fate."

"Let us pray that is not the truth," I said, lifting a hand to cross myself and ward off his curse.

"I mean not I think Henry would die young," he said, playing with a chain of gold about his shoulders. "But I come to think sometimes that you are here to make right what went wrong with me, with our family before this. Will's death was an accident, but some said it was a curse and perhaps it was, perhaps I was punished for my acts of the past. But now, with you, with young Henry, God shows that any such curse is lifted. Will I think at times was my penance for taking a throne from my brother, locking him away. Yet God was merciful. The way is made right again, through my first born child."

"You think I am the antidote to a curse," I said. "An interesting notion, lord father."

"Women often remedy a man's sin," he said. "No matter what men of the Church say, I think it is often the case."

He stopped. He was thinking of my mother. I could see her in his eyes.

As I waited to bring life into the world again, we heard of a death. In isolation in his prison in Cardiff Castle, my uncle Curthose died.

"Woe to me that is not old enough to die," my father said when I came to him on the morning the news reached us.

"You have become poetic in old age," I observed, frowning.

"Lines my brother wrote," he said, staring from the window, "not me."

"You read the poems of Curthose?" I was surprised, perhaps more than I should have been. I knew Curthose wrote poetry in captivity, but I did not know my father read it. Rare had been the times my father mentioned his brother's fate. Robert was there in stories of youth, of course, but of his imprisonment, those long years of isolation where Curthose had done all he could to stay sane whilst locked away, my father had always said little. I had supposed he had tried not to think of him, Robert, that force of misguided energy. If he had read the poetry penned by his lonesome brother, this was not the case.

"I did," he said, looking to me, offering a smile that was more sad than anything. "I think he wanted me to, so I would know what I did to him. I took much from him and although that could not have been helped considering the danger he posed to me, to my throne, I could do this for him. I could read what he had written, so he would be speaking to one person in the world, so he had a connection still to life."

It was a curiously thoughtful act for my father. What was stranger still was that he had memorised lines. But my father was a surprising man, many men are. They seem so easy to read that it is a simple thing to underestimate them. When creatures are taught to hide much of their emotion, besides anger, which always men are permitted to express, there is much hiding beneath the surface.

"You regret not freeing him, now he is gone to God?" I asked, sitting beside my father at the window. Curthose had lived to a great age, teetering on the edge of eighty years when he died. I wondered if my father thought he himself would last so long. If he did, young Henry could take the throne without it ever having to pass to me.

"No. I regret that his imprisonment had to happen," he said. "I do not regret my choice to make it happen." He smiled, putting his hand on mine. "As age creeps upon you, when I die and you take my place, you may find this too," he said. "That we know we cannot change what was, that we believe we made the right choice, but the regret and sadness we feel does not lessen for knowing those things. There is much I regret, much I pray to be forgiven for, yet many of those sins I ask to be forgiven are sins I know I could not have avoided, not if I was to survive, not if those I love were to."

I wondered not for the first or last time if one of those sins was murdering Rufus, as well as imprisoning Curthose.

"I wish it were possible that you could have seen him as a youth," my father said. "Robert was a man of charisma. We all fell for him a little, we who were younger. Always there was something of the fool about him. He had not Richard's calm, that collected grace and wisdom our other elder brother possessed. And he had not Rufus's fire and determination, but Robert was a man like our father in one important respect. Where he led, men would follow, and often to their detriment and death."

"You inherited that too," I said.

"That is what you see in me, is it?" he asked, affection on his face. "Detriment and death?"

"I see in you a creature born to survive," I said. "And I mean that in the best way. You have lived long and suffered much, had to start again and start out with little, and it did not stop you. Perhaps it could not. There are some who fall into fate and what it decrees, and some who shape destiny to their own demands. You are one of those men."

"I think you and I are more alike than we like to think," he said. "For I see that, too, in you."

"Those who cannot go on fall to the wayside," I said. "Perhaps they find peace. Then there are those of us who know not what else to do but get up, continuing walking, no matter how slow the pace."

"Our ancestors were Viking," he said. "Men who had their eyes on other horizons than the one they stood under."

"And women too," I added.

He patted my hand, and it remained upon the soft top of my hand. "Without women," he said. "Man would be nothing."

Days later my father told me he had sent instructions for Curthose to be buried in a tomb in St Peter's Abbey, in Gloucester. Robert was to be buried with the honour due to his rank as a prince of England and lord of Normandy, and as a crusader.

His tomb would be painted and on it would be the effigy of a knight. Curthose had died an old and broken man, his dreams gone and his son dead before he could know any true glory, but if a stranger looked upon his tomb they would not know that. They would see a man who died a knight, a warrior. They would see the eldest son of the Conqueror frozen at the most lauded moment of his life, when he had vanquished the foes of God in the Holy Lands. Perhaps they would see him as my father always remembered him; as a young man awash with fire and ambition and possibility, about to ride out and challenge the world.

And on Robert's tomb there burned candles, as there did on my mother's tomb. They were paid for by my father, and kept there by his coin. A light would burn on his brother's grave for the rest of my father's life, and beyond.

# Chapter Twenty-Eight

## Rouen
## Normandy

## Spring 1134

"I cannot," I wheezed, my voice a whisper, hoarse and low. There was blackness before my eyes. It was a more welcome place than the one I was in. The dark was soothing. There was peace there. Here there was only pain and bright, glaring light. There was only noise and agony. I did not want to be here. I wanted cool dark water to cover me. In the darkness I could hear my brother, calling, telling me all would be well, it would hurt no more if I went to him.

I was dying.

"Please, my lady," said a fraught, tearful and terrified voice. "*Please*, you must push. If you do not you will surely die, and the child."

My child... my mind was wandering. I had forgotten. The pain... that was why there was pain, why I was so tired. I had forgotten the hours, the minutes, days I had toiled. I was in labour and had been a long time. My strength was almost spent. The child was stuck inside me. My daughter would die without ever having lived. I would go with her. We would join my brother, be at peace. It would be better there, in that cool darkness, in that bliss. Here was too much of pain and suffering. "I cannot," I whispered.

I could hear women praying, asking Saint Margaret to save me. I choked, my body throwing me upright as they tried to pour vinegar and sugar water down my throat. It was supposed to aid me, it almost made me drown.

"Hold her up," said a voice.

Hands took hold of my shoulders. I lolled like a doll made of grain, the pouches for arms and neck stuffed too thin.

"Push, Domina," said a voice. "Please, Domina, push." It was Ermengarde.

I could do nothing. My head fell against a shoulder. A weak noise came from my mouth. "There is nothing left in her," said someone behind me. "Can you find an arm? The head? Something to bless with water so the soul of the child will not be lost?"

"She is not going to die!" cried another.

"She is. If she cannot get the babe out and we cannot either, they both will die and the child is unbaptised. To limbo it will go."

It was all so far away, but although the darkness reached for me with soothing arms, I knew to fall into them would be to abandon my child not only to death, but to eternal limbo. She had not been baptised, not unless they had managed to get an arm or part of the head from my body. Without skin to bless with water, my child would be lost to the sight of God. I would go to Heaven. I had been baptised. My child would be lost, my daughter floating between worlds. I could not allow that to happen. I could not let her fall into a world between worlds, where I had always felt I stood. Not an innocent soul like her.

I pulled all that was left of me into my heart. I sat up. I heaved against the pain again, pushing with all I had. Something tore. I felt a warm rush of blood pouring down my legs. Into the dark I almost fell again, but pain held me back.

"Not so hard, Domina!" shouted a woman. I knew not whom.

"Hush your mouth, fool!" said another, a floating voice. "The child must come now. Damage we can deal with, wounds mend. The child must come out or they both die. The Countess knows this!"

Again and again I pushed, my slippery hands awash with sweat and blood clasping those of the women trying to aid me. Dimly I could hear them talking of using hooks to grapple the baby, pull her from me. It would kill her, but might save me.

"Do not," I croaked. "Do not kill my baby, my little girl."

"She may be dead already, Domina."

"You do not know that."

Another hour, how I lasted another hour I know not. And then out my child came, miraculously alive.

"A son, my lady!" someone called.

I did not hear more than the first word. Into darkness I fell, gratefully.

*

"I wish to be buried in the chapel at the Abbey of Bec," I said again weakly.

"Your father will not allow it, Domina," said the frightened voice. "He says you must be buried in Rouen, with your royal kin."

Anger made me open my eyes. I could not move my head, or body, but somehow although I could not move, my father always could move rage inside me. "This is my last wish. Do I not have the choice of where my earthly remains lie?"

I had already made provision as to where my goods would go. Most would be left to Geoffrey and my sons, and some choice items to my ladies and those who toiled so hard to save my life. Those poor women. So long they had worked. They had saved my child, saved my life in the chamber of birth, but I was slipping away slowly now. I was still on the verge of death.

I had left money for the completion of a large stone bridge I was building over the Seine, in Rouen, and I had ordered that much of my money was to go to religious houses, to Bec more than anywhere. I wanted the monks of Bec to pray for me. I believed them most devout of all men of God I knew, and thought my soul would be safe in their hands.

But my father, since he had always had power over me in life, thought it was his right to have dominion over my death. Choice he thought to steal from my hands. Even in death I was not to rest in peace where I wanted, but where he wanted me. Was nothing ever to be mine? Was I never to know a moment of freedom?

It was days after the birth. I did not have a daughter as my father had predicted. Oddly I had believed him without question. Yet questioned him I should have, for I had a second son.

They had brought my baby to me, but I had passed from consciousness the moment I saw a glimpse of his eyes. I had not held my child once. It would have been dangerous to put a newborn into the arms of a near-corpse.

For what felt like days I had only caught glimpses of the chamber in which I lay. They forced potions of root of rock parsley and leek down my throat, slick with oil, and rubbed vinegar on my source of life. They were trying to draw out the afterbirth. They thought it had not all come from me, making me sick.

I saw them take bloodstained sheets to burn. "The Empress will not stop bleeding," I heard Ermengarde say as she pressed pads to my source of life, as other women held me up to make me drink. I moaned as down my throat bitter potions poured, then there was sweet treacle, good for dampening burning blood. I winced but did not flinch as stinging wads of herbs, agrimony and betony, were pressed to me, trying to stem the bleeding.

And then fell fever. Hot and feral was my mind, my dreams vivid yet confused. I screamed and fought my covers, then collapsed a moment later, exhausted. I allowed demons to tear my skin from my body and monsters to suck my eyeballs. I tried to fight at times but at others I surrendered. I had not the will to struggle on.

I smelt henbane smoke, there to relieve my pain, then afterbirth burning in the fire; they said it had taken long to come from me, and would kill me if it stayed inside. On the hot chamber air floated soot and blood, ash and flesh, as the pyres of our ancestors must have smelt upon the foreland, smoke drifting off over the sea.

And the sea, the sea was in my dreams as between life and death, slumber and waking I passed. I knew not where I was, but as fire fell from me, as I was burned on that pyre, it felt like water had come. A soothing darkness tumbled over me. I had been destroyed, through fire I had passed, on that shore I had been lit and my body had burned, and then into water I had been pushed.

*"Bid brothers of battle build me a tomb, after my pyre has fallen to ash, on the foreland by the sea, that shall linger as a reminder of me to my people, looming high on the horizon at Hronesness, so those upon the waves under sail shall afterwards name it Beowulf's barrow..."*

Part of me was upon the sea, ashes floating on the surface, a ghost of myself tumbling in the rolling water. It was cool, and dark and wonderful. There was no distinct sound, no noise of the busy, careless world. Over my ears flowed bubbles and water, weed like silk caressed my hands, my cheeks.

I was in the throat of the world, perhaps the belly, ready to pass to the womb. I would rest where I had been born, bones reaching out through the earth to take hands with Heinrich. I was ended, and yet this was not the end. In the darkness of that water there was more.

I had woken dry of mouth, vacant of mind, staring at people in the chamber. It took me a moment to understand I *was* awake, that this was not a dream. The water had felt more real than this moment of waking did. I blinked and let out a slight groan from broken, parched lips. A head, fallen at my side upon the bed, darted up.

Geoffrey.

White as wave froth was he. "She is awake!" he shouted to people behind him. Suddenly there were many faces and more hands, all prodding. I tried to bat them away but I could barely move. My mind recalled the freedom of the water and mourned it. There all had been easy, here it was hard. That is often the way; death is easy, life a struggle.

"Tend to her!" Geoffrey commanded, his voice snarling, biting. "Make the Empress well or deal with me!"

I stared at him. It had been a long time since we had been enemies, but the fraught concern in his voice and upon his face was sincere. He was terrified I would die.

I thought it strange, and stranger still when I was told he had been there all the time I had been sick, waiting for me to wake. Only for brief moments had he gone elsewhere, to see our sons, check our new baby, named for him, was well. It made me think he cared for me, for my own sake. He had an heir and a spare now. Although there was some argument that without me young Henry's claim to the throne was more fragile, as there was a link missing and few wanted Geoffrey to become the metal that bonded young Henry to the English crown, it seemed my husband was in fact concerned for *me*, for *my* life. He did not want to lose me.

Women held me up, made me drink tea of ground elder and feverfew to control the flames in my blood and purify me. Doctors fed me barley broth to cool the fire inside me, and cut my veins to let my blood, to take away excess humour in the brain. They wanted to slice my nose at the ridge, but Geoffrey made them try a lower point where I would not scar. I ate potion of plantain and knotgrass with dragon's blood, which they said would stem the remaining bleeding. More dragon's blood, an expensive treatment, was applied to pads and put between my legs.

I heard Geoffrey had argued with my father. My father had insisted I lie in Rouen Cathedral. Geoffrey had told my father my wishes would be fulfilled.

It seemed the man who once cared only for thwarting me was the only one willing to carry out my wishes.

*

I woke again, ate a little broth. Geoffrey sent men to the chapels to ring bells and let Anjou know her Countess was awake, and recovering.

But when I woke, amid rejoicing there was warning. One of the doctors whispered to Geoffrey. He and others thought this was a moment often granted by God; a person near death would wake for a while, a few hours, perhaps a few days, and afterwards would sicken and die. This time should be used he said, to set my affairs in order, for me to confess, receive the last rites whilst I could answer properly. Remembering that Heinrich had only been able to blink in response, I agreed. I said again I wanted to be buried at Bec, but my father did not agree.

"You are an heir of the English throne and that of Normandy!" he shouted in my sickroom. "You are royal, and will be buried with royalty!"

He sounded furious, but there was a glint of calculation in his eyes. I knew what he was up to. My father thought to tug me into life using rope of anger, a harness he would set about my shoulders and pull me into life with. I closed my eyes. Eventually he went away. As I heard his steps leaving the chamber, rushes rustling on leather, I found I did not care anymore. I was too tired. I felt there was no blood in me. I felt every weak pulse of my heart. It had had too much. It was time to fall at the wayside. Others would carry on, I could not. My child was safe. I was risking not his soul. I would die, finally I would know peace.

Let them lay me where they wanted. I knew where my soul would go. To that shore where the boat I had laid my brother into in my dreams waited. To that sea where the dragon spirit of Clito flew in the skies. Was Curthose there now, too? Would those men, my kin, build me a barrow upon the shore, burn me and place my ashes in a tomb as often I had dreamed, or would I be put to the sea like my brother? Would I fly as Clito or swim as selkie?

Would I find my mother on the sands, waiting for me? My grandmother, my grandfather, Bruno too? Would I swim in the sea, a creature of water in death as I had been in life? I knew not what destiny death had in mind and I did not care. All were enticing. I could feel salt breeze on my cheeks, feel the memory of winter wind and snow biting my flesh. I could feel the heaving waves and the sighing sea rushing, hissing, up those sands towards me, lusting to touch me, to draw me to it. I wanted that embrace of cold and comfort as no other thing in the world, or so I thought.

"You cannot die," said a voice.

I opened my eyes. It was dark in the chamber, a fire glowing in the hearth the only light. Geoffrey was watching me, his bright blue eyes both dark and brilliant in the dim light. "You cannot die," he said again. "You said you came back for duty, not love, but both of those callings are here, and you swore to uphold them.

"They need you," he said. "Our sons, for duty and for love, they need you. Without you, what do they become? Without you, they may perish in this world, destiny unfulfilled, lives empty. A mother always you wanted to be, and now you are one. Be their mother. Do not die."

I closed my eyes, too weak to answer, but when the sound came washing to me in sweet dreams, I turned my head from the call of the sea.

# Chapter Twenty-Nine

## Rouen
## Normandy

## Summer - Autumn 1134

"Finally may I boast of something other men take for granted," my husband said. He was by the window of the chamber in which I was sitting, eating an apple, one leg up on the stone sill, looking carefree and bold. The scent of lavender from outside where it lined field edges wafted into the chamber, rushing to cleanse the air. Distantly there was a sound of singing, people cutting the first of the hay with scythes in the fields. If I could from the window gaze, I would see flashes of white and silver light as blades swung, catching the sun, looking effortless, as through crisp, golden stalks they slashed, preparing for winter.

I breathed in the lavender perfume. "Which is?"

"That my wife listened to me, and what is more miraculous, obeyed."

I laughed. Geoffrey cast me a wry grin and took another bite of apple. There was victory in that bite, a lust of life, pleasure in the taste of present. We had reason to be merry, light with each other as friends may be when times are clement and the Fates are kind. Summer was rich and hot outside, and I was alive. What more can one ask than to be alive? At times when we take life for granted, when people have not seen the shadow of death, it is easy to want more. When you have recently brushed so close to death that you smelt the corpse of your own future, life is more than enough.

I was alive, blessed. I had two sons, a husband who was my good friend and had fought for me against my father. I had a future, something I had thought lost until not long ago. Long had been my recovery, and bitter fought each scrap of strength returning. It had been exhausting to recover from exhaustion. I had been weak as a newborn mouse, but not as blind. For the second time in life I had escaped death.

Twice I had survived. Men on a field of battle might have done worse. I was not only fortunate, God had smiled upon me, offered mercy, allowed me to return that I might live, be a mother. There would be other wishes, more to ask, for I was human and therefore insatiable, but for now I was content.

In sickness I had passed through the last days of May. As fae were out and about grooming the beards of goats and working magic, I had sipped broth and been fed capon, rice, and herbs upon herbs. As I was bled and ate restoratives to flush out poisons and spirits that had made me sick, I had missed women clasping their fists about thumbs to ward off demons, and common folk scattering primroses about their houses to fend fae off. I had slept through many days and missed cups and plates being stolen by spirits of other realms, made more powerful in the month of May. Through much of magic and life had I slept, but I was alive as was my child. My second son had been named Geoffrey for his father. We had agreed this before I went into my rooms to prepare for the birth, for if this child was a son he would be heir to Anjou as young Henry inherited England and Normandy after me. It was fitting the heir of Anjou have an Angevin name, and I wanted my second son to be named for my second husband, as the first had been for the first. I felt I owed Geoffrey that much. If Heinrich had been honoured, so should Geoffrey be.

Had I borne a girl, she would have been named Matilda, for me and for my mother, but my father had been wrong. Another son had been waiting to be born, not a daughter.

Whilst I was sick my second son could not come near me and my people had taken care of my poor little boy. My young Geoffrey had been taken down stairs before up, for luck, when he was born. Whilst I had been insensible after the birth, my breasts had been covered in nettle and cabbage leaves to drain the milk I had not the strength to offer my child. My women had taken care not to bind me tight, so I would not suffer the same fate as Sybil of Flanders. And care had been taken with young Geoffrey. He was special in ways other than his destiny within Anjou.

This boy, born in the chime hours, would be able to see the dead if he chose, they said, and would never be bewitched, for the time of his birth protected him.

Through June I had slept, sometimes tottered about, but still I was in my bed a great deal. As hot winds blew through the castle, I was more often asleep than awake, but I was almost ready to leave my bed. Indeed, I was as sick of my chamber as I had been in body after Geoffrey's birth.

Another Geoffrey, now the elder of the family, turned to me, throwing his apple core from the window so it bounced down the sloping sides of the castle below and plopped into the moat. "I shall not become accustomed to you obeying me," he said, his grin infectious. "I understand the circumstances were exceptional."

"I promised to obey when we married," I agreed. "I did not specify how often."

Geoffrey laughed; a pleasing sound. Since I had indeed obeyed him and not died, my recovery had been slow but steady enough to please all. My father claimed credit, of course, putting it all down to his refusal to allow my bones to lie where I wanted them. But it was not due to him that I had survived. Geoffrey had reminded me, at a time I needed it most, what was most precious to me here, in life. He had bonded me to it, so I was tied as a rope to a stake. It was just in time. That which I had treasured and lost had been calling; siren song of ghosts upon the winds of death. The voices of those I loved and were gone might well have carried me away had Geoffrey not reminded me of my children.

Since I had awoken, two days after the night I had found him talking at my bedside, there had settled something between us. I feared him no more. I found I trusted him. It had been creeping upon me for some time, but his words of intervention at a desperate time secured it. When I first returned to Anjou, he had said I would need proof, and I believed I now had that. Geoffrey was indeed my husband. We had not love, but there was a bond.

Something like friendship had come to me, a tenderness towards him, and gratitude. It could be said he owed much to me, but I knew that I owed life to him. My husband, the boy I had despised, the man I had feared and hated, had become my saviour. The twists of life are strange, yet sometimes wondrous.

I do not mean that I loved him, nor ever would, but I looked on Geoffrey now not as before. And that was why, when I rose from my sickbed in the dog days of summer when Sirius rose and set with the sun, and when the argument about my dowry, those castles long ago promised and never delivered arose anew, I did not defend my father. This time, I sided with my husband. I joined him in an attack on my father to get what was promised delivered.

Both men were shocked. To my father, I had so long been his tool that to find me working for another was unthinkable. That I was suddenly in support of him over my father was almost inconceivable for Geoffrey.

"The castles were promised as my dowry," I said. "They must be put into the hands of my husband. It is a slight upon Anjou, upon Geoffrey and on your honour, Father, that this has not happened already. It calls into question our marriage, in some ways, for the deal brokered has not been upheld."

"Those castles will be valuable to your sons, in time," he said.

I narrowed my eyes. "And in the meantime, their father can be custodian of their inheritance," I said. "If you were waiting for there to be an heir, there now are two. My husband and I are working for the future of our sons, and ourselves, lord father, and you are standing in the way. If I hold no possession in Normandy, no castles, no defences, then when the time comes I and my sons will be vulnerable. My husband is a proved knight, a leader of men. With him in possession of those castles our claim to Normandy can be secured, as will the future of my claim to the throne. Without those castles, when the time comes we will have to stake a claim without having a secure foot in Normandy. For the sake of holding on to the present you would make the future, my future and that of my sons, insecure."

"You would trust *him* now?" my father asked, gesturing at Geoffrey who stood looking as though he might not so much draw sword and strike my father, but might bite instead, like a dog. Holding back his rage, stiff with pride that was deserved, Geoffrey looked a man in truth. "This boy you would trust with castles in Normandy?" Father went on.

"I trust the man I married," I said. "The Count of Anjou will keep faith with you, as he will secure the future for our sons."

I could feel pride radiating from Geoffrey, rich and strong as the anger in him. "If you will not hand over those castles," I went on, "then your barons must swear an oath of fealty to Geoffrey and to me, in lieu of the properties. They occupy something that belongs to us, therefore as any lord who occupies land or property of another, must swear themselves our vassals."

I thought my father might explode. My demand, although reasonable, would make Geoffrey and me overlords in Normandy, on a par at least equal with my father. Raising equals was not something he was keen to do, which I understood, but without a scrap of England in my hands, without a crowning ceremony as heir, without any hold in Normandy, I was left vulnerable upon the death of my father, as were my sons. I had to have some hold on Normandy or England, or when the time came I might find myself fighting to gain control of any land or castle. My father's terror of sharing power was making my future insecure, weak, and he was placing all faith of future upon the word of men, a string all too easy to break.

"If you will not allow the Norman barons to swear," I said. "Then you must. As overlord of Normandy, but one who owns property which belongs to us, you must swear fealty, thereby binding your vassals to us."

Father appeared lost for words, or perhaps there were too many fighting to burst from his mouth all at once. It was, however, a way to secure a peaceful transmission of power. Father had to see that he needed to honour me and my sons, as well as Geoffrey, within his lifetime, or when his life was spent we would struggle to gain our rightful places.

"I will place your brother, Robert, in command of Dover," he said. "That should assure you, for if he holds that port you can land and claim England with ease."

"That is not enough," I said. "Why do you fear me? Is it that you cannot bear to think of the future, not because you will be gone from it, but because in that future you will have no control? If I am your heir, Father, then you must acknowledge me as such. Let go these castles, put them into our hands, secure our future and you will see that we are friend not foe. We are all now working for a future where young Henry takes the throne, when he is of an age to. Work with us, with me. Do not stand opposed."

"I will have no man sworn to me swear himself to you," he said. "And the idea I would, I! King of England and Duke of Normandy, would do such a thing is *obscene*."

"To other men you have sworn fealty," I pointed out. "To Louis of Francia you have sworn yourself in the past, for the throne of Normandy. So why will you not to me? Because I am your daughter, your heir, or because I am a woman?"

"Because it would dishonour me."

"You will hand over those castles, have your men swear or you will swear," I said. "And you will, as a sign of good faith, release the castles of William Talvas back into his hands." Talvas was one of Geoffrey's vassals. My father had taken possession of some of the castles which belonged to his father, a notorious rebel lord who once had sheltered Clito. Talvas's father had died in goal, and Geoffrey wanted his castles to revert to the son.

"We will talk of this at another time, when you are in possession of a more clement spirit!" my father shouted.

"You are the one screaming, lord father," I said. "I am perfectly composed. I admit to anger, but not loss of senses, or wit."

"You are furious!" he shouted. "I see it upon you."

"Then after my father I take," I said coolly. "Men are permitted anger and women are not? What fools are they who think such! My anger has purpose and control, therefore is not useless or dangerous or squandered as yours is. You cling to those castles not for any good reason, but because you cannot let go, cannot allow us to climb to be seen as your equals in power. Those castles would secure my smooth succession in Normandy and therefore that of your grandson, but you will not relinquish control to aid another, even for me, even for the grandsons you claim to love."

"I do love them!"

Of course I believed him, but I shook my head and left. Geoffrey came after me. "You should not alienate your father," he said. It was not a command, but advice, as all his words were in those days. "He might name another heir."

"And cut young Henry from the throne?" I asked, stopping in the narrow, dim corridor to look at him. The scent of wet stone was in my nose. "I think not. My father would rather die. Our son is in his heart. You never met Will, or saw my father's eyes when he looked upon him. When my father looks at Henry, he sees Will. A ghost of love is hard to stand against. It takes more power, more strength than ever my father will possess to refuse the love he has for our son. It is an echo of his son, a distant call of a love he lost and has missed every day since."

"As you loved the Emperor."

I hesitated, for there was a catch in his voice, but it did no good to be dishonest with Geoffrey, not if we were to work together. "I think at times there is nothing more powerful than love lost," I said. "Nothing more powerful than the bond between us and the dead. How can the living compete with love of long ago? Each day it is absent it becomes more perfect in our minds."

"How do the living compete with the dead, for the love of others?" he asked, almost to himself.

I shook my shoulders back. "Father will surrender, in the end," I said. "He will have to. He can do *homage en marche*, acknowledge our overlordship upon the borders of Normandy and that can be done without loss of authority. He will come to see the truth of all I have said. He is leaving us and the future of our house insecure by his stubborn refusal to cede even the smallest amount of power. He is not a fool, though he may act like one at times. He will surrender."

Even as I said it, I wondered.

Geoffrey nodded. "Thank you, for supporting me in this matter."

"You are the father of my sons," I said. "Whom else should I support?"

Geoffrey laughed, a short laugh, but a good one. "It is good you are on my side."

It was more than a simple matter of sides, than our pact, more than our sons. It was more than my father trying to bury my bones somewhere I did not want to lie when I had thought I was to die.

The reason I stood against my father and with my husband was many things, as it was one. It was indeed my future claim and the security of my son's inheritance, the dishonour being done to Geoffrey and to me, but other reasons ran older and deeper, more personal. It was a moment in childhood where my father had come to the chamber where Will and I were sitting. I was before our father as he entered, yet his eyes had gone straight past me to my brother. Little as I resented my brother to be loved, I resented that I was not loved as he was by our father. In death, Will had become the perfect heir, the perfect King. I would always be defective, always the second choice, not just because I was a woman, but because I was too like my father. He trusted me so far, and no further. He could not surrender a small part of his present to secure my future. In so many ways, he was still looking past me.

That was why he was able to use me, to bargain with me, to see me as a stepping stone. I think I was loved, at times, by my father, but more often I was something to use. But if I had been that before to Geoffrey I was not now. In gratitude for being seen as more than that, I became loyal to him.

As a lord takes to a knee and swears fealty to another, so we had sworn to one another. We had found a place where our kingdoms, our interests, met; in our sons. For them we were united, a bond neither of us would break. We had made peace at the borders of our souls.

And I was content. Without the burden of love pulling at me I was freer than ever I had been in my life. Unshackled to a man, I was myself. My sons could claim me, no other man could or would. Some will think that an empty life, but it felt not so. I had loved, I loved, but where I loved I was careful. My heart had learned caution, my head sense. What was important was my sons. I knew why Melusine took her youngest sons with her and left her elder. The elder had the destiny all wanted. Sometimes I wondered what she had done with the younger, taught them magic? Let them loose upon the world as sorcerers? Perhaps even now they stand in Avalon, with her, looking back upon the world of man through the mists that surround that lost isle in the marshes.

Melusine could not grant all her sons the life they needed in the world of men, so she took two with her. I would do better. I would make this world bow to my sons.

And the world would start with one man. My father.

# Chapter Thirty

## Rouen and Le Mans
## Normandy

### Winter 1134 - Spring 1135

You might think that we would have left Normandy after that argument, but I did not. I stayed, and Geoffrey left. I stayed to argue with my father and I knew I would have more success if it was between me and him. We had been practising long, after all.

Geoffrey went back to Anjou to make other preparations, just in case, and I stayed on to begin the fight to make my father see reason. My uncle David seemed to be aiding me, perhaps without knowing it, as we had word that he had captured the rebels who had risen against him. After a few years of hard fighting, David captured his nephew Mael Coluim, and with him so fell the rebellion. *"It demonstrates the high worth of a loyal family to the reigning King,"* David wrote in a letter to me and my father. *"For what troubles cannot be created by those who share blood and are not loyal?"*

I hoped my father was listening.

As well as arguing with my father about castles, fealty and rights he should be granting now rather than leaving us to scrabble for later, I brought Henry and Geoffrey to him. They were the soft edge of my argument. If my anger and fear could not move him, I hoped my sons could.

Watching my father with my sons was something akin to my heart breaking and mending in the same sweet-bitter moment of pain and joy. To watch him jiggle little Geoffrey up and down, take young Henry in his arms, was as a balm to every moment of hurt that always being second in the eyes of my father had caused, yet it cut me again too, for although these were my sons, the same thing was happening again. I was being passed over for a male heir.

I was as a second where a person holds their breath before starting to talk, a necessary but unwanted moment of silence before the chatter of men broke upon the stage once more.

This was the second time this had happened to me. Should that have made the pain easier to bear, or harder? Before, my brother had been the one my father waited for. I was born first, yet was less important, and now I was less important than a child who knew nothing of the world. Had Henry not been my son, had I not wanted greatness for him too, perhaps stronger resentment would have come to me. My feelings for my son were pure and uncomplicated. I am sure most parents understand the sharp silver dart that is their love for their offspring. I wanted the best for my children, wanted Henry to take the throne. But towards my father my feelings were mixed, as always they had been. I resented that I was not enough, could never be enough on my own. I wanted my turn on the throne to be more than just a waiting game until something better, and therefore male, came along.

My father, naturally, did not need to know that I intended to be more than a guardian. The notion that I intended to rule and demonstrate I could rule well might disturb him, perhaps make him consider a new guardian, like Robert. But I was becoming increasingly sure not only that I could rule, but that I wanted to. I had noted much over the course of the years, changes that could be made in the system of justice, in trade, that I meant to put into practice when I became Queen. I meant to rule, not just hold England and Normandy. I meant for my people to once more name me the Good Queen Matilda, as they had in the Empire, and as they had lauded my mother.

Another was evidently thinking of her legacy. Adeliza had come to Normandy. Joyous to see her, I had embraced her long and hard, and we had taken to talking in our chambers each day, often in the morning when we sat, informal in thick cloaks of embroidered cloth, sharing warmed wine and honey cakes. She gave me a gilded brooch of silver with *ave maria, gracia plena* about the rim. I gave her a ring of gold set with a round sapphire.

I suspected my father had sent for her to talk to me and get me to see reason, but if he had commanded her to do such a thing she did not. Adeliza was my friend and I felt she was on my side in this matter. It was not hard to be. My father was being as thick-headed as a boar. So whilst she was supposed to talk to me, make me accept the chains of my father's absolute dominion, we talked of other matters.

She had completed her hospital for lepers. Monks of her new order were to tend to these unfortunates, administering last care and rites where they could do no more, and feeding others with bluebell bulb juice, or scarifying the flesh and adding hellebore to effect a cure.

She had hesitated about it, as my mother had been famed for her founding of a similar establishment, and my friend and stepmother was always cautious about taking on something that would invite more comparisons, many unfair and unjust, with my mother. "But I decided that to not do something good for fear of what people thought was a fool's game," she said. "I shall ask for no praise, indeed I desire none, but whilst I am Queen I should use the small power I have for good."

"All you do is founded in goodness," I said. "There are those who think only and ever of themselves, and others who are so selfless I wonder how they remember to breathe. You are one of the latter, Adeliza."

She flushed, but looked pleased.

"You *are*," I went on. "There is, I have found, much darkness in the world, in people, yet when I stare into the night I am reminded that there is always a little light, all the brighter for the darkness that holds it. And there need be only a little light, for in the vast darkness of the world just a little is needed that we might find our way."

"Domina, you are of the light too."

"Sometimes I wonder," I said. "When I was a child I felt that way, but I wonder at times. I do not think I am all darkness, of course, but there is much of that in me. Some I know I will need. I see this when I look at the choices kings and princes must make. When I am Queen all I do will not be of the light, and that is something I have to learn to accept."

"It is hard indeed for those who rule," she agreed. "There is much your father keeps from me to protect me, but many choices haunt him. Made as they were, and are, for his kingdom and people, they weigh upon him. But that, Domina, is what the Church is there to aid us with. A path to forgiveness will be made, through prayer, through good works."

"It would be a better thing to do nothing for which we had to beg forgiveness and do penance," I said. "But that would be a world ideal, and only the angels and the dead know that grace." I said nothing to my stepmother about my argument with my father, but I wondered if this was her way of saying he was regretting his choice to withhold the border castles.

"We must do all we can, the best we can, and be gentle with ourselves," she said.

"I will make mistakes," I agreed. "And men will note them more when I make them than if a king did." I sighed. "I fear the choices I will have to make. I fear to fail."

"It is rare that failure is so complete it cannot be rectified," she said, touching a pendant of rubies and diamonds at her throat. "As the spider makes a web which is perfect, only for it to be destroyed, she makes another the next day."

"Weavers have an endless task," I said.

"Your father lost his first wife, his son, his heir, but he made it right, promoting you, and now you and your sons will take the throne." Adeliza nodded. "You will weave the web begun by your father."

"And I must hold the strands steady for my Henry," I said. "And that is why I fear, dear friend. To fail for my own sake would be shameful, but to fail for my child would shatter my soul."

I hoped she would pass those words on to my father, and from the slight smile and nod she offered me, I knew she would. Adeliza was a good ally, as good as Geoffrey in many ways. I had a woman in the inside camp. She was not about to betray my father, especially not outwardly, but she was working for me. If peace could be kept, it would be because of her, not my father or me.

To keep Adeliza weaving her blanket of peace, there was something I did not admit; that I wanted not only to hold the throne for young Henry, but that I wanted to be Queen regnant.

The desire to rule, to know power, to hold it in my hands, was in me. To finally be the one who was looked to first. It felt unworthy, for all expectation was that a mother should only wish things for her children, not for herself, that a woman should want things only so they might benefit others, men in particular. But why should I not want this for myself? Every king got to nurture his ambition, mould the crown to his head and make gold bend to fit his skull. Why should I not do the same?

# Chapter Thirty-One

## Angers
## Anjou

### Summer 1135

*Farewell,* I thought. *And may your temper be a more clement creature when we meet again.* I pulled up my horse as I reached the top of a small hillock. The road was before me, long and dry. It led to Anjou.

I stroked my horse's neck and he whickered with satisfaction. "At least I please you," I said.

Was it me? Did I manage to bring out the monster in men I met? First in Geoffrey and then my father. It might even be argued that I had in Heinrich, for my wish to care for him had turned him into a beast. Yet all I had done with my first husband, all I had asked for with the second and with my father had been reasonable. Geoffrey would admit that now if I asked. I doubted my father ever would admit such a thing.

Past homes and hovels I had ridden for days, my sons in the carriage behind me, along with a collection of large cages holding my favourite falcons, of which two from Ireland were particularly valuable. They sat on silver perches, wild bright eyes on my sons as they slept, those innocents curled up in beds of soft fur in the belly of the creaking carriage.

I thought of the days and months I had travelled by carriage when I was a girl of eight winters on my way to the Empire and Heinrich. It seemed another life, that of another person. Had I ceased to sorrow for my first love? Never entirely would he be gone, but had he not left life and me I would not have my sons, creatures more precious to me than anything.

I could smell bonfires that had been lit, celebrating Midsummer, more than a week ago. Those fires were to welcome the coming of the harvest and celebrate the sun before the long descent to winter, but they also protected against agents of evil. Even now people would be taking ash from those fires to sprinkle about their houses, or wear in charms. Smeared on wood, they would protect the cribs of new babes. Those fires had been lit to encourage the sun not to wane too fast, to stir her power with that of the world of humans. They were lit always windward of crops, smoke pouring, purifying the coming harvest. In the flames herbs and plants would have burned; flowers that looked like the sun, or were red, yellow or white, like the sun. The Church claimed such fires were lit for Saint John, but the fires were older than he. I could almost see the shadows of young men and boys who had leapt through the centre of the fire to prove their courage, see the shades of girls who had divined their futures using fallen ash.

On we rode, the scent of the passing of summer in our noses. Dovecots cooed, noisy and busy with fluttering birds in nesting boxes inside, their flint, circular towers glistening with the morning dew. The grass was sparkling with spider web, threads woven low, glittering gold and silver, as though of metal made.

Men were already digging out the dovecot dung, excellent for herb and garden beds. Women were out collecting wild fruits and berries. Men were trapping songbirds with lime and nets. On a bridge sat an old couple sharing a pipe of coltsfoot, a remedy for weak lungs. We passed carts trundling from ocean to market, barrels of fish, some in water and some in salt, creaking on their backs. Scent of pottage rich with fragrant summer herbs like fennel, parsley, sorrel and orach, and thickened with oats, beans and cabbage was on the air along with the perfume of flowers and a whiff of dung. Women tending beehives looked up, wiping sweating brows covered by veils to protect from the sun. Animals were on the road, herds of sheep and goats and hogs heading to market bit by bit, so they did not all fall down in the hot sunlight and die before reaching market and their deaths. We had passed a poor woman, shaven headed and humiliated, marched through the streets as people jeered. She had been found to be an adulteress. No man was punished with her, although some man too must have committed a sin. Past small gardens and large where onions and beans were waiting to be pulled we rode, onward and away from the kingdom of my inheritance, to the land of my marriage.

I had left my father as once I had my husband. I went to Anjou where once I ran to Normandy. Once more the circle was complete. The story had twisted about, eaten its own tail.

Refusing to hand over the castles of Normandy promised to Geoffrey, and rather than handing property back to Talvas, exiling him, my father had chosen what course our always strained relationship would take. He and I had embarked on several flaming rows. Servants had fled and knights had taken to arms as we screamed at each other. People thought war would break out between Anjou and Normandy when I left. They were not being dramatic. It was a distinct possibility.

"What will *ever* be good enough for you?" I had screamed at him, my rage high not only because of the dowry but for so many other reasons of neglect and abuse through the years. "Will died trying to outdo you, do you understand that? He died trying to prove himself! Would you have me do the same? Or would you hand the throne and crown to my son, now, when he is too young to accept them, when men will rule him and rule through him? Would you do all this just to avoid me following you?"

"God's eyes!" my father swore. "You are stubborn and foolish! Those castles are mine, and enemies of the realm I am entitled to punish as I see fit. I am *King!*"

"And I am your heir!" I bellowed. "Have a care for the future of your kingdom and relinquish some power to me or your line will lose all, Father!"

He did not listen and I could not make him listen. Had I been a man he would have admired the way I stood up to him, the courage in me and my persistence, but he did not.

"You are an *unnatural* creature!" he screamed into my face. It was the last thing he said to me before he left my chamber, and I left the castle. I could not reason with him and I would not become his prisoner. I had left quickly that day. I did not think he would try to take our party by force, not as I had Henry and Geoffrey with me, but I could not be sure. I had sent word ahead, by the fastest horse I could find, to Anjou. Geoffrey had dispatched knights. They were now all around me.

The borders had swiftly become dangerous. Geoffrey was preparing to lay siege to castles held by my father's men. My father was rallying troops to do the same to us.

*Am I to blame?* I asked myself. Certainly some had to come to my hands. I was not blameless. As hot tempered as my father, I had demanded where a natural woman would have begged, but he had told me to be not woman, not even man, but emblem. I was to show strength. I had. I had made reasonable demands, and only asked for what he had offered us in the first place. He was the one who could not surrender control, who could not see the danger he was pushing his own daughter and his grandsons into.

And yet even as I told myself this, there was a gruff call inside me. As I crossed the border of yet another land, on yet another journey, I had to wonder whether always I would rouse monsters in men, by refusing to bow to them. Would I always be on the borders of what was normal because I asked for more respect and rights than my sex dictated? Was I never to be understood, always on the outside, looking in?

\*

As I reached the castle of Angers there was news. "Your father is prowling like an enraged cat up and down the borders of Normandy and Anjou, but he has made no move against us," Geoffrey told me. His fingers were playing with a ring-brooch of gold and garnets holding his cloak to his shoulder. And his fingers were not all that was restless about him.

"Go, spend time with your sons," I said with a smile, watching his feet twitch. "There is time later in the night for us to talk of troubles with my father."

I smiled as I watched Geoffrey almost race to the nursery to see his boys. I thought what I had said was truth. We had time. Trust us my father did not, but he would make war on us only if we made the first move. It would put young Henry and Geoffrey in danger if he did, and he was not about to risk them without good cause. But he was also not about to let me believe he had surrendered. I think he thought to teach me another lesson.

Over the weeks that followed, Father strengthened his castles, confiscated lands where he could. Border patrols were increased. Geoffrey responded by doing the same in Anjou and by allying with dissident Norman lords. Poised we were for all out war with my father if it came to it, but neither side made a more overt move than needed to be. We were teetering on the edge, but not plunging over.

"Two dragons shall succeed, one of whom shall be slain by darts of malice, and the other shall perish under the shadow of a name. A lion of justice shall succeed, whose roar shall cause the towns of Francia and the dragons of the island to tremble. In his days gold shall be extorted from the lily and the nettle, and silver scattered abroad by the hoofs of lowing kine." Geoffrey closed the tome he had read to me from.

"The usual nonsense," I said. "Prophecies always are gibberish."

"People say the lion is our son," he said.

"Others claim that is my father," I retorted.

It was a prophecy from the *Prophetiae Merlini*, by a man named Geoffrey of Monmouth. The prophecies of Merlin were popular at that time. Supposedly written hundreds of years before our times, they spoke in allegory and riddle about the present and future. Many thought them genuine. I did not.

"The book says the lion's children become fishes," I said. "That is a reference to the death of my brother." I had been further annoyed that the books spoke of "whelps" of the lion who would bring carnage upon the kingdom. Clearly I was the whelp.

"And they think you will rouse rebellion," said Geoffrey.

"I would like to avoid that, but if it comes to it, that is what will happen," I said. "We cannot go on with an insecure future. Father must cede some power or we must challenge him for all power. That is the way of it."

Allied, Geoffrey and I were close at that time. I was grateful to have him in more ways than one, for without such a general at my side I would not have thought to stand so bold against my father. We spent time together, reading, looking over our plans, talking of our sons and the future. We avoided the past. There was no sense in looking there; it was not where we were, or where we were going.

One day I stood on the battlements feeling sad and resigned. Supplies were being shipped into our castle, and others all about Anjou, to prepare for sieges if they occurred. Barrels of honey and salt fish and meat, apples and grain, beans and wheat were rolled into cellar and store room, in case we needed to wait out an attack on us. I had watched Geoffrey drill his men, training them with wooden swords. They were always busy. I remarked on it when he joined me later, and he said, "The well trained soldier is eager for action, the untrained fear it."

I smiled. "You have been reading your Vegetius again," I said.

"Rare is the time it is out of my hands, these days."

"Unless a sword is there instead," I said. "*He who desires peace should prepare for war.*"

"We are prepared."

"I still hope my father will not attack. He might endanger young Henry, and therefore all his plans for the future."

"I would rather think the worst, and be prepared."

"That is well," I said. "I think the worst, and hope for the best."

Geoffrey looked as though he was about to say something, agree with me, but he simply nodded. I saw hope ignite and die in his eyes. Perhaps he too wished for things not possible. He left. I went back to watching supplies trundle into the baileys. Fodder for horses, stocks of wine, vinegar, flocks of fowl all came, stewards checking lists as they entered the gates. There would be rations until we knew if war would come.

On the walls, hides were being made for archers. There were fighting platforms already, but these would be improved, and shelters for archers added so we could shoot freely from the walls. Long beams, clad with iron, were being made to push siege towers from the walls as well as men who might think to tunnel at their bases. The chime and clash of the blacksmith's hammer sounded continuously, and more than one, all that we had had been pressed into service. Piles of stones for slingers, hosts of arrows and bolts for crossbows were being gathered or made, ready to repel those who would climb ladders up the high walls. If men broke in, they would find themselves in long channels, people overhead throwing stones and spears down on their heads, slaughtering them.

Supplies and stores would come each day, defences be built and improved, until we knew if we were to go to war with my father. I thought about going inside, but I did not. Some impulse in me could not take my eyes from the preparations for war. *This is where our rage takes us, is it, Father?* my mind asked.

Suddenly I knew how he had felt about his brothers. *"Did you never think to make lasting alliance?"* I had asked once. *"Lasting alliance, loyalty... such things as these most men can only dream of,"* he had said. Perhaps it was not possible because they would not share power and if one will not share and others need what they hold tight and covetous to their breasts, then there will be a fight.

"I regret that I have to do this," I said to the wind. "But I know it has to be done."

Was this yet another lesson, perhaps the most valuable yet he had taught me?

*

Late that night I was still there. Geoffrey came to me as I stood on the battlements, the night wind running cold fingers through my hair. As the dark and I were friends, so too were the night and I. Companions not of hearth and home, but spirit and light, darkness and soul, understanding each other perfectly, asking for nothing but the solace of the other's presence. All things of eternity are lonely. Ask the sun why he shines or the moon why she glows. Ask the stars why they strive so hard to dazzle, ask the wind why it howls into the ears of men at night.

For a while we said nothing, standing there. I glanced to one side and I saw he was watching me; those eyes so shocking in daylight were gentle and terrible as a wolf's by night. "You are like Artemis," he said quietly.

"Yet hardly have I hunted in weeks," I said.

Ignoring my jesting tone, Geoffrey went on. "I thought it before, when I was young, when we were first married. I was in your bed one night and you had fallen asleep. I did not let you know I was awake, but I watched you in the moonlight, eyes closed, your dark hair escaping its cap and I had the thought that you were cold as the moon, and as beautiful."

"I am surprised you let me sleep, you were not one for giving grace to me then."

He turned to me, those blue eyes dark fire in the moonlight. "I watched you sleep because in that moment you felt like mine. As though because I was there and I alone could see you, because I could hear your breathing and see your chest rise, that you were mine, *my* wife. I never felt that way in daylight, but in night, there seemed a chance."

I said nothing.

"Is it not enough, Matilda? All I have done, all I do?"

"It is enough."

"Enough for you to love me?"

"Enough for friendship."

"Is that all we are ever to have? No more than that?"

"Forgiveness and friendship I can offer," I said. "But absolution and forgetfulness I cannot. I saw to the dark heart within you.

That I know now there is one, too, of light, does not make your darkness lighter or me less wary."

"There is light and dark in all things."

"Yet in some I have not seen it, and so can imagine it not there," I said. "But I cannot un-see what I have seen, un-imagine what I have felt. As we are now, we are equal, respectful, and here is as far as I trust to go with you. Here is the wall, as far as you are permitted into this kingdom."

"And if I wanted more?"

I turned to him. "If you had my love, what would you do with it? For how long would it be something prized? A long time you wanted to possess me, Geoffrey, and never did you manage it by domination and cruelty. A long time more you sought other tactics. You have offered alliance and friendship and I will respond in kind, be your ally and your friend, but trust you with my heart I never will. You forget that I know you. However much you are grown there is still that boy in you, that dangerous boy, that monster you seek to restrain. You have tied the dragon to a wall, but you have the key to his chain."

"You do not trust me?"

"I do trust you, but I remember the creature you were."

"Can a man make no mistakes, and have them forgiven?"

"Can a woman trust completely where once she feared?" I shook my head. "I have forgiven you the past, but forget I cannot."

There was silence a moment.

"Besides," I said, "it would not last, if we loved. You tire easily of toys even now. The book you are halfway through is not as exciting as the one waiting. If I dared to love you, you would forget the love you have for me. There are other arms, and legs, where you might nestle. I begrudge you them not, spend all the time you want with them. But I will never be such to you. Ally, friend, mother of your children I shall be, but trust you with my heart I never will. You are nothing safe, Geoffrey. There is a feral thing in you I trust not. I respect it, in many ways, mistake me not, for it makes you great in war, in leading men. In many ways I think that thing, when you have harnessed it, will be your greatest power. But it is not something I will trust. You have my duty, my loyalty, for our sons I will never cease to toil and you have earned my respect, husband. I trust your judgement, I trust you with our sons and their future, but my heart cannot be yours. I do not trust it would be safe in your keeping, and I am not one to take risks with something so dear to me, not now."

I saw his jaw clench. Dark tenderness, tinged with the fateful sorrow of knowing it would never be expressed, rose in me. It had nowhere to go. Reach out to touch his face as I wished, lace a fingertip down that sharp cheekbone, along that jaw, along that slight scar I had made, show tenderness at that moment, and I would risk too much. A kind of love for him was in my heart. I lied when I said all I had for him was duty, alliance. Geoffrey, that spoiled boy and now a man more than my match in loyalty, perseverance and fire, had a piece of my heart. But I would not let him see that. A union of that kind between us would bring about destruction of one or the other. Two dragons fighting in a river would be as our love would. That could not be, for the sake of our sons never could it be.

His hands grasped the wall. "You should not linger long out here, it is cold," he said. He turned and made for the door.

"I promise I will not," I said. "I am not one for risks."

I heard the door to the tower close, his steps hurrying down the stairs. I could feel a place in my heart where his heart, wounded once again by me, was pulling at mine. Both were bleeding a little, but allow him what he wanted and bleed more we would. This was not a love that could be.

There are some loves that conquer and build and some that do nothing but destroy. Two dragons fighting in a river we would become indeed. A fire too hot to go near, a distance that had to be kept. As raw and bitter and deep as our hatred had been, so would love, if unleashed.

We had to remain on the banks, in our own territories. With one on either side, no man would make it through to threaten us. A clutch of eggs held safe in a nest amidst water and weed would be granted the time to hatch.

I touched the adder-stone hidden under my clothes, next to my heart. If I held it up now, I would see not a future of which many maidens dreamed, of love for a man that would solve all problems, banish all demons. That was not my fate.

If I held that stone up to the dying light, in cobalt blue and dove shadow I knew I would see the grey eyes of my son. And before them would be gold; the glitter of a crown, a crown that was mine to wear before I placed it upon the head of my beloved son.

# Chapter Thirty-Two

## Angers
## Anjou

### Autumn 1135

Dragon and damselflies zipped across watery flats by day, wings as diamonds in the streaming sunlight, as trees turned yellow and brown and gold. Apples were thick on the branch and ground, falling in winds that rose warm yet cold at the same time, as water mixed in a bath of copper. Men tramped to the orchards each day, basket after heavy basket of apples coming back, so boys of the stores could wipe them and place them in dark barrels to store for winter.

It was the fertile time of the year, and my body responded. This time, however, my husband looked more concerned than delighted when I told him I was again carrying his child. "So soon?" he asked.

"When we spend nights in bed together, there *are* likely outcomes." I gazed from the window. In a valley, far away, was a cloud fallen. The mist of the valley, not white but lightest blue, shone under a pale grey sky. It was a realm of smoke and ghosts, hazy as the past, as memory, and as my recollection of love.

Men were gathering the last of the apples. We needed plenty if we were to war with my father. Apples are good for a siege. In the sunlight, some looked golden, like the fruit of the trees in the Garden of Hesperides. A many-headed dragon named Ladon had been guardian of that sacred garden, placed there by Hera to defend the golden apples and the walled paradise. Heracles killed Ladon, shooting arrows laced with the blood of the Hydra, another monster he had slain, over the high wall, into Ladon's flesh. Coward's victory that it was, Ladon died, and Heracles stole the golden apples the dragon had protected all his life. Broken-hearted, Hera placed her dragon in the heavens. Ladon is the constellation Draco, snaking about the night skies, curling about the North Star, protecting it, as once he guarded the treasure of the goddess.

The ground buzzed with furious wasps on the verge of starving to death in winter, clustering on the browning fallen fruit that winds had brought down by night. Apples were in every dish, along with pears, fresh and crisp raw, silky and sweet in pies, slippery on the tongue. Later in the winter, as we snaked towards spring, they would be leathery and dry from long months spent in barrels, their flesh sharp rather than refreshing, but now everyone ate them with relish, and young maids saved their peel to take to some place out of sight where they could throw it to the floor and foretell their future husband's name, or profession, from the shape the peel assumed.

It was not maidens alone who thought plants had magical powers; evidently Geoffrey thought they did too. "I had thought… you said you were taking herbs to slow the rate we had children?"

"I was," I said. I had been taking them as the edge of war, we both had thought, was not a place to give birth. "But these methods are by no means foolproof." I was touched to see his creased brow, more than I would admit. There was much I would not admit to Geoffrey then. "You are concerned."

"You almost died the last time. I thought, if we took precautions, we could find pleasure and there would be a space between our sons."

"Perhaps God is being wise, so sends all our children quickly before we can fall out again."

He laughed. "You do not seem as worried as I."

"I feel hale, healthy. I have faced death in childbed once. I will not say I have no fears, but I know my duty, as you reminded me, is to live for our sons."

"I want to start insisting on precautions, but I fear that this will make you rebel and do the opposite," he said.

"I will take more precautions this time than last."

"No travelling," he said. "Please hear me on that matter at least, and gentle exercise, and good food."

"I will obey," I said.

"I am glad to hear this time you mean to stick to your marriage vows," he said, smiling.

"This is one of the times I will," I agreed. My face became more serious as I sat at his side. "I will be careful, I swear it."

"Allow me to do things," he said. "A state horrific for men is when they cannot act when they need to."

"It is no less worrying for women," I pointed out. "We are simply more often restrained and unable to do anything."

"For the sake of my sanity," he said.

"I will order my own women to attend me," I warned, adjusting my brooch of diamond upon my breast.

"That is well. Allow me to seek out apothecaries and physicians who can advise both of us. If any of your cunning women like not the potions or herbs they recommend, you do not have to take them, but allow me to do things. I would like to order the goods for your lying-in chamber and birthing room. I want to ensure that all you need in case of an emergency is there this time."

"That sounds entirely reasonable," I said.

"You are my good friend, wife," he said, his voice catching on the word 'friend'. "I will not risk you."

He was telling me that he loved me. Geoffrey had pride, there was no extracting that from him. It was in his blood. He was not about to express love to me again and risk being hurt again. But his love was expressed, as the love of men often is, in actions more than words. I sometimes pitied men for being raised to express emotion only for brothers-in-arms and not for the women they loved. It was not true of all men, there were young men and poets who dared to speak, but so much of men was bound up inside them, kept hidden. Yet they felt as wide and deep as women, their hearts ached with love and sadness as ours did, they fell to sorrow, cherished tenderness. Yet they were taught not to show such, so a part of them was forever bound in shadow and in chains. Part of them always was a slave.

I, a woman, could well understand. So much of me and women like me was restrained, held back and hidden. We screamed in a silent darkness, unable to be truly free. But men, for all the freedom they had in the world, all the power, were not truly free either. They too were trapped by the expectations of the world. What would we become, we humans, if we were not watched, if we were alone, naked in the wilderness? I wondered at times why Adam and Eve donned clothing when awareness fell on them. Was it because they were aware suddenly of the judgement of the world, rather than the dawning of wisdom? If left alone, without eyes watching, would we be free, be innocent, be ourselves?

Not long after, another chose to express love in actions rather than words. Despite his distrust of us and our intentions, when word was sent to my father that I was with child once more, he pulled his men back from the borders.

The risk was small they would disobey him, but it seemed he would take no chance that some bored or overeager guards or knights might tarry into Anjou, take action that might draw Geoffrey from my side, or launch us into all-out war.

"It may be for another reason," Geoffrey said.

"To lull us to slumber so he can attack?" I asked.

Geoffrey nodded. "As the Minotaur was hidden deep in the labyrinth, so should the designs of a general be hidden from his enemy. There was a reason that monster was one of the legionary ensigns of the past. I suspect your father is hiding a monster, waiting for us to relax that he might unleash it."

I nodded. "I understand, and it is your role to think the worst. Do what you think necessary for the protection of Anjou and our children."

Geoffrey would. His men believed in him utterly, they called him the leopard of Anjou, and although Geoffrey had confidence in them and his abilities, he was cool and collected when he assessed his troops. He gleaned all there was to know about the enemy he was to face, assessed strengths and weaknesses. To see him pondering maps to check the best ground, to see him compare troops of the enemy against his own was to see a man devoid of the spoilt, feeble and fragile boy I had known. In time, I thought men might well see genius in him, as time nurtured his strengths and more weaknesses fell from him.

"But you think it not the worst?" he asked.

"I do," I said.

In truth, as I was told his patrols were being pulled back it was almost as though I heard my father's voice, whispering on the wind, wishing me well, telling me and my child to be safe.

# Chapter Thirty-Three

## Angers
## Anjou

### Winter 1135

I must show you things I never saw, otherwise this part of my tale you will understand little and think dull. For as I waited, days unfolding as they did at any other time, things of moment were occurring elsewhere.

Often this is the way. We think of life as only existing before our eyes, and are surprised to learn that elsewhere something has happened that affects us. It is hard for us to think of all the places of the world in which people live, get on with life whether adventurous or dull, sorrowful or happy, each day. The world is too large for our small minds, so we often become insular. Perhaps that is why it is a great shock when we learn that something has happened somewhere else, changing our lives, these intimate little shells, for good.

I must take to the skies, become the creature I had felt within me, this dragon. Sister of Melusine must I be for a time, my dragon-tail licking the wind as it soars over my scales, silver as a serpent, my feet treading clouds as they might tread water, carrying me through river and sea to my hoard of treasure.

Follow my tail through the skies. Watch my breath plume, ashes and fire flowing from my tongue. We head to watch my father.

That winter my father had gone to England and in the same season he left England again. As he came across the sea, the elements of the heavens moved with him once more. Night blocked out day for hours, and stars were seen about the darkened sun. The earth shook. Men thought the end of days had come, but soon the light returned and the earth became still. Soon they forgot and went back to their lives.

It was the 25th of November when my father rode for his hunting lodge, a little castle in the forest. Huntsmen were sent out to assess the game for the next day. He went to his hunting lodge in the Lyons-la-Forêt, near Rouen. He was feeling hale and reasonably happy, despite our estrangement and ongoing border troubles. He had loved his siblings and warred with them, so understood the ways of family and power often are complicated. Pleased about the latest child to grace my womb, he said to intimates, my brother Robert amongst them, that in time I would remember my duty and we would be reconciled. There was never time we had not been. In the most trying and difficult of circumstances we had always come back to one another, gathering like seeds of dandelion on grass, wisps of white and seed and fluff clinging to one another as the wind tries to blow them apart. Always I had submitted to his will, and would again.

He was certain I carried another son, and told his men so. All these years I had had no children and I was now handed a surfeit of heirs. The barons could not object to me as Queen, as my father's heir, with an heir of my own and two spare sons to offer to England and Normandy. Father said he would wait and I would understand the errors of my ways. Not about to forgive his daughter for making war and disobeying him was he, but he was pleased to hear how fertile I had become. We humans may feel happy and discontent at the same time, feel different and opposite emotion about the same matter. We are complicated creatures, at times. He was feeling happy, so ate well and heartily. His favoured dish, lamprey, were served various ways and he ate many.

That night he became ill.

Six days later, he was dead.

He had time to make confession to the Archbishop of Rouen, and to ask my brother Robert, who was at his bedside, to take money to abbeys he favoured to pray for his soul. Then, on the first night of December, my father died.

For those with him, it was not only a shock because death always is, but because my father had hardly been ill in his life, at all. Nothing had seemed able to stop him, not sickness, not battle, not even arrows of the Welsh or of his bastard daughter had managed to take his life, but now, an eel did. A little cousin of monsters who guarded treasure, of snakes of the deep, came for my father.

He told men where he wanted his body sent, where his money should go. But of me and my inheritance, he said nothing. I knew nothing at the time. I was still in Anjou, preparing for war with him, or peace, whichever came. Robert would tell me, much later, that my father had said nothing about who was to follow him. He did not, at that last moment of life, secure my place as heir. Perhaps he was too angry. But he did not, either, name another. Therefore I was still his heir, as was young Henry.

Later men would lie, say he had named another to take my place. No matter what I believed of my father, this I never believed.

If I could make a wish, I would become the dragon I imagine myself to be so I might show you this time, for I wish I could see with those eyes. I wish I could see my father one last time.

We parted at conflict, angry at each other. Perhaps it was fitting. We always were troubled in life, and so it had ended that way too.

In blissful ignorance I carried on in Anjou, taking care of my children, of myself as I entered the first stages of pregnancy and spent all my time either vomiting or ravenous. I did not know that my world had altered, that I had become an orphan, that I should be now claiming the throne I had been promised.

But someone else heard that the world had altered. My cousin, Stephen of Blois. He heard fast, for Boulogne was close to where my father died. And in a moment Stephen was upon horse then upon the waves, heading for England and the treasury, on his way to secure the crown.

My crown.

My cousin of Blois was a thief.

It was a family tradition. My father had done the same. No matter there was an heir, that Stephen had an older brother with a better claim, that I and my children existed, he raced to England, to the treasury and to the crown. My father had followed the same path as his brother lay in a pool of blood. I, held fast by ignorance and by my body, remained in place as Stephen acted.

Crown not claim, made a King.

Death had stolen my father. My kinsman had stolen my future.

In a moment, my world had changed. And I knew nothing of it.

# Chapter Thirty-Four

## Anjou and
## Normandy

### Winter 1135

Outside, feet firm on frozen paths about the castle a magpie was hopping, black eyes bright. His banded tail bobbed, excited as he found something to eat amongst the snow. A flash of black and white and he was away into the skies, something wriggling desperately in his sharp beak. But a moment and he had what he wanted.

"We must secure the castles of Normandy," I said, turning from the window, glancing down at my stomach, as yet little swollen, with mixed feelings. I could not curse my belly, my unborn child. Such an act would revolt me, but how I could curse that being a woman held me back from sailing now, to England, to claim the throne.

My stomach lurched. I swallowed vomit. I had been being sick all morning. That was enough. I had work to do and could not do it with my head in a bowl. I thought I was two months with child. Each time I came to this time in pregnancy I became ill. But this time it irked more, perhaps I had more to be sick about, and I vomited long and hard each morning, heaving against my own belly and the changing whim of fate.

News of my father's death had come. When first it had been revealed I could not believe it. Something in me still did not. Strange it was, for I never had problems knowing my brother and mother had died when I was told, but with my father it seemed impossible. There are some people who seem impervious to the touch of Death, some who are immortal. My father was one. I could not feel sorrow, not in the way I had for my mother and brother, because in truth I did not believe he was gone.

And in dreams he was alive, and in dreams he turned to me and smiled, arms open, heart too, as they never were in life. In dreams I was his daughter as I had never felt when we were awake. Even as heir, named to follow him, I had never felt a sense of belonging. I was a possession to my father, and to belong is not the same as to possess. To belong is to know where you should be, and need to be; it is to become a stone glimmering upon the beach as light froth and water flow over you, tumbling you up and down the shore. To be possessed is to be picked up, taken away from salt and sea, from the rippling wind, so you dull and fade, become just another stone, lost to beauty and to life.

In dreams I did not belong to my father, but I *belonged*. I was bonded to him yet free. I was loved, without condition or circumstance, without necessity to fulfil some dream, complete his legacy. In dreams my father told me he loved me. In dreams, I believed him.

I needed to be in England. Although I was assured that the barons, having sworn many times to uphold me as heir both before my marriage and after, would hold the throne for me, I needed to be in England to stake my claim. And I could not. I was held captive by pregnancy. Risking death the last time I had faced childbirth, I could take no risks now, and not only for me and the child I carried. My Henry was too young to hold the throne for himself and no baron of England or Normandy would accept Geoffrey as regent or guardian. Robert might be able to act for my son if I died, but young Henry would be in a precarious position without me, always in danger. I could not risk death. That meant I could not go to England until the child I carried was delivered, six or seven months at least. That was dangerous. It was not uncommon knowledge that I was with child, or that I had suffered badly the last time. That left England in a situation precarious too.

Nothing did I know then of Stephen. I did not know my crown was already stolen.

*Captive you are*, I told myself, *but we will do all we can until your body releases you.*

Normandy had to be secured. It was full half the Empire my father had left, and I was in a position to make sure this half was secure. Geoffrey was not merry about it, as he wanted me taking no risks at all, but I wrote to him saying I would make a base in the Argentan, if he would ensure Anjou was secure. If this was done, we could send word to England to make sure that the rest of the Empire would follow. Not many days later, I went to Normandy. I was more acceptable to the Norman barons than Geoffrey was. Send my husband and they might think that he was attempting to take over, become Duke, something they wanted not.

Two months with child, I rode carefully and slowly for Normandy so I could start to secure castles promised to Geoffrey and me long ago, by my father now dead. I sent men ahead, to prepare the way. Fortunate it was the men of Normandy knew me and were loyal, for they knew much I did not. I could have made a worthy prisoner had they been disloyal. For there, in Normandy, I found truth. There, I learned of Stephen.

He had heard of my father's death, and had raced to England. Taking possession of the treasury, he had claimed the throne. "News is, Domina, that the Count of Boulogne means to have himself crowned before Christmas Day," said the man who told me.

I dared not open my mouth. My fury was so great that if I tried to speak it would rush from me and devour the world. I cursed that it was thought unnatural for my sex to wield a sword. Gladly I would have taken iron into my hands and struck off the head of my cousin of Blois. That snake slithering in to steal my throne, my crown, my future, freedom and dreams!

"What have the barons of England said to him?" I asked. "Stephen swore himself to me, swore to uphold me as they all did. "

"It would appear men of England will accept him as King, Domina," said the man. "Their loyalty is as strong and hale as their memories, it would appear."

Had rage possessed hands mine could have stretched over the seas and throttled the life from Stephen, thief of Blois. And I had thought him a good man, a man of honour! Honour! What honour was there in what he had done? To steal from a woman, because she was a woman. If I were a man he would not have dared do as he did. And other men would not have supported him.

But because I was a woman, they had.

And I could do nothing. I could not will my rage and fire into existence because I wanted it. I could not grow a tail and fly to England to open my mouth and swallow that craven little fool who had the audacity to claim a throne that did not belong to him! Did he think he followed in my father's footsteps because he rushed to gain the treasury and be crowned before the other claimant to the throne could come? Stephen was not even eldest son of the house of Blois! He had no right to what his clammy, grasping little hands had taken!

But because he could rush to England and I could not, he had his way.

This was why men might be thought beings of action, because held prisoner by their bodies they were not. Stephen had rushed for a horse, for a boat. Unhindered by anything, save the feeble nature of his claim, he had stolen my crown.

I could almost hear my father laughing. No doubt he would find my present rage amusing. Perhaps he would think this just revenge for me defying him before his death.

Yet all my father had asked I had done, no matter with how ill a grace. And now, he had doomed me. Pregnant, sick, unable to travel upon the sea for fear of losing life, I was hindered from the path of destiny by the body of woman. Were I a man, unconstrained, not subject to bear life from within, able to live where I wanted, able to leave breeding to another, to a wife, these problems would not have been mine. But as woman they were.

And the English barons had not upheld me. They had not seen Stephen coming and laughed in his face, told him there was a child of true blood and lineage who already owned the throne. No, the little bitches had rolled over to show the invading hound their quinnies.

Not one man in England spoke for me, the heir they had sworn over and over and over again to uphold. Not one. Men of high birth they were, "And low courage," I said, bitter.

One man outside of England spoke, but not for me. Robert favoured my son for the throne, but Henry was only two years of age. Since I was a woman and my son an infant, the barons upheld Stephen.

If it proved anything to me, it was that no claim, no blood, no oath sworn before God could make a woman Queen when there was a man, any man, to take her place as King. What else it proved to me was that I knew men not at all. I had feared some barons would not support me, never that my brother Robert would not. I sent word to him in Rouen. He was still there, waiting to take the body of the father we had shared home to England. I asked him to support me, reminded him not only of bonds of blood and bone we shared, but friendship. I had nothing in return.

At night, as I stood on the battlements, I wondered if I knew anything. Anything of the world, of people. They knew nothing of me, it seemed, for I was as easy to brush aside as a speck of dust. I had lost England, the future I wanted for myself and for my child.

"And yet not lost," I said to the night. "This is no end to the tale. This is no surrender."

*

On the 22nd of December, Stephen was crowned. It was poorly attended, but mattered not. What mattered was the crown, the throne, the oil upon his head marking him so God would see him. God did not strike him down, and so there was a new King of England.

But one man who I had relied on proved himself early. In late December my uncle of Scots invaded England with an army. There was much David was attempting to secure for himself, and for Scotland with this act, but I believed him when he announced he was doing so for me. Alternative motives he might have, all men do when they do anything, but I had no doubt that one of those motives was me, was the love and loyalty he felt for me because of his love for my mother.

"God rain blessings on my uncle of Scots!" I cried when I heard. At least one man was willing to act for me, to uphold vows he had taken.

I knew that had I been a man the barons might have held the throne for me, that Stephen might not have attempted his rush to England. Fragile though the throne might be even for a man it was more so for a woman. And fragility was what mattered. That was what they thought me, what I became in their minds. No woman could hold a throne in her own right. A man was a better bet, in the long run.

And a man was something they were more comfortable with.

That is the truth of it, most of the time. We humans, we see faces in all things. In bushes and in leaves and in trees we see the shape of cheekbones and eyes. We look to clouds and see faces looking down on us. We see not only what we want to see, but what we need to see.

Men did not want me on the throne because I was not of them. It mattered not my birth, experience, my heirs or my intelligence. What mattered was that I was less than them because I was woman, not man. It would have been the same had a man of the villein order staked a claim. Men could not see themselves in me, so they could not believe in me.

They thought it would shame them, to bow to a lesser being, to something God had cursed with pain and blood, yet still mysteriously allowed not only to live, but to bring all life into the world. They thought to uphold me as Queen would make them appear feeble, that to bow to a being with a cleft between her legs would make them seem weak. They were soon to find there was much they did not understand.

It would be Easter at least before I was ready. Easter: a time of rebirth; the death of the old and life of the new. That was the truth of the message of Christ. For as Jesus was part of God, he was also partly mortal, for how else could he die if he were not? There is resurrection in all of us, we can begin again, renewed, cleansed. We may accept all parts of ourselves, darkness and light, and choose which to act upon. We can find strength even in the most fragile moments, even in death.

I was become dark with memory, with lost and found dreams, with betrayal and loyalty. And still I dreamed. Still in the dark chamber of my soul there burned a light everlasting, lit by love and kept alive by hope. Guttering and flaring was that light, but still alight it was.

I would become that which they could not predict. Women were peace weavers, and fate weavers. Child of water that I was, I would weave a blanket of destiny from strands of water. I would build my own cloth. Into myself I would take the monster, the maiden, the knight, the dead and living. From water I would rise to claim earth. In dark cave in hidden glen would this creature roar. When it was time, I would come. *Take hands with the dragon*, I told myself.

My dragon was a monster, yes, it held much that was dark but it guarded me from darkness that lay beyond, darkness that was darker than dark. It was said once that a snake-dragon encircled the world, protecting realms of man from those of chaos, but I thought that only a half truth. Perhaps they hold some back from chaos for the power in that realm is too great for some. But I think they protect us from a different kingdom.

Chaos holds possibility, but inertia nothing. From the void of nothingness and no one my dragon guarded me. From dangers of disappearance, the loss of what was sacred of self, my monster protected me, I knew that now.

And dragons do not gather wealth for greed. What they guard is treasure unimagined. The power of transformation, of chaos, the ability to transcend, these are the treasures the dragon within us guards; things not to be used lightly, and never to be disregarded. If we can face them, they let us tap that power, their power. Monsters, dragons, selkies, they are made monstrous by those who fear their power and who fear change. I did not fear power, and change was coming, for England, for Normandy, for the world and for me.

I would take hands with the monster inside me. I would drink from the chaos and possibility I contained. From me would be born a creature the world had not witnessed, one of light and dark, neither swept away nor hidden. A creature of male and female and no sex with the right and might to rule. From me would fall the Countess of Anjou, from me would rise another being.

This is the lesson Melusine taught. Let maiden take hands with monster, and, neither denied, let them take flight as one. As one being combined may we fly the world of man and expectations of mankind to live as we see fit, unfettered and free.

I could not call myself Queen, for that title had been stolen by Stephen's wife, my once-friend and companion, Matilda of Boulogne.

Matilda, Empress, daughter of the King of the English, I had called myself.

"I am Matilda, Lady of the English," I said to my people in Normandy. "And the throne is mine."


***Here ends Melusine, Book Two of The Heirs of Anarchy. In Book Three, Shipwreck, Matilda must challenge her cousin Stephen for the English crown, and for the right to rule.***

# Author's Notes

This is a work of fiction. Although I try to stick to known facts, there are certain elements I created in this book. All conversations are fiction, although where the words of the characters were set down in historical record, those words are used. The characters of the people involved are my invention, although based on study of their lives and actions. I used a great deal of sources for this book, and mean to include those in the bibliography at the end of the series.

I include a few notes on the book here. For those who do not know the story covered in this book and future ones in the series, a warning: I discuss matters that might spoil the tale to come.

Edward "the Confessor" is so called in the book to distinguish him from other Saxon Edwards, and to avoid confusion. He did not take on the name "the Confessor" until Rome considered canonising him, around the year 1161. This was within the lifetime of Matilda, so since this book is told as the Empress looking back on her life, she would have known it, but during the time period this book covers the Confessor was not yet the Confessor.

Matilda's loss of weight due to stress in her marriage I used as a reason for her inability to conceive in the first years of her union with Geoffrey. This is entirely my theory, as are the problems they encountered with each other. What actually happened in the first years of their marriage, exactly why she went to Normandy (some sources say she was cast out by Geoffrey, others claim she left him of her own accord) is unknown. Whether cast out or if she left of her own accord, their marriage was not happy to begin with. There is another theory that she was sent out of Anjou due to the rebellions that occurred in the first years of Geoffrey's rule, which is also feasible. They were not, however, an amicable couple. The fault for this is put on Matilda by some sources and on Geoffrey by others, but the truth probably lies in the middle. He was probably threatened by her titles, family and position, and she was certainly insulted to be matched to someone lower than her in status and age. This is not a recipe for a happy marriage. The arguments they have in the book are based on the issues they had, such as her dowry being withheld, in the form of the castles, but the contents of the arguments and all their conversations are my invention. Later, when she returned, they appear to have come to some kind of understanding, as they had children rapidly and also worked together well as allies. Geoffrey's love for Matilda and her affection for him are my inventions, although I do believe there was a bond between them forged of strong feelings.

Poor nutrition, remembering that the nobility ate far more white bread and meat than vegetables, legumes and grain, could also have affected Matilda's fertility.

Just as Geoffrey's feelings for Matilda cannot be truly known, the love Brian Fitzcount is said to harbour for Matilda is based on rumours which came about later. It may be entirely false, and may have been spread by her enemies in an attempt to discredit her. Brian may have been loyal as many other men were, because he believed in her and her claim. I chose to accept the rumours, as there are no such rumours about many other men who followed her, but there are about Brian. If he did love her, or was attracted to her, that does not mean she reciprocated his feelings or that anything happened between them.

Matilda's view of herself as defective for her lack of a child is certainly not my idea of childless women (being one myself) but was intended to show how then, and now, women can be viewed by others (and by themselves if they come to believe such things) as incomplete because they do not have children. Matilda certainly yearned for a child. The fact that the only time she was ever recorded as crying in public was at the christening of her first son, Henry, goes to show a great wealth of emotion that was connected to him, and he was always her favourite child, perhaps because he came first, proving to her and to the world that she could have children, and perhaps because she had wanted him for such a long time. I do not personally believe women are in any way incomplete for not having, or choosing not to have children. I was trying to show a pressure which existed upon women, both at the time of this book and now.

Matilda naming her first son for Heinrich is my invention. Generally it is believed she named him for her father, but even if this is so it is possible to name a child in honour of more than one person.

Some ages of the characters are subject to interpretation. Birthdays were not marked particularly, not as they are today, so with some, particularly the women, it is hard to know how old they were. Matilda the Empress was probably born in 1102 in February, the first child and daughter of Henry I and Matilda of Scotland, although there are sources which speak of an earlier daughter who died young. These reports appear to be unreliable, so I took her as the eldest child, and recorded no other legitimate sibling but William.

Queen Adeliza may have been a great deal younger than she is in the book, as she is recorded as being a "young maiden" at the time of her marriage to Henry I, which might indicate she was twelve years old. If she was that young it might explain why they remained childless, as she might have been too young to have her menses, although it would seem pointless for the King, who needed a son, to then choose her as his wife. Women's private bodily functions were not private when they were being selected as wives. I thought it more likely she was young, like Matilda, but not too young. Another explanation for their lack of children, as I mentioned for Matilda, is poor nutrition, which may have caused infertility on a wide scale in society, or simply that Henry, an old man by the standards of the day, had become infertile. Since Adeliza went on to have children, the last explanation seems fairly likely. I made Adeliza around the same age as Matilda as I wanted them to form a bond, as sisters and friends, which would make later events more understandable. I left the age of Matilda of Boulogne a little vague too, as there are various dates suggested for her birth. She was about half her husband's age, making her somewhere in her late teens to early twenties in this book.

A whole host of noble and royal houses claim the fairy Melusine was their ancestor. The house of Anjou did, and the story fitted with something I wanted to explore in this book to do with understanding the various powers within a person. Likewise, many of the fables and myths I have used come from all over the world, and are present in many cultures. Being a lover and devotee of fairy tales, I enjoyed this part of the research and book a great deal. As a side note, unicorn horn is mentioned in the book and the reason this often was found on beaches is because it was narwhale tusk.

I have longed to write about the Empress Matilda for a long time. I find the notion that England and Normandy might have had a Queen regnant so early in our history fascinating, and cannot quite stop wondering how it would have affected the future, the Tudor dynasty especially. Would Henry VIII have accepted his daughter Mary as Queen? Would Anne Boleyn and Elizabeth I figured in our history at all? Of course it would depend on the success of Matilda as a Queen, but still, the questions and theories come and remain for me. I also found Matilda herself intriguing. Although by no means perfect, like the rest of us, she had many strong and vibrant characteristics, which I admire.

# Thank You

…to so many people for helping me make this book possible… to my proof reader, Julia Gibbs, who gave me her time, her wonderful guidance and also her encouragement. To my family for their ongoing love and support; this includes not only my own blood in my mother and father, sister and brother, but also their families, their partners and all my nieces who I am sure are set to take the world by storm as they grow. To my friend Petra who took a tour of Tudor palaces and medieval places with me back in 2010 which helped me to prepare for this book and others; her enthusiasm for that strange but amazing holiday brought an early ally to the idea I could actually write a book, begin a career as an author. To my friend Nessa for her support and affection, and to another friend, Anne, who has done so much for me. To Sue and Annette, more friends who read my books and cheer me on. To Terry for getting me into writing and indie publishing in the first place. To Katie and Jooles, and Heather, often there in times of trial. To all my wonderful readers, who took a chance on an unknown author, and have followed my career and books since.

To those who have left reviews or contacted me by email or Twitter, I give great thanks, as you have shown support for my career as an author, and enabled me to continue writing. Thank you for allowing me to live my dream.

And lastly, to the people who wrote all the books I read in order to write this book… all the historical biographers and masters of their craft who brought Matilda, and her times, to life in my head. I intend to include a bibliography at the end of the last book in this series.

Thank you to all of you; you'll never know how much you've helped me, but I know what I owe to you.

Gemma Lawrence
Wales
2020

# About The Author

I find people talking about themselves in the third person to be entirely unsettling, so, since this section is written by me, I will use my own voice rather than try to make you believe that another person is writing about me to make me sound terribly important.

I am an independent author, publishing my books by myself, with the help of my lovely proof reader. I left my day job in 2016 and am now a fully-fledged, full time author, and proud to be so!

My passion for history began early in life. As a child I lived in Croydon, near London, and my schools were lucky enough to be close to such glorious places as Hampton Court and the Tower of London, allowing field trips to take us to those castles. I think it's hard not to find characters from history infectious when you hear their stories, especially when surrounded by the bricks and mortar they built their reigns and legends within. There is heroism and scandal, betrayal and belief, politics and passion and a seemingly never-ending cast list of truly fascinating people. So when I sat down to start writing, I could think of no better place to start than a subject I loved and was slightly obsessed with.

Expect *many* books from me, but do not necessarily expect them all to be of one era. I write as many of you read, I suspect; in many genres. My own bookshelves are weighted down with historical volumes and biographies, but they also contain dystopias, sci-fi, horror, humour, children's books, fairy tales, romance and adventure. I can't promise I'll manage to write in *all* the areas I've mentioned there, but I'd love to give it a go. If anything I've published isn't your thing, that's fine, I just hope you like the ones I write which *are* your thing!

The majority of my books *are* historical fiction, however, so I hope that if you liked this volume you will give the others in this series (and perhaps not in this series), a look. I want to divert you as readers, to please you with my writing and to have you join me on these adventures.

A book is nothing without a reader.

As to the rest of me; I am in my thirties and live in Wales with a rescued dog, and a rescued cat. I studied Literature at University after I fell in love with books as a small child. When I was little I could often be found nestled halfway up the stairs with a pile of books in my lap and my head lost in another world. There is nothing more satisfying to me than finding a new book I adore, to place next to the multitudes I own and love… and nothing more disappointing to me to find a book I am willing to never open again. I do hope that this book was not a disappointment to you; I loved writing it and I hope that showed through the pages.

This is only one of a large selection of titles coming to you on Amazon. I hope you will try the others.

If you would like to contact me, please do so.

On Twitter, I am @TudorTweep and am more than happy to follow back and reply to any and all messages. I may avoid you if you decide to say anything worrying or anything abusive, but I figure that's acceptable.

Via email, I am tudortweep@gmail.com a dedicated email account for my readers to reach me on. I'll try and reply within a few days.

I publish some first drafts and short stories on Wattpad where I can be found at www.wattpad.com/user/GemmaLawrence31 . Wattpad was the first place I ever showed my stories, *to anyone*, and in many ways its readers and their response to my works were the influence which pushed me into self-publishing. If you have never been on the site I recommend you try it out. It's free, it's fun and it's chock-full of real emerging talent. I love Wattpad because its members and their encouragement gave me the boost I needed as a fearful waif to get some confidence in myself and make a go of a life as a real, published writer.

Thank you for taking a risk with an unknown author and reading my book. I do hope now that you've read one you'll want to read more. If you'd like to leave me a review, that would be very much appreciated also!

Gemma Lawrence
Wales
2020

Printed in Great Britain
by Amazon

44875444R00199